INVESTIGATING
MR WAKEFIELD

For Mary

ROB GITTINS

INVESTIGATING MR WAKEFIELD

y Lolfa

*The characters in this book are entirely fictional
and are not intended to bear any resemblance
to anyone living or dead.*

First impression: 2016
© Rob Gittins & Y Lolfa Cyf., 2016

Cover image: Niclas W
Cover design: Matthew Tyson

Paperback ISBN: 978 1 78461 239 9
Hardback ISBN: 978 1 78461 262 7

The author wishes to acknowledge the award of a Writer's Bursary
from Literature Wales for the purpose of completing this novel.

The publishers wish to acknowledge the support of
Cyngor Llyfrau Cymru.

Published and printed in Wales
on paper from well-maintained forests by
Y Lolfa Cyf., Talybont, Ceredigion SY24 5HE
e-mail ylolfa@ylolfa.com
website www.ylolfa.com
tel 01970 832 304
fax 832 782

What's she like when you're not watching?

YEARS AGO, I read this story. It was about a man who played a trick on his wife.

2 .

'THANKS FOR AGREEING to this.'

The blonde nodded at me, a coffee in front of her, her companion fiddling with a digital Sony Cyber-shot by her side.

'We're really grateful. We want to do a series of these sort of interviews.'

She smiled.

'Local celebs.'

'And that's me?'

'You'd be amazed who lives down this street. Actors, playwrights, chefs.'

'I don't act, write or cook.'

'You take pictures.'

'Used to take pictures.'

'The actor we interviewed yesterday hadn't stood on a stage for six years. People are still interested though.'

The blonde smiled again, almost apologetically this time.

'It's only a local paper I know. One step up from a free sheet. But if we can get a series together we might attract a syndication offer so like I said, we're grateful.'

I settled back in my chair, casting a wary glance towards the photographer. Being on the other side of a camera was still a new experience.

'So what do you want to know?'

'First of all, how did you start?'

'Taking pictures?'

'What was your first camera?'

I paused, ambushed a little by that, memories suddenly, involuntarily, before my eyes.

'Just a simple Instamatic.'

'And how old were you?'

'Ten.'

'A birthday present?'

'That's right.'

'From your parents?'

'Grandfather.'

The blonde looked up at me, registering something in my voice, a reluctant admission perhaps.

'The Instamatic was the first camera I owned. The one I fell in love with belonged to him too, a Brownie.'

'You fell in love with a camera?'

That was her companion looking up from the Sony. He'd finally found the power button.

'I took one look through the viewfinder and that was that. The world through a peephole. You can see out but no-one can see in.'

The blonde eyed me.

'Next up was a Nikon, then a Leica – not a patch on the Leica M9 I still use now but it's got sentimental value. Then a Canon EOS which I still use for portraiture work and, of course, a Hasselblad.'

'So you still use film?'

That was her companion again. He made it sound like an offence punishable by hanging.

'Why abandon what was already perfect?'

The blonde permitted herself another small smile as he just stared back at me, blank.

'I'm serious. Film has a higher HDR, it can take up to three bracketed RAW digital files to achieve the same sort of tonal range. Also, zoom in on any digital picture and what do you see? A soup of square pixels. Do the same with a film image and you'll see a mosaic of random crystals which looks a lot more natural. And you don't need electricity, so when all the power in the world runs out and you can't charge your D-SLR you can still create photographic negatives and turn them into prints.'

I paused.

'Oh, and I forgot. The chemicals smell good too.'

The blonde cut across, extracting what was obviously for her the salient point in all that.

'Sentimental value. Does that mean you've kept them all?'

I stood, nodded towards a far door.

'I'll show you.'

It used to be the spare room. At one time we'd earmarked it as a possible nursery. Not that anything was ever said, just half-hints and coded references to the fact there was no balcony, that the window was set high up in the wall; all very child-friendly. Over the years, as the junk piled up inside and the emotional clutter piled up outside, the half-hints and coded references stopped. The day I cleared it out and rechristened it my darkroom marked the end of something, but neither myself nor Tia had ever sat down and worked out what. Probably now, we never would.

A pair of professional stainless steel sinks had been installed along with a unit of customised cabinets and worktops. The walls were reskimmed and painted steel-grey. The high window had been bricked up. And then – the finishing touch – a light trap revolving door had been fitted, guaranteed to create the perfect blackout.

'Impressive.'

That was the blonde. The photographer was back in our open-plan sitting room, probably still trying to work out which end of the lens to look through.

I nodded.

'Not much good without the rest of the kit though.'

'The rest being?'

'A Leitz 35mm enlarger, Kodak tray rocker.'

'Mechanised?'

I nodded again.

'And a Kindermann rapid dryer.'

'And for the prints?'

'Galleria bromide paper, Ilford brand lab chemicals.'

'And don't tell me. Delta 3200 for the film.'

'You know your stuff.'

'Last night I didn't know Kodak from Kit Kat.'

'So what changed?'

'I like to do my research.'

I hesitated, but let it pass. In any event she'd already turned to some prints tacked up on the wall.

'I like these.'

She picked up a couple of landscapes, brooding shots of the river under low cloud taken from one of the strange little beaches that occasionally bless the Thames, visible sometimes only for moments before the tide or, more usually, the swell from the river traffic, submerged them again.

Then she picked up a couple of close-ups, plants struggling up out of the mud, something almost heroic in their defiant claim to existence. No matter how many times the wash from the water blasted them against the quaysides and wharfs they still re-emerged, bruised and battered perhaps but usually intact, waiting for that one moment when the rest of the river was quiet and they could blossom and bloom. And that was the moment I'd caught them.

The blonde lingered over the simple images. Then, finally, came a grudging acknowledgement.

'I can never manage close-ups.'

'What camera are you using?'

'A Holga.'

Another reluctant admission. She obviously knew a little more than she cared to acknowledge.

'Not even with a macro lens?'

'Still looks like someone's washed over the whole thing with a paintbrush.'

'OK, try this.'

I hunched forward.

'Attach the lens anyway. Doesn't matter if it hasn't worked before, just do it. Then take off the back of the camera – .'

'Take it off?'

For the first time there was some sort of instinctive reaction, surprise replacing the more studied responses she'd affected so far.

'Tape a piece of greaseproof paper – or tracing or waxed, even parchment if that's all you can find – where the film would go.'

She nodded, her eyes now not leaving mine.

'Next, set your Holga to the B setting. Then set it up in a darkroom – it doesn't need to be anything professional, a windowless bathroom will do. Then light a candle, making sure you keep the lens in line with the flame. Then hold down the shutter. When you see the image of the flame on the paper, move the camera backwards and forwards. It might take you a few attempts but finally you'll have it, the flame in perfect focus.'

'So now I've got a flame in focus in a bathroom?'

She didn't sound impressed.

'Then you measure the distance from the flame to the lens. Write it down. If you stick to that distance when you're outside, doing any other close-up, the image is always going to be pin-sharp.'

I nodded at the close-ups of the plant life on the Thames mudflats.

'Like those.'

She studied them a moment longer.

'They're terrific.'

'Thanks.'

'Not too sure about these though.'

The blonde stared at some portraits taken in and around a hospital in Laos. I'd never have been given permission to shoot pictures like those in the UK. A man with no eyes or legs hunched over in a corridor, a woman, her features obliterated by a surgical mask by his side. Tia had always hated them and from the expression on the blonde's face it looked like she wasn't alone.

'Don't you ever feel it's exploitative?'

'To record something that's real?'

'It feels disrespectful.'

'They didn't even know I was there.'

'That's even worse, isn't it?'

'What's worse is when you line up your shot, assemble all the people who are going to be in the picture, arrange that side of the frame, then the other, checking the light's right, waiting for the exact moment the sun comes out from behind a cloud, whatever. And then you press the shutter and what have you got?'

'You tell me.'

'A lie.'

'Because?'

'Because you have to get them in the instant before they know you're watching. That split-second before they see the camera. Once they see it, once they know you're there, they're gone. The best shots are always accidental. Very often you don't know you've got it until you get back to your darkroom, start working through the prints, then you see something your eye didn't pick up but your camera didn't miss.'

She'd wandered off, her mind elsewhere.

'So you don't like it when people start posing?'

If I hadn't been so caught up in all that evangelical shit I was spouting I'd have seen it coming.

'I don't like it.'

'Because it's wrong to manipulate images?'

Too late, there it was, the trap-door opening right under my feet.

I gave a tight smile.

She really had done her research, hadn't she?

3

Half an hour later I manoeuvred the Duke out of the underground parking bay. Tia had sprayed herself into her leathers, black with red stitching, matching helmet. The geek in the accessories shop had told her it was the Emma Peel look and was rewarded with a stare of total incomprehension. I had to buy Tia the complete boxed set of the Sixties TV classic before she even began to understand what the hell he was talking about.

There's lots of bikes in the world and then there's this one – The Ducati Streetfighter 1098s. The press blurb said it was a bike that could only be described using superlatives. For once the overheated publicity department weren't just blowing hot air.

170hp with a dry weight of just 169kg in a machine that utilised more World Superbike technology than any bike before. 1098 Testastretta Evoluzione engine, top-of-the-range suspension, lightweight chassis, the first road bike to be fitted with a full race-spec traction control system.

And it didn't just have the looks. A totally ballistic 87.5lb-ft (11.7kgm) of torque, Öhlins suspension, fully adjustable 43mm Showa forks and with an additional special low friction titanium oxide treatment applied to the sliders.

OK, admittedly it was wasted on the clogged streets of the sinful city. Most of the time it just raged, impotently, a few short metres down to the next set of reds. But it was all still waiting there, straining to be unleashed and early one morning, two days after taking delivery, I'd let it have its head. With Tia on the back we'd slipped along the Highway and into the Limehouse Link. There was nothing else on the road. One practice run through the tunnel and then the real thing. Within two seconds of dipping down into the lighted yellow causeway, the engine was screaming, the rev counter already rocketing towards the red line. Another couple of seconds on and walls were flashing past at what seemed like the speed of light. At any moment I expected a sonic boom to shake the sleeping residents of the Basin above from their early morning slumbers. A police outrider joined the link at the first exit but he didn't even bother. He'd never have got within touching distance and probably didn't even want to try.

I pulled up the Duke by the Hospital Club a couple of streets away from Covent Garden. Tia jumped off, taking a small bag from the pannier that I'd – just – allowed to adorn the naked street art posing as a machine. As Tia had pointed out she couldn't really spend her whole working day prancing around in black leathers even with all that red stitching.

Tia worked for an events company in Covent Garden itself. They were a loose, rag-tag, collection of designers and PR consultants who worked together to stage basically anything a client required. If you had a gallery to launch they'd plan every moment of the opening evening right down to fireworks over Tower Bridge if inclination and budget stretched that far, complete with a guest list that was automatically updated with the latest wannabe-celeb. If you needed to publicise your latest book, film – even, in one case, a newly-refurbished mainline railway station – they were your one-stop shop.

No one commission was the same. Every event was different, which was why Tia loved it. She always said it was like reinventing yourself every time someone stepped through the door. A client starts talking about the event he has in mind and for a moment you're totally naked, no point referencing the event you'd just put on, the amazing evening you'd organised two months before, they'd probably been there. So had a vast majority of the potential guest list. With the prices her company charged each client expected, indeed demanded, exclusivity. Something different from the rest. So every time that door opened Tia and her merry band of designers, PR consultants, ex-models and office gofers had to re-design, from scratch, the wheel.

That's what that interview was all about. Normally I'd run a mile from anything of the sort. With everything that had happened I'd developed something of an aversion to all matters journalistic. Google my name – Jack Connolly – and you'll soon see why. Page after page scrolling out across cyberspace, updated every few seconds at one time it seemed by more voices, more opinions, from simple punters to national politicians, all keen to jump on the bandwagon, express their view on one of the burning matters of the moment.

Tia had received a new commission for a performing arts school on the outer fringes of Shoreditch. A couple of ageing rock stars had endorsed it, not only with their names by way of support, but also with cold hard cash. The problem being it involved the building in question in a change of use – from a local community centre – and there'd already been some rumblings of opposition so Tia wanted all local opinion makers on side. That included local and national press, hence the blonde and her male companion who weren't exactly in the running for the Pulitzer Prize, but who could now be counted on to write a more or less glowing endorsement of the new venture that was taking shape on their home turf.

A couple more interviews with the ageing rock stars themselves, maybe an invite or two to the right sort of launch parties and the new school would be hailed with as much fervour as the Second Coming.

It wasn't just the launch itself that was important as Tia knew only too well. It was everything associated with it. Not missing a single trick.

But today there was going to be a detour. It was why I'd been pressed into unleashing the Duke. Tia wanted to show me something by way of thanks. It was another thing she'd learnt in her new incarnation as fixer of the weird and the wonderful. I'd done a couple of shoots for some record companies in the past and the mantra went something like a musical scale: Every Good Boy Deserves A Favour.

Tia led me past the street performers, cut through the covered piazza, weaving in and out of a crowd watching a juggler on stilts. A small child started to cry. All he could see were a pair of long legs in front of him with, seemingly, no body attached and he really didn't like the way the world had suddenly distorted before his eyes. On the other side of the square, Tia headed into a small alley I'd never noticed before before pausing outside a nondescript-looking shop. Then she turned, flashing that dazzling smile of hers.

'Here we are.'

Tia hadn't always been in this game. I'd first met her when she was just another arsy kid working the basketball courts and playgrounds used as blank canvasses by a hundred other similar souls. She'd just come back from Cape Town where she'd left her tag. Before that she'd hit a wall on the Paris-Versailles train line as well as the Amtrak line in New York. Her life in street art – graffiti to some – urban vandalism to others – started like most by stealing into train yards, toting a holdall containing up to a hundred spray cans, selecting colours largely by touch before spraying carriages in the pitch dark.

Initially, it was as much about the excitement, the thrill of the forbidden, as the finished product. As Tia always said, they bring you up on superheroes and then expect you to stay home and watch quiz shows. Everyone needs a buzz and nights spent breaking into train yards or riding subways in foreign cities was hers.

But for a time it looked like it was going to be something more than that. While local councillors fumed, while the British Transport Police set up a special unit to pursue the taggers, while a street artist from Bath was charged with causing, allegedly, sixty grands' worth of damage to his home city, the large corporations started moving in.

Red Bull, Adidas, Puma, Lee and 55DSL all started incorporating graffiti into their marketing campaigns. And where big business led, so the art world started to follow; Black Rat Press, Elms Lester off the Charing Cross Road and Stolen Space near Brick Lane, well-known haunt of customised bank note man, D*Face, to mention a few. And once the Hollywood A-list started frequenting their auctions everyone really did start waking up and smelling the coffee.

All of a sudden this wasn't vandalism any more. All of a sudden this was collectible and in a way not seen before. Up to then it was the usual sort of trajectory if you wanted to make it in that sort of world. A stint at Art School – finishing was optional but beginning was more or less compulsory – followed by a couple of gallery shows. They'd be shared, you'd be one of a handful of similar hopefuls all trying not to look too hopeful and trying not to look too obviously delighted when one of your pieces was bought by an influential collector or media conglomerate, although the resulting invitations to cool parties would usually summon up the ghost of a grin.

Everyone was still cautious though. There'd been false dawns in the field before. Norman Mailer – no less a heavyweight – had written a book about graffiti back in the Seventies. Jeffrey Deitch had urged collectors to invest in a whole graffiti-covered train and then mothball it although there were few takers for that particular flight up the flagpole. In the same year Stash had his first on-canvas show at the Fun Gallery but it still didn't herald anything like take-off for what seemed to be a movement destined, like so many, to be strangled at birth.

Then came cyberspace. And all that Myspace did for bands, the internet did for graffiti. Within a few months it had become a full-blown movement and Tia had become the subject of a feature in *Sleazenation*. One week later, she was mixing with Adam Neate and Swoon. One week on again and one of her pieces sold for ten thousand and that was already underpriced. Not bad for a girl from the Island whose Dad rode the river clippers all day as a conductor.

The problem was she started to lose touch with all that gave her work that impetus and excitement in the first place. Once it had started to become absorbed into the mainstream, once it had become the object of the sort of interest the artists themselves used to pillory in their creations, once the council started licensing areas where the artists could practise and perfect their art free from interference or prosecution, something started to change. Some of the established names rode the flow but Tia was finding it harder and harder.

Partly it was that first sale. Another collector wanted something similar, another wanted something exactly the same. She started to lose interest just as the rest of the world started to take an interest in her and the rest of her bandit band of spray-can saboteurs. Which is when I made what, in retrospect, turned out to be a mistake.

We'd got together a few months before. I'd been sent on an assignment to shoot some of the new breed of street artists in action and had a whole load of paint flung over me by Tia who'd mistaken me for an undercover cop and thought my camera was her one-way ticket to a date with the local magistrate. By the time the confusion was cleared up I had bright yellow hair and looked like a canary, but it wasn't all bad. It turned out Tia liked canaries. At least she said she did. That night, back in my bed. And she seemed to mean it.

For a couple of months after that we travelled as I accepted assignments in far-flung parts of the world. I took my prints back home. Tia left her tag behind.

I made sure images of some of her better efforts were spread around the new style magazines that were then springing up almost weekly. I even managed to include a couple of her pieces in the background of one of the urban assignments I'd been asked to complete, a photo report on a township near Soweto that wanted to send a team to compete in the Homeless World Cup.

From there it was a short step to the next. Music had always gone hand in glove with graffiti, particularly Hip-hop, Rap and Deejaying. Lots of bands wanted street art adorning their posters that would then be pasted the length and breadth of the Old Kent Road. Tia had submitted some designs to one of the up-and-coming companies and they were being picked over by the management team of a new band that, so rumour had it, were about to break big. I knew the management team in question and pushed her designs along a little. It wasn't just altruism on my part, I genuinely thought her work had the edge. But maybe, as Tia was to later point out, I was just a tiny bit blinkered when it came to any independent assessment of her talent.

Tia secured the commission. And all of a sudden she was buzzing again. She worked all night on some modified designs she was going to present the next day. She went in early the next morning to the agency, was let in by the arriving receptionist who made her coffee. As she handed Tia her morning mocha she added one small bit of bile.

It was only a throwaway remark. The remark referenced Tia, her designs and her boyfriend. It wasn't explicit but it was clear enough. Tia was only there because of who she knew, not because of what she'd done – certainly not what was in that thin folder she was currently carrying. The receptionist wasn't exactly impartial herself, it turned out her boyfriend was on the rejected shortlist, meaning she very definitely had an axe to grind.

There's a French movie called *Shoot The Piano Player*. It's about this musician who plays piano in a cheap bar. Charles Aznavour – later to become a famous crooner – plays the lead. He used to be a concert pianist and was destined for greatness, but then he discovered that in much earlier days his wife had slept with an impresario to kick-start his career. For her it was an act of love but he didn't see it that way. He walked out on her, feeling all his achievements to be tainted. She committed suicide. It didn't quite go that far with Tia. But something still seemed to change inside her that day.

The designs were received OK, she just needed to do some more work on them, that's all. The usual stuff everyone gets, doesn't matter whether you work in fine art or fine dining. They gave her a deadline of the next day which passed without her making any sort of contact. That was cool, deadlines were meant to be broken. Then the next day passed and the next. The more she looked at her original designs the more she decided she liked them. The more the band looked at them the more they decided they did not. It never got to any sort of massive face-off, the band and their management just found someone else. Over the next couple of months they played a couple of festivals, mainly in Europe, but then they did what so many bands did around that time and since; faded away. Tia's short-lived career in the music game did much the same.

We never really talked about it. I was busy then, away a lot. But then she went off for a week, I didn't know where at first. At first I thought it was to regroup, rethink, lick her wounds, whatever.

In fact she'd gone to paint her final goodbye to it all. Her last, great big fuck-you.

Tia travelled to Bristol and picked out the shabbiest, shittiest end terrace in one of the run-down suburbs fringing the city centre. She made sure it was visible from one of the main train lines as well as from the elevated arterial road route into and out of the city. Then she spent three nights working on stencils in a small bed and breakfast which didn't even provide a breakfast to go with the bed.

Tia picked the longest night of the year although she had a pretty shrewd suspicion she wouldn't need all those hours of darkness and she was right. She was out of her lodgings and at the shabby, shitty house by midnight. A few moments later she'd smashed the bulb on the only street light that provided any sort of illumination on that particular example of the city's not-so-exalted housing stock. Five minutes later, she was hard at work. Three hours after that she was back in the bed and breakfast. By the time daylight dawned and the first of the trains had cranked along the nearby line and its passengers had peered, blearily, out of the windows – and by the time the first of the cars had choked their way along the elevated arterial overpass as well – the whole area was buzzing.

A favourite local son had done it again, it seemed. He'd left his calling card on what had never been intended as a local landmark but was now, very definitely, one of the most prominent. It was a typically cute design too. A window had, apparently, been let into the wall through which could be seen a picture-postcard beach and palm trees. The contrast with its actual surroundings was acute and, it was assumed, ironic. In fact it was a prediction but none of those early viewers could have known that then.

Art lovers flocked in their hordes. Galleries received thousands of hits as they registered the latest addition to the canon on their websites. A local coach operator started advertising sightseeing tours for those wise souls who didn't particularly relish the thought of parking their upmarket vehicles anywhere in the immediate vicinity.

Meanwhile the owners of the house stared in some bemusement at the newly decorated pine end of their previously-unremarkable home, a bemusement that soon turned to something else when they were enlightened as to the likely value of the windfall that had apparently been visited on them overnight from the gods.

There was an attempt to contact the favourite son to verify once and for all the provenance of the piece but all such enquiries were met with the usual stonewall. The artist in question, according to an email that finally arrived at one of the enquiring galleries, was away polishing one of his yachts.

It was always going to be a long shot anyway. The artist was a famed recluse who would never confirm or deny authorship of any of his work. It was up to the art establishment to decide. And they decided. The mural was the genuine article.

One day later the previously-bemused, now totally switched-on, home owners announced the auction of the mural with the house thrown in for free. The house sold the next day for six hundred grand to a Ukrainian collector who demolished it brick by brick and transported it to a gallery just outside Odessa.

Two weeks later, two hundred grand appeared in Tia's bank account from an unnamed and unidentified source which she put down as her share of the deposit on our Narrow Street loft.

She went back just once after that to have a farewell drink with her old school friend, formerly of that same end terrace, who'd by now put her share of the proceeds into a picture-postcard beach house on St Kitts.

Tia opened the door of the small, nondescript-looking shop which gave onto a smaller, even more nondescript gallery space. Nothing was hanging on the walls and there was nothing on the floor waiting to be hung on those whitewashed walls either.

Then a man came through from the back with an accent I later identified as pure Bronx but which sounded, on first acquaintance, as if he'd been the recent victim of some seriously heavy-duty torture. The man with the vandalised vowels took us into the back room and opened up a large display drawer. He took out the first item that came to hand, the only item in that particular drawer in fact.

Say 'One Sheet', 'Subway', 'Lobby Card', 'Insert' and 'Half Sheet' to most people and their eyes are going to glaze over. Say it to a certain type of movie freak and their toes are going to start tapping. A bit like mine were tapping right there and then in the back room of that shop.

Ever stood in line at a cinema, looked at the posters around the lobby advertising the current big hit? What do you see? A cheap piece of advertising? Something to lure you inside, let you know who's in the movie, who directed it, who produced it, something that's just there to promote the product, boost the box office, to be taken down and stored when the movie finishes its run or, more likely, simply canned? Try telling that to Richard Amsel, to Bob Peak, to Drew Struzan or to the Hildebrant brothers. Tell that to Saul Bass. Or to the Grandfather – maybe even the Great-Grandfather of them all – Jules Chéret.

The world was a different place when the movie was born. Illiteracy was rife, what mattered were images that could be understood by anyone, anywhere. One face on a movie poster could have an audience flocking to a theatre in droves. And once a star's contract began to specify the size of their image and exact placement of their name, the modern age of the movie poster had well and truly arrived.

But still no-one was collecting them. Still they were just disposable ephemera. But then the major studios turned over the distribution of their movie posters to the National Screen Service who established a dating and numbering system, usually found on the border of the poster. And then the collecting craze began.

That's what I was looking at now. A simple number – 74/94. It was a reflex reaction to double-check even though I knew from the half-smile on the face of the man with the strangled larynx that this was well and truly the real thing. Then I looked at the poster itself.

First, the by-line –

He was 25 years old.

Then at the boy standing by a tree.

He combed his hair like James Dean.

A girl sitting next to him.

She was 15. She took music lessons and could twirl a baton.

The young couple sitting apart, no contact between them.

For a while they lived together in a tree house.

A gun in the boy's hand.

In 1959, she watched while he killed a lot of people.

The Internet Movie Database – something of a Bible for movie insiders – provided a simple summary of the plot which, like most summaries of just about every decent and even half-decent movie you could mention, said absolutely nothing at all.

Dramatization of the Starkweather-Fugate killing spree of the 1950s, in which a teenage girl and her twenty-something boyfriend slaughtered her entire family and several others in the Dakota badlands.

In one sense I understood nothing about it. I didn't understand Kit and why he felt compelled to kill, first, Holly's father and then go off on his subsequent spree. I didn't understand Holly's attraction to him aside from the fact, as Tia had often pointed out, that the young Martin Sheen was undeniably hot.

Not that Holly seemed to find him all that hot. Their first sexual experience on the bank of a local river provoked just one response from her;

Is that it?

And Kit didn't seem exactly overwhelmed. He didn't see what everyone made all the fuss about either.

Everything seemed to float on the surface for the two lovers, including the characters they encountered and the situations they endured. They seemed as much of a mystery to each other as the landscape they traversed, human and otherwise. At the end justice finally caught up with Kit and he was taken away by the police. All he was concerned about were the arresting officer's clothes and hat.

I'd watched it so many times I could even tell you all the mistakes, the anachronisms or – to use a technical term – the goofs.

At the beginning of the movie, Kit meets Holly after a long day as a garbage man and his white T-shirt is spotless. Kit then asks Holly to take a walk with him, at which point his T-shirt is magically dirty.

Although the film takes place in the late 1950s, there's a modern Ford car dealership sign visible in one of the shots.

A passenger train that passes Kit and Holly at one point is pulling Amtrak cars. Amtrak wasn't established until 1971.

Even though the film takes place in 1959 the soldiers at the end of the movie can be seen with M14 rifles, which replaced the M1. First deliveries of the M14 were made to the US Army in July of 1959 and weren't in wide circulation until 1961. It's unlikely, to say the least, that National Guard units in Montana would have been among the first recipients. Also, the rifles lacked any magazines meaning the troops were carrying unloaded weapons.

In a voice-over near the Montana / South Dakota border, Holly says –

... at the very edge of the horizon we could make out the gas fires of the refinery at Missoula, while to the south we could see the lights of Cheyenne, a city bigger and grander than I'd ever seen.

I'd been there. From anywhere along the border, Missoula would be over six hundred miles to the west, and Cheyenne would be some three hundred miles to the south. Nothing short of a satellite would allow you to see both at the same time.

Who cares? I didn't. Maybe in the only sense that mattered I understood everything. But I still watched it time and again, examined it frame by frame. Tia said I was trying to explain the inexplicable. She was right and she was wrong. It might have been what I was trying to do but nothing was inexplicable as I'd assured her in turn. You just needed the right vocabulary that's all. I hadn't found it yet when it came to Kit and Holly but that didn't mean I wouldn't.

The business side was concluded pretty quickly. Tia had already paid for the poster, it was just the aftercare we had to sort out and that was all pretty routine. The man with the speech patterns from Mars was a professional after all.

He knew better than anyone that this particular beauty was never going to be dry-mounted. The dry-mounting process requires that the poster be, effectively, glued to a backing and the only way it could ever be removed from that backing in future would be courtesy of a professional restorer.

The poster would be going into a glass frame – it was for permanent display after all although it would never be exhibited in direct sunlight or under UV lights – but it would have an acid-free backing board and would be matted so it never came into direct contact with the glass.

The poster would then be linen backed using the double-mounting process meaning it would first be pasted – using a vegetable cellulose paste – to Japanese rice paper and then mounted to linen or duck cloth. A poster should never be mounted paper to cloth. In the worst case scenario, the constant rubbing of the poster against the cloth could actually result in its complete disintegration.

4 .

I WALKED OUT of the Covent Garden shop on a high. It wasn't just the present itself. It wasn't just the fact that another much-prized and eminently-collectable One Sheet – of *The Wild Bunch* this time – might be coming in soon and the movie poster man advised me to keep calling back and I told him I would. It was the fact that Tia did it all the time. We'd been together five years and she never stopped thinking. What would I like? What would please me?

The year before she'd found an autographed copy of the *Badlands* screenplay signed by Sissy Spacek. Not content with the certificate of authentication she tracked down the lady herself. She'd fixed up a transatlantic call where we could talk one-on-one. An amused Ms Spacek had been forced to deal with some pushy individuals in the past but nothing it seemed compared to this clearly-driven caller from deepest, darkest, Tower Hamlets.

My only regret was not taping the call. Memories are now inevitably fading. It would have been good to have those moments preserved as if in aspic, ready to summon up at a moment's notice, pore over each half-hesitation, each pause.

Similarly, I wanted to preserve this moment, savour the high. It seemed too ordinary somehow to climb back onto the Duke and simply head home. I checked it was secure, paid the equivalent of a minor ransom to park it up for the next few hours, then cut down to the Strand, then along Fleet Street towards the distant dome of St Paul's.

At Tower Bridge I paused. The quickest way back to the loft was along the Highway. If I preferred the scenic, but slightly longer, route I could have cut down Wapping Lane and taken the River Walk. I stared across Royal Mint Street sensing, if not actually seeing, the alternative.

And decided to take a sentimental journey instead.

I cut through the Georgian Peabody and Whitechapel Squares, always the most gentrified part of the manor. You couldn't even see the otherwise ever-present overhead DLR from there. The communal area in front of the upmarket apartments was dominated by a playground where no children ever seemed to play. Here, silence was indeed forever golden.

Then it was Grace's Alley. Even when I was growing up it had a magical ring to it which had nothing to do with the fact, as we learnt in the nearby school, that it was a memorial to the local Cistercian abbey that stood by the river. It was much more to do with the fact it was still home to Wilton's Music Hall – still extraordinary, still exotic – though for how much longer was anyone's guess. A theatre company had now made it their home and were staging rehearsals as the sounds emanating from inside attested, but the only thing that was ever going to guarantee its survival was a return to its heyday – already too long in the past – as a venue for regular shows.

Then I came out onto the Square, three tower blocks dominating the open space.

This was where I was born and all I could remember, from my earliest days, was a feeling of being squeezed somehow. The new developments had already started, grouped around News International to the south and the gradual spread of Whitechapel – the new Whitechapel – to the north. Shadwell was fast becoming colonised by the new developments springing up in and around Limehouse to the east and as for the west, Tower Bridge had always marked the division between the have and have-nots. Old time residents would sit on benches on the walkways and look at an ever-multiplying panorama of cranes on the skyline and predict the destruction of the three tower blocks within a few short years.

A lot of the people I'd grown up with had stayed around. It was that kind of place and I hated it for that very reason. It squeezed you on the outside and on the inside too. Maybe it was down to being a Square. Wherever you were it felt like the whole world was looking at you. Maybe that was why I'd picked up that first camera. With that held to my eye – and as I'd perhaps incautiously explained to the blonde – no-one could see me.

Dozens of businesses had since sprung up along the nearby Cable Street, nestling in the old railway arches. Mini-cabs, car hire, storage outlets, mobile food vans. It should have felt vibrant but it didn't. It felt dead. And my new-found sense of well-being was fast fading. And it was about to disappear completely.

There was a row of strange little links houses on the eastern side of the Square. Some were little more than prefabs although they did have small gardens to the front and rear. They looked onto more permanent structures opposite that boasted coach lamps and brass door knockers. As I passed, one of the prefab doors opened and out stepped the Professor.

He wasn't, needless to say, the genuine article. It was a name he'd been given in school and it had stuck. He'd even played up to it for a time. He took the occasional class of younger kids when a hard-pressed teacher was forced into playground duty to cover for some absent teaching assistant. Later, the police reckoned he'd started abusing them when he was still just shy of his tenth birthday. The first time they put it down to an immature response to the shy adoration of unformed minds. By the time the sixth or seventh parent had made the same complaint it was clear he was just a plain and simple nonce.

He still had the same high forehead. He still had the same glasses, dark frames, thick lenses. And he still had the same line in wit.

'Well, well, Pinocchio.'

Everyone knows the story of Pinocchio, right? Years ago there was a carpenter named Geppetto who made a boy from wood. Then the Blue Fairy came along and made the wooden boy come alive which was fortunate because that was his dream.

Pinocchio wanted to be a real boy but in order to become one he had to endure a series of tests. His curse was that his wooden nose grew every time he was under stress, particularly when he was telling a lie. When he told the truth, his nose shrunk back.

The Professor – his defence mechanism already up and running it seemed – told tales about us all when we were growing up. It was a classic way of diverting attention from himself. This boy was a thief, that girl was a slag. For some reason he'd latched onto the notion that I was a liar. I genuinely couldn't remember why. Maybe I'd told a lie at some time, who hadn't?

We'd lost touch over the years although I followed some of his seedier exploits in the local paper on the few occasions they'd been mailed to me by a mother – now dead – keen to keep me in touch with what she called my roots. Roots were all the Professor should have had any sort of contact with too, preferably from the wrong side of a shallow grave.

The problem being that the last couple of years had given my childhood nickname all the gravitas of a prediction by Nostradamus. I may not have been made of wood and my nose might not have automatically elongated and retracted, but in the eyes of everyone I knew, everyone I'd ever worked with, everyone I'd ever shared a drink with in some foreign bar on some assignment somewhere, I was now well and truly labelled a liar.

The Professor eyed me. He didn't get a lot of excitement or enjoyment in his life these days. Too many beatings in too many not-so-secure units had left him more or less crippled and, certainly now, impotent too, but before he could speak again

I turned away. It never made sense to trade insults with a man who looked at small children and saw what he saw.

The problem being that when he looked at me he saw something else too. Something difficult to deny. Something recorded in every journal I'd ever worked for. Something enshrined in every cyberspace hit that contained my name, something I was going to have to live with for the rest of my days which meant my childhood companion and myself shared something in common at least. No-one, it seems, ever escapes their past.

Which was when a much more appealing voice cut across from that same past.

'Hey, the Leica Legend.'

The Professor scowled at the interruption. Standing behind us was a brunette in an outfit that hadn't ever been within spitting distance of any local High Street. Trudie Rosa might have come originally from a similar estate, in her case down on the Island where she and Tia went to school together, but she now ran one of the smartest film sales agencies this side of Burbank.

Trudie also had a daughter in one of the local schools – private, not state – which was where she'd just been and she was about to hop on a shuttle from the City Airport across to Berlin where she was to close a deal that night on worldwide distribution for a new art-house flick that wasn't going to stay in art houses for long if the redoubtable Trudie had anything to do with it.

All that didn't come out immediately. That came out over an overpriced Americano in the lobby of a nearby chain hotel. Trudie reckoned she'd be needing a pretty massive launch party soon – red carpets, Leicester Square, rent-a-celeb, the whole bundle. She was going to get in touch with Tia when she got back to see if she could arrange something. Maybe I could take some of the stills? If I wasn't too busy chewing the cud with the lowest of all local lowlifes and taking trips down memory lane?

Trudie wasn't just an old friend to Tia, Trudie had stood by me too, hadn't blocked my calls and had always returned them if she was away or out of the country. But she still couldn't quite make the offer sound anything more than it was. Charity. Trudie and the Professor occupied different planets but there was still that same hesitation in her voice when the conversation skirted on the thin ice of the not-so-recent past.

She didn't want to push me under, like the Professor. But she knew it was there, as we both knew it always would be.

I let myself back into the loft half an hour later. I'd walked Trudie past the security guards randomly, ever more randomly it seemed, stopping cars and cabs as they headed towards the bars and offices of Canary Wharf. Then we'd walked down the wide boulevard, past the sterile and antiseptic small mall of newsagents, coffee shops and chain outlet restaurants before taking a right and then a left to the station.

Trudie told me to tell Tia she'd be in touch when she got back. Then she repeated her offer that I take the stills at the launch party. She couldn't think of anyone who would do it better.

Her nose didn't grow and she held my stare, steady. But she was still lying about the last bit and she knew it and so did I.

I poured myself a Jack Daniels, took it out onto the balcony that ran the whole length of the loft. I looked down at a clipper that had just pulled out from the pier a few hundred metres to the left, dodging the smaller tug that made the short hop across the water every ten minutes or so during peak commuter hours from a waterside hotel on Surrey Quays. It ran every twenty minutes during the evening and weekends and it kept pretty good time too because I'd once spent weeks checking on it.

I'd spent those same weeks checking on the larger clippers too. They'd start at six in the morning on weekdays coming up from Woolwich. They'd come into sight of the loft as they were approaching Greenland Pier some sixteen minutes later before moving on towards Tower Bridge roughly fifteen minutes after that. The last service of the day would come back into view around half-past midnight and I'd watch it disappear around the bend in the river heading all the way back to Woolwich as the clock turned one in the morning.

Weekends were more leisurely with a start from Woolwich around 8.30 a.m.

I knew the timetable by heart because it's all I did for all those weeks. I sat on the balcony, a bottle of Jack Daniels at my elbow, emptying the bottle, checking the appearance of the riverboats against a pocket timetable. For a while it totally occupied me. Once the west-bound boat passed I knew I'd have the east-bound to track in just a few moments. And by the time the service stopped completely the bottle was empty and I was unconscious. I woke early, but always with the comforting realisation that within a fairly short space of time the river would come to life again and the routine would resume.

You didn't need to be any sort of half-decent shrink to realise I was blotting things out. Taking refuge in mind-numbing tedium so as not to open that same mind to what was waiting to ambush it again.

Tia understood. She left me largely alone, just checking on me from time to time, making sure I wasn't sitting too close to the edge of the balcony too late at night after too many sips of that Tennessee whiskey, that sort of thing. She knew I'd work it through, get it all out of my system in time. I did the former but still wasn't too sure about the latter.

I'd been sent on an assignment to a war no-one believed should be fought. But the rights and wrongs weren't my job. Some of the journalists could – and would – write opinion pieces: should we be there, why were we there, what were the costs, long and short term, of our involvement? My opinion didn't count. I was there to create a testament to events as they unfolded. The way I saw it I was following in a fine and honourable tradition of photographers who operated in similar arenas like Robert Capa and Felice Beato. There, as I was about to discover, the similarity would end.

'Never Again' – the headline blazoned across the front pages. Eight British soldiers had died as a result of what had been called friendly fire, an oxymoron only just excused in the general panic and hysteria that followed. A five-star General went on record to say it would be his personal quest that the deaths would not be forgotten. The sound never would, as all who had the misfortune to hear it testified.

It was a cross between a scream and a roar, a fierce rattling of fire from two B-1B Lancers flying low overhead, aircraft that shouldn't have been in the British-controlled area at all. They were sweeping across at approximately five hundred feet looking for something to fire at and they found it.

The two American pilots turned their guns on a convoy of British vehicles from the 1st Battalion Welsh Guards, instantly killing one man who'd just celebrated his twenty-sixth birthday, fatally injuring four others and wiping out two armoured reconnaissance vehicles. Two civilians, each waving a large white flag, were also killed.

Within seconds, the planes came back a second time. By now the forward Air Controller was screaming over the radio, 'Check fire, check fire'. At the same time, near-hysterical calls were being made to Air Assault Brigade headquarters to find out what the hell was going on.

The B-IB Lancers were on their third approach when they were finally told by the American Air Patroller to stop firing. Usually, they'd stay on patrol to provide air cover while helicopters came in to evacuate the casualties, but they didn't. They baled out.

Anger swiftly replaced the initial stunned disbelief. All the 1st Battalion's vehicles were clearly marked with fluorescent panels on the roof. No-one could even begin to understand how the pilots hadn't seen them or the flags that also clearly identified them as part of the coalition air force.

One of the 1st Battalion's vehicles was still smoking the following morning. The bodies inside couldn't be immediately retrieved as the vehicle was fully loaded with ammunition, turning it into a tinderbox. When the rescue mission was finally attempted, chemical suits has to be worn because of the depleted uranium in the American assault weapons.

Trooper Steven Rohl, 19, the driver of one of the destroyed vehicles, survived with only a hole in the shirtsleeve of his bullet-proof vest made when shrapnel entered and exited without touching his arm. In the immediate aftermath of the attack he'd simply walked away. As he made clear to anyone who'd listen, he couldn't figure it out. The soldiers who'd died had wives, children, people who'd mourn them. He had an elderly mother and a sister he hadn't seen for three years. Why couldn't it have been him?

I had a drink with him that night in the makeshift mess bar. And we spent the night talking recipes.

Steven came from a small village just outside St Davids – not St David's as he was keen to point out – in the west of Wales. Any further west and you'd be looking at New York. It was way off the beaten track, miles from anywhere, the kind of place where you had to make your own entertainment and Steven knew exactly the kind he wanted to create too.

When Steven was small his mother had taken him to a local tearoom for his birthday. It was the smell he remembered best – warm, stuffy almost – but sweet. All the smells of childhood wrapped in a great big bow and served up in one small space. He'd been served tea in a large china pot that arrived with a three-tier silver tray and a selection of cakes and pastries. Steven had been given the choice, it was his birthday after all. Steven had picked up the first one that came to hand, taken a bite, and that was that. He was transported.

The tearoom closed a couple of years later. People didn't take tea any more it seemed. But maybe that was because the tearoom had been taken over by a chain that knocked out factory-made pastries and cakes bought in from a catering unit that also supplied all the local hotels and guest houses. They'd lost the sweet smell of baking dough that wafted from the kitchens out onto the street, that stopped shoppers and day trippers and small children and wafted them back inside.

And that was Steven's dream. To reopen that shop. To restore it to its former glory, just as he remembered it. Every spare penny he could save, Trooper Rohl was now saving. When he had enough for a deposit he was going to apply for a small business loan and start turning that dream into a reality.

Steven was aware himself of course that he was simply attempting to re-create what was in all probability his happiest childhood memory. The combination was pretty irresistible after all – a birthday, a doting mother, a silver tray that must have looked like it contained all the treats the world could offer. But Steven was also hardnosed enough to have spent all his spare time reading up on recipes and now he reckoned he'd found his secret weapon, which was the ultimate cake. Called, appropriately enough I suppose, a Welsh cake.

I'd never heard of these cakes till that night in the makeshift bar thousands of miles away from the country of their origin. But, and courtesy of some coasters picked off that same bar, Steven enlightened me. The cakes were about the same size and shape. They were made from flour, butter or lard, eggs, sugar and currants or raisins and were also known as bakestones because they'd traditionally be cooked on a Welsh *maen* or bakestone which was a cast-iron griddle. They could be served hot or cold and dusted with caster sugar, a bit like the English scone. But unlike scones they weren't usually eaten with any sort of accompaniment.

They were pretty well perfect as they were, according to Steven. But he had a variant on the theme that really made them special because Steven cooked them with plain flour, usually wholemeal, rather than the standard self-raising variety and baking powder, which resulted in a much flatter and crisper cake. He also added grated apple to the mix which helped keep the cake moist for longer.

As for the taste, Steven's eyes just grew dreamy. No other description seemed necessary.

He didn't mention the events of the day or his dead companions all evening. All he talked about were his cakes. Maybe that's why no-one saw it coming. All that seemed to be on his mind that night was the future.

The next morning, unarmed, he walked towards an enemy position, two hundred metres across a road that had become a no-go area. Even the hunting birds stayed away. A couple of colleagues tried to get to him but his body was ripped to pieces by a hailstorm of bullets before he'd covered even a quarter of the distance towards his date with death.

It was suicide. Pure and simple. Totally needless and pointless. Another useless death. And something happened inside me. Maybe it was seeing those other totally needless and pointless deaths the day before. Maybe I just wanted one death at least to count.

The Army were already preparing their own sanitised account of what had happened. I prepared my own. Steven's body was still where it had fallen, his killers had turned tail and had run. I walked across, retracing his last steps, put a gun in his hand and composed the shot. From a low angle you could see the position he was, apparently, attempting to storm.

All I wanted to do at that stage was send an image home to his elderly mother, his estranged sister.

Look what he was.

Look how he died.

Trying to make a difference – trying to make his life, his time out there – count.

The photo was picked up for syndication. It was blazoned across national news bulletins in the UK and the US. It was even nominated for a couple of Press Association prizes. By that time it had become too late to correct the misapprehension, but I didn't want to. That simple trooper was going to be remembered as a hero as so many others should have been so remembered but weren't. Where was the harm in that? But it was a naïve question and I knew that even in those first few days of the picture flashing its way around all those different agencies throughout the world.

I'd penned a few lines about the tearoom to accompany the picture. Some enterprising home-based journo had tracked down the actual place and written a supplementary feature about it, interviewing a few people from his home town at the same time about its now-dead son. Maybe it was a slow news day or maybe it just captured some mood, who knows? For the next few days the press and TV were full of it. There was something in the tale of the burly soldier who went into battle dreaming of tearooms and cakes that seemed to resonate with everyone. Ever mindful of a bandwagon and ever desirous of hitching a ride, a tribute was paid to Steven by his local MEP. A couple of tabloids made him the face of the war that week. A food programme on cable TV even reprinted his cake recipe.

I got the call late on a Saturday night. Far too late to do

anything about it even if I could, as they knew. They'd pulled this sort of stroke many times before and would do so many times again. They knew their trade and in the opinion of the journalist who called me that night it was just a pity I didn't know mine, and I suppose he had a point.

The press, UK and worldwide, has always operated on a system of levers and pulleys. The pendulum effect. Build your star up to the sky and then push the pendulum, watch it start to swing all the way back down again. Destroy what once you'd created. Turn into dust the dreams you'd made – albeit temporarily – real.

Steven had become an unlikely hero and that had made for good copy but now came the real story. The feet of clay. The confidence trick exposed. The latest sorry saga in the ever sorrier tale of one of the sorriest wars the country had ever been duped into fighting.

A couple of soldiers in the unit had broken ranks. Why? Jealousy was a possible motive, but unlikely. More likely they'd just endured enough lies to last them what was probably destined to be a pretty short lifetime. It started as the odd whisper here, a small rumour there. But it was enough.

The next morning the headline screamed out from the newsstands. The specific words didn't really matter although they were pretty damning in themselves. Words like, fraud, cheat, usually are. Worse, everyone seemed to agree. It was the sense of let-down that was the problem. Of being conned. Of putting faith in what turned out to be a gilded creation, all glister and no gold.

For the heavyweight Sunday papers the real story behind Steven and his death was a metaphor for the whole war itself, a PR exercise designed to sell the gullible electorate a false view of reality.

For the tabloids it was a pure and simple con. Questions were asked in the House. The former tearoom featured in the profile was daubed with yellow paint, the traditional colour of the coward. Steven's sister – who hadn't spoke about him all through the previous media aggrandisement – gave an interview to a daytime TV show hinting darkly at yet more poison to come. How, after all, could you trust a man who spent his days dreaming of making pastry?

I didn't have a network of support around me at the time to help field it all. I'd been proud to call myself freelance for the previous few years which gave me all the freedom I craved, but no safety net if the world ever turned hostile and cold. The upside was the newspapers didn't have to censure their own structures or staff. It was one rogue element in the journalistic firmament that was to blame, one single cancerous growth on the press politic and everyone knew the best treatment for that.

Cut it out.

Excise it.

Remove it from existence; which they did.

Then came the hatchet job on a couple of my other stories too. They were mainly motivated by professional spite – nothing being more satisfying in some circles than the sight of a colleague once riding high now brought low. A couple of comments here, the odd raised eyebrow there, and that was enough to not only spike some pictures that had yet to make an appearance, but question those that were already out there.

Was that picture posed too? Was there just a little too much artifice about that composition? It was all part of the general falling out of favour, a career in freefall. Once it starts there's no stopping it, although I tried. Initially I rushed into print defending stuff I knew was the genuine article but all that did, if I'd stopped to think about it, was draw even more attention to the implicit admission that the Steven portrait was anything but.

And that's all people saw. The stain in the corner of the landscape. That finally spread to engulf it all.

After a while I did what Tia told me to do. Sit on it. And sit tight. Don't speak out, don't try and defend what was, in most people's eyes, the indefensible anyway. Ride the punches, accept the law of the rollercoaster and maybe – just maybe – one day I'd ride it all the way back up to the top again. That day seemed a long way off when she first said it but I accepted it. In truth, I had little choice.

A month or so after the story broke I received a letter of thanks from Steven's elderly mother. She was the one sole voice of support but as she was, by then, already frail enough to be living in a respite home it didn't exactly provide much of a bulwark against the rest of the hostile tide; but it was something.

What did it teach me? Aside from an encyclopaedic knowledge of the daily comings and goings of river traffic on the Thames? At first I couldn't see too much in the way of a useful lesson. But gradually, up on that balcony, walking the river path, taking the clipper itself into the city, haunting the parks and surrounding streets, I came to see what I suppose you'd call the bigger picture.

Forget everything else. Forget career, forget recognition, forget the approval and respect of one's peers. There was only one thing that mattered and that was truth. No matter how unpalatable, no matter how harsh, no matter how inconvenient. All that mattered was that every word that was said, every picture that was painted came out of something that could stand up anywhere, in any situation and in any company or context and be recognised as simply, incontrovertibly, and unexceptionally true.

Outside the window, a commuter clipper hooted across to a pleasure cruiser. They'd staged strictly unofficial races up towards

Tower Bridge before and it looked like another was about to start. High above, a plane banked as it headed away from City Airport, making for the North Sea and maybe Rotterdam or Berlin. Maybe it was the plane carrying Trudie across to her festival. Maybe right at that moment in time she was looking down at the river and already regretting her altruistic offer of work. Or maybe, knowing Trudie, she was just getting on with business and not wasting a moment in anything so time-consumingly useless as regret.

The phone rang – the loft phone – meaning it had to be either Tia or a couple of close friends. We'd changed the number after the Trooper Rohl incident. Previously I'd been quite proud of having it listed. It didn't matter how far I'd travelled from my roots it was still not so far away that I'd gone ex-directory. A couple of hundred nuisance calls later from just about every crank you could imagine and some you really could not and I'd changed my mind.

'Hi.'

It was Tia.

'Guess what?'

'Come home. Tell me instead.'

I was missing her.

'Tomorrow.'

'Tomorrow?'

It was like the floodgates bursting. Pent-up excitement positively spilled down the line.

'We've a meeting up in Edinburgh tonight. They're launching the new Sony blockbuster at the festival.'

'The one with the wave that drowns Manhattan?'

'The one with the mega-wave that drowns Manhattan.'

'The one you said looked like a pile of shit?'

'The one I said looked ground-breaking, genre-busting and a one hundred per cent sure-fire hit.'

'Clever lady.'

Tia laughed, the sound rippling. For a moment I felt a stab of jealousy. Not at the prospect of an evening mixing with studio stalwarts, just at the enthusiasm, the sheer joy in her voice. How long had it been since I'd felt like that about anything?

'We're getting the late shuttle. There's a presentation at midnight which we're sitting in on. Then they want proposals by the weekend.'

'Don't get swept away.'

'Trudie'll keep me in check.'

Outside the loft window, the world suddenly seemed to dip in volume.

'Trudie?'

'She's one of the sales agents coming up with us.'

I stared at the phone, that same warm smile still suffusing Tia's voice.

'You know Trudie. If anything's going down…'

I looked, instinctive, out of the window, just caught the last of a vapour trail as a plane disappeared over the horizon, Europe-bound.

Then I turned back to the phone, tried to keep my voice calm.

'Yeah. I know Trudie.'

5

THE NEXT MORNING another call came through on the landline. But it wasn't Tia calling from Edinburgh. Or wherever she might have been, I couldn't now be sure. It was the man from the movie poster shop.

It turned out they'd hit a small problem. When they were preparing the poster to be linen-backed they'd found a couple of pinholes. Nothing too serious but he thought I should know. He also wanted to know if it would be OK to carry out the standard repair which involved placing acid-free archival tape on the back of the poster and colouring in the front of the tape to match? I told him that was fine. He told me it wouldn't affect the price. Then he hesitated and wondered if he could talk about some other business too?

One hour later and for want of too much better to do, I was back in Aladdin's Cave and my head was filling with his strangled vowels. If the exile from ZIP Code 10453 was surprised at the speed of my response he didn't show it. Or maybe he did and I didn't notice. Maybe I'd not noticed quite a few things lately.

The shop, although only open for a matter of days, already had a fully operational website which had attracted a respectable number of hits. But he'd had an idea. What if he could take some of the posters out on location, matching the poster, wherever possible, to a relevant landmark or area?

A still of the poster for *Passport to Pimlico* in – guess where? A shot of the poster for *Absolute Beginners* at the entrance to Old Compton Street. Just something to give the whole thing that little extra zing. What did I think?

I thought it sounded like a monumental waste of time and told him so.

His smile began to fade a little.

'Just trying to push along the stock a little.'

'Do you think that's how Saul Bass saw his artwork? Stock? To be pushed along a little?'

'I've never met Mr Bass.'

'Take an educated guess.'

'I'd have thought he'd have welcomed any opportunity to have his work publicised.'

'Like on a sandwich board?'

'Look, it was only an idea.'

I swallowed, hard. What was I doing? I'd listened to hundreds of wackier ideas in the past from countless magazine editors and had always extricated myself with grace from each and every one. A light comment here, an amused observation there and I was on my way with relationship and, perhaps more importantly, self-respect intact.

'Yeah. I'm sorry.'

For a moment the half-smile was back, though his eyes remained wary.

'Bad day?'

I responded, struggling, but responded nonetheless.

'Bad night.'

'While the cat's away, right?'

I felt myself tensing again.

'Excuse me?'

'Do it myself all the time. Poker's my thing but my wife hates it. It's not the money.'

He smiled, gesturing around the shop.

'Look at this place, do you think this spells high-roller?'

He shook his head, wry.

'It's the principle, that's what she says. Doesn't matter how much money's in the pot, it's still pissing it away and this from the woman who'll drop a couple of hundred on a makeover every month and believe me, she is not in the first flush of youth.'

I tried to sound casual.

'Which is probably why she wants the makeover.'

'And that's exactly why I like my poker games. Whatever keeps you going, right?'

'How did you know by the way?'

'Know what?'

'That my partner was away on a work trip last night?'

'I didn't.'

'You just said.'

'I knew she was away, I didn't know it was a work trip.'

I stared at him.

'She told me. She called just before I closed up to pay for the framing on the One Sheet. Told me she was going away for a day or so and to call her on her mobile if there was any problem with the card.'

I let myself out of the shop five minutes later. I'd promised to put some thought into his somewhat-desperate idea to attract new trade. He told me he was grateful. He was still looking at me in that half-quizzical way but at least we were off the subject of absent partners.

Back in the loft I poured a Jack Daniels, went out onto the balcony. A tug hooted, perhaps at myself, maybe at another passing boat. I'd become something of a fixture so far as river life was concerned over the last year or so. But I didn't look down. I didn't even check the time of the eastbound clipper as it passed between the loft and the tug heading downriver. I did some thinking instead.

Why would Tia have lied to me? Why say she was travelling up to Edinburgh with Trudie when I'd virtually waved Trudie

A Review Copy From

Dufour Editions, Inc.

Chester Springs, PA 19425-0007

Tel. (610) 458-5005, Fax. (610) 458-7103

factotum@dufoureditions.com

Investigating Mr Wakefield
Rob Gittins

FICTION / Mystery & Detective / General

Publication Date: Dec 05 2016

ISBN 978-1-78461-239-9

Paperback Original, 408 pages, $16.00

Published in Wales by Y Lolfa Cyf., this book is exclusively distributed in the U.S. & Canada by Dufour.

For the convenience of your readers, please cite both imprints,

Y Lolfa / Dufour Editions, in your review.

We would appreciate a copy of any review or mention.

off myself on a Europe-bound shuttle just an hour or so before?

The first question was, why bother? I knew she was going away for the night anyway. She didn't need Trudie as any sort of alibi.

The answer, presumably, was that Trudie made the trip sound more convincing, something more genuinely connected with work.

Which meant that it might not be anything to do with her work at all. Maybe she wasn't even going to Edinburgh. Maybe Tia hadn't even gone out of the city. But she wouldn't have gone to all that trouble for just a simple night out with a few friends.

So what had she been doing?

And more to the point, who with?

I stared out over the river. We still had a few male friends from the old days, ex-colleagues of mine who would call round from time to time, share a drink, shoot the breeze. There was one friend in particular she'd openly describe as hot, although I was putting a metaphorical line through that name even as I considered it. Tia was too open about him for starters. If she'd really found him hot she'd never have said a word. Tia always was the deep one. Wild horses wouldn't have dragged an admission of genuine interest out of her. Until she tired of simple contemplation and decided on a little action instead.

That left those colleagues, acquaintances and friends she didn't talk about which made this a real needle in a haystack quest if ever there was one.

There were old boyfriends of course. One – a relationship only recently finished when we'd first started seeing each other – had been something of a threat in the early days. There'd been a few late night drunken phone calls from a variety of pity-party bars as well as occasional appearances from him on our doorstep. But he soon – literally – faded from view. From that point on there wasn't anything or anyone specific to worry about, aside perhaps from her reaction whenever she talked about anyone from the past. She'd always come over misty-eyed and wistful as if she was experiencing genuine pangs of regret at a relationship that had ended too soon. But I realised soon enough that she'd talk like that about anyone and everyone she'd ever met, liked, had contact with, worked with or shared a bed with, be they male or female. Tia always wanted to hang onto everything and everyone, never wanted to let anything or anyone go. It didn't mean anything, as she herself said, it was just the way she was and over the years I'd come to accept it.

I put down the Jack Daniels, went back into the open-plan living room. I picked up the phone, dialled Tia's mobile. As expected, it went straight to her answer service.

I picked up the bottle of Jack Daniels again, staring at it heavily as I registered it was empty. For a moment I conducted a silent struggle with myself before I put down the bottle, headed down the stairs, across the small courtyard and took a left through the gates. There was a convenience store along the street that sold just about everything a soul could need, which – in my case – was another bottle of the finest Tennessee could offer.

As I stepped inside, a couple of temporary residents from a serviced apartment across the street were trying to pay the congestion charge and weren't even remotely beginning to understand that they couldn't do it any more. They did so on their last visit a few years before, they were pointing out, so why couldn't they do it now? The shop assistant was trying to explain, as patiently as he could, that times change.

I went to the left of the counter to the hard booze counter at the back. A single bottle of Jack Daniels was squatting on the top shelf which convinced me, momentarily at least, that there might still be a God. I turned back, bottle in hand, to be confronted by a vision of what, at one time, I believed to be one of his angels but that was in another country, as the old saying had it, and I really thought this wench was well and truly dead.

At least to me. Only she wasn't. She was staring at me with much the same look of surprise that had also rooted me to the floor of that shop.

By the counter the couple from the serviced apartment had finally grasped the fact the world had moved on in the last few years and they'd have to find a different way of paying their daily ransom for driving in this strange city.

Around the corner by the hard booze shelf, my world in contrast had just stood still as a young, slim, Japanese girl kept staring back at me for a moment, before breaking into a smile.

6 .

Natsuo – the young, slim, Japanese girl in question – had come into my life six years before and in somewhat strange circumstances. I was living at the time in a small flat in Shepherd Market, looking out onto a street corner where the occasional novelist – and even more occasional peer of the realm – Jeffrey Archer had allegedly flashed his headlights at a local prostitute, guaranteeing him yet another fall from grace but visiting upon her an ultimately sadder fate.

Not that it had succeeded in dissuading a whole platoon of like-minded men from making nightly visits to the very same spot. The vast majority of the working girls in the area had already begun to operate out of walk-ups rather than advertising their wares out on the street, but obviously word hadn't got round. Most of the women working in the local restaurants, art galleries and clothes shops fielded at least three or four imprecations from evermore desperate drunks each night.

I was doing a regular run each day up to Finchley Road. I was employed as stills photographer on a movie that was shooting in a large warehouse on a nearby retail estate. Every day at seven in the morning I'd get on the Tube at Green Park and travel the few stops north via the Jubilee Line. Every evening, also at seven, I'd do the reverse trip. For a couple of weeks you could set a clock by my movements. I always chose the same carriage for the return journey too, third from the rear. It opened straight opposite the exit that took me up onto Piccadilly before I took a right along Half Moon Street and then cut back into the market itself. For those few weeks I was well and truly Mr Routine so maybe it wasn't all that surprising that Natsuo grasped hold of the wrong end of the stick.

Natsuo had arrived in England from Tokyo some couple of years before. She'd scammed a job working a geisha club that was opening in a basement at the southern end of Tottenham Court Road. Once through customs she'd taken one look at the basement and the club and had hightailed it out of there. She found some bar work in an upmarket hotel just off the Strand and then took a job as a hostess in a casino near Piccadilly Circus. For those two years she lived the life of a single girl to the full.

Then the free sheet came into her life.

At the time, Natsuo was living with a flatmate who'd injured her back during a stint at a pole dancing club. Every morning Natsuo accompanied her to a physio session in Finchley Road, leaving her with another friend for the day before coming back to collect her in the evening. For those couple of weeks her routine never altered either. And it seemed that someone had noticed.

In the free sheet at that time there was a lonely-hearts section where travellers could leave messages for fellow travellers who used the same Tube or bus. Natsuo had taken to reading it each night and she wasn't alone. I'd noticed, with some amusement, that of all the people in that carriage, at least half turned to that page before anything else. I'd been known to take the odd look myself.

Then, one evening, about four days into her regular stint of acting the concerned carer and right in the middle of the listings was a notice for the gorgeous Japanese girl who travelled to Finchley Road from Green Park around seven in the morning, returning around seven again the same night and asking if she'd like a drink sometime.

An intrigued Natsuo showed the paper to her friend. Was that her? Was she the girl who'd been singled out? On her next

Tube ride home she couldn't help stealing glances around the busy carriage, wondering – did he place that message – or maybe him?

The next day there was another listing in the same section of the paper. *Our eyes met, you know they did, you looked round the carriage and saw me, so come on, please, just that one drink?*

And this was a tease. Irresistible. Natsuo and her friend speculated in hushed tones again, was it him – or him? It was fun, giggly – there were lots of truly dreadful candidates and possibilities in truth – but there was one guy at the end of the carriage who could have been just checking the progress of the stations on the on-board display; but who could – maybe – have been stealing some glances in her direction too?

The next day and emboldened by the support of her grinning friend, Natsuo approached. She brandished the free paper and asked the man she'd just approached if this was him, had he been leaving her these messages?

I looked up, startled and not a little shocked – who the hell ever talks to, let alone directly approaches, anyone on the Tube? And then I had to tell her with deep regret – and not a little embarrassment – that actually, no, it wasn't me at all.

And if I was a little embarrassed, Natsuo was mortified and no wonder. She'd just approached a total stranger in a train carriage packed with other total strangers.

Oh God…

And because she was so mortified and so embarrassed and because she so obviously wanted the earth beneath that Tube train to open and swallow her up, I offered to buy her a drink anyway. And after much to-ing and fro-ing Natsuo agreed – although she insisted on buying me a drink instead to make up for the unwarranted intrusion. We took the up escalator at Green Park, cut down Piccadilly, found a table in the Shepherd Tavern and talked – and talked. By the end of the evening we'd agreed to meet each other again. Which meant, out of the most awkward of circumstances for her in particular, something might have just started between the two of us.

But that still left the original messenger of course.

Myself and Natsuo had our first official date the very next night and it went well. A simple meal in a tapas bar in Down Street. She was fascinated by some of the stranger photographic techniques with which I was experimenting at the time and one in particular ambushed her imagination. It was the one I called the Doppelgänger.

For this technique and for the best results, you use a Horizon and, shot correctly, it allows you to meet the twin you never had. You first needed low light conditions and then you set the Horizon to its longest exposure. Set it up on a tripod – although a hard surface would do – and then stand to the side as the lens starts to move.

Next – and make sure you're quick – press the button, then sit, stand, dance, jump; whatever. Keep doing it until the lens has passed, but as it'll do so in less than a second you can see why you have to be quick. Then hop, skip, moonwalk, backflip, whatever – until the lens passes back again and you've just added your own double to the world. And if you use Coloursplash flash during the movement it's going to give great highlights as well.

Natsuo loved it. So much so that she created literally dozens of doubles of herself which she later hung on every wall in her flat.

The other trick she perfected – again using the Horizon – was the long shutter release. She'd already fallen in love with the bendy buses that were clogging up the crowded London streets around that time, although I was always unsure if it was the name that appealed more than anything else. Maybe bendy bus sounded filthy in Tokyo.

I took her to the middle of Piccadilly Circus, put the camera on a tripod and then selected a long, slow, shutter speed. The lens moved from left to right letting the maximum amount of light onto the film. Catch a bendy bus just at the moment it turns a corner in front of you and it elongates impossibly – and ultra-comically – as Natsuo's response never failed to confirm.

Two kids and a camera. It was perfect. And it could – indeed should – have stayed that way too. But the next day there was another message in the lonely-hearts listings. This one again was addressed to the gorgeous girl who travelled each day to Finchley Road etc., etc. And the message was simple.

You Should Have Picked Me.

Natsuo ignored it.

The next day there was another message in the same section.

You Really Should Have Picked Me.

And Natsuo was now getting a little unnerved – these new messages did seem a bit abrupt after all – but she decided to keep on ignoring them. The next day she was walking out of the Tube station with her friend on their way home and there was a message spraypainted on the wall opposite the station.

Pick Me.

And now Natsuo was beginning to get concerned. A couple of fairly innocent messages were one thing but this was becoming intimidating.

And so, well-mannered girl that she was, Natsuo decided to frame a reply. I even helped her with the wording. By now she was a regular overnight guest at my Shepherd Market flat. Using the same lonely-hearts listing, and referencing his original approach, Natsuo told her messenger she was flattered by the attention but really wasn't interested. She had a boyfriend already and so really didn't want to meet anyone else.

Two days later she came upon the same slogan spraypainted

on a wall near to her actual flat which was a good three or four streets away from the Tube station. The same two words again.

Pick Me.

Which was when Natsuo grew really concerned. This guy, whoever he was, knew – roughly at least – where she lived. And so I came up with a plan which was maybe not much of one but was a plan at least.

The trips to the Finchley Road shoot had stopped with the film wrapping due to lack of cash. Eventually footage would find its way onto a couple of websites which made everyone involved as pleased as punch the money ran out because the talent, it was pretty clear, had run out some while before. But Natsuo was still making her regular trips, so for the next few days I rode with her.

We didn't make any sort of big demonstration about the two of us being an item but we did sit close together, I did take her hand as we chatted animatedly to each other. The message, if her mystery admirer was watching somewhere in that packed carriage, was clear. Back off. The girl is spoken for. She doesn't want to know.

Two days later I was mugged. I was about fifty metres down Half Moon Street when someone stepped out from the shadows by the old Naval and Military Club behind me and smashed me across the head.

It could have been a coincidence. Muggings happen all the time, even in wealthier enclaves – sometimes especially in those wealthier enclaves. I'd once done a photo-shoot for a documentary on street crime and as one of the habitual muggers who'd been interviewed had pointed out, there weren't many ladies who lunched walking the streets of Southall.

The odd thing being that nothing was taken – and the attack did take place just a short time after mine and Natsuo's very public display of unity on the Tube.

One day later a note was pushed through her door. It was from the mystery admirer which meant he now knew exactly where she lived. Unlike the slogans daubed on the walls the note wasn't threatening or aggressive. He just begged Natsuo to meet him, just the once, that's all he was asking, just once and then he promised he'd leave her alone if that's what she wished.

For Natsuo and myself, all this had very definitely accelerated what had now become a quite intense relationship, bonding us in a way that maybe wouldn't have happened if we'd just been hanging out, taking walks in the park, going for the occasional lunch in Nobu. And my reaction to the request was simple. No way. The guy was obviously crazy, Natsuo simply couldn't meet him, anything could happen.

But Natsuo was torn. What if she refused and he refused to give up hassling her? She couldn't live like this, wondering day by day, minute by minute, what was going to happen next. At least if she met him there was a chance she could talk some sense into his obviously-deranged head.

Natsuo, in short, was absolutely insistent that she had to resolve this and to end what was fast becoming something of a nightmare and I finally gave in but with one condition; that I go with her. By now the strange, quirky little Japanese girl had not only found her way into my bed, but my head as well. There was simply no way I was going to watch her walk away, alone, for a rendezvous with some clear maniac.

I told Natsuo she should propose some neutral venue only I'd be there at the same time. I wouldn't interfere and I wouldn't approach. I'd just let her meet with and talk to this character, but I'd be there all the time in case things turned even more strange than they were at present.

Natsuo duly replied to the message, suggested the meeting place – a gastro-pub just off Brook Green – and a day and a time was fixed. I travelled to the pub with her but we separated on arrival. Natsuo made her way to a far table, sat down, alone – and then waited. And waited.

Finally, just as she was about to give up a barman approached, asked if she was Natsuo, which wasn't such a brilliant deduction – there weren't that many young Japanese girls in that pub that lunchtime. Then he gave her a message. Apparently the person she was waiting for was out in the beer garden.

All that I discovered later. I was looking for a madman breathing fire and wearing horns. I wasn't taking much notice of a barman chatting away to my girlfriend as he collected glasses from her table. Natsuo was stunning, sheer white skin with dyed blue hair. She attracted a lot of attention wherever she went. It wasn't surprising that she was apparently attracting more of the same in that quiet bar.

I didn't even take much notice when Natsuo stood and headed, apparently, for the toilets. I was still keeping watch on the front door scanning each and every new arrival.

After ten minutes Natsuo hadn't returned and I was beginning to get edgy. She was a girl who took pride in her appearance but this was a touch excessive even for her. I went towards the toilet door, then stopped as I saw the door to the beer garden, open. I didn't even know, till that point, that the pub had a beer garden. A quick tap on the toilet door established there was no-one inside. A hurried conference with the barman established the content of the conversation he'd just had with Natsuo. I dashed outside to the beer garden only to find it completely empty.

Even more eerily, the garden was walled. There was only one way in or out and that was through the pub. Natsuo had, apparently, walked out into that enclosed beer garden and then vanished into thin air.

I checked the rest of the pub in seconds including the toilets, not content with a simple tap on the door this time.

Nothing.

I checked the surrounding streets, trying Natsuo's mobile all the while which kept going straight to her answer service. She wasn't anywhere in the immediate vicinity and none of the passers-by I stopped seemed to have seen her either.

I briefly contemplated calling the police. But what would I tell them? We'd met on a Tube train under a confusion of cross-purpose, before Natsuo had been targeted by some mystery admirer she'd never even met. She'd travelled to see him and had then disappeared from a sealed, walled, garden. Something told me the eyes of the local duty sergeant would have well and truly glazed over before I'd made it even halfway through that strange-sounding story.

I dashed back to the Tube and went to her small flat in a portered block just behind the Royal Academy. I'd been there once before, waiting in the hall while Natsuo collected some clothes. The doorman took some persuading to let me in and would only allow me up to her flat if he came with me. We cut across the small courtyard in convoy, past the individual marked parking bays and an entrance to the underground garage, then on into the flat complex itself.

Natsuo's flat was on the second floor. The doorman waited for the lift but I was already halfway up the stairs and he was forced to follow. I got to the front door about thirty seconds ahead of him and by the time he arrived I just knew I wasn't going to get any reply from inside.

'Open it.'

'What?'

'Open it or I'll kick it in.'

'I'm fetching the police.'

'Fetch them. By the time they arrive that door's going to be off its hinges unless you take your master key out of your pocket and let me have a look inside.'

I pleaded.

'Please. You'll be with me all the time. But I've got to get in, I've got to find out where she might be.'

He looked at me for a long moment while his brain computed options. I looked at the door while I tried to work out whether to use my foot or my shoulder. Then he reached into his pocket.

'You've got five minutes. And don't move out of my sight.'

He opened the door and we went inside.

In truth I'd no idea what I was looking for. Natsuo had no idea who'd been hassling her so why I thought there might be some clue among her things I didn't know. Maybe I just had to feel I was doing something.

There was nothing in her desk aside from bills and circulars all stacked neatly. Her bed was made and was as neat and tidy as the rest of the flat. Nothing looked untoward or out of place. It looked like a show apartment in fact, a place for everything and everything in its place.

Then I noticed the wardrobe door. It was hanging slightly open which was odd in itself. It spoilt the neat lines of the rest of the flat, made the place look uncharacteristically untidy. And something – white – seemed to be gleaming in the darkness inside.

The doorman followed my look to the partly-open wardrobe and he shifted, nervously, on the balls of his feet. All of a sudden the atmosphere became charged as we both stared at the door. It was as if, somehow, it was looking back at us.

Or something was looking at us.

From inside.

Or someone.

I didn't move for a moment. When I did it was to try and get a better look without actually opening the door, like a child hiding from a television programme they really don't want to watch, totally unable to tear away their eyes.

That same whiteness gleamed inside. And something else too, there seemed to be a touch of blue as well.

I closed my eyes for a moment, then approached. For another moment I hesitated, my hand on the wardrobe handle, then I flung back the door. I didn't move or make a sound but the doorman let out a full-bloodied scream of shock.

Then he stopped as he saw what I was now seeing; a life-size white doll, the palest skin, wearing a blue wig, its face painted, its lips the brightest red.

For a moment I just stared, unable to work it out.

Was it some sort of message, had it been left there by the mystery pursuer?

Then we both wheeled round as a voice broke in from the door.

'I see you've met Kuniko.'

Natsuo moved into the room, past the staring doorman, came up to the wardrobe and smiled inside at the doll.

'You can do so many things with her. Shout at her, scream at her, hit her, beat her, do that to a human being and they'd be black and blue, maybe worse.'

Natsuo leant forward, kissed the life-size white doll full on its painted lips.

'Kuniko never complains. Never answers back. She just takes it. Anything you want to do, she'll let you.'

And, suddenly, here she was again, years on, but the same white skin, the same blue hair, looking as timeless as a piece of porcelain.

I seated myself opposite her in a nearby converted harbourmaster's house that was now part of a restaurant chain. The willing staff tried their best but the food tasted like something mass-produced and anonymous, which couldn't have made it any more different to my new lunchtime companion. The one thing I'd realised about Natsuo – both in the immediate aftermath of the painted doll incident and since – was that she was a complete one-off, never to be replicated or imitated.

'I read about your troubles.'

'You and the rest of the world.'

'Self-absorbed as ever I see.'

I conceded the point.

'Maybe not the whole of the world.'

'Just the part that matters, right?'

Natsuo looked down at a steaming plate of mussels the waitress had just placed in front of her. She speared a piece of the meat from inside a shell, just holding it up, making no move to eat it.

'I've been thinking about you lately.'

'That's nice.'

Natsuo didn't even seem to hear me.

'It's odd – strange – I don't normally think about things like this.'

'Like what?'

For a moment she didn't speak and, as the silence stretched, I began to think that perhaps she wouldn't respond at all.

Then she looked at me.

'I've been wondering whether I made a mistake.'

I kept silent waiting for her to elaborate. I wasn't a mind reader. And even if I was would I really want to climb inside the mind of a creature like Natsuo?

Natsuo looked at me as if I was another piece of mussel meat. Something to be observed, considered, then digested. She seemed oddly, uncharacteristically, reticent; almost – and weirdly for her – coy.

'Were you the one that got away?'

Then she fell silent.

And, for the rest of the lunch, silent she largely stayed.

Half an hour later I was walking back to the loft. I hadn't bothered buying the Jack Daniels. I didn't seem to need it now. Maybe my mind wasn't consumed by all-matters-Tia any more.

It had, of course, all been a game. Everything always was so far as Natsuo was concerned. Nothing should ever be as it seemed, no person should ever be as you expect. Once you got to know someone, once you discovered everything about them, what was the point in keeping on with any sort of relationship? If you could no longer be surprised by someone all that would be left would be atrophy.

It all derived from physics so Natsuo believed; Newtonian interpretations and those, later, offered by Einstein. In the former there were laws which were immutable. The Victorians translated that into their artistic view of the world. People had characters that were fixed and similarly immutable. They might hide those characters away, dissemble, evade; but they were still there to be divined or discovered.

When those laws changed – when the physical world became no longer ruled by such a literal and immutable world view – then artists became much less certain about the notion of character. Natsuo, in particular, didn't believe there was such a thing. The world was forever shifting and so were its inhabitants. So she wanted to uncover how that person could change, preferably before her eyes, in response to a million different situations and if those situations didn't exist then she'd manipulate the world around her to bring them into being.

As she did with the imaginary boy on the Tube, a part of the intricate fiction she weaved around me. As were the messages spray-painted on the wall. The mugging in the street was nothing to do with her of course, that was a simple occasional hazard of life in any modern city. But it was entirely characteristic that she would build that into the web she was creating to see how I would react, what I would do. Twisting and turning me all the time, so I was putting more and more of myself on open view, providing Natsuo with more angles to examine, more reactions to absorb.

Natsuo, quite simply, hated the idea that each person had a distinct personality or sets of rules for his or her life. For Natsuo it wasn't the great stories of theatre or film or novels that appealed, it was those creations who would say exactly contradictory things at almost exactly the same moment.

She didn't expect us to stay together after I'd effectively broken into her flat. She'd had boyfriends in the UK before and none of them had lasted the distance. There was a moment, staring at her stroking the white-faced doll, listening to the doorman breaking out into a volley of abuse, when I was tempted, like him, to turn and walk away, glad that I'd seen this girl for what she really was even if I didn't have a single clue what that might be.

But all I knew at that moment was that I wanted to find out precisely what she was – which was a doomed endeavour of course. How could you ever know the unknowable?

In the end it was probably that rather than the game playing that finally killed us off. Natsuo refused to believe we could ever know each other and I found that impossible to reconcile with what I knew was a growing and deepening closeness. I truly believed we were in love. But if I could never know her then how could I be sure?

I let myself back into the loft, looking down at another clipper heading upriver towards Tower Bridge as I did so. Instinctively I checked the timetable. It was running to within a couple of minutes of the published schedule. The world was moving at roughly the speed it should.

I was calming all the time now. And all sorts of rational explanations were starting to take the place of the wild imaginings of just a short time before.

Maybe Trudie had originally been included on the guest list for the Edinburgh trip. Maybe she'd cancelled at the last minute having discovered a much more interesting opportunity in Berlin. Maybe there was no big issue – and very definitely no big lie – involved here at all. Maybe Tia would have walked back in, I'd have given her the third degree only to have the wind totally taken out of my sails by the simplest possible explanation.

Trudie cancelled.

Trudie changed her plans.

Now what exactly is your problem?

Which really would have opened a can of worms. What was so wrong that I'd wound myself into a panic like that? What did it say about me? More importantly, what did it say about us? Whichever way you looked at it, whatever angle you studied this from, it didn't look good. Natsuo might have taken a scientific interest in a hitherto-unsuspected insecurity finally blasting its way to the surface. Tia would simply have been seriously pissed off.

In the end it was always the way. The simplest, most obvious explanation usually prevailed. It was the same in photography, the most complex set-up usually led to the largest deception. To stand before something with a mind uncluttered, with prejudices and preconceptions set to one side, that was when you usually managed to get something truthful.

The phone rang behind me. On the way to answer it I passed the empty bottle of Jack Daniels and made a mental note to throw it out. I didn't want anything alerting the returning Tia to anything amiss.

'It's me.'

For a moment I couldn't speak. Something – guilt, love, a combination perhaps – swept over me and Tia hesitated.

'Hello?'

'Hi.'

'For a moment there I thought you'd forgotten me already.'

'There's been times these last few hours.'

'Meaning?'

'If you'd had to listen to that crazy Yank and his even crazier notions for publicity stunts, you'd understand.'

'The poster man?'

'The very same.'

I told her all about his wacko ideas and she laughed. Tia was at the airport in Edinburgh and had just been told the plane was diverting to Gatwick from Heathrow. There'd been a fire just off the M4 and all flights were being diverted away from the immediate area for the next hour or so. It meant she'd be delayed by a couple of hours getting home and hadn't wanted me to worry.

I asked how the trip had gone. She said it had gone fine. She'd get the train from the airport and tell me all about it when she got in.

On an impulse I went down to the underground garage and wheeled out the Duke. I put her helmet in the pannier intending to wait in Arrivals and intercept Tia before she could get the shuttle between the terminals and board the London-bound train.

As I put the helmet in the pannier my hands made contact with something. I scrabbled round in the bottom for a moment, then brought out a key.

I looked at it for a moment, my mind blank. It wasn't the key to the loft or to any of the internal doors in the complex. And it wasn't a spare key for the Duke. It was totally the wrong shape and besides, neither myself nor Tia would have been stupid enough to conceal a spare key to the bike in one of its own panniers.

I looked at the mystery key, a little unnerved in truth. Then I put it back in the pannier, rolled the Duke out of its parking space, firing it up as the automatic gates opened.

7

I RODE DOWN into the Rotherhithe tunnel. There were a number of routes I could have taken to Gatwick. A dark ride through an old, leaking, badly-lit tunnel wasn't the most scenic but it had one advantage over one or other of the bridges I'd have otherwise taken. If the traffic was light I could kick down again at the tunnel entrance, just like I'd done all those months before in the Limehouse Link and sweep through the tunnel as if it was Mad Sunday at the TT. The sound, as ever, was like nothing else. The howl of the exhaust seemed to bounce back off the tunnel wall, amplifying all the time.

The traffic was virtually non-existent. I dawdled on the way in, letting a family saloon get a good couple of hundred metres ahead. Then, my own personal space mapped out in front, I hit the loud pedal and snaked underneath the water like a turbocharged eel.

A tramp was at the exit directing traffic. Or maybe he was just waving. He had a big smile on his face which split into the widest, happiest grin when the driver of the family saloon tooted his horn in appreciation of his efforts and a young girl in the back seat waved at him.

'What the fuck?'

I affected wounded outrage as Tia stopped and stared at me. She'd just come through Arrivals, past the bored customs officers, round by the shops and into the usual waiting press of people waving placards bearing misspelt names. Among them, on this occasion, was someone Tia had very definitely not been expecting.

'I risk life and limb.'

I maintained the air of wounded outrage as Tia kept staring.

'Put the best part of a hundred miles on the Duke – and think what that's going to do when I try a part-ex with that slimy dealer up on Commercial Road and all he can talk about is how much these things depreciate.'

I shook my head, more in sorrow than in anger.

'And all I get is – .'

I didn't need to complete it, Tia did it for me.

'What the fuck?'

We collected the Duke five minutes later. Tia loaded her overnight bag into the pannier. I meant to ask her about the key as she did so but then a diversion wiped it from my mind. A security operation was being mounted on both the arrival and departure levels. Maybe they were preparing for the entrance or exit of some VIP or other or maybe it was just an exercise. Whatever, one of the officers obviously decided we merited a closer look and signalled to us to move away from the Duke and stand a short distance away while he radioed in the bike details to check whether it was being sought in connection with any recent international terrorist incident.

While he was doing that a female officer isolated Tia and started asking her questions – where she'd been, what had she been doing? Which was ironic, in a sense.

At a loose end – no-one seemed too interested in where I'd been or what I'd been doing – I watched another officer operating some kind of spycam on the crowds that were streaming almost non-stop from inside the airport. He'd pick individuals out apparently at random, following them as they moved towards waiting cars or cabs or, beyond, towards the short and long stay car parks.

Most of them didn't seem to see him but there was one man who did. He was in his early thirties, carried a small case, wore a good suit, expensive shoes. He didn't look like a terrorist and there seemed no reason to pick him out aside perhaps from his taste in clothes. The wages of a police officer weren't bad these days but they still wouldn't stretch to emulating this particular traveller's style.

The spycam tracked him all the way towards the car park. The man kept his head down, didn't look round, although his face very definitely sported a thin glistening of sweat. Then, just before he dived into one of the lifts he glanced sideways at Tia as she stood talking to the interrogating police officer and nodded at her, briefly.

Without taking her eyes off the officer, Tia nodded – equally briefly – back at him.

It was odd. And, in a way, curiously intimate. As if she'd been conscious of his approach all the way from the airport building.

I looked after the mystery man but he'd already been hidden by the closing doors of the lift. I looked back at Tia but her eyes, aside from that brief nod, still hadn't left the face of the police officer. I looked back at the officer operating the spycam. This time he was pointing it straight at me.

Ten minutes later we were back on the Duke and heading for home. There was an intercom system, meaning we could talk, but neither of us used it. We both liked the sensations around us too much – the wind, the noise, the feel of the air on our faces. Talking seemed to break the spell somehow.

We arrived home in something approaching record time. For once the main arterial routes into London were flowing smoothly. No incidents to report, as the bulletin readers on the local radio stations were wont to say.

So what was there to report? I'd been so calm earlier – seeing everything, I believed, so clearly again. The mystery man in the airport had changed that, although even now my mind was beginning to ask questions.

Had I really seen the quick nod that seemed to have been exchanged between the pair of them? Or had it just been some trick of the light? Had he seen someone else entirely? Was I doing what I'd done with Trudie all over again, inventing conspiracies, seeing potential treachery where in truth none existed?

For the first hour or so it was catch-up time and there was a fair bit to catch up on too. For most of the delegates it had been a freeloading junket but Tia was at work. Meeting this person. Pressing the flesh. Oiling the wheels.

The blockbuster with the mega-wave was going to be launched with a charity premiere. They'd already drawn up the list of usual suspects who could be counted on to attend and wear the odd outrageous costume. There were a couple of genuine stars in the movie – cameo roles in truth although it wouldn't stop their names being emblazoned on the slip cover of the DVD once the movie had bombed theatrically as everyone knew it would.

Tia had already been making a million and one phone calls on the diverted flight and had secured the hire of an exclusive West End nightclub for the venue along with liberal quantities of the latest variation on the more fashionable illegal narcotic, meaning the whole thing would be virtually guaranteed to go with a swing.

It didn't sound like Tia had a spare second, as I remarked.

She didn't, she replied.

'So how was it for everyone else?'

'How do you mean?'

'The rest of the deal-breakers?'

I paused.

'How much of the pie did Trudie manage to carve for herself?'

Her smile began to fade.

'Trudie?'

'You said it yourself. If anything's going down…'

I shrugged.

'Don't say the Piranha of Poland Street didn't grab the odd territory or two?'

I held my breath and prayed Tia wouldn't notice. Was it my imagination or was she looking at me in a slightly different way now?

Closer?

More intent?

'Did I tell you about the Spanish deal Trudie cut last week? She'd been pipped to the post by some Danish sales agent so she went to the producer of the movie, showed him documentation that the Danes had sold the French rights twice. The producer goes ballistic, the Dane goes into a flat spin, how could that have happened, it takes him two days to sort out the mess – .'

I finished it for her.

'Which is when he discovered he hadn't done anything of the sort, the whole thing seemed to have been some total misunderstanding on the part of a low-level sales agent in Lyons that nobody can now seem to trace by which time Trudie had stepped in and grabbed the deal for herself.'

Tia grinned.

'What an operator.'

Then she paused.

'She'll be gutted.'

For not the first time in the last twenty-four hours I tried to keep my voice calm.

'Why's that?'

'Trudie never made it.'

'Oh.'

'She had some festival to go to over in Europe.'

I opened a bottle of Barolo for supper. Tia wanted to know if it was a special occasion and I told her it was. She was home. We took out a room service directory and picked out the menu from our favourite restaurant, a Spanish place tucked in amongst the new-builds on the Island. As a setting it was grim which was maybe why they put such an effort into the food.

Every week they flew over the finest ham from Huelva, a fishing port about a hundred kilometres to the west of Seville. Myself and Tia had gone there once on a touring holiday of Andalusia. The main highway from Spain to Portugal by-passed it and that's what the town felt like too. Cut off. I'd mentioned it to one of the waiters who served us swordfish in a beachside restaurant where the wind blew non-stop up and down sands that seemed to stretch for ever. He conceded the point with a wry smile fringed with approval. Look at the rest of the Costas, he pointed out. Wouldn't you prefer to be cut off from them too?

That night we'd found a hotel in what we thought was a small village just outside Seville itself. Walking round the next morning it proved to be more of a small town but there wasn't a lot of incentive to stray out of the hotel in truth. The building used to be an old olive press and, after that, home to an obscure sect of monks. The bedrooms were housed in a main building which was open to the skies in the centre. A small bar gave onto a garden where the best breakfast in the world, so they claimed, was served. After the first morning we found it hard to disagree.

Beyond the garden was a pool that stretched into another pool and then another. When we were staying there it was just myself, Tia, and two other couples in residence. We smiled at each other at breakfast and as we met around the pool, but for the rest of the time the two of us just read and lazed and took lunch in the poolside restaurant. We both agreed it was one of our happiest times together.

Tia wasn't to know it but I was feeling exactly the same right now. Her casual remark about Trudie and her absence from the sales junket felt like a cloud lifting from a troubled sky.

The room service company called with a problem. The restaurant didn't have the usual paté so would we settle for foie gras instead? At the same price? Putting ethical reservations aside for once, we agreed. According to the menu, we'd just saved ourselves around thirty pounds. It felt like some sort of victory. An advantage gained.

Tia went to take a shower. I went out onto the balcony and watched the clippers passing on the river. One of the boats hooted and I waved. A small party of schoolchildren sitting outside on the rear deck waved back excitedly. They'd been trying to get some sort of response all the way up from the Eye with no success. A girl – not from the school party – kissed her boyfriend as they stood, Titanic-style, at the front of the boat. I smiled, then turned as the buzzer sounded. Room service must be early.

Only it wasn't room service. It was something even more welcome. A courier struggled up the stairs with a large package. It was the movie poster, linen-backed and framed. I signed for it, unwrapped it, then propped it up against the dining table, checking all was OK. The courier gave it an approving glance as I did so, his only reservation being the visible fold in the centre. I started to explain that movie posters were routinely folded back then. In fact, if it didn't have a fold you should be ultra-suspicious but then I stopped. I'd sound like an anorak and I knew it.

Besides, it seemed to give him a certain amount of pleasure. He wasn't so obviously begrudging as some of the delivery drivers who called into the complex but he still loved pointing out a flaw in what must have seemed, if not a paradise of a setting, then something fairly close. A small victory. An advantage gained.

I turned back to the water and watched the river police from

Wapping checking some debris on yet another of the small beaches the low tide had temporarily exposed. Then a second buzzer sounded from the door and I moved back inside. This time it was the room service company. I checked the delivery, signed the docket and gave him a tip. Strictly speaking, service was included but even better service was guaranteed next time if you treated the man who actually delivered the food as well as the person who created it. The food chain had many links and each was as important as the other.

I put the hot cartons in the oven, low heat and went to call Tia. The sound of the power shower stopped just as I opened the door. Perfect timing. She could slip into the dressing gown I'd taken from behind the door and then eat the food while we huddled up together on the sofa.

The bathroom was filled with steam. Tia was checking her hair in one of the floor to ceiling mirrors. She smiled as she saw me holding out the bathrobe.

'The food's here.'

'Shame.'

I looked at her.

'Had a different sort of starter in mind?'

'Maybe we can make it dessert instead.'

'They've already delivered dessert.'

Tia eyed me.

'But it's cold. It'll keep.'

Tia smiled and turned, holding out her arms for me to slip her bathrobe over them. As I did I paused, only for a second, nothing that she'd notice.

In the middle of her back was a scar. It was small, not the sort of scar that would have been caused by a knife. More the sort of scar you'd get from a fingernail digging into your back. It was red, meaning it was recent. It also hadn't drawn blood, meaning if it was a fingernail then whoever was responsible hadn't dug deep. But they'd dug deep enough. And they'd done so sometime in the last twenty-four hours.

We went through to the kitchen. I took out the food and arranged the toast and foie gras on the salads the restaurant had packed in separate containers and we ate while we watched a couple of pleasure clippers out on the water. Music pounded from the on-board speakers. Party girls in off-the-shoulder frocks shivered on the upper decks and sipped champagne. The night was going to turn a lot colder and they were going to turn a lot colder too but from the expressions on their faces nothing would have dragged them inside.

Tia recognised the look of eager anticipation and her own face turned wistful as if she was remembering that feeling, reliving it once again.

Or was it something else she was reliving? Something that had nothing to do with the scene out on the river or the mini-dramas being played out on the upper decks of that pleasure clipper?

Something much more to do with the small scar that had suddenly appeared on her back?

8 .

I WOKE EARLY the next morning, went out onto the balcony. Tia was dog-tired and, despite her earlier and best intentions, had gone to bed soon after food. By the time I'd joined her she was all but dead to the world. It had been a long trip. I'd made all the right noises, smiled in all the right places, said all the right things. That kind of thing takes it out of you, as I pointed out.

But none of those things gave you a small, red, angry scar in the middle of your back, the sort of scar it's difficult to get backing into a car door or manoeuvring around a chair but the kind of scar it's very easy to collect if you're too close to a fingernail and your back is exposed to the same for some reason.

Like, if you were in bed.

With someone.

Who had occasion to touch you on your naked back.

When I was sure she was soundly asleep – and already hating what I was doing – I opened her overnight bag. There was nothing incriminating inside and I didn't expect there would be. I was looking for something else instead.

Tia kept two mobile phones. One was for work and one for her personal use. We frequently swapped personal mobiles if we were out or if a battery had died on one or the other so I had a shrewd suspicion that if she wanted to hide any calls she wouldn't take them on that phone. But what was on the work phone?

I scanned the log, frustrated. There were dozens of different numbers but none of them meant a single thing to me. And I could hardly dial each one asking and how and in what way they knew my partner?

I checked the inbox on the text menu. Nothing. Everything had been deleted but Tia had a habit of doing that anyway. Her service provider didn't allow a lot of space for texts and she'd frequently had to spend an irritated ten minutes or so deleting an unwanted backlog just to permit another incoming text to be delivered. Now she was in the habit of reading texts and deleting them almost immediately.

I checked her incoming answerphone messages, but as expected they'd all been deleted too. But as I was about to replace the phone, one number caught my eye.

I recognised it straightaway. It was Trudie. And it appeared among her recent log of calls.

I clicked on the number and accessed the details. Trudie, it seemed, had called Tia the previous evening, presumably after she'd landed in Berlin. I'd no idea what the call was about – maybe the premiere she'd mentioned to me – but it suddenly ushered in a new and unwelcome possibility.

Previously, I'd imagined my simple query about Trudie had elicited an equally simple and transparent response. But if Trudie had called Tia on some work matter or other and had mentioned, as she would have done, that she'd seen me then Tia would have been alerted to any potential danger. So she could have been planning her story all the way down on the plane.

When Tia woke she immediately called the office and accessed her voice mails. She had another million and one calls to make following the Edinburgh trip and was going to be away most of the day. I hesitated, making sure she registered it. Always attuned to every tiny shift in mood, she wanted to know if there was a problem? Finally, and after a bit of coaxing and with a show of considerable reluctance, I mentioned the party.

A friend of mine – one of the few who'd stayed a friend – was having a launch for a book of photographs he'd recently shot in some African village. They'd probably end up reprinted on some calendar or other. I'd received the invitation a week or so ago and meant to throw it away. It was just about the last thing I wanted to attend and the fact a few old faces from the even older days would be there was even more incentive to add it to the rest of the recycling. With one thing or another it was still in my wallet and now it had become a test.

Tia was surprised I wanted to go. She understood the potential embarrassment and awkwardness. I acknowledged her reservations, admitted I'd felt them too, but how long did I keep living this hermit-like existence? When should I finally step out and face a world of which I was once so much a part?

All bullshit of course. Anyone who was really anyone wouldn't be within a first-class flight of that sort of gathering, but it was giving Tia food for thought.

Tia should go into the office. She should follow up on her trip. Maybe there was another reason she wanted to go into the office today too. Maybe something to do with the mystery man who'd nodded at her at the airport yesterday.

But this seemed important to me. And she could follow up on her calls some other time. If it was a straight tussle between a work commitment and something to do with our home life then I usually knew which one Tia would choose. Right now I hadn't a clue. The next few seconds or so were going to tell me whether this relationship of ours was in any sort of trouble.

Fifteen minutes later we were on the Duke turning right towards the towers of Canary Wharf before weaving in and out of various rat-runs on our way up to Hoxton. Tia had passed the test and now I was booked for an excruciating hour enduring the stares of wannabes, has-beens and college lecturers, surprised I'd fallen so low as to actually be there in the first place.

Or maybe no-one would even know who I was. The world had moved on in the last few years even if I hadn't quite managed to get past movie posters and river clippers. What had happened might have been huge in my universe, but maybe – and as Natsuo had already pointed out – it really wasn't of such all-consuming interest to anyone else.

I came round a few hours later on the floor of the loft feeling like I'd just gone ten rounds with Tyson.

It hadn't started too badly. There was a respectable crush of people there by the time we arrived and Tia knew a few of them. Who didn't Tia know? For the first half-hour or so the air was thick with talk of launches and events and no-one even paid the photographs hanging on the walls of the gallery a second look. They didn't deserve it in truth and I think everyone knew that too. I managed a few words with my old photographer friend who, extraordinarily enough, was rather too concerned with this event in his own life to worry about past events in mine. Bet his home was simply racked with mirrors.

The problem began as I was trying to check my watch without making it too obvious and wondering how to signal Tia that we should be making tracks without making that too obvious either. Apparently, royalty had a code of some kind. A handkerchief taken out of a bag, a key phrase spoken at a certain time and everyone knew it was time to get the hell out of there. I'd read about it in some paper somewhere and not for the first time wished I'd paid a bit more attention.

'A bit studied, don't you think?'

I turned. He was standing behind me, a familiar smirk on a face framed by trademark floppy hair. Toby Vine. Even the name sounded impossibly affected. Which was nothing compared to the man himself.

'You can almost see him in every shot.'

Toby was a professional dabbler. We'd been on some of the same shoots in our early days, an activity Toby always subsidised with his corporate lectures. Or maybe he used the lectures to subsidise the shoots – I'd never actually worked out his priorities and neither, perhaps, had he. His impressive workload was augmented by appearances on late night TV and radio art shows. He was the default rent-a-mouth when it came to pronouncing on all matters photography so far as the media was concerned. He'd been there, done that, at least in his own mind, had a waspish line in wit and if that covered a lifetime's disappointment at his own failure in never pushing any boundary himself then no-one cared or enquired too deeply.

I should have just ignored him but I couldn't. One of the programmes he'd hosted had been devoted to myself and my fall from grace. He'd prefaced it by praising me to the skies; always a worrying sign. Then he'd proceeded to orchestrate the most savage death by a thousand cuts I'd seen outside a recent re-run of *Ben Hur*.

'Maybe a bit more of the passive spectator might help, don't you think?'

'I don't think a photographer can ever be a passive spectator.'

'You don't think an overly emotional involvement compromises the compositional eye?'

'Where did you get that from, a fortune cookie?'

Toby eyed me, amused. It had obviously taken him even less time than he expected to wind me up. Something in him thrilled to the realisation that I was still locked in my past. It must have made up for his own niggling suspicion he'd never had one.

'Something Cartier-Bresson once said actually.'

Cartier-Bresson. We were in a small gallery looking at travel snaps and he was talking Cartier-Bresson.

'And Avedon, I think.'

A man who wasn't even fit to lick the boots of the great

Avedon let alone invoke his name in support of a typically specious argument.

'Where did that brilliant white on black shading come from? That separation of subject from landscape he's such a master of?'

'I prefer the roadside drifters stuff he does.'

'My point exactly.'

I had a shrewd suspicion it would be. Toby had spent a lifetime appropriating the opinions of others and passing them off as his own.

'The way he manages to get all that detail into the shot and yet you still get such an amazing sense of all that – .'

He paused, searching his mental database for the right phrase, culled from the most apposite article.

'Emptiness.'

'Good word.'

'What?'

I'd actually managed to stop him in his flow.

'Exactly the word that just floated through my head just now too.'

Toby smiled, thinly.

'You always were more of an Arbus guy, I suppose.'

'And you're not?'

Toby Vine had once worshipped at the toenails of Arbus.

'These days I go for more clarity in the composition.'

I shook my head in disbelief.

'Hold the front page, the famous Christmas tree shot lacks compositional clarity.'

Too late – far too late as it turned out – I decided to ignore him, began to move away, but Toby stopped me.

'I read something the other day and thought of you, you know.'

Why did I pause?

Why not keep moving across to Tia, to safety?

Why not ignore the trap door just for once?

'Cartier-Bresson again. The moment of selection and the moment of regret. Regret that the image hasn't translated into the picture we believed it would be, the moment we see where we've failed. And I was thinking, maybe you had it right after all. You didn't like an image so you changed it. No honourable failure for you, right?'

Toby smiled, thinly again.

'Only kidding.'

The launch was a bit of a blur after that. I remember a speech, I remember trays of wine, I think I remember commandeering a whole tray at one time, I remember Tia trying to suggest, quietly, when I was talking too loudly to some camera geek, that maybe we should be going now and I remember telling her I was enjoying myself. Tia told me I was so far from enjoying myself I might as well have a sign around my neck proclaiming it to the whole wide world and I asked her how the hell she knew that, how the hell did she know anything, she didn't know me, how could she, how could anyone know anyone?

By now I was rambling and it wasn't long before Toby moved in for the kill. He wanted to witness this at first hand. A public disintegration. That really was going to sound sweet in some green room. He might even get a late night special out of it linked to an article in one of the Sunday supplements.

I didn't allow him the luxury. As soon as that floppy hair waved in front of my face I did what I'd wanted to do for years. His mocking smile was first obliterated by a full glass of cheap red wine followed closely by my fist.

Toby fell into a stacked display of books bringing down some of the framed photos on the wall at the same time. A photographer from the publishing house, sent to record the event for the trade weeklies, made himself a little extra by taking snaps of the whole thing before making follow-up phone calls to a couple of tabloid editors. Their readership wouldn't really know who I was, not in terms of face recognition anyway, but Toby was on television. How far do the once-mighty fall. In his case it was considerably less than five or so feet off his subtly-built-up heels, but it was probably a lot more interesting than anything else that had happened during that launch.

Not that Tia found it all that interesting.

The next thing I knew I was being frogmarched towards the door and into a waiting taxi before I could even begin to wonder where I'd parked the Duke. Tia didn't say a thing and we didn't speak all the way home either mainly because I was having trouble forming words. When we arrived back at the loft, and after having me poured me out of the taxi, I fell over a low table.

Tia just looked at me, spread-eagled out on the floor. She still didn't speak, just turned and walked back out again. I shifted on the floor for a moment or two, then went to sleep.

When I woke it was almost dark and Tia wasn't home. Something told me she wouldn't be home till the early hours and even then there was unlikely to be too much in the way of conversation. All my words of a few hours before were swimming around inside my head and it was an odds-on certainty they were doing the same inside hers right now too.

How I'd had enough of this hermit-like existence.

How I wanted to touch base once more with a world that had been my world for so long.

How maybe that simple launch party would be the first step.

I'd known it to be evasions and lies and now she did too. I knew what was behind it all. I just hoped to hell she didn't.

I couldn't stay in the loft so I went out, started walking,

following the line of the previous rat-runs north. I found the Duke exactly where we'd left it, which it very definitely would not have been before gentrification sprinkled its stardust over that neighbourhood.

I unlocked the pannier and reached inside for my helmet. Then I paused as my hand closed on something.

There was another key inside. Not the one I'd found previously. This was different, more heavy-duty. This one came with a metal strip attached, a set of numbers embossed along the whole length.

2208.

Four simple numbers.

That didn't mean a thing to me.

9.

I RODE THE Duke back home taking extra care to observe the speed limit and not be too cute when it came to carving up any lines of stationary cars. It was odds-on these days that at least one of those seemingly-innocuous family saloons would suddenly sport flashing lights and a wailing siren. The last thing I needed with all that cheap wine still swimming through my system was the not-so-tender attentions of the local thin blue line.

I paused, dutifully, at the head of the first line of cars, drawing far more attention to myself in all probability than the myriad selection of couriers who roared past, weaving in and out of each and every available half-square inch of fast-shrinking road space.

I looked to my left at a tramp huddled in a shop doorway, a plastic cup in one hand, the other hand clutched round the lead of a dog I could swear I'd seen at least twice before with different street dwellers. I'd heard they'd taken to sharing them out. Not many of them actually wanted any sort of live-in companion but there was no question that takings tripled with one sitting alongside. Maybe there was an agency somewhere that hired them. Maybe I should set one up if not. If recent events were anything to go by I wasn't going to have too much else to occupy my time.

As I moved away the tramp looked up and straight at me. It must have been some trick of the light, my face was hidden by my black, reflective, helmet but he still seemed to stare straight into the very centre of my eyeballs.

I let myself back into the loft and decided to take belated charge of what had become a strangely unsettled and unsettling life these last forty-eight hours. Tia was a reasonable person. If I apologised, referencing the Toby encounter as an excuse for my madness at the launch, she'd be fair-minded enough to acknowledge that I did have too much time on my hands these days, that demons and ogres were bound to fester in a mind too little occupied with the normal and the everyday. It might even be the start of something better for the two of us, the first step towards a new beginning. My rent-a-dog business maybe.

I made a mental note as I rehearsed all this not to attempt to lighten it with any sort of levity. Something told me this had all the hallmarks of an encounter that could backfire spectacularly. There was little point in my helping it along with an ill-advised stab at humour.

Did I call in advance to warn her of my visit? Something told me that would be something of a doomed strategy too. I probably wouldn't have even penetrated the first line of defence at the moment, her answerphone. Far better if I simply turned up at the office, asked to see her, said my piece and then left.

I took the DLR into Bank. On the way I looked across towards my home Square as I passed by Cable Street, the community still just about hanging on but for how long?

I'd once watched a documentary which had featured Hampstead only a few generations before, all rolling fields and rural splendour. Times change. Communities appear, disappear, are re-invented. Nothing stays the same. I'd changed, had become re-invented, I'd always assumed for the better although the last couple of days had maybe questioned that fond illusion. So what if this was all to be swept away in some modern-day version of the Highland Clearances? Would it matter? Who would care?

I walked from Bank to the office. Lights were blazing brightly inside. From down the street came the sound of music as some event or other was celebrated in a local bar. Through the window

I could see the over-qualified receptionist who was working that desk for just one year as she made every contact she could, mentally filing away the addresses she encountered day-in day-out as part of her career plan. Then, behind her, a door opened and the light inside the office seemed to increase in intensity although perhaps that was just the blood suddenly pounding through my head; because then I saw Tia.

It was like an Exocet had exploded deep inside my gut. Everything seemed to be moving in slow motion. And all that had happened, all Tia had done, was open a door, handed the receptionist some papers, laughed at some exchanged comment or other and then turned and moved away.

It was so simple. So natural. So uncomplicated. And in that totally unremarkable moment I loved her more than I'd ever loved her before. Or maybe I'd just remembered how much I loved her when I seemed to have spent the last couple of days forgetting that ineradicable fact.

So what was I doing? Why the hell was I inventing conspiracies, searching for treachery when somehow – deep down, at some primeval level of instinct – I knew for absolutely sure there was none?

Had my life become so screwed up in these last couple of years I'd only be satisfied if the world around me somehow reflected that? Did I need it in some way? And part of me was already thanking whatever deity may or may not rough-hew our ends that at least all this was still only inside my head, that I'd not actually confronted Tia. OK, she'd seen me screwing up at the launch but we'd get over that. An unexpected reaction to a toe dipped too early in a world still difficult to cope with, a too-early exposure to the viperish likes of Toby Vine.

I turned away, not able to deliver my simple apology just yet, needing time instead, cut through the piazza behind Tia's office.

The buskers were changing over outside the covered market while inside another party of kids were screaming in delight as the same clown on stilts swayed high above them, tottering so it seemed on the very point of collapse. Small parties of tourists took snaps from every possible angle.

I moved on, then paused as I saw the entrance to the alleyway that led down to the movie poster shop. I hesitated a moment longer, then – on an impulse – headed down there. Maybe the *Wild Bunch* One Sheet had come in.

As I came up to the entrance I slowed. A couple of crates were outside and for a moment I stared in disbelief. This wasn't exactly a high crime area but if someone had simply dumped a couple of cartons of collectable movie memorabilia outside the door then the man with the leaky larynx really needed to change his courier.

The shop was locked. Stacked by the cartons were some other items – shelving and brackets. It took me a moment to realise that the man from across the water was probably heading back there. The shop had closed.

Then, suddenly, the door opened before me. A couple of shop fitters came out, made for a van at the top of the alley. Inside, the shop had already been furnished, floor to ceiling, with different shelves and some stock had already been unpacked. Posters dotted around the walls proclaimed its new retail interest which was nothing to do with celluloid collectables.

By a newly-installed till, a banner on a wall proudly proclaimed a new name: The Surveillance Store. The shop was now going to be less about celebrating the past than capturing the present and not only capturing it but recording it on all manner and type of devices it seemed.

The shop fitters returned with more shelving, one of them shooting me a half-quizzical glance as they passed. Then they moved back inside, closing the door behind them, cutting off the view, substituting it with my own staring face reflected in the glass doorway.

But something else was suddenly reflected there too. As the door closed I saw people passing through the piazza behind. The busker who'd just finished his stint was heading away. An old lady had paused to catch her breath, leaning over a small shopping trolley she was using partly for storage, partly for support. And behind them, glimpsed just for a moment, was Tia with the mystery man from the airport, laughing and joking, her head flung back as they walked on.

All of a sudden everyone seemed to be moving at half-speed again, all of a sudden all I could hear was the sound of blood roaring in my ears and this time there was no spontaneous outpouring of submerged feeling flooding through every vein in my body, this time there was something darker.

All Tia was doing was walking along, probably on her way to some meeting or other. All she was doing was talking to someone. He was probably a colleague from the office. So why did it root me to the spot as if I'd suddenly been turned to stone? And why – again – did it all look so horribly, piercingly, intimate?

There was an upper level in the covered market. From various vantage points it was possible to look down on the small cafés on the ground floor. For the next hour I watched Tia and her companion share a coffee, their exchanges marked all the time by that same laughter, that same easy, natural, companionship.

Tia didn't look as if she had a care in the world. As if all the troubles of the day so far had been forgotten.

As if she'd turned her back on all that.

Moved on.

10.

I'D COME ACROSS the story a couple of years before.

I'd been engaged on another film shoot. From the very start of filming one of the key elements is the press pack – a documentary-type portrait of the movie from day one to the final wrap and beyond. Publicists would pore over every still, selecting images for this magazine, that journal, this TV feature, that chat show. Sometimes images from the press pack would be included on the all-important poster. Compiling it was my job.

The stills photographer was supposed to be present all the way through the shoot but the one who had been engaged had jumped ship, sussing – shrewdly as it happened – that the producer was flaky, the finances even more so and that the plug was about to be pulled on the whole thing. He'd had an offer to cover an overseas tour of the latest boy band sensation, and even though they themselves probably wouldn't last much more than a year or so, that was going to be a hell of a sight longer shelf-life than this rapidly decaying turkey. Did I ever, I sometimes wondered, get involved in anything else?

The producer, in denial, had agreed a fairly exorbitant fee. The shoot was already losing time hand over fist and in one of the fallow periods while everyone was waiting for the near-hysterical writer to work his way through yet another totally new set of scenes, I broke the vow of a lifetime and actually read the script.

It started well, probably the reason the producer had managed to wing the money he'd raised so far. It wasn't original, but I'd been around enough movie shoots to realise by now that scripts usually derived from some other source than the imagination of a contemporary writer. Scripts came from books, TV shows, graphic novels, even comic strips. It seemed to make the movie execs feel safe if the script they were shooting was proven in some way, if it had a life previous to its present incarnation. Partly that was because it might attract its previous audience, but it was also because someone else had first taken the risk in presenting the material to the world and that risk had been rewarded. Riding on the coat-tails of someone else. According to most of the people I'd ever come across in the movie world it was the only way to travel.

The original story was also out of copyright which was another huge plus. While those same execs would pore over newly-published novels – or sometimes just the galley proofs submitted by eager publishers in advance of a first appearance on a bookshelf – they knew it was going to cost, and usually big-time too. Before they even set up the first catering unit they were going to have to write a sizeable ransom in the form of a cheque for the rights. But if the author – as in this case – had the decency and grace to die just over a hundred and fifty years before then that made life so much simpler.

OK, they'd still have to hire a writer to actually turn the material into something that approached a script – and another writer to rewrite that first attempt – not to mention a third, fourth and fifth to redraft successive attempts, not to mention hiring yet more writers to execute what were euphemistically called polishes – but at least they saved themselves that initial hit. Dead authors were just about every film studios favourite beast.

The story – or source material – was written by an American author called Nathaniel Hawthorne. He'd written a few stories back in the nineteenth century and a couple had already been filmed although that wouldn't stop anyone filming them again.

After reading this particular story I started digging into the life of the man who'd written it. Tia said it was yet another example of an obsessive nature and maybe she was right. I couldn't ever be content with simply dipping in and out of someone's life and work. Once I started I had to know everything about them, had to read everything they'd written. How else could I understand them?

Tia's response was simple. Why would you want to?

Hawthorne was a novelist as well as a short-story writer and a central figure in what came to be known, somewhat fancifully, as the American Renaissance. Most countries had them in most centuries so it seemed. His best-known work was probably *The Scarlet Letter* published in 1850.

The man himself was born in Salem in Massachusetts. His father was a sea captain and descendent of John Hathorne, one of the judges in the Salem witchcraft trials of 1692. He died when the young Nathaniel was four years old.

Elizabeth Hathorne, his mother – Nathaniel added the 'w' to his name when he began to write – withdrew to what was described as a life of seclusion. It seemed she didn't like her son mixing too much with a world that had already taken one man in her life and she pushed him towards more isolated pursuits. His childhood seemed to have left him overly shy and bookish, perfect training perhaps for what was to become his life as a writer.

Another of his ancestors, William Hathorne, was a magistrate who had sentenced a Quaker woman to a public whipping. Hawthorne was later to wonder whether the decline in the family prosperity and prominence during the eighteenth century, while other Salem families were growing wealthy from the lucrative shipping trade, might not be some sort of retribution. Like another of his contemporaries, Edgar Allan Poe – who oddly didn't have too much time for Hawthorne – he took a dark view of human nature believing, as he wrote in *The House Of The*

Seven Gables, that the wrongdoing of one generation lived on in their successors.

From Salem the family moved to Maine where Hawthorne was educated. In the school and among his friends were Longfellow and Franklin Pierce who became the fourteenth President of the United States.

From 1825 onwards, Hawthorne contributed to periodicals and journals. The *Democratic Review* published a couple of dozen of his stories and he obviously needed that vote of confidence too because Hawthorne had burned his first short-story collection, *Seven Tales of My Native Land*, after several publishers rejected it. He even paid for his first novel, *Fanshawe*, to be published and while it didn't do well it brokered an introduction to his long-time publisher Samuel Goodrich.

Already Hawthorne was exploring many of his favourite themes such as hypocrisy, witchcraft, the Puritan guilt, and the sins of fathers. But the treasure of intellectual gold, as he called it, wasn't providing food for his family, and food became a pressing concern that year.

In 1842 Hawthorne had married Sophia Peabody, an active participant in the Transcendentalist movement. Hawthorne first settled with Sophia in Concord, but a growing family and mounting debts saw them return to Salem and intense disillusionment on the part of the would-be scribe.

Hawthorne was simply unable to earn a living as a writer and in 1846 he was appointed surveyor of the Port of Salem. He wrote to his old friend Longfellow that he felt like he'd locked himself in a dungeon and couldn't find the key.

All that I gleaned from numerous biographies and all manner and types of internet references. But, oddly, almost none of them referenced the story that had so ambushed my imagination that day – the first thing I'd ever read by him, a tale with just a one-word title.

Wakefield.

In some old magazine or newspaper, I recollect a story, told as truth, of a man – let us call him Wakefield – who absented himself for a long time, from his wife.

It was an odd story and the style wasn't exactly usual either. The story speculated on the real-life identity of its hero as if the tale really was based on fact. As for the reasons that lay behind his extraordinary actions, the only clue the writer gives the reader is that Wakefield has a little strangeness.

And some.

And so he goes. He leaves his home, he leaves his wife with no hint as to the charade he's about to enact, no thought of preparing the woman with whom he's chosen to share his life for the ordeal she's about to endure.

To be fair to Wakefield it seems little more than a prank at the beginning. He only intends to stay away a relatively short period of time – maybe just a couple of nights – enough time to panic her, stampede her presumably into a huge display of grateful affection once the wanderer returns.

But he's made the break. He's crossed the line, strayed into territory most normal people would regard as unacceptable. And it's clearly heady stuff, intoxicating almost.

But he soon discovers he has a problem. Wakefield wants to see how his wife's coping. He wants to see the pain of separation etched on her face. He wants to see in her eyes the love he feels for her reflected back a million times. He wants to bathe in it all.

But how can he do that? He can't actually see her. He can't get even remotely close enough to her. So his mission seems doomed from the start.

Everything then gets more and more odd. Wakefield dons a disguise and follows her. He takes to walking past their house late at night, hoping for a glimpse inside, trying to espy in the pose she strikes as he passes the window the extent of her suffering.

One day there's sudden excitement as a doctor calls at the house. Has he provoked some sort of emotional or physical collapse? Wakefield's torn. Half of him wants to rush to her bedside. But he doesn't. Something restrains him but he doesn't know what. Slowly, the visits made by the doctor become less frequent. Finally, his wife is seen moving around inside the house again, eventually venturing outdoors, but looking changed, a shadow indeed of her former self.

As is Wakefield. For he knows now, if he didn't before, that even though his former home is not that far away from his current lodgings, it's actually in another world.

One day Wakefield and his wife come face to face. She's walking to church, dressed as if she's now a widow. Perhaps, in her mind, that's now what she is. There's a crowd milling around outside the church itself. In the crowd is the ever-watching Wakefield. As the crowd moves, as some obstruction forces a flow and then an eddy in the press of people, Wakefield is pushed against her. It's only a fleeting contact, his shoulder pressing against hers; but for a moment husband and wife are touching.

There's another moment – not then – when his wife pauses, some association sounding perhaps, some instinct stirring. But that's a short time after she's moved away, as she's about to head on into the church. Then she looks back at the still-milling crowd, but by then Wakefield has gone. He's back in his lodgings, almost in a fever. At the moment his wife is scanning the crowd, unable to translate into anything like coherent thought the confused messages inside her head, Wakefield is throwing himself on his bed, all the miserable strangeness of his life, as Hawthorne describes it, revealed to him at a glance. In that moment he truly believes himself to be mad.

Wakefield told himself at the start of it all that he'd go back soon. Perhaps he believed it. But he doesn't. In the story Wakefield stays away for more than twenty years. He keeps seeing his wife, keeps watching her – from a distance – bears witness to her growing older before his eyes as he too is now growing older. By now, as Hawthorne puts it, he's well and truly given up his place among the living without being admitted among the dead.

And then, one night on his usual walk past his former home, he sees – through the window and illuminated by the open fire – a shadow of his wife. For a moment he sees almost a grotesque caricature dancing above the room. And acting on a sudden whim, Wakefield approaches his front door, takes his key out of his pocket, fits the key in the lock and walks back into the house he left more than two decades before.

And what happens?

We will not follow our friend across the threshold.

We don't know. We never find out. Hawthorne, presumably, wasn't interested. But sitting on the set of that film shoot, engaged and energised for the first time in days, I was most definitely more than interested. For some reason that tale reached deep inside me. And from that moment on all I wanted to know was what had happened next.

11.

TIA CALLED ME a couple of hours later. I tensed as I heard her voice on the other end of the line. We'd hadn't exactly parted, those few hours before, on the best of terms. At least I assumed we hadn't parted on the best of terms. How could I know? I was flat out on the floor, barely able to speak, certainly not able to stand and very definitely unable to make any sort of amends for a scene I couldn't even begin to explain.

'Hey.'

It was a reasonable start – literally – in that Tia actually sounded reasonable. Friendly, even. It might seem odd to read all that into just one word but when Tia was seriously pissed she could invoke the wrath of the gods in a single syllable.

'Hey.'

I responded, still cautious.

'Good day?'

Now there was a hint of amusement in her voice.

Amusement?

'The usual.'

'Assaulted any more TV pundits?'

'Nuked a couple of newsreaders. Wasted a DJ down on the Island.'

'Station?'

'Three, I think.'

'Classy.'

'Maybe Two.'

'Populist.'

Tia giggled.

'How about you? How's work? What time will you be back?'

'We've a client to meet in Euston. Shouldn't be too late.'

We talked for a little longer. It was the same tone, light, almost playful. I asked Tia if she wanted me to make her anything for supper and she told me to order something from a new addition to another room service menu that had just come out. She also told me to open a bottle of the Pinot Noir from the Napa Valley we'd found on a Stateside holiday the year before and asked me to record some arts programme that might be interesting, work-wise, in relation to some event they hoped to stage.

It all remained casual, warm. The events of the day were wiped, so it seemed. And as I put down the phone, my face still instructing my mouth to smile, I knew, without a shadow of a doubt, that we were indeed now in trouble.

12.

IT WAS ONLY one small store. But it felt like you could keep track on the whole world from all that was stacked inside.

There were surveillance trackers, theft trackers, fleet trackers, listening devices, spy phones, spy cameras and even – a neat touch – anti-spy software too. If you really wanted to cover all angles, all bases.

I'd walked into the shop, as casually as I could, at ten the next morning. Tia had come home at roughly the time she said she'd return. I'd already opened the Pinot Noir and she talked about the upcoming event in Euston. It wasn't going to be particularly glitzy – no A-list Hollywood celebrities – and it wasn't even the type of launch that was going to attract the Z-list wannabes either. But it was work and the agency were grateful for anything that might come their way. Times were still tough.

I complimented her on her choice from the take-out service. We'd finished the bottle and, at her suggestion, gone to bed. What followed wasn't the most passionate of encounters but there was nothing amiss about it either. At breakfast I'd enquired – again as casually as I could – about her movements for the next week or so. No particular reason. No underlying intent. At least that's the tone I hoped I'd injected into my voice. Tia told me she'd check her diary when she arrived in work and let me know.

There was just one member of staff in the shop when I walked in, a twenty-something male assistant sporting a shock of black hair, combed upwards, almost in the shape of an old-fashioned beehive. He wore forbidding dark glasses lightened by an easy smile. From his accent he was from Essex but he could just as easily have hailed from Leamington Spa. The days when people carried their accents around with them like a badge were long gone. Now they were interchangeable like items of clothing. What was the point of moving somewhere new if you didn't re-invent yourself along the way?

The assistant was called Dom. He didn't say what it was short for and maybe it wasn't short for anything. And he wasn't the assistant, he was the manager. And he didn't bat an eyelid when I mumbled something about wanting some information for a project I was doing. I might also have said something about doing some research. It didn't really matter what I said because he wasn't listening. He'd probably heard it all a hundred times before and the fact the mumbled excuse needed to be made in the first place meant he should certainly mistrust it. Anyway, why should he care? He was in business. Supply and demand was all he was interested in, not the many multi-coloured motives that may or may not lie behind it.

Dom told me to take a look round. He often found that was best with new clients. It was a neat touch being called a client rather than a customer. A bit unsettling too, as if there was already some semblance of professional collusion between the two of us. Maybe there was and he'd just acknowledged that rather more quickly than I had.

So I stared, blankly at first, then rather more raptly and within a shorter time than I might have expected, at the first shelf as I became introduced to the world of the tracker.

The first of the goodies on display came in the shape of a gift, perhaps for a birthday or Christmas. But it also came with something of a sting in the tail.

This tracker was built into a watch – a number of styles and shapes were supplied. It was fully functioning but came with its own phone number. The GPS tracker determined its location and would then send a text message to a mobile phone with a map link and coordinates.

All you then had to do was click on the link and a map would download showing the precise location of the watch and wearer. OK, you'd need GPRS connectivity, but even if you didn't have that you could just type the text message into a facility such as Google Earth and there it was. The location of that wristwatch – and its wearer – at any moment in time. Particularly handy, said the blurb on the box, if you had children or an elderly parent and, for your own peace of mind, wanted to know where they were at all times of the day or night.

Or if you had a partner you distrusted.

The downside being what you do if your partner doesn't put on the watch that day? Or decides it's the tackiest thing they've ever seen and rather than hurt your feelings drops it down the nearest drain and all Google Earth can come up with is the inside of some sewer somewhere?

I moved on to the next shelf. Now it was more difficult for the manufacturer to claim any sort of altruistic purpose such as care and concern for an elderly parent.

This particular tracker was tiny, little more than the length of the smallest adult finger. It was designed to be attached to a vehicle. Once recovered it recorded every journey the vehicle had made courtesy of signals received, apparently, from no less than twenty-four satellites orbiting the earth. The internal computer determined the location of the device within two and a half metres, recording data every second, and you didn't only find out where the tracked person was at any point in time. You could even, if you were so bothered, work out their fastest speed on any given journey, where they stopped and for how long.

This miniature logger was powered by two triple-A batteries and could be placed inside, outside and even underneath the vehicle. The magnet mount was also water resistant. It would record up to one hundred hours of data and would even suspend activity when the vehicle wasn't in motion.

I reached out, took the tiny box down from the shelf and moved on to the next section.

Listening devices.

And there really were some neat boxes of tricks in this little lot.

First I picked up a totally ordinary looking adaptor. Just a common or garden double plug on the outside, but containing a GSM Bug inside. Plug in to any standard socket and straightaway you're listening to everything that anyone's saying in that room. You just dialled the number on the SIM card inside the plug from anywhere in the world and it would automatically and silently connect. You could even plug an appliance into the adaptor and it would still work fine.

I was starting to enjoy the euphemistic descriptions on the packaging. This one advised the user that the device they were holding was a high-quality surveillance product that offered long-term audio monitoring in an area of concern without arousing suspicion.

In other words, let's see if that wife of yours really is entertaining friends at home or whether that husband who says he loves you is actually screwing the au pair while you're away.

Unless that wife of yours plugs her hairdryer into the adaptor or that husband of yours fires up his noisy X-Box within a metre of the device drowning everything else out. As with the watch, I put the double adaptor back on the shelf.

I looked at outsize wall clocks that doubled as listening devices – in matt black finish or natural wood – but I couldn't see Tia accepting anything like that anywhere in the loft no matter how stylish the finish. If she wanted to live in a station as she'd probably have pointed out, she'd bunk down in St Pancras, although even then she'd make sure she was within quaffing distance of the champagne bar.

There was also a device that would have enabled me to

listen through walls which didn't exactly get to first base either. Our neighbours seemed pleasant enough on the few occasions we'd passed on the stairs but I really couldn't see them permitting me my Gene Hackman impersonation in their living room.

There were also all manner and sizes of mobile bugs – most small, for obvious reasons – that could be placed just about anywhere in the loft. The problem being that's exactly what they looked like; bugs. They may have come in the smallest of packages but the loft was ultra-minimalist which was another way of saying we didn't really have much in the way of furniture. It wouldn't be easy hiding even the smallest device in that open-plan space without risk of fairly early detection.

Then I saw the picture frame. Now this was cute.

It was a totally ordinary picture frame. The kind we had hanging up all over the loft, records of encounters from long ago, myself and Tia with friends and acquaintances.

'You can hang it on a wall, stand it on a unit, a shelf, anywhere.'

I almost physically jumped. I'd been so locked in my own world for the past few moments I'd as good as forgotten there was someone in that shop with me.

'The bug's built into the back of the frame. Dial its number, it's programmed to answer after two rings.'

'Two what?'

I couldn't help it and Dom smiled.

'Only kidding. We call them rings but they're silent. Once the device answers you can hear everything that's happening in a fifteen-metre radius. No geographical restrictions, call in from anywhere.'

Dom studied the box.

'Battery life is about two weeks but that will shorten depending how often you dial in. Sound quality's excellent though.'

Dom melted back to the till, as quietly as he'd materialised at my side, one last parting shot over his shoulder as he went.

'Comes in a variety of sizes.'

I reached up to the shelf, took down the picture frame, added it to the basket. That was the Duke and the loft taken care of. But how to maintain surveillance when the subject was on the move?

From the next shelf two garishly-coloured lines of writing screamed out at me from a box.

The 3480 Spy Phone.

And this one was simple. Give the phone to a loved one, bask in their grateful thanks, then dial in from a pre-programmed number and listen to whatever's being said by the user. There were no visible signs that the phone wasn't anything but a standard mobile or had this feature installed.

Alternatively you could just put the phone in spy mode, and leave it lying around as a bugging device. Again, just dial the pre-programmed number to listen in.

The problem being that Tia was more than usually picky when it came to mobiles and that was nothing to do with any latent fear of being spied on. It was more to do with fashion than function although she'd deny that with her last living breath. The chances were that any phone I dared buy her would end up in some forgotten corner of her deepest desk drawer at work.

I moved on. The next section was jammed full of gizmos that allowed the user to eavesdrop on a target computer and this looked much more promising as most of them looked to all intents and appearances like a simple USB stick. It would record all emails and instant messages and would store a record of all passwords, internet activity, and everything else that was typed into the target PC or Mac, even recording online conversations conducted in chat rooms. It stored four million keystrokes and the memory remained intact even when unplugged according to the characteristically breathless prose on the side of the box.

'Undetectable by spyware programs too.'

That was Dom once more at my suddenly-tensed shoulder before he drifted away again.

I nodded as he did so, feeling like a punter in a porn shop. This already felt like a private undertaking to be conducted well away from outside attention. So please, just fuck off.

The USB tracker went into the basket too which just left the last section.

Spy cameras.

And now we really were into big boys toys and was I already loving these little beauties? I'd have bought the whole lot just to look at them and show other people, although that might perhaps have sabotaged the point of the exercise.

There was the Tissue Box Camera & DVR. An actual, real-life tissue box with everything you'd need for covert recording – a hidden 480TVL Sony CCD camera with wide-angle lens, built-in long-life battery, three different recording modes, both video and audio, a 2GB SD card which would accept up to 32GB and remote control.

Serious shit in other words.

The Tissue Box permitted three different recording modes; motion detection, scheduled or continuous recording. All recorded footage was time and date stamped and the unit could even be connected to a TV for viewing the recorded footage in widescreen. Alternatively, just remove the SD card and use a reader to play back the footage on your laptop using KMPlayer.

I looked all round it for the spy hole. There wasn't one and that was as in not anywhere. So how the hell did the camera record? Simple – via a standard board lens in the product casing which worked a bit like the tinted windows you'd see on customised cars – you can see out, but there's zilch chance of seeing in – all powered by a built-in rechargeable 12v long-life battery capable of maintaining the unit for two to three days from a single full charge.

And the final touch? It came supplied with two packs of tissues, for authenticity.

Really neat.

Next up, the radio alarm clock, the sort of clock you'd see on any bedside table in the country, in reality the ultimate covert camera system: another 480TVL high resolution camera and good-quality mic for recording audio too.

You could set the camera to record manually – starting the recording via remote control – or, again, on detection of movement or even at a specified time. It recorded onto an expandable SD card and, as with the card in the tissue box, recordings would be time and date stamped and could also be played back through a TV or laptop. It was all powered from the nearest mains socket meaning the system could run twenty-four hours a day, seven days a week with no need to change or recharge batteries.

And the finishing touch – because they all had finishing touches, I was beginning to realise – the unit had a built-in projector so the digital time display could also be seen on your ceiling or wall in the dark.

That went into the box along with the tissues. OK, it was possible neither would actually be used. Tissue boxes tended to be dumped in the bin the moment the box even remotely neared exhaustion so that was probably a no-no. And Tia might wonder why the hell I'd suddenly put a clock radio on the bedside table when all we'd ever bothered with in the past were time displays on our mobiles but again, what the hell?

Boys and toys again.

Then I found the pen. Now this was undeniably more practical, mainly because there were always so many lying around the loft.

And it looked like any other pen too. Maybe a bit chunkier than most but nothing that would really mark it out as meriting any special inspection. Ideal for covert video and audio surveillance and also for interview recording. Now let that slimy broker tell you that he really had spelt out the small print. Just play back the conversation and watch his blood pressure soar.

And the finishing touch – because they all etc., etc. – it was actually a fully functioning pen as well. You could have written out the entire works of Andrew Marvell had you but world enough and time.

I looked round the shelves again, feeling more and more like a kid in a sweet shop, then turned as the door opened. And then I stopped as if I'd been slapped across the face.

A fifty-something man was with Dom. He was sweating slightly although seemingly more from excitement than nerves. He was bent over some newly-delivered package which Dom was demonstrating and looked as if he was about to foam at the mouth. For a moment I saw the shop and its contents as the paradise for the perverted it could so easily become and it was like standing outside my body and seeing myself for the first time since I'd walked in.

What was I doing?

What was I thinking of?

What if someone I knew had walked in and not this fifty-something?

What would I say, how would I explain?

I put the basket down, quickly, contents still inside. I hurried past Dom towards the door. As I exited, I just caught sight of his eyes following me all the way.

THAT WAS CRAZY. I must have been crazy. It was the old problem, too much time on my hands, too much room in an empty mind for imaginary ogres to assume human shape.

Tia and I were solid. Rock solid. I could cite innumerable examples of that undeniable fact.

Take just one of the very latest.

Take Eddie.

It was the first chance of work I'd had since Trooper Rohl. Tia had just started in the agency and was still getting established. We were asset rich, but cash poor. I'd already defaulted on a couple of credit card payments and we'd also had to suffer the humiliation of an early morning call from a debt collection agency. Then I suddenly got the chance of a shoot in South America.

I'd come to the attention of a commissioning editor due to some experimental stuff I'd been shooting. Partly as a result of all the new time on my hands, I was becoming something of a pioneer in the strange and sometimes spooky world of partial winding. Photography, as every camera freak could tell you, has always been the tool of choice for capturing a moment, freezing that moment in time – but what about a collection of moments? What if you wanted to squeeze, for example, five frames into the space of three? That way you can capture a mixture of images, of people and places, scenes and faces so that one image, in panoramic format, tells the story of a whole day or at least several moments in that day as opposed to just the one.

Assume you're working with an LC-A. The camera can be adapted to suit. First, start with the basics. Shoot your first image.

Then, before winding on, press the rewind button and hold the rewind handwheel steady at the same time. Now, wind the film on just a fraction and then release the button and the wheel. Finish winding on until your LC-A is ready to shoot again and keep doing this over and over again.

Health warning – when you're developing the film don't let the lab cut it. Some of them will wonder what the hell you've been up to and try helping you out of the apparent mess you've created. It happened to me on a couple of occasions and it's painful to see images you've laboured to bring to life stillborn at birth.

Tips – you'll need a flatbed or drum scanner to get a whole strip scanned. Also, direct light and high contrast situations don't give the best results, aim for similar backgrounds that are going to merge well. Get all that right and you're approaching something really special. Just imagine being able to capture the same face on one strip of film as that person hears, first, good news and then bad, as they experience genuine delight and then, moments later, total devastation.

The commissioning editor believed this technique would suit the contrasting experiences to be encountered on the South American shoot perfectly. It was also the sort of career opportunity that could be a genuine way back for me.

But it was going to cost to put together a relevant portfolio and for a time it looked like the opportunity might vanish before my eyes. Which was when I collected together all my cameras, laid them out on the floor and did some long, hard, thinking.

I'd hardly looked at some of them in years. I'd certainly not peered through the viewfinder of most of them in anything that even remotely approached anger in even more years. They still had sentimental value but what was that? How did that stack up against the sort of chance that was now on offer? After a couple of hours – and despite the misgivings of Tia – I decided it didn't stack up at all, packed up the pick of the specimens on show and took a trip into Whitechapel.

In the old days – days I didn't remember – they'd be called pawnbrokers. But maybe the name was just too redolent of times past, its echoes too Dickensian. Now they were called by a variety of other titles, Money Converter, Money Matters, Money Exchange were just three I'd seen. But they all performed the same function. Bring us your unwanted items and walk out with cash.

Tia had come with me to provide moral support. Despite my new resolve she knew it was going to be hard to part with cameras that had been with me, in some cases, longer than some of my adult teeth. Her decision proved to be a mistake. None of what subsequently happened would ever have done so if she'd simply stayed home that day.

It was pretty obvious from the moment we walked into the shop that the owner, a forty-something we only knew by his first name at that point – Eddie – was struck by Tia. Which wasn't surprising. It would have been more surprising had he not. Tia was hot and I was used to the stares of strangers. What I wasn't used to was his reaction to her partner.

It was equally obvious right from the start that Eddie didn't exactly rate me. In his eyes I was obviously just another of the local unfortunates and at that point so indeed I was. So what was a woman like Tia doing with a chancer like me?

Eddie was openly contemptuous of me – openly leery towards Tia – and more than a little dismissive of all I had to offer in every respect from the start. He didn't have a great deal of power in that first meeting and any leverage he had was exclusively financial but he used every ounce of it to try and make headway with Tia.

In truth it was more pathetic than offensive. Ordinarily neither of us would have let the likes of Eddie even remotely bother us. To take him seriously really would have been breaking a butterfly on a wheel. But Eddie had caught us at a bad time – insecure and unsure of our place in the present and even more insecure and unsure as to where we were heading in the near and distant future. And all the time Eddie stoked the fires, evermore obvious in his dismissal of a man who could put a woman like Tia through an experience like this, ever more leery in his clumsy pursuit of Tia herself.

We'd been to the shop a couple of times. He was forever inventing reasons why we had to call back – a check on this, a valuation on that. It was obvious to us both that the real reason for these return calls was nothing to do with his business but everything to do what Eddie clearly hoped would soon become his pleasure.

Tia even suspected he'd photographed our visits – there was an array of CCTV cameras dotted all around the shop. At the time I'd understood and accepted them as necessary security devices. In his world you were bound to come across the odd strange – sometimes exceptionally strange – customer, although few were likely to be as odd as the proprietor himself. Tia didn't want to think what other, more private, use he made of the tapes he recorded and I didn't want to give him chance to do so again if Tia was right. So when the next call came from Eddie, checking some spurious detail on one of the cameras in advance of his release of our cash, I took a solo trip down to his shop.

Eddie was less than pleased to see just me. And Eddie seemed to realise that any future visits were also going to be made just by myself too. I thought that was the end of the matter. A foul-tempered Eddie – his business-hat finally donned – agreed that I'd have my money within the next two days and I left more determined than ever to make a success of the upcoming shoot so myself and Tia would never, in our lives, have cause to cross the path of a character like that again.

As I let myself out I glanced up at the CCTV camera monitoring the shop doorway and permitted myself the smallest of smiles, something I was sure Eddie would understand if part of the point of those recordings was indeed for him to savour, later, the power he held over those who crossed his threshold.

The next night Eddie called round to the loft. This was, needless to say, very much forbidden territory. I wasn't even aware Eddie had our home address. We hadn't yet properly concluded the deal thanks to his now-habitual delaying tactics and so there was no reason to complete the bill of sale – the ostensible reason for his visit. But it wasn't the reason at all. It was self-delusion of a type that would glaze over the eyes of Narcissus, a belief that somehow, maybe, the man might have a chance.

Tia was alone. That could have been good fortune on his part but somehow I doubted it. I hadn't planned to go out that night but an acquaintance had called out of the blue and I'd gone with him for a drink. The only way Eddie could possibly have known I was away was by keeping watch on the loft from some vantage point somewhere, perhaps from the all-night café across the street. That prospect was simply too creepy to contemplate but – and as with so much else so far as he was concerned – the cap very much seemed to fit.

Tia hadn't wanted to let him in. Then she hadn't wanted not to. She didn't want to acknowledge – to him or to herself – that he unsettled her in any way. And so she'd opened the door, ignored his hints that she fix him a drink, stood the whole time as he rambled his way through the feeble reason for his visit before showing him the door.

On the way out he'd brushed her breast with the back of his hand. Maybe he thought the gesture would be irresistibly arousing and in a sense it was, although not at all in the way Eddie expected. A second or so later Eddie was in a crumpled heap on the floor outside our door. Which is where he was five minutes later. After another ten minutes he did manage to stumble to his feet only to sink to his knees again which is where he remained for ten more minutes. By the time the pain in his groin had subsided to the point he could even begin to contemplate standing at least halfway straight, fully half an hour had elapsed since his not-so-subtle attempt to caress Tia which – he was now beginning to appreciate – was somewhat ill-advised.

I arrived back a couple of hours later by which time Eddie had disappeared. Whether he'd actually made it home by then was a moot point. It wasn't much of a walk but he would have been making snail-like progress all the way. For the rest of the evening Tia luxuriated in her description of our fallen tormentor. It was a sweet moment of victory in a life that had become tainted lately by defeat and, small and insignificant as it was, we savoured every moment.

The next day I called in on him. We had business to conclude but I'd have called anyway. Physically, I expected the same old Eddie. Tia hadn't hit him that hard. He'd be OK by now even if he'd be moving a little more stiffly than normal for the next few days.

But the worm – or worms – had turned. The relationship had been redefined in some way. The old order had changed. How would Eddie react? What person would now eye me as I opened his shop door, crossed that threshold, approached him at his counter?

For a few moments it was all I expected. His eyes ducked my silent stare as I paused in the doorway and looked across at him. He didn't look up as I approached. When, finally, he met my eyes there was more than a touch of the wounded animal in the look. I allowed myself a brief surge of satisfaction. But I should have known. That was when animals were at their most dangerous. When they were wounded was the moment they're most likely to strike back.

Eddie concluded the paperwork on our deal, the paperwork that – according to him anyway – had brought him to the loft the previous evening. That visit and the end to that visit weren't referred to once but still hung heavy between us like a veil. Everything we said, every gesture was filtered through it. As was the next move in the power struggle.

Eddie pushed the paperwork across to me along with a cheque. For a moment I stared at it, unable to take it in. Something was wrong. It took a while to grasp the extent of the discrepancy between the agreement we'd signed and the cheque that had just been pushed across the counter. I went back to the agreement, evermore conscious of his eyes on my bewildered face, stopping as I realised.

Eddie had altered the figures. After we'd signed the form. He'd run off a new agreement, transposing my signature from the old. To anyone who didn't know, it looked like the original document. It was a simple but devastating subterfuge. The new agreement paid out roughly half the previous sum. I'd just sold my precious collection of cameras and still wouldn't have anywhere near enough to embark on the South American shoot.

'What's this?'

'What's it look like?'

'This isn't what we agreed.'

'Why did you sign it then?'

'I didn't sign this.'

'So what's that?'

Eddie pointed with a grimy fingernail to the signature at the bottom of the page.

'Scotch Mist?'

'You've altered it.'

Eddie sucked in his breath, injured innocence.

'Fighting talk.'

'It's not the agreement I signed.'

'Strange that. Because I've only ever seen one agreement.'

Eddie tapped the piece of paper again.

'And that's it.'

Things became a bit heated after that. But it was a battle very much stacked in Eddie's favour. He was on home turf for one thing. He was also burning with a misplaced, but still white-hot, sense of righteous indignation. In his mind we'd been fair game. A kill that had somehow revived and turned on him. And now he'd turned too. In Eddie's world life was composed of minor setbacks and small victories. That knee to his balls was a more than usually significant example of the former. Standing across his counter, staring into my now-wild eyes, he was relishing a more than usually significant instance of the latter.

I could sue. Of course I could. There was a good possibility I might have won too, once I'd paid out money I didn't have to engage experts I couldn't afford. So I either took the money and tried to raise the remainder some other way or I walked away and left with nothing. If I did the latter I wouldn't even leave with my cameras. I hadn't realised before but now I could see they weren't in their usual place beneath the glass display on the counter. They'd be in the back of the shop somewhere – or out of the shop completely – hidden from view. There was a default clause in the contract allowing Eddie to keep all goods and chattels – fine phrase – in the event of the vendor breaking the terms of the original agreement.

I left with nothing. I didn't even take a copy of the new contract I'd supposedly signed. I'd given away a collection of cameras that were intended to launch myself and Tia into a brand-new life and had walked out with just the memory of a mocking smile by way of payment. I walked around for hours, just moving, not really thinking, during which time Tia had tried calling me at least eight or nine times.

I walked into our loft just before midnight and told her what happened. Tia didn't respond. She just went very quiet, as if her whole being had suddenly stilled somehow which, as Eddie was to discover, was not good news.

Wounded animals were indeed dangerous. But a wounded Tia was even more so. On the inside she was boiling. On the outside she was ice cold. It was a potent combination, one I'd seen in her from the very start. That stroke she'd pulled with the graffiti and the house in Bristol was a classic example. Maybe it's what attracted me to her in the first place. That combination of distance and passion. The burning desire to hit back, to exact vengance, allied to pure, cold, reason. If it wasn't so sexy, it would be chilling.

It wasn't just the fact we'd been cheated out of what was rightfully ours, that Eddie – out of sheer pique – was attempting to sabotage our whole future. It was that Eddie had decided to turn the whole thing into a game in which he made up the rules. Unlike Natsuo, Tia didn't like games. And she particularly didn't like games in which the rules of engagement kept shifting. She preferred direct action which is what she now determined we would take and quickly. If Eddie could keep track on our movements, could work out when one of us would be in and would be out at any given time, on any given evening, then we could do the same. And if Eddie could make unannounced visits to our home then we could do the same to his.

In other words it was payback time. Whatever Eddie could do, Tia decided we could do so much better.

Of course Tia wasn't going to sit in some pavement café near to his flat and wait for him to emerge, blinking as he always seemed to do for some reason, out onto the street. If Tia was going to do this then Tia was going to be in control right from the start.

It wasn't that difficult to extricate Eddie from his flat. Times being what they were, he was receiving a fair few calls back then, asking for a valuation on this item or that. The more portable of the items would be brought into the shop but there was also the occasional house clearance to view. These were especially tempting. Most houses contained at least something that sparkled amongst the dross as Eddie himself had boasted on more than one occasion.

Tia engaged an actress friend to make a call. Eddie listened intently as she explained how she wanted to clear out the apartment of a now deceased aunt which was stacked full – so far as she could see – of the most appalling junk. Eddie dissembled as, all the while, he tried to find out just what he was dealing with here. The actress, who clearly had a fine future ahead of her, played her new role to perfection, apparently walking round the apartment while she spoke to Eddie who was now almost salivating on the other end of the line as she told him all about this piece of furniture, that painting, this ornament, that watercolour.

The postcode was the clincher. It would be hardly likely, after all, that one of the more exclusive streets in St John's Wood would have been furnished out of a pound store. There had to be something there worth a look.

Eddie made an appointment for that very evening. It would take him the best part of an hour to cross the city, he'd probably hang around outside for at least another half-hour in case his caller had been delayed and it would then take him almost another hour to get back. So we had between two and three hours to get into his flat and to recover what was rightfully ours either by way of goods or – fine phrase again – chattels or, even more preferably, by way of cash. Eddie, we suspected, wouldn't deposit all his takings in a bank. He wouldn't want the taxman to know the real extent of his earnings. Far too much potential for too many awkward questions. He had to have some hiding places where he secreted his store. A couple of hours or so should give us ample time to find it.

Eddie duly left his flat an hour before the appointment. He dodged a couple of skateboarding kids, turned a corner and was gone.

I looked at Tia who looked back at me. I was excited, my breathing shallower than normal. Tia, as ever, was ice.

Getting in wasn't difficult. Eddie had an alarm but it wasn't exactly state of the art. Cutting the electricity supply was easy enough and posed no danger of detection so long as the power source was reconnected within one minute – to the box, not the sensors. We'd already worked out that a tiny, silent, generator – the kind the indie film outfits tended to use on guerrilla film shoots – would be fit for purpose and so it proved. Two minutes after cutting the supply and reconnecting the small generator we were inside. The generator was good for just over an hour, probably more. By that time an increasingly impatient Eddie would be pacing the pavement of the upmarket enclave and we'd be heading home, the scales of justice more or less evened up.

The problem was that all our thinking about Eddie and his secret store of cash proved, pretty quickly, to be misplaced. Maybe that explained the less than effective alarm. Eddie might well have squirreled away a small fortune somewhere but it wasn't in the flat. There were only six rooms – kitchen, sitting room, hallway, bathroom and two bedrooms. It was furnished sparsely and the floors were concrete. There were no paintings on the wall that might hide hidden treasures, no dummy drawers or false bottoms in the wardrobes or kitchen cabinets. Which meant either Eddie was broke – which we knew, from personal experience he was not – or he really did deposit all his takings at the end of each day in the local night safe – which we still thought was unlikely. Which meant he had a hiding place in the shop instead and that, we knew, would be guarded more securely than the Federal Reserve.

Not that any of this was remotely fazing Tia. There was still a relatively decent TV system with the latest plasma screen, a half-decent music system as well as some other electrical bits and bobs which by themselves wouldn't amount to anything particularly princely but would go some way to compensate a pauper.

There was also – and how sweet was this? – my collection of cameras now about to be restored to their rightful owner.

The removal of all the items was going to make us rather more visible than was strictly desirable but, and as with most districts in London, it wasn't exactly the kind of area where you'd find a high preponderance of good neighbours keeping an eye on the property of others.

There was an alleyway leading from the rear door of the flat onto the street. One end of the alleyway gave onto the High Street, the other gave onto some waste ground and across that another street. Tia made a call to another friend and secured the use of a small van, no questions asked. The van was parked on the street fronting the waste ground within fifteen minutes. By then Eddie was probably contemplating calling his wasted night a day but it'd still take him almost an hour to get home.

Ten minutes later and the first of the trips from the flat to the van was under way and a plasma TV screen was inside. Five minutes after that and Eddie's music system along with various portable radios – state of the art DAB examples – were in there too along with my cameras. I retraced my steps to the flat for the final trip of the night, allowing myself for the first time to feel a sense of exultation.

Left alone I might have cursed my luck and crawled under a

stone. With Tia by my side I hadn't. Together, we'd emboldened the other. Together we'd hatched a plan, had amended that plan admittedly but – ultimately – had executed it. I would never have done that with anyone else. In that moment I knew what others meant when they talked about finding a soul mate. I'd previously dismissed all that as the ramblings of the delusional or desperate. But now I knew it to be true. Previously I'd believed people to be interchangeable. If one relationship failed then there was always another ready to take its place. Some relationships were preferable in one way, some in another, but there was always someone else waiting in the wings.

Only there wasn't. Sometimes you found a person who couldn't be replaced in any way. I'd found someone who would not countenance the thought that I might be beaten. For the first time in a life that had previously been marked by anything but, I began to understand the powerful appeal of commitment, of monogamy, of devoting oneself to just one person knowing that one person would do exactly the same.

14.

TWO DAYS AFTER my visit to Dom and his strange surveillance store, I waited till Tia was having a shower and then – and still with the same sense of self-revulsion – opened her handbag again. Reaching inside I took out her phone. I was only going to need about five minutes according to the software but I wanted to allow myself a little longer. I might make a mistake, have to reprogram some step or other. Or I might change my mind halfway through and decide to abandon the whole thing.

I had done as Dom's eyes seemed to have silently predicted as I left the store that day. I had returned, although I'd made only one relatively low-level purchase. And for this purchase to work it was essential to get access to your quarry's own phone which made it problematic if the subject was a work colleague or some distant acquaintance. For a wife or husband or partner it was perfect; especially one who had no suspicions that their movements might be tracked and I was pretty certain Tia would have absolutely none.

I'd remained careful not to float any casual-sounding questions about her work colleagues. I hadn't quizzed her, just that little too closely, on her movements when she came home at night. I'd displayed none of the telltale signs of the potentially jealous partner so why would she even begin to suspect that partner might be watching her when she was out of sight?

Besides, Tia was something of a technophobe. She'd just about mastered the TV remote although even that had taken something of a crash course in patience and tact. Electronic devices were a closed book to her, to be admired for their design statement rather than investigated for the uses to which they could be put.

I took her phone out onto the balcony and placed it next to my laptop which was already connected to the target website.

There were the usual warnings and boxes to tick. The software was developed, apparently, with the primary aim of tracking stock as well as monitoring staff movements so long, of course, as this didn't constitute any infringement of civil liberties or intrude on the personal privacy of the persons monitored in this way.

Yeah, right.

I ticked all the boxes indicating that I'd read and would comply with all the specified terms and conditions and then used my debit card to buy some GSM credits. The debit card was in my sole name and was linked to an account I used only sporadically and which was actually registered to a previous address. Statements anyway were only delivered by email so there was very little chance of Tia stumbling across them.

Almost immediately her phone – which I'd switched to silent – illuminated with a text message. The message was for Tia and asked if she wanted to add me to her Buddy list. To accept she simply had to reply to the text message with the word, Locate.

Why not? We were already buddies, weren't we? Or was that what I was about to find out? Either way, I dispatched the suggested text. Almost immediately the handset illuminated again, warning Tia that this agreement allowed others to know where she was at any given moment in time and that, for her own safety and peace of mind, she should be aware of that. I deleted both the text messages making sure her phone hadn't stored them in her Archive folder. Some deleted messages were held there for a day or so just in case they needed to be retrieved.

I heard Tia coming out of the bathroom and put my laptop

into sleep mode. I waited till I could hear the muffled roar of the hairdryer through the wall, then walked back into the sitting room and replaced her phone in her bag. Then I walked into the bedroom.

Her bare back was facing me, the scratch now fading. I asked if she had any change, I needed to get some items from the convenience store and there was always a *Big Issue* seller outside who never seemed to have change for notes.

Tia told me to take some from her purse but I brought her bag in to her and asked her to find some instead. A man should never rummage in a woman's handbag, as I pointed out. It might not be one of the Ten Commandments but it should be. Who knows what I might find? A grinning Tia threw the purse at me and I let myself out of the loft.

Tia was heading out as I came back in, a bag of groceries – and the latest *Big Issue* – in hand. She was going up to Islington for a drink in a theme bar with Ben from the sales team and Ingrid from promotions. Ben was doing a pitch for the launch of a similar new theme bar in Piccadilly the next week and wanted to check out the competition. He also wanted to rehearse his pitch in conditions that would approximate to the real thing. Apparently the owners of the theme bar held all meetings in the place itself which made for interesting sales conferences if a stag or hen party was taking place at the same time.

I kissed Tia goodbye, drank in the smell of her freshly-washed hair, waited till I heard the taxi door slam down on the courtyard, then watched as the driver took a left and disappeared from sight. Then I went back into the sitting room, retrieved my laptop from the balcony, powered it up and checked my list of GSM devices.

In pride of place there it was, the latest addition, a new mobile number. I hesitated a moment, conscious even at this late stage of crossing a somewhat significant Rubicon, then clicked on Locate.

For a moment as I waited, I had a momentary stab of panic. What if Tia hadn't switched on her phone? What if she'd decided she didn't want to be disturbed that day? I hadn't even considered that before. Everything I'd done, all the preparations I'd made would come to nothing courtesy of something as simple as an off switch.

Then the screen fired into life. A map appeared of the area immediately surrounding the loft, a shape that resembled a person-shaped blob clearly visible in the centre of the screen. I stared, rapt, at Tia moving through time and space, far out of range of the human eye, well within range of the electronic tracker, the spy in her handbag.

Then the picture froze and I tensed. Had I done something wrong, had the software failed on only its first outing? Then the picture assumed shape again and I realised it was taking snapshots on a default setting. I could program the space and distance between each one. I could even choose a five-minute delay meaning I didn't have to stare at that screen continuously, just check back from time to time.

But I didn't.

FOR THE REST of that day her routine was exactly as Tia had predicted. Her taxi took roughly the route I'd have expected as it headed north for Islington. There was a brief moment of excitement when the on-board coordinates on the tracker map suddenly started showing south-east as opposed to various degrees of north but a quick check on the monitor – and a subtle adjustment of the volume on my laptop – and I was soon listening to the cabbie and a trademark rant against unnecessary road works, incompetent council employees, useless private motorists and a world in general that conspired to make his life just that little bit harder every day.

Situation normal in fact. Just like everything else for the next few hours.

The cab stopped, finally, outside the bar in Islington. For a few moments Tia paused on the pavement as she met Ben from the office, as they discussed the bar and speculated on its likely clientele. After a few moments they were joined by a woman I didn't know but who I guessed was Ingrid, who added her own voice to the general inquest.

Then the acoustic changed as they headed inside and for a moment I thought I'd lost them again as all volume momentarily dipped to be replaced by the sort of aural snow you used to get on an old analogue TV. But then the satellite shifted a millimetre or so in space or whatever satellites do, and I could hear Tia now sitting in the bar, spreadsheets on a table in front of her apparently, along with photographs of past successes in the events world and design swatches for the next.

Tia left her mobile in her handbag when she went to the toilet and for a few moments I was treated to some bitchy office gossip from Ingrid who really didn't appreciate Tia being sent along to watch over her like this. Ben tried to reassure the edgy Ingrid that Tia was just some extra help, another pair of eyes, but he was having an uphill struggle if Ingrid's evermore monosyllabic and clearly-unconvinced responses were anything to go by. Then Tia returned and Ingrid launched into a fulsome appreciation of her hair wanting to know where she had it done and while she was on the subject of all-matters-Tia where on Earth – if it was on Earth because in Ingrid's eyes they might well have wafted down from Heaven – did Tia find those shoes?

Again, all pretty standard stuff.

Then they ordered lunch. Ben ordered tuna melt with fries, Ingrid a selection of hummus and olive flatbread and Tia debated long and hard the respective merits of the house burger – was it the actual house burger or one brought in from another house entirely, or more probably out-sourced from some catering outlet – or should she go for the whitebait with garlic aioli? Eventually the choice was made. Ben had switched to the whitebait, Ingrid stuck with the hummus and Tia had switched to the tuna melt although all agreed they could sample the other's chosen fare, partly in the service of research, partly in the event of second thoughts.

Again it was all so ordinary as to be mundane. Except it wasn't. It was anything but and for a time I couldn't work it out. One of the selling points of the software was that it allowed you to get on with your life while the surveillance was under way, that it offered the purchaser the facility of simply checking in from time to time.

But I couldn't take my eyes from it all. I could no more have left that monitor and gone into my darkroom, checked out some prints I was planning on running off, than I could have walked to the moon.

What an extraordinary feeling it is to watch someone when they don't know you're watching. Particularly when that someone is as close to you as close can be and you're seeing them with other people, talking, laughing, eating, as you've seen them talk and laugh and eat a million times before but never, ever, quite like this.

There was a department store in New York that once experimented with a new type of Christmas window display. While Bloomingdale's decked out its windows with the usual tinsel, holly and Christmas trees this store constructed the living room and bedroom of a small apartment in theirs. Then they put two models inside the makeshift flat where they simply did what all young female flatmates would do. They watched TV, they fixed snacks, they read, they surfed the net, they talked, they pored over magazines and they tried on clothes.

The moral majority tried to get the display banned. The police were none too happy either but that was due to the record crowds the ultra-ordinary display was attracting forcing the few pedestrians who didn't stop and stare out from the sidewalk and into the road.

The reason for the record crowds was clear in the view of the moral majority who – judging by the numbers assembled daily on that sidewalk – might not have actually been in the majority at all. At odd times of the day or evening the girls, as girls are wont to do when trying on clothes, would undress down to their underwear.

That always provoked a loud cheer as such things always would. But for the rest of the time the girls did nothing out of the ordinary and, to be frank, even stripping down to a bra and pants was hardly extraordinary. Had these people never been to a beach? A public swimming pool? Never watched a wife, a lover getting dressed?

But the crowds watched, rapt. They stared in mute fascination at a life apparently going on, oblivious, on the other side of the glass divide. The more mundane and ordinary it was the more compelling it seemed to become. Some people actually drifted away during the underwear interludes as if all of a sudden it had turned into a show, something they could see every day of the week in the movies or a theatre. It had become artifice and therefore had ceased to be interesting.

Some people became just that little bit too interested. A couple of particularly engaged souls tried to tap on the window and attempted to engage the models in conversation but the girls ignored them and in truth the eager punters would have been disappointed had they not. The point was not some sort of social interaction. The point was to watch. Silently. Surreptitiously. Observe the minutiae of another life. Stand back and dissect that life in its every detail while all the time remaining apart from all that was unfolding before your eyes.

Tia spent the next two hours in the bar. I was treated to a rehearsal of the pitch Ben planned to make and in my opinion it needed polish. That was also the opinion of a tactful Tia and Ingrid too although when he went to the toilet they both agreed that it didn't need the odd nip and tuck, it required fairly drastic surgery. Ingrid offered to have a word in his ear on the way home and Tia gratefully accepted the offer. She had something else to do, she said, somewhere else to go.

There was something in her voice when she said that and I suddenly leant forward. If I'd been rapt before I was positively energised now. What did she have to do, where else did she have to go? Ingrid was clearly picking up the same vibe and she was probing now, albeit lightly, playfully almost, speculating on what this seemingly pressing engagement might be?

Tia insisted it was nothing; Ingrid pointed out that if it was nothing she should have no problem in saying what it was; Tia said she wouldn't be interested. Ingrid made it clear she was very interested and was becoming more so by the moment; Tia was by now in fits of giggles at being pressed so hard. The returning Ben wanted to know what was going on, clearly wondering if it was something to do with him. That sent Tia off into yet more fits of giggles, Ingrid now joining in and Ben couldn't help himself, he started giggling too. The only person in the whole world who wasn't laughing right now it seemed was a couple of miles away in a loft, listening to his partner now approaching hysterics and totally unable to work out why.

Later, waiting for a cab outside, Ingrid conceded defeat. Whatever it was that Tia had planned for the rest of the day, Ingrid hoped she'd enjoy it. Tia told her she would. Then Tia got into the cab, closed the door and – before I could hear her tell the driver where she wanted to go – turned off her phone.

I stared at the now-blank monitor, blinked stupidly in sudden and intense frustration.

What the – ?

I stood up and patrolled the loft, checking the monitor every few seconds. Nothing. I tried closing the laptop down and booting it up again just in case that particular piece of software had crashed; a faint hope I knew because everything else was fine. The software was fine too. The program loaded without incident, there was simply nothing to report. There was little the software could do when faced with an off-switch as the instructions on the box had already made crystal clear and that's what Tia had done.

She'd pressed the off-switch. She'd cut herself off from all contact, had effectively divorced herself from the world. On a working day, having just left a meeting, when she might have messages to check, when anyone from her place of work might need to get in touch with her, when Ben might want to call her to rehearse his rewritten pitch, Tia had decided that she didn't want to have any contact with anyone.

Or had decided she did want to have contact with someone. Someone very special.

And didn't want to be disturbed.

I paced some more, walked out onto the balcony and stared across the river, tracked a clipper as it passed below, heading down river, about to call at Canary Wharf. A conductor was trying to chat up the girl manning the catering outlet, a man was staring down from the rails into the water as if contemplating whether or not to jump.

I didn't even give them a second glance. There was only one life I was interested in and that wasn't a life playing out down on that river where I could watch, observe, take note. It was taking place in a different universe entirely. Where I couldn't watch, couldn't observe.

I headed back inside as a new thought assailed me, picked up my mobile and dialled her work number. What if Tia hadn't turned her phone off? What if her battery had simply died? She was always forgetting to charge it to the point I'd even suggested she carry round a spare battery but as she pointed out, with ineffable logic, if she couldn't remember to charge the first battery why would she pay any attention to the second?

I waited for a connection to be made. The phone rang once, twice, three times, then her voicemail cut in.

Tia wasn't there. I checked my watch again computing times from Islington to her office. Even allowing for unnecessary road works, incompetent council employees and a world in general that conspired to make life just that little bit harder every day for London's finest, any cabbie would have had her there by now.

So why wasn't she there? And thinking all this through just that little bit more clearly than I'd been managing in the last few moments or so, wasn't it just ever so slightly coincidental – if I was still pursuing the battery option – that it should die just at the very moment Tia got into that cab? As opposed to, say, a few seconds before? Or a few seconds after?

But it didn't die a few seconds before or after, it died at the moment, the exact moment Tia closed that cab door, just before she could speak to the driver, just before I could hear her tell him where she was going.

A ring sounded on the doorbell. I wheeled round, paused to control my breathing. It wasn't the entry phone so it was someone from the complex, a neighbour perhaps. It wasn't exactly the kind of place where people popped in for an idle chat or to borrow a cup of sugar if anyone still used it these days, but we'd had the occasional caller asking us to keep an eye out for some delivery or other.

I composed my features, opened the door, then stopped, staring at the mystery man from the airport, the Covent Garden coffee shop man, as he, alone on the doorstep, stared back at me.

16

B Y TEN THAT night the party was in full swing.

From one end of the loft to the other it was wall-to-wall PR execs and events coordinators. Put like that, it could have been a vision from the far side of hell and in a different world and time I might indeed have turned tail and run a mile from it all. But this was a different world and time again. A world in which Tia had sprung a surprise party on me as well as offering me a chance to meet all the people she'd come to know over the past few months and who, so far, hadn't had the chance to meet me in turn.

She'd been planning it all day. The only proviso was that she wanted to invite people she actually liked, which was why Ben and Ingrid weren't among the invited number. And why Mr Mystery Man was. The man in the airport, the man in the coffee shop, the man I stared at as he stood on my doorstep just a short time before.

Now he was standing before me again, this time in the company of an impossibly beautiful, stick-thin blonde. The mystery man was Joseph, the co-owner of the agency where Tia worked. The stick-thin blonde was Nikki, the other co-owner and Joseph's current partner. They both loved having Tia in the agency and both seemed genuinely delighted to now be meeting her partner. Joseph also talked warmly about a couple of exhibitions I'd put on in the past. Nikki talked even more warmly about some magazine shoots I'd done. And I was beginning to get that all-too familiar feeling again.

What had I been thinking of? Why had I read so much that

was sinister and mendacious into a simple goodbye nod at an airport and a shared coffee?

The rest of the party passed in something of a blur. Not the kind of blur I'd experienced at the photo launch, not the Toby Vine-inspired black fog of bitterness and petty jealousy. A pleasant blur. A comforting blur. The sort of blur where faces merge and each one is smiling. Where each conversation wraps itself round you and you float inside some sort of protective cocoon, not worrying what you say or what anyone else might say because, somehow, you know they're on your side and you'd be on theirs too if there were sides but there aren't, the night is just made up of people you want to be with and who want to be with you and that again was down to Tia and her decision to build this bridge, to make this gesture and I knew why.

He's down. He's been acting like an asshole. So let's make him feel better. Let's lift him out of all the introspective loathing and self-loathing and just have a good time. What could be simpler? What could be more perfect? To paraphrase a bad English magician, not a lot. Or maybe that was an exact quote, I didn't know. I went to ask Tia but ended up asking one of her colleagues – not Joseph, he was out on the balcony watching the river traffic with a couple of other people from the office – and we spent five minutes trying to decide before spending a further five minutes trying to mimic the exact intonation of the bad English magician in question as he delivered his deathless catchphrase. It was that kind of party.

Then I saw Tia bending over my laptop which I'd abandoned at that ring on the doorbell. Tia was staring at the screen and frowning.

I was at her side in an instant, bad English magician and catchphrase wiped, the blur of the party wiped too, everything now in crystal clear focus, my voice feeling like it was at least a few dozen decibels too high which it wasn't, but it was still loud enough for Tia to turn and stare at me along with a couple of her colleagues helping themselves to one of the bottles from the case of mid-range Barolo I'd broken out mid-blur time.

'What are you doing?'

Tia stared at me for another moment. My voice might not have been as loud as it sounded in my ears but the tone was sharp, far sharper than I'd intended or the situation warranted.

'My phone's down. The battery died, I just wanted to check my emails.'

I stared at the laptop. Tia had indeed accessed her office server, the home page clearly visible on the screen. But right beside it was the small arrow that would reveal all recent history, a record I would normally have erased making sure to go into the hard drive and erase the associated cookies too. It would have been easy meat for some techie to retrieve it but it would have taken the sort of time and effort that was well and truly beyond technology-averse Tia.

But I hadn't had time to do any of that. And all Tia would have to do now was click on that small arrow and my recent surveillance program would be up there on the screen. She'd pause, then stare at it for a moment, puzzled initially perhaps, but she'd realise pretty quickly that this was something strange, something out of the ordinary, nothing to do with my work such as it was these days. And by that time maybe she'd have been joined by some of her friends who'd be more intrigued than puzzled and who would very definitely know more about computers than Tia and who'd be able, with a couple more clicks of the mouse, to access all recent activity, maybe even replay some of the surveillance footage the software had stored on the hard drive.

And then Tia would stare at the screen, listening to herself, to her day, to all her movements from the moment she left the loft and maybe it would take her a moment longer to realise what it was all about, but then she'd know – as all her colleagues would know – and then they'd all realise just why my voice had suddenly shifted an octave higher and I was staring at her with those fixed eyes.

'Nothing important.'

Tia clicked off the computer, closed the lid, smiled at me.

'Let's party.'

As Tia did. For the next two hours. Non-stop. She drank, she did a couple of lines of something very tasty that one of the guys from the office had brought back from Lebanon, she danced, she shimmied, she glowed and she did all that inside the loft and out on the balcony where she waved to a passing pleasure clipper and danced in time to the music pounding from the top deck.

My friend from the bad English magician conversation rejoined me and we discovered a lifelong common devotion to all matters Zappa. He was more into the later stuff – *Apostrophe* and the like – while I was still hooked on the early incarnation of the great Mr Z when he was still with the Mothers. We discussed the relative merits of *Absolutely Free*, *Freak Out!*, the sublime *Uncle Meat*, the flawed experiment that was *Cruising with Ruben & the Jets*. We both agreed that *Fillmore East – June 1971* was fun but swore undying love to each other as we agreed that *Hot Rats* was just the most perfect album that had ever been released although we did clash, ever so slightly, on the relative merits of 'Peaches en Regalia' – his favourite – against mine, 'Willie the Pimp'.

One thing led to another and I broke out a rare pressing of *Lumpy Gravy* I'd managed to source from some mail-order record geek. It wasn't a modern-day pressing but the original vinyl, always so much thicker than their latter-day counterparts. I played it on high days and holidays and, today, on party days. Tia always said that she knew it was an original by all the hisses

137

and crackles and the way the stylus would jump every now and again. Myself and my new lifetime companion – for such we agreed we now were – solemnly agreed that some people simply have no soul.

Then I brought out the real prize, an *Old Masters Box One*, the first in a series. Originally five box sets were planned, but only three were issued. The first box set consisted of the first five albums and a bonus mystery disc consisting of previously unissued material that at the time was unavailable elsewhere.

The icing on this particular cake was the particular edition of *We're Only In It For The Money*. When FZ eventually won the legal battle to gain possession of his original masters they'd deteriorated so much that he chose to overdub the original rhythm tracks courtesy of bass player Arthur Barrow and drummer Chad Wackerman.

At one point we were joined by another colleague attracted by the wailing of Jim Black, Roy Estrada, Billy Mundi, Don Preston, Bunk Gardner and Jim Sherwood and – the prune – Ray Collins. He told us he was scheduled to see Zappa and the Mothers at the Free Trade Hall in Manchester, 1971. He was in an agony of excitement for weeks beforehand. Then some lunatic pushed him – Zappa that is, not the office colleague – off the stage at one of his London gigs and Zappa had broken his leg, cancelled the Free Trade Hall gig and broke the heart of at least one adoring fan in the process. It wasn't all doom and gloom though. He was sure, somewhere back home, he still had a vinyl of one of FZ's more esoteric signings, Wild Man Fischer. He just about resisted my attempts to get him into a taxi and to go home there and then to find it but it was a close-run thing.

In between I'd catch sight of Tia, moving from guest to guest, filling a drink here, breaking open another bottle of Barolo there. Occasionally she'd smile across at me, a shared complicit moment, then she'd be gone. Around midnight the doorbell rang and more reinforcements arrived in the shape of a launch party down the road that had broken up early and had been summoned by Tia to carry on at our place. They melded into the existing group as if they'd been there from the start. I didn't find any new Zappa fans in among the new arrivals but it was a small blot on what was otherwise a pretty special sort of landscape.

I went to fetch another case of wine, walked back into the loft to see Tia heading out onto the balcony. Joseph was standing by the doorway talking to one of the new arrivals. As Tia passed, Joseph held out his hand to open the door for her. For a moment as she moved on, his hand was hidden from view from everyone in that room and everyone out on that balcony aside from me.

Only I saw the tiny, almost instinctive, gesture as he brushed his fingers, light as gossamer, across the top of her hand as she passed by.

Only I saw Tia momentarily pause. Only I saw the fleeting half-blush that stole across her face.

Only I saw the quick but dreamy smile that illuminated, just for a millisecond, her lips.

17.

F OR A FEW days after the party I prowled the loft. Time and again I replayed the moment two paths had crossed, wishing now I'd used all those toys in that shop to record the moment from every angle so I could assess it the more effectively, examine it all the more clinically. All I had to rely on was memory and the moment that picture washed again before my eyes – and as in the airport – the doubts started.

Did I really see what I thought I'd seen? Could I absolutely trust that momentary image? Moonlight was rolling in from outside at the time, shadows were being cast all over the loft, so could I really be one hundred per cent certain that what I'd seen was a hand touching another hand? Was it possible it was some trick of the light, an apparent caress where in reality all I'd seen was simply shadow with no substance?

After the third evening of standing in that same doorway, at that same time, assessing angles, even recording images of the moonlight outside as it fell into the room, I decided I had to take action. One way or another I had to know, not just about that moment, imagined or otherwise, but every other moment, imagined or otherwise, too.

I still had the tracking device installed on the mobile. I'd activated the software on my laptop a few times in the days since the impromptu party but it made for largely frustrating listening. Tia would be where she said she was going to be, she would meet the people she told me she would be meeting and they were the same conversations she reported with those self-same people when she returned to the loft at night.

Occasionally I thought I'd caught her out. Now and again there'd be a slip, the odd encounter not reported, the occasional conversation not referred to in her trawl through the events of her day. I'd press her, as casually as I could, on some detail or other immediately before or after the missing moment, watching her as closely as I dared, waiting for the moment I could see deliberate evasion in her eyes.

Tia passed every test. It might have taken a few moments, but she'd then talk, easily, naturally about that hitherto-missing encounter, that person she saw out of the blue, that unexpected acquaintance she'd bumped into on the street.

And as the days passed, as each encounter turned out to be even more innocent than the last, the frustration deepened and I began to work out why. The problem was that all these incidents and events took place in public where Tia could be seen, where she was aware of people watching her, although she couldn't know who was also watching back in the loft. So she was on her guard, not wary exactly, but poised, controlled, always maintaining a public face as opposed to the more private one I craved to study when she believed no-one was around.

And so the solution was obvious. I had to watch Tia and record her movements, not when she was out in the wider world but when she was home, by herself, when I might catch the moments that could betray her, the private conversations she might conduct when she truly believed that no-one could see or hear her, the times she might let her expression lapse into something that might provide some sort of window onto... what?

Frustration?

Despair?

Some evidence of general unhappiness that might lead, via

some careful detective work on my part, to a specific cause or reason? I didn't know.

But I had to find out.

I'd already run across the rather obvious problem with the tracking device in the mobile phone. Mobiles could be switched off. In fact mobiles usually were switched off when the owner didn't want to be disturbed and as that was exactly the moment I wanted to study the movements of my partner all the more minutely that was more than a little frustrating.

So I retraced my steps to Covent Garden – again – hesitated for a moment outside the Surveillance Store, checking – once more and via my reflection in adjoining shop windows – that I wasn't being observed by anyone I knew. For not the first time I felt like a suburban visitor to a Soho sex shop. Then I took a quick, deep, breath and headed inside.

Dom was at his usual place by the till, talking to a man who could have been a suburban visitor but who, I discovered later, was a sales rep for one of the larger electronics company that had recently moved out of cut-price computers and into the surveillance field instead.

Dom hardly glanced at me as I walked past and didn't seem to recognise me from my previous visits. I moved to the first of the shelves I'd studied before, cast a – now rather more practised – eye over the enticements on offer and then picked up once again a mobile tracker, little more than the length of a small finger, designed to be attached to a vehicle.

I paused, box in hand. In truth, it wouldn't advance my cause that much to find out where Tia might be at any point in time on the rare occasions she took out the Duke – or to work out her fastest speed on any given journey – or where she might have stopped and for how long. But it would provide some sort of corroborative evidence – or otherwise – for her own later résumé of her day, for the times her mobile might for one reason or another fail to record her activities. The tracker was taken down from the shelf, was added to a small basket I'd picked up by the door and this time it was going to be checked out, not abandoned out of some last-minute attack of conscience or nerves or doubt.

Next I moved on to another item I'd studied before, the picture frame, the type of frame we had all over the loft.

'You can hang it on a wall, stand it on a unit, a shelf, anywhere.'

Again, I almost physically jumped. Dom was at my shoulder once more, the sales rep now exiting out through the door, Dom rehearsing what I was coming to realise was a well-oiled sales spiel of his own.

Then Dom paused, some dim recollection apparently stirring.

'Have I seen you before?'

I hesitated. Something told me the question was rather more rhetorical than Dom was letting on.

'I was in last week.'

'And you probably heard all my jokes then, right?'

'Probably.'

Dom smiled an easy smile.

'Give me a shout if you want to hear any new ones.'

Dom melted back again to the counter. He was one of the few people I'd ever met who seemed to dissolve across a floor space. He didn't seem to move, he seemed to become invisible and then somehow materialise again a few feet away. Maybe it was a trick of the light. Or maybe it was one of the conditions of employment in his line of work.

I checked the box again. Dial the bug and it was programmed to answer after two rings – only of course, as Dom had previously pointed out, those rings were silent. Once the connection to the bug had been made I'd be able to hear everything that was happening in our open-plan sitting room and out on the balcony. Walls weren't an issue, they might as well not exist. The battery life, on standby at least, was about two weeks but that would shorten depending on how long and how often the device was activated but the downtime – when Tia was away from the loft – would provide ample opportunity to recharge. The frame would also take any A4-sized picture. I added it to the basket.

I moved on to the next section already knowing once again exactly what I was looking for and there it was, the simple USB stick. But once plugged in it would record any and every online conversation conducted in any and every chat room, all emails, any instant messages etc., etc. Somewhat worryingly, I was becoming almost word for word in my recollection of text I'd read only the once before.

The USB tracker went into the basket too which just left the last main section to plunder and already I felt my breath quickening as I approached.

Spy cameras.

First there was the Tissue Box Camera & DVR, the actual, real-life tissue box with everything you'd need for covert recording.

Next up was the radio alarm clock, the ultimate covert camera system with its 480TVL high resolution camera and good quality mic for recording audio too.

I added the tissue box and the radio to the basket as well.

I'd now covered all her movements when Tia was out of the loft and I'd covered her movements inside with both audio and video trackers and I'd now also be able to monitor her laptop activity courtesy of the USB stick which I could easily switch for the one she was currently using. It'd be the work of moments to transfer all the data from the old stick to the new and I knew Tia rarely removed the device from the onboard port. Tia had once lost an entire account by not backing up her work and was almost pathological when it came to that sort of thing.

I took the basket to the till and Dom smiled that easy smile of his again.

'Find everything you were looking for?'

I nodded, tempted – briefly – to offer some sort of explanation for my purchases, just about biting it back at the last moment. How many similar explanations had he heard as he stood at that till? How many customers had stood before him giving in to the apparently all-conquering urge to confess before they'd even committed the sins they were contemplating?

And if they gave in to that impulse standing before a total stranger, how would they cope with the larger subterfuge to come?

'Everything.'

Dom nodded.

'There's help lines for each of the devices, details inside the boxes. And I'm here most days if they're unavailable. Some of these guys have their own staff on call twenty-four-seven, but a few outsource to call centres and quality can be a bit variable.'

'Thanks.'

I paid for the items in cash. It seemed to be the normal way of conducting business. There was an electronic reader for credit cards but something told me it didn't see much use. The entries on the credit card statement would be suitably anonymous but there was little point in taking unnecessary chances. Dom asked if I wanted to take the items with me or would prefer them to be delivered but I think he knew the answer to that question as well. He packed them in an anonymous carrier bag. No store details on the side for equally obvious reasons.

I headed for the door, bag in hand, then stopped as I saw a camera incline slightly in my direction. It was the type of security camera you'd see at the exit to any shop up and down any High Street. I'd no idea why it suddenly looked sinister but it did.

From the till, Dom – who seemed to be wired in somehow to just about every thought process of everyone who walked into the shop – called over.

'It's a dummy.'

I looked back at him.

'You're not serious?'

'One hundred per cent.'

Dom shook his head, more in amusement than anything else.

'We stock the latest gizmos on the market, we could keep track on almost everyone on the planet with just half the toys we've got in here and all we've got to cover it is a camera that doesn't work.'

Dom nodded in my direction again.

'Or maybe that's just what I was told. Maybe they just said that to lull me into a false sense of security or something.'

Dom smiled again.

'That's the trouble with working in this kind of place. Who are you ever going to trust?'

His tone was as light as ever. So why didn't it sound all that light to me?

I walked out of the shop, turned onto the piazza, stopping dead as I came face to face – for the second time in as many weeks – with Natsuo.

18

'YOU EXPLAINED IT all once.'
  I frowned, trying to remember. Which particular technique was she talking about? What specific trick of the trade?

'The long shutter release stuff?'

Natsuo shook her head.

'Something to do with the right way of taking shots of two or more people, of getting depth into the shot.'

I was sitting opposite Natsuo in the same pavement café that had played host, some days before, to Tia and Joseph. I could still see them, heads bent close together, fingers cupped around their latte and macchiato.

I looked back at Natsuo keeping their former table in my eye line, almost expecting its previous occupants to suddenly reappear and reanimate that same space once again.

'Using what camera?'

'The fish-eye.'

I nodded.

'That's perfect for getting a wide expanse of view.'

I hunched closer to Natsuo warming, as ever, to anything with a photographic theme.

'But the problem with the fish-eye is if you stand two people side by side – the classic pose shot – the type of shot you see all the time in family portraits or weddings – it's going to look flat. So get them to stand one behind the other, not too far away, just enough to mix up the angles. It makes it look almost 3D and you still get all that width to either side.'

'And if I did that at the same time as that other trick you taught me?'

'What other trick?'

'All that double exposure stuff.'

I could see instantly what she was getting at. Now we really were getting into seriously freaky territory. Correction, seriously Natsuo territory, although maybe that was the same thing.

To get a double exposure on a fish-eye you had to almost trick yourself into it, which you did by deliberately forgetting to wind the film. It's a contradiction in terms of course. How can you deliberately forget as Natsuo had pointed out, calm and logical as ever when I first attempted to explain the technique. It didn't make sense. To forget is an aberration, a lapse of concentration or memory, to deliberately do so is the opposite. It's just such a habit, winding on film, almost second nature, it requires a very specific act of will just to use the MX button – multi-exposure for those still to be inculcated into all matters fish-eye – and then put it back in your bag and – try – to forget about it.

I could still remember, from years before, the excited child taking over from the adult as I explained it all to Natsuo. She was expecting plain old fish-eye pics although she knew from my own excited manner – her anticipatory enthusiasm was infectious – that she was in for something really special.

I'd taken a typical fish-eye landscape shot from the roof of a nearby building, currently under renovation as most of south Mayfair seemed to be back then. The builders hadn't batted an eyelid as a camera geek and a Japanese girl with blue hair had sashayed past them on the stairs and made for the roof. It was that type of area back then too. Or maybe they just couldn't give a shit. Whatever, we were up on that roof and I had my shot and a moment later – one deliberate act of memory loss completed – I had the shots of Natsuo I wanted as well.

A short time later we were back in a small café on Shepherd Street. It was a favoured haunt of all the local taxi drivers – always a good sign – and the police manning the local beats – even better. Taken together they composed the toughest imaginable audience and if they returned time and again the place really must have something. There was a steep stairway that led to a basement where the air was thick with the smell of all-day breakfasts and coffee so strong it caught at the back of your throat. But there was another small seating area too at the very top of those stairs, just a couple of high chairs and a tall table from where you could watch the world walk in and walk by and it was where we usually encamped ourselves.

But today, for once, Natsuo wasn't watching the human floor show that flowed before us. Today, all she wanted to see was the double sneak exposure I'd tricked the fish-eye into creating and I knew, after all the build-up, that it had better be good.

Behind the counter a blonde female exile from somewhere in Eastern Europe surfed effortlessly amongst the punters standing, sometimes three or four deep in the small space between the counter and the always-open door, juggling at least three or four orders at a time – a bacon ciabatta here, a few slices of toast there, a serving of lasagne heating in a microwave as another serving of meatballs folded into huge strips of fettuccine was pushed across the open counter.

By the coffee machine a younger version of the blonde exile stared at the torrent of orders that were piling up before her disbelieving eyes, knowing she could never in a million years cope with anything like it, glancing – in the few seconds' grace she could steal between knocking out coffee and tea – at the thin women in skin-tight clothes moving past the window, heading for appointments in hotels along Park Lane, wondering – she had been briefly tempted on her arrival – whether she should have opted for that way of earning her daily crust instead, knowing she never would, knowing too that in a year or so she'd also be surfing effortlessly amongst those orders, her life measured out by endless portions of spaghetti.

At the high table on her high chair Natsuo stared at the picture I'd taken out of my slim bag.

For a long moment Natsuo just stared at the image, didn't move her head, didn't blink or in any way betray herself with any sort of reaction, instinctive, unconscious or otherwise. For that moment she resembled some sort of statue as the steam from the coffee machine, the yells and exhortations from either side of the counter washed over her. For that moment she was caught up, totally, in the image she herself had created without ever intending to do so.

Natsuo was floating, disembodied, in a sky that seemed caught between night and day. The edges of the frame were ink-black but a semi-circle of light, just off-centre, held out at least the promise of the sun. At the point the semi-circle levelled into the landscape you could see houses and office blocks. But then, to the left of the frame, again off-centre, was Natsuo, not the whole of her body, just her face, part of her neck, the blue of her hair, the white of her face, bleeding into the buildings below, before darkness at the far right of the frame descended once more.

It was almost Gulliver-like. As if Natsuo had suddenly acquired superhero status, reigning over a world that seemed unaware of her hovering presence. As if someone had suddenly parted the clouds and for a second you could see what lay behind, a figure that had always been there; an almost divine presence that had suddenly assumed human shape.

Natsuo still didn't speak as she picked up the printed image and walked out of the café. I stared after her for a moment as she negotiated the crush at the door which seemed to part, instinctively, as she approached. There was something about her that always made others give way. Outside the café she turned left, passing a small shop selling milk and produce and which also, improbably, housed a basement stuffed floor to ceiling with a collection of household implements and tools. By the time she was crossing the road past the final outlet on that short street, an upmarket hair salon, I was behind her and could see where she was going.

Shepherd Street continued on into a small mews terrace lined mostly with short-let houses and apartment-style hotels. The large tower blocks of Park Lane looked down on it in the near-distance. On the corner of the small street was a photo-shop and by the time I'd followed her inside Natsuo was already at the counter, print in hand, explaining that she wanted this blown up, as large as could feasibly be done and then backed onto stiff board and framed and Natsuo wasn't talking A4 here, she was talking movie poster dimensions.

Natsuo hardly seemed to see me. And she never directly referred to the sneak double exposure I'd suckered the fish-eye into taking. She just paid for the blow-up and then Natsuo went off with the fish-eye. I didn't see her for two whole days. She must have shot a small mountain of similar prints in that time, prints I never saw although I saw the original once it had been blown up into the outsize image and backed and framed. It occupied almost one whole wall of her small flat and was grotesquely out of proportion with everything around it. Which suited the image perfectly of course.

Natsuo hadn't talked about that image for the remainder of our time together – or indeed any of the remaining images she shot from then to our break-up, which was why it was something of a surprise that she should be doing so now. It was also something of a surprise that she should be seeking any sort of technical advice given the length of time she'd spent manipulating similar images in the days and weeks following that first experiment on the Shepherd Market roof. By the time we'd finally gone our separate ways she could have given a masterclass.

'It wasn't an accident.'

I looked at her.

'The other day. In that shop.'

Natsuo paused.

'I was sort of seeking you out.'

I stared at her, still didn't respond. She'd made that enigmatic reference of regret the last time we'd met. Was this more of the same? Natsuo had always been a character who, once she'd moved on, simply kept moving. If all this was about rekindling an old flame she'd changed a lot.

'I wanted to see you. Only I couldn't tell you why. It seemed stupid.'

Natsuo smiled, wry.

'So I started talking all that shit about me and you.'

I leant forward, wary. Natsuo had always been the original manipulator. Nothing was ever as it seemed. What seemed evident on the surface was rarely the same underneath. So it was perfectly possible that all this was part of some new game.

And yet those clear, ice-grey, eyes seemed troubled. There was a frown creasing her forehead that hinted at genuine turmoil inside. Either the ultimate game player had found a new and even more convincing way of executing a habitual charade, or Natsuo was finally falling prey to all-too-human emotions she'd previously refused to even acknowledge – doubt, confusion, fear.

'I started seeing someone. A few months ago. Still am seeing him. It's odd. For the first time, I can't see an end to it. I always could, I could always see a time we'd have moved on. But this time – .'

Natsuo paused, didn't finish the sentence, didn't need to. Now she really did seem to be stepping into uncharted territory.

Natsuo looked back at me.

'You know him.'

I kept staring at her, my mind now racing through possibilities, each more ludicrous than the last. I even briefly contemplated the possibility of some new union between my old lover and my current nemesis. Natsuo and Toby. That really would have been a liaison forged in some mismatched hell. I dismissed the thought as quickly as it popped inside my head, but who else could it be? I'd lived such a hermit-like existence these last couple of years, had cut ties with so many former friends and acquaintances, who was she talking about?

'But Tia knows him better.'

Slowly, the mists began to clear and in more ways than Natsuo could possibly have imagined.

'He works with her. Well, technically I suppose she works for him.'

'Joseph?'

Natsuo nodded.

'I didn't realise the connection. Not at first. Then I saw you dropping Tia off one day at work. That's how I found out what had been happening with you.'

Natsuo smiled, apologetic.

'I don't really keep up with the papers.'

I nodded back, cautious.

'Tia never said.'

'I don't think she knows. We decided to keep it quiet, we didn't intend to hide away or anything, but it just seemed less complicated, I suppose. Your ex-girlfriend hooked up with the boss of your new partner. And anyway – .'

I finished it for her.

'It wasn't any of our business.'

Natsuo looked back at me.

'I didn't think it would last. Joseph's not really my type. Anyway it's not exclusive, he sees other people, so do I.'

One phrase stood out for me in all that. Something I never thought I'd hear her say. Something that made her sound almost ordinary. Like everyone else somehow.

'Your type being?'

Natsuo inclined her head, accepted the point. She'd always previously denied the existence of types.

'And that's why you came to see me? You wanted some sort of advice?'

I stared at her again, floundering once more, a familiar sensation when it came to all-matters-Natsuo, but she shook her head.

'I told him about the fish-eye. The double exposure. Showed him some of the shots I'd taken, he was impressed. He thought they might have commercial possibilities. He even asked me to talk to a couple of the creative guys in the agency, see if they could use them in any of the campaigns. He started experimenting with it all himself, taking the camera out onto the streets, mixing up all sorts of images, he's got quite an eye for it.'

Natsuo hunched forward. I still had no idea where all this was going.

'A couple of months ago I was in his house. He had to go and fetch something from the office, some artwork that had been delivered for some pitch or other. I started looking round, I don't know why, I wasn't exactly snooping, I was just curious I suppose. I'd never been alone in his space before.'

'And?'

'I found these.'

Natsuo pushed a couple of prints across the table, images from – I'd later discover – a copied download. There were two images on each print, although neither image would have occupied the same space in reality. These were classic double exposure shots, pictures yoked together from at least two clearly distinct settings. As a piece of art – or craft – they were impressive. The colours from one bled into the other neatly. The dispassionate observer would have found much to admire in their composition but I wasn't a dispassionate observer and neither was Natsuo and for the first time since we'd seated ourselves in that small pavement café I began to understand what this was all about.

The images were of Joseph and Tia. And there wasn't just the one image, there were dozens of them, Tia in different poses and settings, Joseph in different poses and settings again, but the two of them yoked together through the trickery of the fish-eye, sometimes Joseph hovering over Tia, almost predatory, sometimes Tia behind Joseph, as if she was following him, stalking him, sometimes their faces blurred into the other.

I stared at the images for another long moment, then looked up at the watching Natsuo.

'That's why I wanted to see you.'

Natsuo nodded back at the pictures.

'I want to know if that's just a simple experiment. Or if something else is going on.'

19.

E XACTLY ONE YEAR earlier, I'd been standing in a plain room with blue curtains in an anonymous office block in Paris having an out-of-body experience.

In the space of just a few moments I was, firstly, a retired heavyweight boxer and then a shop mannequin called Claude. Life, fairly freaky anyway in the last few months, had just become even more so. Normally I'd need to have invested a substantial sum of money in some mind-altering substance to even begin to approximate an experience like this. But this was an experiment and it wasn't costing me a penny. And I was loving every single, unsettling, moment of it.

We were in a research clinic headed by one of Tia's old flatmates. He'd trained as a behavioural psychologist in which role he'd frequently press-ganged friends, family, flatmates and sundry acquaintances into all sorts of curious experiments back in England. Now he'd moved to France but nothing much seemed to have changed. Within moments I was the guinea pig in an experiment designed, so far as I could understand, to convince people they inhabited a body other than their own.

The clinic had funded the research in the belief that it might improve the general field of robotics as well as assist in refining the design of prosthetic limbs. It could even help psychiatric patients with a disturbed sense of self – those with anorexia or bulimia nervosa for example. There were even suggestions it could be used for confronting racial or sexual prejudice. I didn't quite understand that last claim and didn't really care. Because this was quite simply a blast.

The clinic specialised in experiments with naïve subjects,

defined as people who didn't know what to expect. I knew a little but I was about to learn a lot more.

First, special goggles were attached to my head with small screens inside the eyepiece. Then, Alix, the head of the facility, stood in front of me wearing a headpiece with a pair of cameras on top. The pictures from the cameras were relayed wirelessly to my goggles meaning I could see a stereoscopic image of myself from the point of view of someone standing in front of me. The image looked just like the person I'd seen in the bathroom mirror that morning. But he was in fact nothing to do with me.

My brain was telling me it was my hand squeezing the hand of the man standing opposite me, that these were my fingers tensing but it wasn't my hand and these weren't my fingers, it was the hand of the retired heavyweight boxer and they were his fingers too. Before I could even begin to get used to my new identity – if such a thing were possible – everything changed again.

Now I'm the mannequin. Now I'm inanimate, now I have no fingers, no hands but looking down I'd still swap his well-honed torso and six pack for mine. Alix takes out a pen from his pocket and strokes that well-honed torso. My brain tells me he's stroking me and I tense slightly but that's nothing compared to what's about to happen next.

Suddenly, from nowhere, Alix has a knife in his hand and he slashes it across what I still believe to be my stomach. My gasp of shock, of terror indeed, fills the room, reverberates off the walls and I look towards the curtains expecting them to be sprayed red, geyser-style, by my blood, but how can there be blood? I already know I'm a mannequin and that knife was nowhere near my stomach, it just looked as if it was and my brain did the rest, reacting instinctively as if it were under attack.

The experiment concluded, I was returned to the body I'd never actually left. I bid goodbye to the boxer and the mannequin as well as to Alix and his goggles and cameras and his out-of-body box of tricks.

But for those few moments I was the boxer and the mannequin. I was both of them. For those few moments I felt what it was truly like to inhabit another skin, feel their emotions, monitor their responses, taste their sensations.

Alix said the overpowering look on his subjects' faces when they were similarly returned was one of relief. Now they could slip back into a skin in which they were comfortable rather than continue to inhabit another alien identity.

I nodded and smiled in all the right places and didn't contradict him. But I felt the opposite. All I wanted to do was stand opposite Alix again – and again – assuming different personalities, experiencing over and over just how it felt to be another human being.

20.

B Y THE NEXT morning all the security devices acquired via the strictly cash transaction in Covent Garden were being installed around the loft.

The computer was the first port of call. Tia had never got to grips with laptops although she used one at work. But she still preferred to transfer everything over each evening to an ancient but trusty desktop. Laptops might be mobile but that meant they could be dropped, crushed in a rush-hour scramble on the Tube, have coffee spilt on them during some overexcited sales pitch.

Tia had once invested in an electronic address tablet and had spent a whole day inputting names and numbers from a dog-eared old address book scarred and scored with different names and addresses entered over the last five years via a whole kaleidoscope of different coloured pens. At the end of the day she'd treated herself to a massive vodka and Ribena – Tia always did have curious taste – one sip of which she managed before spilling the rest all over it. For a moment nothing happened but then the screen started to splinter. Tia frantically dabbed at it with a cloth but nothing was going to stop the slow process of disintegration now playing out before her. Within thirty seconds the screen was a maze of cracks and all the names and addresses so carefully inputted over hours had turned into the equivalent of computer mush.

I removed the USB stick that was permanently resident in one of the ports, copied all the information onto the stick supplied by Dom. Then I inserted the new stick which was virtually unrecognisable from the old – they came in a variety of shapes and sizes for just such an eventuality. From that moment on every keystroke made on that computer would automatically be recorded on mine.

Phase One complete.

The next phases were completed just as easily. The picture frame complete with bug was substituted for an existing frame that was hanging in our open-plan sitting room. It wasn't an exact match but the chances of Tia noticing the switch were virtually non-existent. The border was a slightly flatter shade of white but the frame was in direct sunlight for a good few hours of the day. Even if she did notice the slight colour change it could easily be put down to global warming.

Next came the tissue box which again presented few problems. Tia had several dotted all over the loft. The bathroom was the obvious location but something inside me baulked at that. It may seem strange to confess to scruples at a stage as late as this, but something just didn't seem right about spying on her somewhere as private as that. Besides, what could she possibly get up to in a bathroom – surveillance-wise anyway? On the grounds of taste and practicality I placed the new tissue box in the bedroom instead. It could be moved of course but I still had another piece of kit to take care of the pictures.

This was the trickiest of all. The USB stick, the picture frame and the tissue box replaced existing items inside the loft. Tia had walked past such items every day for a few years so any chance of their inviting comment or – worse – inspection were slight. The radio alarm clock was different. This was new. Up to that point, Tia had always relied on the alarm on her mobile for wake-up calls. And in my case job offers hadn't exactly been flooding in for more time than I'd now care to remember so I hadn't had too much need of early morning alerts.

So how to explain the sudden appearance of a state of the art radio/alarm system on the small inbuilt table on my side of the bed? After struggling with various possible explanations for a few hours – and having got precisely nowhere – there was a buzz on the intercom from a delivery driver outside the gate and all of a sudden the gods of contrivance had delivered my explanation too.

The clock, I would claim, was a freebie present that had arrived with a latest consignment of wine hauled up the stairs by the – now sweating – delivery driver. I'd unpacked it, plugged it in and listened to the cricket as I sampled a rather nice Pinot Grigio from, of all places, Romania.

Two hours later, the returning Tia wasn't in the slightest bit interested in the new adornment to our bedroom, being much more interested in that Pinot Grigio from, of all places, Romania. She took a large glass with her into the bathroom having taken a tissue from the rogue box to wipe away some make-up just moments before. On the way she passed the substituted picture frame without even giving it a second glance.

I waited till the shower was running before slipping down to the underground garage and fixing the mobile tracker to the Duke. That was the safest task of all. The bike had all sorts of strange devices attached to all parts of its lightweight frame and Tia had never shown the slightest interest in any of them. When it came to propulsion, she was interested in motion, not investigation. While she didn't take the Duke out often, when she did feel the need for a solo trip on some open highway, I'd now know exactly how long she'd been travelling, how long she'd taken to get to her destination, how fast she'd travelled and how often she'd stopped. It wouldn't tell me exactly where she'd been but, together with the tracker on her mobile, it would still be a pretty effective means of keeping tabs on her.

I moved away from the Duke, then paused. On an impulse I returned, opened the pannier. But this time there was nothing inside. No keys, no accompanying code. I still had no idea what either of those two keys were for or what that four-digit code was all about; but at least perhaps I'd now taken the first step along the road to finding out. I closed the pannier, retraced my steps back up to the loft and let myself in just as Tia was emerging from the shower.

Tia nodded at a small gym bag I'd propped by the door.

'Going out?'

'Working out.'

'You mean, just as I was thinking about grossing in front of the TV you're heading to the health club?'

I smiled, trying to keep my voice as casual as I could manage.

'Coming?'

Tia pretended to consider the question seriously for a moment.

'No.'

I grinned, lifted the gym bag which contained a pair of swimming trunks, some body soap and my laptop.

'But if you're going back to the early morning stints I might join you.'

I looked back at her. Years ago I used to head into the gym when it opened – around 6 a.m. – for a work-out, keeping company with the City boys.

'That's what it's about, right?'

'What?'

'That new alarm clock? You're getting back on a keep fit kick?'

I paused, then nodded.

'Right.'

I let myself out of the loft, turned right, passed a pub that – according to local legend – used to be a haunt of the youthful Charles Dickens. The story was he'd be taken in by some adult relation or other, made to stand on a table or stool and sing, literally, for his supper. The pub looked out onto the street on one side and the river on the other. During the summer I could look down from the loft balcony onto the decking and check out the daily specials on the blackboard. In the years we'd lived there they'd never tempted us once but maybe now I was on the brink of a whole raft of new experiences to rank alongside bugging my home and spying on my partner.

I took a cut through an alley onto the river walk, passing the Thames on one side and an inlet flanked by converted warehouses on the other. When the tide was in, the inlet was a place of some considerable beauty, water lapping against the lower levels, wildlife swimming up to the windows. When the tide was out it was an evil-smelling mudflat, the receding water revealing a whole repository of abandoned detritus from shopping trolleys to cans, bottles and wastepaper washed up by one tide, about to be washed out again by the next. The tide was out and I held my breath as I passed.

Out on the river a clipper tooted as it approached its next stop and I stepped around a small army of approaching cyclists, cut across a small park-like area fringing the walk and headed past a tiny beach revealed by the low water at the foot of a steep bank of steps.

A few metres further along, past a range of fast-food outlets, I cut up some more steep steps into the health club. Signing in, I glanced sideways at a whole bank of computers. A seat I'd allocated myself in my mind in a far corner, its back against the wall, overlooked by no window, was occupied. I decided to have a quick dip in the pool while I waited for the occupant to vacate it and head away for a trawl of the daily papers kindly provided by the management in exchange for the current monthly fee that would dwarf a sizeable mortgage for most. I cut down some more stairs – the journey to the changing rooms was enough exercise in itself – changed and headed for a spa area beneath the actual pool, entered a warm water area pummelled along the whole of one side by power showers, squatted underneath and let the water cannon down onto the back of my neck.

If truth be told, I was glad of the delay. Now it had come to it – and despite my early experiment with her phone – I was nervous. Tia was home, alone or so she thought. Her every movement was – or should have been – totally private. She was unobserved. She could do whatever she wanted, secure in the knowledge it would remain her business and hers alone. Now, finally, I was about to find out what my partner was like when, apparently, I wasn't watching.

Half an hour later and I was back in the small café area of the health club, by a window looking out onto the walkway next to the Thames. On reflection I'd decided not to use one of the in-house computers from the bank that lined the walls. It would have been more anonymous than using my own admittedly, but there was always the risk of some acquaintance or other coming up on me as I maintained my surveillance and not being able to close down an unfamiliar monitor as quickly as I could my own. There was also the danger of some future nerd taking up residence at my computer of choice and accessing a previous program despite my best efforts to conceal my tracks.

Freshly showered, I put a large mocha on the low table in front of me. From my position in the café I was facing the stairs and the small counter from where drinks and snacks were dispensed. No-one could come up to me without my seeing them first. I hesitated one last moment, powered up the laptop, then accessed the software that would enable me to monitor the sitting room loft via the bug in the picture frame. For some reason I wanted to work up to the radio alarm clock and the video as well as audio option.

The moment I logged on I almost physically winced. A sudden wall of sound assaulted my eardrums, so loud I glanced sharply around the small café fearful someone might hear it too even through the close-fitting Sennheisers I was using. But no-one looked over. I adjusted the volume to a more manageable level and felt a smile stealing across my face.

Tia was playing Zappa. At full volume by the sound of it. She'd always derided my interest in the Mothers yet here she was, taking advantage of my absence to load *Absolutely Free* onto the turntable. Tia was singing along to some of the wackier lyrics and was word perfect too, meaning this obviously wasn't the first time she'd indulged this guilty pleasure. For a moment I forgot all about the task in hand and marvelled again at the collective talents of Ray Collins, Jim Black, Roy Estrada et al.

Then, as 'Call Any Vegetable' gave way to 'Invocation & Ritual Dance of the Young Pumpkin', I started to refocus.

Tia had stopped singing now, all I could hear was the music starting up although there was something else – a click, perhaps of a kettle knocking off – a door opening, perhaps from the sitting room to the bathroom, but then I heard the sound of another door being pulled back on a runner meaning Tia was either going out to or coming in from the balcony.

Then the music suddenly stopped and I leant forward. Now I couldn't hear a thing. No clicks, no doors opening or being pulled back, suddenly there was total silence and it was deafening.

I switched software, activated the audio bug in the tissue box and some strange rustling noise confirmed that Tia was indeed now in the bedroom. What she was doing was more difficult to work out from sound alone so I switched software again, activated the camera inbuilt into the radio alarm clock, praying – despite all assurances to the contrary – that some light somewhere in the device wouldn't suddenly activate and I wouldn't find myself staring at a startled Tia staring back at me.

The picture took a second or two to assemble. But when it did it was pin-sharp. It took in most of the room meaning the device was fitted with a fairly decent lens. From the vantage point of the bedside table I'd have seen any activity on or in the bed in pretty vivid close-up but there wasn't any activity on or in the bed. Tia was sitting before a mirror at the far end of the room and the rustling sounds I'd previously heard were being made by the tissues she was carefully wiping across her face, removing all final traces of her make-up.

Had I been so minded I might have reflected on the unconscious irony. Tia was removing all trace of artifice, of innocent subterfuge in a sense, just as I was perpetrating one of the most extreme instances imaginable of the opposite. But I didn't. I just sat there, a short distance from the home we'd set up together and watched her.

'Hey.'

The voice cut across my reverie and I took a second to snap back to reality. I tore my eyes, reluctant to the last, from the screen towards the figure that had suddenly appeared before me.

Trudie Rosa smiled, easy, casual, back.

'What are you doing, don't you live something like six metres away?'

I nodded.

'Five at the most.'

'But you're working on your laptop in here rather than in your million-pound luxury apartment?'

'Tia's thrown me out. Just had time to grab this.'

I indicated the laptop.

'Left her throwing the rest of my possessions into the river.'

Trudie grinned wider as I closed down the laptop as casually as I could, nodding at one of the nearby local papers at the same time.

'Just been scanning the local accommodation listings.'

We shot the breeze for a few moments longer. Trudie offered me her floor and I told her I was grateful. All the time I was computing rather more sensible explanations for the moment Trudie would inevitably tire of the verbal fencing, but luck was obviously on my side that day as we were interrupted by a small, slight figure sporting a cowboy hat and a pony tail. I'd no idea which latest screen sensation had suddenly appeared in front of us – or even which side of the camera he habitually inhabited – but Trudie immediately lost interest in matters domestic so far as I was concerned and took her new companion across to the counter.

As she did so I expelled a breath, unaware I'd actually been holding it virtually all the way through that exchange. A moment later I stood – and with Trudie exchanging evermore extravagant air-kissed greetings with the now shyly-smiling owner of the cowboy hat – picked up my laptop and headed up the stairs, went back out onto the walkway and headed home.

On the way I passed a man blessing the river. He had his arms stretched out as if in supplication and his eyes tightly closed as he muttered imprecations. Most people were hurrying by but I paused for a moment, looked out over the same stretch of river which at that moment seemed angry somehow, vengeful even. Water coursed from one bank to the other, smashing against the bulwarks and wharves before cannoning back again.

The Thames, of course, always moved in that way, never in anything like a straight line. I once read somewhere that at least ninety-five per cent of its energy was lost in turbulence, the majority of that in the extended section I was looking out on at that moment along with my new companion, his arms still outstretched, eyes still closed, mouth still muttering his strange entreaty to a God to whom only he seemed to have access.

In its infancy, at its source, the river was undefiled, innocent somehow, clear in its composition and flow. Some miles down its course, by the time it had become contained by the city, it had assumed this totally different character, something darker, if not dank. I'd always thought that the story of the river in that sense mirrored the more general story of human history, but the river moved on, regressed, returning finally to its source, back to purity and clarity once more; the reason why baptisms had always been instinctively associated with water perhaps.

The pilgrim – for such I'd now decreed he must be – stepped forward, took some bread out of his pocket and moved to the edge of the bank. For a moment he looked as if he was getting ready to feed the birds but he wasn't. Even my desultory trawl through local history was enough to enlighten me as to his true mission. Bread cast upon the Thames had always been a tribute to the water goddesses and a test. If the bread sank she'd accepted the offering and would renew her blessing on the supplicant. If the bread continued to float the offering had been rejected. The pilgrim watched the bread intently for a few moments, tensing as it continued to be tossed along at the mercy of the current. Then, slowly, the bread began to sink beneath the water and the pilgrim closed his eyes again, began muttering once more his incoherent, mumbled, imprecations.

I let myself back into the loft a short time later. A film crew was setting up outside the pub where the youthful Charles Dickens used to sing for his supper. From the size of the crew and the elaborate preparations that were being taken to light the upcoming scene it looked like a Hollywood blockbuster had just rolled into town. I was later to discover the production in question involved a celebrity chef on a walkabout.

As I walked in I glanced instinctively across at my stack of vinyl records on the floor by the retro turntable I'd found in a junk store in Camden. Tia was out on the balcony and I checked, quickly, that they were back in the right order.

I'd always liked to stack the LPs in their order of release – so *Freak Out,* released May 26, 1966 would be followed by *Absolutely Free*, released June 27, 1967; which would be followed by *We're Only In It For The Money*, released March 1968; followed by *Lumpy Gravy*, released May 1968; followed by *Cruising with Ruben and the Jets*, released (and what a prolific year this was for FZ) on December 2, 1968; followed by *Uncle Meat*, released April 1969; followed by *Hot Rats*, released October 1969.

One by one the records presented themselves as I flicked through them, falling like counters exactly in the order in which I'd originally stacked them. Then the balcony door opened behind me and I turned to see Tia coming back into the loft.

'Just seen Trudie.'

'In the health club?'

Tia couldn't help the note of amusement now creeping into her voice. Trudie was razor-sharp in her professional persona. She was less than honed in matters of personal fitness.

'Working. Networking. Whatever. She was hooking up with some twelve-year-old. Buying him a milkshake.'

Tia giggled and fixed us both an espresso, two extra shots. We ordered a take-out from a new Italian deli/café that had just opened up along the Wapping Wall. Then we watched a movie and went to bed.

For the next day it was the same pattern, the same the day after that, a pattern repeated over and again in fact. Of course there were variations. Left alone, Tia would select different music to listen to, occasionally singing along and, even more occasionally, dancing along as well. Zappa, I discovered, was something of an aberration, there really were only a couple of tracks she seemed to like, the rest were simply ignored.

I didn't realise before just how much she seemed to need background noise when she was alone. Left to my own devices I tended to prefer the sound of silence but I did have other diversions in the form of river clipper timetables and arranging a vinyl collection. The moment I left the loft something would be turned on, a TV, a radio, a CD player, it didn't seem to matter.

There was little discernment in the choices made. Everything seemed to serve the same function. It was background – wallpaper – while Tia got on with whatever she was doing which was pretty much all she'd do when I was there save for the acoustic pounding out in the loft behind her. She'd check emails and compose replies. I traced them all courtesy of the rogue USB stick and, while bright and chatty and animated, none could be construed as overly affectionate or even remotely intimate. She responded to instant messages all of which I studied on my screen as she read them on hers but none were from people I didn't recognise and none of her replies were anything other than straightforward responses to questions or comments.

There were no emails or instant messages addressed directly to Joseph and none that seemed to come directly from him and there were no phone calls to him made in my absence either. If the concerns Natsuo expressed about Joseph had any foundation in reality, if his new experiments in photography betrayed any secret relationship then it wasn't revealed through the actions of my partner when she was alone.

The various bugs dotted throughout the loft unearthed no other furtive callers either. I left Tia alone for a day and a night during this time, travelling across to the West Country to visit some old friend. I asked the friend if I could call Tia from his landline on the evening of my arrival, feigning a dead battery and a poor mobile signal. The loft phone boasted caller display so she'd have seen the number before she answered, would have known that I was most definitely a hundred or so miles away, that there was absolutely no danger of being disturbed if she'd decided to entertain anyone. But there was nothing revealed by the bugs and no-one revealed on the camera that recorded our bedroom, all night, from the radio alarm clock on our bedside table. Just Tia – perhaps more restless than usual – perhaps less quick to drop off to sleep – but very definitely alone.

With the bug on the Duke it was a similar story. She took it out once – early the very next morning – which did briefly quicken my pulse, a sudden animation that faded just as quickly when I remembered a long-standing arrangement, to which I'd agreed more than readily, that the bike would be used as a prop for an album cover for a new indie Brit band. Visions of the iconic VW Beetle used in the Abbey Road shoot had swum before my eyes, potentially boosting its second-hand value into the stratosphere. The shoot lasted less than ten minutes as an email from Tia to her office later confirmed. Two key members of the band didn't show and all in all it looked like another dream had turned to dust as Tia kick-started the Duke into life and headed home.

The problem, as I soon realised, was akin to that of an unstressed building. Tia was being placed under absolutely no pressure. There was nothing happening that might expose any sort of fault line, that might widen any hidden cracks so they suddenly became visible. It was still perfectly possible that Tia inhabited some other life but while she was in the loft, while she was engaged in the ordinary and the everyday I was never going to bear any sort of witness to that.

I needed something else, I needed to introduce some new element into the mix. I needed to see her raw and naked, in some extremity of emotion somehow, to see the façade cracked. I was seeing nothing that I wouldn't have seen watching from just a few metres away. We might as well have been in the same room.

Of course, it was perfectly possible there was an eminently

good reason for that. As the old saying goes, if it walks like a duck, talks like a duck and looks like a duck then the strong probability is it ain't no penguin. If Tia betrayed no hint of an alternative existence, no suggestion of another life hidden from general view, then perhaps she really did have no alternative existence and maybe there was no other life hidden or otherwise. Maybe all this, in other words, had been a total and complete waste of time and effort, not to mention cash which wasn't going to be as easily replaced these days. Maybe I'd simply suckered myself into something that existed only within the confines of my own imagination and maybe the reason I could discover no treachery or mendacity was simple; there was none.

Then something happened.

21.

EARLY THE FOLLOWING afternoon, I'd called Dom from the loft. He spent some time telling me about a couple of new toys they'd just taken in which he thought might be of interest given my recent purchases. Finally managing to cut through the sales spiel I told him the situation had changed, that I was no longer interested in this kind of surveillance but before I could make any arrangements for the return of the items I'd bought – they all came complete with a thirty-day returns policy – Dom launched into yet another well-rehearsed pitch.

Dom obviously thought my phone call was Phase Two of the journey into paranoia amongst the clientele he habitually encountered; that far from wanting to eavesdrop on others I was now concerned a similar exercise was being mounted with regards to myself. Which was why the new Multifunctional Bug and Camera Detector might apparently be just up my street.

This detector, so I was assured, utilised the latest technology in tracking down wired and wireless spy cameras and – clearly the main selling point – any concealed wireless bugs that might be hiding in your bedroom, meeting room or office.

It worked in three different modes: IR laser, Vibration alert, and Audible alert. The IR Laser option was used to detect the spy cameras themselves. Detection was based upon the principle of optical augmentation, meaning that if a hidden camera was illuminated and viewed with the IR Laser LEDs a strong reflection from the hidden camera would immediately reveal its position to the user up to a range of some five metres. It was also surprisingly small and could fit easily in any pocket.

After a few more moments of the same I managed to cut across and tell him exactly why I'd phoned.

Dom paused.

'You want to return them all?'

'Yes.'

'Are they not satisfactory in some way, we've plenty of alternatives if any don't suit for some reason?'

'The devices are fine.'

'They're still fit for purpose?'

'They're fit for purpose.'

'In the interests of market research – and please understand this doesn't affect our returns policy in any way – could you tell me why you're bringing back the items in question?'

I hesitated. Strictly speaking I didn't have to answer but it was a reasonable enough request in the circumstances. But what could I say? I'd suspected my partner of what, exactly? Even now I wasn't quite sure. Leading a life she hadn't told me about? Keeping from me a secret of some kind? Conducting a relationship of which I was unaware? Or did I say that I'd simply wanted to get to know her better? Listening to it all playing out inside my head was difficult enough, I really didn't want to compound all that by confiding the same to a relative stranger.

Dom must have sensed my dilemma because all of a sudden his voice lowered, becoming almost conspiratorial.

'I really don't want to press you, it's just I've got this form to fill in.'

Dom paused.

'I could just put something like, object accomplished?'

Now it was my turn to hesitate. It didn't matter – why should it, this was just simple office procedure, the sort of corporate feedback you'd expect from any organisation, large or small. But something inside me still grated at the obvious falsehood. Strictly speaking, nothing had really been accomplished.

'Or, abandoned.'

I didn't respond, my silence speaking volumes.

That was more like it.

I turned back to the picture frame, the rogue USB stick and the tissue box. From the half-open door to the bedroom I could see the radio alarm clock, red counters ticking down the seconds.

Dom spoke again.

'Hello?'

But I wasn't listening. I was staring at the TV screen. It had been left on by Tia that morning as she left for the agency. And as I kept watching I slowly replaced the phone, cutting Dom off, ending the call.

It had happened about half an hour previously, a few miles south of Waterloo. It was the nightmare scenario, two high speed trains, one accelerating away from the station, the other just starting to decelerate as it made its approach. The closing speed taking both into account was in excess of two hundred miles per hour. To make matters worse the collision happened on a stretch of track frequented by smaller commuter services mainly from the dormitory towns of Surrey and Kent. As the carriages were flung across the tracks they collided in turn with at least six smaller trains slicing through some carriages, crushing others.

Early pictures from the scene showed a cat's cradle of twisted metal, flames and smoke although, at this stage, few people aside from the first of the emergency services who'd just arrived. No-one knew yet what had caused such a catastrophic accident and no-one was particularly interested either. That was all very much for later. The only priority was helping as many of the crash victims as possible. Early estimates put the number of passengers across all the carriages involved in the multiple pile-up at somewhere in the region of five or six hundred, possibly more. It was impossible to assess as no-one knew exactly how many were on board each train. All that was known at this stage was that there were expected to be many fatalities.

As I stared at the pictures I suddenly realised I'd actually been holding my breath again for at least the last minute or so. Clearly it was becoming some sort of default reflex in times of stress.

Then everything kicked in.

For the next few moments I was back in war zone mode again. Then, all it took was a sudden burst of sniper fire and suddenly I was running. Everyone else would be running away from the action, I'd be running towards it. Now I was running again.

Like then, I knew I couldn't think. I just had to do. No hesitation, no second thoughts.

First; the note, composed in less than a minute.

One minute later, I was out of the loft carrying a small holdall.

Another minute on again and I was wheeling the Duke away from the underground garage.

A moment before I'd sprayed over the rear number plate – typical boy-racer trick. Every wannabe Rossi would do it before taking their bike out for a burn. The paint was reflective and all a speed camera would see was a blur as the bike flashed past.

I didn't fire the bike up until I'd got at least a hundred or so metres away. Past conversations flashed through my mind like tracer fire, one exchange in particular with a neighbour who told me his young son would always wake in an instant whenever he heard the bike rumble into war mode in the garage beneath.

Next, a blip of the starter, not even a hint of the customary twist of the throttle before I hopped on and headed for the Limehouse Link.

In the darkness I could hear distant sirens up on the surrounding streets. Coming up into the daylight, a small army of ambulances sped past in all directions. Ten minutes later

I pulled into a small car park just round the corner from the station concourse.

A bored operative manning a small booth at the exit took no notice as I rode in. Another problem out of the way. The last thing I wanted was a bike freak who wanted to talk about all-matters-Duke.

Then the next problem, the ticket. The charging system in the car park was simple. You punched a button on a machine as you entered, the entry time on the ticket determining the charge. My ticket was clearly useless, the time was stamped on a central strip, a good hour or so after the time of the crash. But there were a couple of other bikes at the far end.

I stood by one of them, one motorcycle freak admiring the prized possession of another. Tucked just behind the left hand grip was its ticket. I smoothed my hand over the grip, retrieved it, the entry time again stamped clear, a couple of hours before. I switched that ticket for mine and headed back to the Duke.

As I stowed my helmet in the pannier, a woman passed. She'd just come out of the station with a small child in tow and was cursing the station staff having just been told some blockage on the tracks had temporarily suspended all services. All eyes swivelled her way as she ranted and raved. Her daughter had a dance lesson on the other side of Croydon, her exam was only a few weeks away, now what was she going to do?

She was what I always used to look for the minute I arrived at the scene of any conflict, a distraction, something to divert potentially hostile eyes. I took my small bag out of the side pannier of the Duke, headed away, making sure I wasn't in sight of any of the nearby CCTV cameras, making for my next stop, a small café a street or so away.

And then, as I seated myself at a quiet table away from the counter, I slowly felt myself start to relax. Up to that point I'd been on automatic pilot. I was in control of the decisions I was making, but it still felt like some force apart from myself was guiding my actions. Or maybe that was some sort of defence mechanism already kicking in. Perhaps I was already constructing ways of attempting to evade responsibility for all I was doing.

But with the Duke abandoned in that station car park I could no longer avoid it. Now it was time to take stock, to go over what I'd done so far and what I would have to do from this point on in order to fully realise my intentions.

2 2 .

I STAYED IN the café watching travellers heading towards and then back from the station, some looking shocked, some simply irritated. There were, it seems, quite a few parents that day keen to take daughters to dance classes. All the time my mind computed future strategies, reviewed those already taken.

All the time too I had my laptop open in front of me, the software tracking the bugs in the loft. I didn't expect Tia to return for at least a couple of hours but I couldn't know that for sure.

Again and again I went over the note I'd composed before I'd exited the loft, left on the small table by the door where Tia always dropped her keys. She'd once read a thriller about a gang of thieves who'd target suburban houses by feeding makeshift hooks through the letterbox to retrieve carelessly-discarded key fobs, but that didn't stop her tossing her own down on that table in exactly the same way. So she'd see the note as soon as she walked back in.

Did I strike the right note? Did it give just the right sort of information? I'd acted in such a rush that now a cold feeling began to sweep over me as doubts crept in. I knew that note would be pored over in the hours to come, every syllable studied and not just by Tia but by some of her friends and colleagues, even by strangers, officers from the emergency services perhaps. There couldn't be anything in there that would make anyone pause, take stock, begin to wonder. I'd taken all possible precautions – had only snatched up clothes I was fairly certain wouldn't be missed – had covered my tracks with the Duke – had only taken a relatively nondescript amount of cash although I had taken the contents of a strictly secret slush fund I kept in case of emergencies. Up to that moment emergencies had been defined as purchases – usually for Tia – that I wanted kept secret from her. Now, and as with everything else, previous definitions didn't seem to count for much.

I could see the note as if it was still before me. I'd printed it out from the laptop as I didn't want any strange shake of my pen to betray any hidden agitation.

Heading down to Brighton for the afternoon.

Casual, almost chatty in style.

Taking the train, should be back around midnight.

I didn't say from which station I was catching the train or what service I was using. I'd kept it all suitably vague. Why shouldn't it be?

Catching the Kean exhibition.

Kean – just the one name, no-one seemed to know if he had any other or whether that was a Christian or a surname – was something of a legend among war photographers. He'd covered most of the major conflicts although always on a strictly freelance basis. He was tied to no publication. No magazine paid his expenses either, meaning he was beholden to no-one in his choice of shots or indeed conflicts and was free to offer the results to anyone he chose. And that was always his choice too. Many an editor had begged for his favours to no avail.

In typical Kean fashion he'd sanctioned a retrospective exhibition of his work, not in some upmarket gallery in the capital, but in a small outlet just down from the pier. A couple of college kids who ran the gallery had written asking permission and out of the blue he'd agreed, surprising them as much as the critics who now had to decamp to the seaside if they wanted to be in on the latest photographic happening. The first night had come and gone with the usual fanfare – minus Kean himself – and Tia would have been surprised if I'd decided to attend that feeding frenzy. But a short hop on an idle afternoon to catch his show wouldn't strike her as being in any way curious or strange.

See you later. x.

Another nice, casual touch and the kiss at the end could become, as I'd intended, unbearably poignant. Even now I could see a tearful Tia tracing the outline of that last kiss with her finger.

I checked the images on the laptop which revealed no-one in the loft and I checked my phone which showed no calls. Tia was still in work, still in blissful ignorance of the calamity in which I'd apparently become enmeshed meaning, with the review of the past hour out of the way, I still had some time to decide what to do next.

I looked round the café which was filling up now with frustrated travellers, most using the place to make mobile calls. I had a table to myself at the moment but that wasn't going to last too long given the press of people being turned away from the station. I didn't have any philosophical objection to close proximity to my fellow citizens, but I did have a couple of practical problems right now. My open laptop for one. The last thing I wanted were strangers sitting next to me ogling the images I was observing on my screen. I needed somewhere more private and I needed it quickly. In fact I needed a proper base for the next few hours at least, probably overnight and that meant a hotel.

One decision made, the next was the location. There was plenty of choice on offer locally but that was the problem. They were all local and already I was preparing the cover story I'd have to tell on my return.

I'd remembered that in the wake of a recent terror bombing centred on the Paris Métro, the driver of the only bus to be attacked had simply walked away. And he'd kept on walking too. Later, he couldn't tell anyone exactly where he'd gone or the route he'd taken. All he – and his massively panicked friends and family – knew was that at a certain point, much later that day, he'd been found wandering some strange streets about five or six miles away from the scene of the bombing, having finally come to some sort of realisation as to what he was doing.

The driver had been in shock of course. His mind had first of all entered survival mode – get away and as far away as possible – and he'd then deliberately avoided all rational exploration of what he was doing as that would have been to admit the facts of an event he couldn't as yet even begin to assimilate.

I planned on doing much the same. Later I'd tell Tia that I'd walked out of one of the smashed carriages, that I couldn't deal with the sights I was witnessing and had walked away just as the emergency services were arriving. With wounded and dying people lying all around they weren't interested in a man who might be one of the walking wounded, but who was at least walking. After that everything became a blur. I'd tell Tia that I remembered sirens and emergency vehicles rushing past me but that was all. The next thing I knew I was in a taxi. The next thing I knew I was in a hotel and all I wanted to do was sleep which I did.

All of which left the choice of hotel. Something in me kept baulking at a local choice. How could I maintain the fiction that I'd blotted everything out when all night I must have been hearing sirens outside the bedroom window?

Besides, study the template. What had the Parisian bus driver done? He'd walked miles, had put as much distance between himself and the scene of the trauma as he possibly could before fatigue presumably overtook him.

I couldn't, of course, walk. This wasn't my home patch, but the chances of stumbling across someone I knew, while not high, were still distinct. It was pretty obvious from the mayhem developing out on the street that the local transport network was fast descending into chaos. Tube lines were going to down along with the mainline links, disgorging more and more commuters out onto the streets.

The cabs were still operating though and as luck would have it one was dropping off a fare just a short distance down the street. Within moments I'd packed the laptop, was out of the door and in the back of the cab almost before the departing punter could collect his change. Which just left one further decision as the cabbie turned and looked at me.

'Where to?'

I'd expected all sorts by way of an arrival committee. I'd half-expected something official, as if in the midst of all the turmoil going on, the powers-that-be had actually devoted time and energy to investigating and decoding my unfolding deception and decided to nip it in the bud. I knew, even then, that was self-absorption of a level to glaze over the eyes of even the most effete of dilettantes; but I was in a strange and dislocated place right now. I even half-expected Tia to be standing outside the hotel entrance, a pitying look in her eye, telling me I really needed help. My clearly-fevered mind expected all sorts. What I didn't expect, were peacocks.

The driver dropped me off around an hour or so later. I'd remembered passing the entrance to the country hotel some months before. I'd taken the Duke and had come across one of the straightest lanes I'd ever seen. The Duke hit 140 mph before I braked for a sharpish corner and as I did so I saw the sign. Why I remembered that sign, why I could still recall the name I had no idea, but for some reason, looking for some sort of current sanctuary, it was the first place that popped into my mind. Unsurprisingly, the cabbie had never heard of it but, courtesy of Sat Nav, he soon located the place and he managed the task with some considerable enthusiasm too. A run out into the country was clearly an attractive proposition for him right now with the streets of the capital rapidly turning into gridlock. None of which stopped him securing the agreed fare upfront and I didn't blame him. The events of that day were proving, all the way round, that there were some strange people about.

I stepped out of the cab, picked up my laptop and small bag, then stopped dead as I felt at least five pairs of eyes boring into me. Cold eyes. Unblinking eyes. Eyes that seemed to stare right inside me and out the other side.

'They shoot them, don't they?'

That was the driver nodding across at our silently watching audience.

'Who do?'

'Toffs.'

I hadn't heard the word for years.

'That's pheasants.'

'What do they do with them, then?'

One of the peacocks – one of the males I'd later discover – suddenly spread his wings, revealing a riot of blue and orange feathers underneath and emitted a noise that could have been a greeting or a warning. By his side an albino example – the female I'd also later discover – simply watched. The males were all pomp and show, the females didn't bother. Yet another example of a world that seemed to be standing on its head right now. I cut short the conversation, the last thing I wanted to do was give the driver even more reason to remember this fare. Then I walked past the still-watching peacocks, past a stack of logs that I'd later discover were simply decorative – the hotel did boast a rather more modern form of heating – and headed on into a small lobby just behind the front door.

A practised smile greeted me although its owner was clearly more than a little distracted. Behind her a twenty-four news channel was playing on the hotel TV feed. Most of the regular shows had been cleared for the evening for the different channels to provide their own updates on the same developing story. The broadcasters clearly knew a ratings winner when they saw it unfolding before their eyes. I asked for a room for a night or so and was offered a fairly bewildering array of options ranging from a suite at the top of the old hotel – I'd been previously unaware there was a new one – to a room in the more modern complex that had been added onto the original building and ran all the way down to a small leisure complex, also newly built.

I opted for the new-build. Had it been left to Tia and myself we'd have chosen the old suite every time. Yet more evidence, if any were later needed, that my actions were demonstrably uncharacteristic, my mind clearly not my own.

I was led by a member of the staff along a bewildering succession of corridors, over-decorated and stuffed with display cabinets featuring the most esoteric of objects – one devoted entirely to thimbles – another to memorabilia associated in one shape or form with Winston Churchill – and past signs indicating meeting rooms named after, so I assumed, local personalities and figures of note. Then we stopped outside a door on a long corridor that resembled in its every detail every other door along that same corridor; at which point my companion handed me my key, didn't show me inside, just wished me a pleasant stay.

I unlocked the door, went into the room, barely taking any notice of my surroundings and immediately unpacked my laptop, fired up the software and logged onto the complimentary wi-fi after inputting a code provided by the receptionist. Then I scanned the loft.

Still nothing. It had taken me just over an hour to get from central London to the hotel but I hadn't missed a thing. Tia was either working late or more likely had fallen foul of the transport meltdown that had by now, according to the brief report I caught on the TV in the reception lobby, engulfed the capital.

I looked up, became aware of a small balcony at the far end of the room. Unlocking the doors I stepped out and looked down onto what would once have been a lawn, but was now a car park. And as I did so I allowed a strange feeling to wash over me, a reassuring feeling of certainty, of knowing that I'd done exactly the right thing.

It was always the flaw in the original story. All Wakefield had done if he'd really thought about it, and at the start of the exercise at least, was occasion his wife unease. It was an unease that grew as the days and weeks ticked by, but by then she was already adjusting to her new situation. There was no one moment when all of a sudden her world seemed to cave in on her. There was no single instance when he could look into the eyes of the partner he'd abandoned and see, with one hundred per cent certainty, the effect of that abandonment, the anguish or otherwise his actions had occasioned. His test was more of the slow-drip variety than the hammer blow I'd put in place, meaning there were actually two flaws in his original plan. He wasn't able to properly assess the effect of his behaviour as the time in which he lived could never provide him with the opportunity to do so. And the timescale he'd initiated was too slow, the process too drawn out which was why, presumably, he'd waited twenty years before returning to the fold.

On both counts I was well ahead of that game. And, if things worked out as I hoped, I'd have my answer in well under twenty hours, not years.

Tia was due home any moment. To while away the time I researched train crashes.

The first one the search engine threw up was the Ladbroke Grove train crash, also known as the Paddington crash, which took place on 5 October 1999 in west London, just a few miles from Southall, itself the scene of a fatal train crash some two years previously.

The link to the Southall crash told me that seven people had been killed and one hundred and thirty injured after the Swansea to London Paddington high speed train, operating with a defective automatic warning system, went through a red signal and collided with a freight train. The driver didn't observe the preceding signals visually, but the automatic train protection equipment – or ATP which overrides the driver to automatically stop the train before passing a red signal – should have prevented the accident. However, while the train was fitted with the warning device it was switched off because the previous driver hadn't been trained how to set up the system. But in any event, and at the time of the accident, automatic train protection was not actually required to be switched on in service as it had proved troublesome.

In the Ladbroke Grove train crash two years later, thirty-one people were killed and more than five hundred and twenty injured when a three-car regional passenger train operated by Thames Trains collided head-on with an eight-coach First Great Western high speed train with a combined closing speed of approximately one hundred and thirty miles per hour.

The first car of the Thames train, the 08.06 from Paddington to Bedwyn, Wiltshire, driven by Michael Hodder, was totally destroyed on impact, and the fuel carried by the train at the start of its daily journey ignited, causing a series of separate fires in the wreckage. The fire was particularly fierce at the front of the high speed train which was completely burnt out.

The immediate cause of the disaster was identified as driver Hodder passing signal SN 109 showing a red aspect – technically known as a Signal Passed At Danger – five hundred and sixty three metres before the impact point. Later, the public inquiry would identify many contributory factors including the Thames Trains driver training procedures. Driver Hodder had only qualified two months previously.

There was also a question mark over the actions of Railtrack, Great Western Zone – the body responsible for the maintenance of the track and signalling – which hadn't taken appropriate action after eight similar SPADs at signal SN 109 in the preceding six years. Many drivers had complained about poor visibility at the scene.

Signal SN 109 had a particularly restricted view as there was a road bridge over the railway line one hundred metres before the gantry on which that signal, together with four others, were mounted. The design of signal SN 109 was also non-standard, in that it was shaped like a reversed L with the red lamp on the horizontal arm rather than below as was standard and it's thought that this, together with the bright sun rising in the east behind the train and shining directly into the signal lens itself, might have misled driver Hodder into thinking the signal was allowing him to proceed.

One year later on 17 October 2000 at Hatfield, north of London, a Great North Eastern Railway high speed train travelling at over one hundred and fifteen miles per hour derailed south of Hatfield station. Four people were killed and a further seventy injured. Although the accident resulted in a lower death toll than Ladbroke Grove or Southall, the historical significance was probably greater since it exposed the fundamental failures of the privatised national railway infrastructure company, Railtrack Plc; and ultimately triggered its partial renationalisation.

In the case of Hatfield, a rail had fragmented when the train passed over it, the likely cause of which was something called gauge corner cracking; microscopic cracks in the rails caused by metal fatigue. Repeated loading would cause those same cracks to grow. When they reached a critical size the rail would fail by separation. Over three hundred critical cracks were found in the rails at Hatfield. The problem was known before the accident and replacement rails were made available but never installed.

Some years later, at Potters Bar, a train derailed at high speed killing seven and seriously injuring another eleven. Another seventy were less seriously injured. A four-car regional West Anglia Great Northern train service from King's Cross to King's Lynn via Cambridge, crossed over a set of points just south of Potters Bar station. As the final coach travelled over the points they moved causing the rear wheels of the carriage to derail onto the adjacent line. The momentum carried the train into the station where one end of the final carriage struck a bridge parapet, sending debris onto the road below. It then mounted and slid along the platform before coming to rest under the platform canopy at an angle of roughly forty-five degrees. The front three coaches remained upright, and came to a stop just north of the station. Six of the fatalities were travelling on the train while a seventh was killed by masonry falling from the bridge.

In the aftermath of each of the tragedies, all interested parties swore they had to be one-offs, that such dreadful events should and could never be repeated, that lessons had to be learnt. I recalled the five-star General saying much the same in the wake of the Trooper Rohl incident.

I stood up and moved to the window. Across from the balcony was a large bank of trees. A relatively new addition to the property, they must already have been ten metres or more in height. They totally screened any view to the south, giving the hotel what the proprietors no doubt desired; an exclusive feel.

Or was there something else at work behind this particular grand plan? No-one could see in, but no-one could see out either. So was that why those trees had been planted? Maybe it wasn't to guarantee additional privacy, maybe it was to prevent anyone in that hotel seeing what lay beyond the man-made barrier. I scanned the foliage looking for any breaks in the branches.

Then a beep sounded on the laptop back in the room behind me. For a moment I kept staring out towards the trees, forgetting why I was there, what I was doing, not even absorbing the significance of the alert from the computer. Then I wheeled round as reality crashed back in.

The software on the computer had detected movement in the loft.

Meaning Tia had finally arrived home.

I knelt in front of the laptop, hitting the space bar, the screensaver having cut in. The screensaver cleared and I could see the bedroom of the loft, the door open to the sitting room – as I'd left it – giving an uninterrupted view all the way down to the front door which was where Tia was standing at present, taking off her shoes, putting down her keys on the hall table within easy reach of the letterbox – how many more times? – before picking up the note I'd left on that small table just a few hours and, perhaps, a whole lifetime before.

Tia moved, note in hand, on into the sitting room. For a moment – a single, intense, excruciating moment – she disappeared from view as she moved to put her bag down on a table – but then she came back in vision once again, note still in hand as she came into the bedroom.

I watched, intent, as she read the note once more, saw the first hint of unease creep over her face, then kept watching as she moved, more quickly now, more purposefully, out of the bedroom back into the sitting room, reappearing again a moment later with her mobile in hand.

My head jerked towards my own mobile which was still switched on! For a moment I couldn't believe my stupidity, I'd done everything else so efficiently, covered my tracks so effectively, yet I'd left my mobile turned on. We'd both talked about it, joked about it even, months before, how the location of a mobile can be pinpointed to within just a few hundred metres – something to do with the signal bouncing off different masts or something; so if Tia now made a connection, even though I was hardly likely to answer, then someone, somewhere, at some point in the future, could study the log of her calls, could work out that while I was supposedly enmeshed in the twisted wreckage of some train carriage my mobile was inexplicably an hour or so away in the vicinity of some country hotel.

My hand snaked out and I just managed to hit the off-button before Tia pressed a speed dial button. For a moment I couldn't catch my breath and so missed her initial reaction when a standard answerphone greeting cut in but I recovered sufficiently to hear the doubt – the fear even – in her voice as she left her message, asking me to call her the moment I received her message. Then I watched as she put down her mobile, looked at it for a moment, then looked at the note still in her hand. Then she crossed the room, opened the doors and went out onto the balcony.

For that time I lost her again and I cursed the fact that the bug in the radio alarm didn't have a swivel facility – although a wildly revolving clock might perhaps have given the game away. But I didn't have too long to wait. Within a few moments a ripple shimmered on the far wall as the balcony doors were opened once again and cooler air from the river buffeted in. Then Tia picked up her mobile, hit a speed dial button again. I listened, as intently as she did, heard once again the standard answerphone greeting from my answer service, then watched as Tia emitted a loud, single-syllable curse before throwing her mobile down on the bed without, this time, leaving a message.

Then she crossed quickly to her large desktop computer and powered it up. At the same time she retrieved my note, read it again as if she might have missed something. Then, with her computer up and running she began to hit the keyboard.

I'd never have seen her screen from the camera inside the radio alarm clock but with the USB stick it was easy. A quick couple of hits on my laptop and I was following every move she made.

Tia had typed in the website address for the national train service. She accessed it pretty quickly, we both used it fairly regularly to check times and book tickets. There was a new notice on the front page about disruption caused by the incident – neat word – in south London but Tia ignored that. She typed in a hypothetical journey from London – all stations – to Brighton. She let the computer work out the terminus then – once the itinerary was loaded – stared at the screen.

So far as the entry point was concerned – the commencement of the journey – she had a choice of two stations, London Bridge or Victoria. Tia put her mouse over each of the destinations in turn and I read them on my screen as she accessed them on her computer. Both journeys would have taken an hour or so, slightly more in the case of London Bridge where the service called at East Croydon, Gatwick, Three Bridges, Haywards Heath, Wivelsfield, Burgess Hill, Hassocks and Preston Park before finally rolling into Brighton one hour and five minutes later so the website claimed, subject to the usual riders and qualifications about driver shortages, snow, leaves on the line or, as in the case of the service that day, bodies and train wreckage.

London Victoria would have taken ten minutes longer with the service calling first at Balcombe before then calling at Haywards Heath and all the other stations called at by the London Bridge service en route down to Brighton. Momentarily, it struck me as odd that a service that called at two fewer stations should have taken longer to reach its destination but it was still a pretty marginal call as to which one I might have chosen. I was on a jaunt, a day out. Ten minutes here and there would have made no difference.

But it made, of course, all the difference in the world to Tia right now. If I'd taken the Victoria service then I'd have missed the crash that had closed the mainline from the capital down to Gatwick. If I'd taken that service I'd still have been caught up in the travel disruption. If I'd managed to get through before the crash then – perhaps around now – I'd be returning to the station in Brighton to be told that there was no service currently running into London and would probably – along with a few hundred others – be attempting to negotiate a fare home with a succession of taxi-drivers who, without wishing such a catastrophe on anyone, would nevertheless be thanking their lucky stars that their services were in such suddenly-expensive demand.

If I'd not made it out of the capital before the crash happened I'd either still be halted in my train – all services south, irrespective of the line they were using, had now been cancelled due to the signalling chaos following the crash – or I was being led from my stranded train onto a succession of coaches that had been hired by the hard-pressed train operators to take similarly stranded passengers on their journey down to Brighton and all points visited en route or – if the individual passenger preferred – back to London.

In both instances Tia could expel the deep sigh of relief I could almost see she was bottling up. In both cases and as with so many that day, I'd been caught on the fringes of a nightmare. I'd have endured some hours of frustration, of delay, of half-heard and often-conflicting stories before being told the truth and returning home.

Then her head jerked up as she heard something outside. I flicked to the bug in the picture frame which was nearer the door and silenced all the others. What had Tia just heard? Was someone approaching up the stairs, had some other friend or acquaintance – or someone else entirely – already been alerted to the potential tragedy somehow and had come to offer comfort, information or – once again – something else?

Then I heard it. Distant, the sound of a powerful engine out on the street, a rasping note to the exhaust, similar to the Duke, but not the Duke, very definitely not my Duke which was, as I knew only too well, neatly parked in that car park adjoining the station. The exhaust note grew louder but then faded as the bike sped past the loft, heading down to the Island by the sound of it.

Tia didn't move for a moment. Then she turned back to the screen.

If I'd taken the London Bridge service then I'd have passed directly over the stretch of track that had witnessed the horrific smash. If I'd approached afterwards I'd have been delayed as in the Victoria scenario. If I'd passed over before I'd be in Brighton, again as in the Victoria scenario. If I'd taken the train that was involved in that head-on crash – the most badly mangled of all the different trains involved in the smash that day – then I'd either be horribly injured or dead. Early reports coming out from the crash scene delivered by whey-faced representatives of the emergency services weren't holding out much hope of there being too many survivors.

So now Tia had two questions. Which service did I take? And what time did I take it? Her hands scrabbled for the note I'd left, stared at it almost as if she was hoping I'd left some clue that she'd missed on her previous readings, something that might tell her the time I'd left the loft, the station I might have picked to begin my journey, the time I might have done so; anything to give her some sort of hint that I might have cheated all that had quite clearly been visited on so many others that day.

Any initial stab of sympathy I felt for Tia's now-clear agitation was short-lived. It was already being overtaken by something else and that was a sudden rush of feeling I could only describe, somewhat inadequately, as rapture.

Already in her eyes I was beginning to see exactly what I wanted to see – panic – fear – a sickening, desperate denial – all the emotions traditionally associated with the potential loss of a loved one. All the emotions heightened when that loss is tragic.

For the third time Tia tried my mobile only to get the same standard answerphone message. By now she was walking round the loft, taking refuge in motion, no pattern or purpose to the way she was currently moving from room to room, simply unable to stay still. Then she paused, smack bang in front of the camera in the clock, staring at the far wall, her mind finally attempting to impose order on what, for the last few moments, had been chaos.

Tia crossed to and flicked on the TV. Her fingers hovered over the remote, ready to access one of the twenty-four-hour news channels, but there was no need. All the major terrestrial channels had now replaced their normal services with live reports from the crash scene.

On the bottom of the screen a number was displayed continuously, the number to be called if anyone had concerns about relatives or friends who might have been caught up in it all. Tia reached for her mobile and – eyes fixed on the screen – began pressing buttons. A few moments later – they clearly had a fair number of volunteers manning the lines – her call was answered.

In truth there was little they could do to help at this stage. They could and did take my name. They could and did take down the little Tia knew of my journey details. They made the reassuring point that many hundreds of people were currently caught up in the travel chaos that had engulfed the capital in the aftermath of the train crash, that roads as well as rail lines were blocked, that the mobile phone companies were struggling to cope with the surge in demand for capacity and that some operators had already restricted callers to emergency usage only which could explain her difficulty in getting through to me by phone.

At the same time as her respondent was explaining all this, he was clearly checking on the names he already had on a list in front of him, the names of those already confirmed dead, because he was able – within just a few more moments – to confirm that my name hadn't yet appeared on any report from the emergency services and suggest Tia call back in an hour or so for a fresh update if she'd heard no news on my present whereabouts in the meantime. He took her numbers – landline and mobile – in case they heard anything before then. He also gave Tia the name of a support group that was taking calls from relatives or friends whose loved ones were confirmed as being caught up in the incident, and also for those who feared they might be, in case Tia wanted to talk to someone.

Tia ended the call. I'd have laid odds that she wouldn't have called the support line – Tia was always more interested in action than reflection – and so it proved. After a couple more minutes pacing the loft, after a minute or two more of staring at the TV screen, the pictures from the crash scene now seemingly on some sort of loop with the same images playing over and over, Tia picked up her bag, collected her mobile and made for the door.

This time it was easy. There was no way Tia was going to switch off her mobile right now so all I had to do was sit back and watch her progress outside the loft as simply and easily as I'd watched her activity inside it. Out on the street, Tia hailed a cab. I heard her hesitate as the cabbie asked where she wanted to go and warned her not to say south London, he just wasn't in the mood.

Tia – who hardly seemed to hear him – continued to hesitate. I could almost see her thoughts oscillating between the two choices currently on offer. Did she choose London Bridge or Victoria? Did she confront her fears full-on by checking out the station that could spell disaster or did she first check out the one that offered deliverance? If she found the Duke at or near Victoria then there was no need to go near London Bridge, she could simply return to the loft and wait.

The cabbie repeated his question, growing impatient. I held my breath as I waited, then released it slowly as Tia finally spoke.

'Victoria.'

She'd hadn't gone for broke. I really thought she might. Which was the first surprise of the evening. Perhaps it was to be the first of many.

As Tia rode along the Highway she used the search facility on her phone to access the internet. Through the minor miracle of the bug supplied by Dom I could follow on my laptop every site she visited.

She first checked the car parks around the coach and train stations at Victoria. There wasn't a massive choice. The first and most popular on offer was an NCP car park on Semley Place next to the coach station itself. It was around a tenth of a kilometre from the train station too making it the choice for most commuters. It also offered twenty-four-hour access.

Tia next hit the second most popular result on the search engine, discovering that there was also a facility on Belgravia Road. This was uncovered and constituted some one hundred and twenty-two spaces. It also offered twenty-four-hour access and had a special rate for motorbikes. Tia highlighted the postcode, typed it into Streetmap and made a note of the exact location.

Then Tia scrolled down to the third choice on offer, this one in Pimlico, around seven minutes' walk from the station itself, further away but potentially a better bet as this particular example was larger, offering some two hundred and seventy-four spaces. Then the phone went silent, no more activity recorded as the cab now approached, so the mobile coordinates were telling me, Victoria itself.

There were meters all around the station of course. I could have used one of those. But something was obviously telling Tia I'd have preferred the relative security of a car park and she was right. A Duke was a prized machine. It would have been the work of moments to wheel it away from a meter and even if a light-fingered biker failed to crack the security code on the anchoring chain there were all sorts of tempting-looking bits that could have gone missing once the careless owner returned to his pride and joy.

In the few moments before the cab pulled up, Tia did a similar search on car parks in and around London Bridge. Now she discovered that the closest would be a facility in Montague Close near to Tooley Street and therefore pretty well adjacent to the station. There was another car park in St Thomas Street in Bankside – another convenient location – one on Weston Street in Bermondsey – another called, elegiacally I'd always thought, London Snowfields, on Kipling Street; and the one I'd actually used, a short hop from the station but still close enough to be called convenient. There she'd find the Duke, anchored by its security chain and sporting the entry ticket showing quite clearly that I'd parked the bike a good hour or so before the fateful train crash a few miles down the line.

Just as the cab came to a halt, Tia fired her mobile into life again as she tried dialling my phone once more. I could almost feel the desperation wafting its way from that decelerating cab all the way across west London and into commuter country out in the hills. But of course all Tia heard once again was that standard answerphone greeting inviting the caller to leave a message, which she did not. Tia paid the driver, emerged from the cab and began her trawl of the car parks in the vicinity of the train and coach stations taking in – just in case – all the meters she could find along the way.

It didn't actually take that long. The car parks boasted around five hundred spaces between them but the sections reserved for bikes were relatively small. And the Duke was pretty distinctive. It took her roughly twenty minutes to eliminate first the Semley Place facility, then Belgravia Road and finally the car park in Pimlico.

Courtesy of the tracker on the phone I was able to monitor her movements via the street coordinates that had come as an optional extra with the software. During that time Tia might have been reduced to an indistinct blob moving along a succession of 3D streets but the software still monitored the way she completed the journey in fits and starts, the way she paused outside each of the three car parks in turn, perhaps summoning up some reserve of strength or courage before heading on into each car park willing the Duke somehow into existence, to be there before her eyes as she turned the corner.

Each time and after each viewing, each trawl, there was also a pause. Again, the software could record that, but it couldn't reveal the expression on her face. I couldn't see the emotion in her eyes which made this part of the observation as excruciating as it was enlightening. I could see what Tia was doing. But to get behind that, to see the effect of it all, would have to wait for later, when she was back in the loft.

After the third and final car park, Tia paused for longer than usual. Or perhaps she was simply having problems locating a cab. Normally a mainline station would be awash with them but these, fairly obviously, weren't normal times.

I stared at the now-stationary blob on the 3D mock-up in mounting frustration. What was she doing? She hadn't found the Duke in Victoria, there was only one thing she should now be doing, and that was diving into another cab and heading up to London Bridge. Then I relaxed again as Tia started to move.

Outside, one of the peacocks – male, female, I didn't know which – started to emit some sort of call, an invitation or a warning, maybe if I'd gone to the window and looked down from the small balcony I'd have found out. But the proverbial – possibly even the literal – wild horses couldn't have dragged me away from that laptop right now.

Tia kept moving up Vauxhall Bridge Road before she cut left onto Rochester Row. I stared at the screen growing puzzled again as the blob that was my partner continued on her way towards Westminster Cathedral. A few moments later she took another right turn this time towards Whitehall.

I stared at the screen some more, realisation dawning. She was walking. Tia was actually walking, perhaps all the way from Victoria to London Bridge. I computed distances in my mind's eye. This was a journey that was going to take her through Whitehall up to the Embankment, past the Hungerford, Waterloo, Blackfriars, Millennium and Southwark bridges before she even came within sight of London Bridge itself.

How long would it take her to complete a trek like that – half an hour – an hour perhaps? Why was she doing it? It wasn't in her make-up to put off something difficult, her initial choice of Victoria and her hesitations at the entrance to the various car parks aside. She was always the type to charge straight in rather than hold back or at least that's what I'd always previously imagined. I stared at the screen but Tia was still moving steadily through Whitehall. There were no pauses, no breaks in the journey when she might have stopped on the pavement, tried to signal a passing cab. Her progress was inexorable, almost metronome-like. And after a few moments I stood up, went back out to the balcony.

Now I could see the peacocks. They were clustered round the female in a group. One of them was displaying its brightly-coloured feathers but the female didn't seem too interested. Maybe it was the sudden light falling from the balcony as I pushed open the window, but she was staring up at me instead.

I looked beyond the peacocks to the trees. With darkness having fallen there were pricks of light visible beyond the trees, the lights of houses perhaps or possibly another hotel. Everything was quiet and still, something that was going to take some getting used to after the loft and the twenty-four-hour floorshow that was life on and by the river.

I stopped, suddenly chilled. Then I rolled round the last thought that had just flashed through my mind as if it was a particularly chewy piece of meat, gnawing away at it, impossible to digest.

Replay what I'd just said again.

It was going to take some getting used to?

How long was I contemplating keeping this going?

I moved back from the balcony and the watching albino peacock and returned to my laptop to try and find out.

The small indistinct blob that was Tia was still moving. She was now walking along the Embankment although it was difficult to tell from the 3D mock-up if she was moving along the north side of the road or the south, skirting the actual river. The software suggested she was walking in the middle of the road itself but that would have been somewhat unlikely. From the little I'd gleaned from the news report on the TV in reception, transport was chaotic in the capital but that wouldn't have meant suspension of a kind that would turn the busiest east-west link in the city into a pedestrian thoroughfare. By now Tia was passing Temple which meant by my reckoning that she still had some twenty minutes to go before she could begin her new trawl. I hunched down in front of the laptop, didn't – this time – head back out to the balcony, just watched her progress, trying to imagine the emotions she must be enduring every step of that tortuously long way.

All I felt was aggrieved. I couldn't help it. I'd invested a considerable amount of thought, time and expertise in all this. Now I was being denied the chance to see the full impact of it all, to watch Tia as she adjusted to a possible new reality and to assess how quickly she was able to do that, if at all. A moving blob on a mock-up of a street map seemed scant recompense and I couldn't help feeling badly treated somehow.

Then I jerked forward, refocused on the screen as suddenly Tia began to move forward at speed, far too fast for her to be walking, meaning she must have finally hailed a cab. Or maybe she'd only just found one. Perhaps I'd read this completely wrong, perhaps there'd been no choice involved, perhaps the streets around Victoria had been closed off for some reason, perhaps the reason she hadn't hailed a cab was simple, none were running and she had to make her way across Whitehall and had to wait until she was halfway down the Embankment before she could even think about finding one.

I opened up a new window on the laptop taking care not to close down the open application as I did so. Having severed a connection it might not be easy to re-establish it. Memories returned again, this time of the July 7 bombings on the London Tube and the way the networks crashed, leaving thousands of commuters not only stranded but, agonisingly for their relatives, incommunicado as well. With the surveillance software minimised I clicked up the news service. Sure enough the police were acting on a tip-off – later to be contradicted – that there might have been a terrorist involvement in the south London train crash. As a precaution the Met were closing down selected streets in the vicinity of a number of stations ring-fenced as potentially at risk.

As I closed down the news service and maximised the surveillance software again all my anger ebbed away. Now all I could feel was a piercing stab of sympathy for Tia compelled to trek halfway across London with only a growing sense of dread to keep her company. If I could have reached out at that moment, stopped her progress, held her in my arms, reassured her all was fine, that I was fine, then I would have done so.

I could have done that by proxy of course. I could have turned on my mobile and attempted to surf the overloaded networks, tried to make contact. But then I would only have had her voice to rely on. I could have heard her relief, but I couldn't have seen it in her eyes.

The now fast-moving blob that was Tia turned right onto London Bridge. In a quieter and more peaceful world and time we'd taken that exact same route, heading for Borough Market. Breakfast would usually be taken in Brindisa before we trawled the various produce stalls. I didn't know why that memory suddenly popped into my head at that moment in time but something told me it wouldn't be shared by Tia. Food was likely to be the last thing she was thinking about right now.

Sure enough all movement was temporarily halted as Tia presumably paid the driver. Then I watched, growing evermore breathless as Tia cut down to the station, taking in, first, the car park on Montague Close, the one near to Tooley Street, pretty well adjacent to the station. As she approached, Tia slowed, perhaps negotiating crowds still milling around the station, then moved on into the car park itself. Tia remained there for another three to four minutes before, that location eliminated, she moved onto the next car park in St Thomas Street in Bankside.

That was inspected and eliminated in about the same amount of time as was the next possibility in Weston Street in Bermondsey. It was now taking her longer to move around – I didn't know why, perhaps she was getting tired or perhaps this was all taking its inevitable emotional toll. After all, every few moments Tia was gearing herself up to encounter a sight she really did not want to see.

Tia moved on again to the next car park, London Snowfields on Kipling Street. Tia lingered longer than normal here, and again I had no way of discovering why. But while she did so I did make a mental note to investigate the origin of the name once this was all over. It was the sort of thing I'd come to enjoy during my enforced retirement. I told Tia it kept my mind active while I waited for the world to turn, for people to forget and for magazine and newspaper editors to move on. She told me, on more than one occasion, that I needed to get myself a life.

I hunched forward, staring intently now, totally focused on the screen. Tia had quit the Kipling Street site and now had just the one car park left to inspect – the one I'd used. End of journey. Mission soon to be accomplished.

Then I had a sudden stab of fear. What if her researches hadn't been quite so forensic as I'd imagined? She'd accessed a number of possibilities, what if she'd somehow missed that one or what if – in her agitation – it simply hadn't registered? What if she was about to head home, happier now, secure in the knowledge that wherever I was, I hadn't been anywhere near either of those two fateful stations, that – with the Duke being at or near neither – I might even have decided to take it all the way to Brighton and was even now riding it back over those switchback Downs?

That meant she'd be heading home. She might try my mobile a couple more times that night but if she didn't get through she'd just assume I'd been enmeshed in the chaos that had engulfed the networks as opposed to the very different sort of chaos I had in mind. Which meant I might have to wait till the morning for any sort of development. Which meant I'd have a whole night in this strange out-of-the-way hotel with only peacocks for company; then I stopped.

The indistinct blob that was Tia was finally moving again. But she wasn't moving back as I feared towards the bridge, away from the station, she was moving towards Trinity Street, towards the car park that housed the Duke.

By now I was having serious problems reining my raging emotions back under any sort of control. I was even having wild fantasies of the Duke not being there, of it having been taken in the last couple of hours by some desperate commuter who simply had to get home, no matter what; then I stopped again.

Tia was now in the car park. And unlike her previous trawls around similar car parks, Tia had now halted completely. And she didn't move for some long, long moments. I tried desperately to visualise the layout of the car park. Could she see the Duke from the entrance? I couldn't remember, but if she couldn't then why had she stopped like that, was she talking to someone? Maybe this wasn't the moment after all, maybe this journey still had some distance to complete and I didn't want to wait for that to happen, not any more, I wanted this to be over, I wanted Tia to be standing there, staring at the Duke, knowing what it meant, unable to take it in.

Then her mobile activated as she began pressing keys and I

upped the sound on the computer, praying Tia was going to get through to whoever she was dialling, that I could listen in to a conversation now, could actually hear her voice.

Her call was answered after three rings. She had absolutely no trouble getting through to the number she'd dialled. If she'd been dialling the office or some friend she wouldn't have stood, as I later discovered, a prayer. But the emergency number being given out all night by all the TV and radio stations, the number for relatives and friends to call if they were worried about anyone caught up in the train crash, was being prioritised right now.

'Hello?'

For a moment Tia didn't speak. I could almost hear the emotion overwhelming her.

Tia's respondent – female this time – repeated the greeting, not aggressive or irritated, far from it, gentle, caring, a soothing lilt to her voice I couldn't quite place at first.

Then Tia spoke.

'I think my partner – .'

She stopped again, struggling to regain control.

'I think my partner's been involved in the train crash.'

'What's his name please?'

Tia gave my name and a few other details as she was prompted, including my age.

'And your name, please?'

All the time Tia was answering, her respondent must have been checking lists in front of her.

'We don't have anyone of that name on the list we've been given. Not yet.'

All Tia heard were the last two words. Because, of course, the list was being updated almost minute by minute. The fact I wasn't there didn't mean a thing, I might not be now but I could be added at any second.

The same gentle, caring, voice floated out of the ether again.

'What makes you think your partner might have been on one of these trains?'

And it was like the floodgates opening. It all poured out, my note, Tia checking the routes I might have taken, then the trawl of the car parks, ending with the discovery of the Duke and – here her voice faltered again – the ticket stuffed into the handgrip recording the time I'd entered the car park, an hour or so before the crash. Just enough time for me to get into the station, buy my ticket, board the train – they were running every ten minutes at that time of the day, Tia had checked – settle into my seat, perhaps sip at a coffee, maybe scan some headlines in a paper, before the train reached full speed out of London.

Tia tailed off. For a moment the woman on the other end of the line didn't speak either. She must have heard a hundred similar stories in the past couple of hours but it obviously hadn't deadened her to the emotion behind every one, the raw emotion she could hear in the voice of her caller right now, the same emotion I could hear right now too.

'You've tried calling?'

'Again and again. His phone just goes straight to his answer service.'

'It probably would anyway, most of the networks are down right now.'

'But it'd ring, wouldn't it? It's not even doing that, it's just going straight to his service as if it's been turned off or it's – .'

Tia faltered again.

' – smashed or something.'

The woman had obviously kept on checking the list, which was indeed being updated every few seconds.

'Still no-one of that name.'

Tia didn't reply and now I could almost see the owner of the gentle caring voice lean forward, reluctant to end the contact, knowing she'd be abandoning her caller to a nightmare, aware she had other, equally desperate, callers queuing up behind and maybe there was actually something practical she could do to help them, even if it was just to put them out of the misery of waiting for news.

'Why don't you go home? If your partner is OK that's where he'll go and if something has happened and the emergency services find any evidence he has been involved in all this then that's the first place they'll contact.'

Tia still didn't reply.

'I can imagine how hard this is. I – .'

The woman stopped, this time her voice catching slightly, the first chink in the professional veneer.

'A relative of mine – my brother – he was caught up in an explosion years ago – we didn't hear for hours, I thought I'd go out of my mind.'

'What happened?'

'It was during what they called the Troubles – as if they were the only troubles we ever had – when they first put those defences up round the city – that's where he worked – .'

Tia cut across again.

'Was he killed?'

There was just a momentary hesitation.

'No.'

Tia cut the call a short time later. She promised the woman she'd do what she advised, go home, sit tight and wait for news. There was nothing else to do and she knew it. She'd keep trying my mobile in case the problem was simply the network crashing and she took the name of the woman too, promising to call her or leave a message if she received good news. What Tia would do if she received bad news she didn't say. She didn't need to.

Intent, I kept watching the screen after the call was cut. I couldn't predict what Tia would actually now do despite all her assurances. She could equally well go into a local bar and drink herself into oblivion as head down the Highway and sit in the loft.

Tia hailed another cab – the traffic chaos clearly not having engulfed this part of London in the way it had nearer to Whitehall – and I watched her progress as she moved east. I lost her slightly as she neared the end of the journey – I suspected I might as the driver took the Limehouse Link, disappearing under the old Regent Canal – before emerging again at the entrance to Canary Wharf. Then he swung left and left again and dropped Tia outside the loft. There was a short delay while she paid the fare, then Tia disappeared again as she moved inside the loft and I lost reception – as we always did for some reason – on the stairs.

Then all of a sudden she was back out of the complex, moving back across the small courtyard again.

I hunched over the laptop. What the hell was she doing? Where was she going? Was this the moment that made all this extraordinary effort worthwhile? Now she'd been placed under the most extreme of pressure, was this the moment she turned to someone else in her hour of need, exposing herself without realising it, justifying the elaborate plans and preparations I'd made, robbing herself forever of any moral high ground if and when she discovered the subterfuge to which she'd been subjected?

Outside the open window one of the peacocks struck up another of the discordant choruses with which I'd been dubiously entertained since my arrival. A small cluster of wasps were milling at one of the windows having not yet discovered the open patio doors leading out onto the balcony. I stood to close them, cutting out the sound of the peacock's progress as it made its way along the front lawn. When I returned to the screen Tia had obviously hailed another cab because now she was moving along the street at pace and there was clearly a lot less traffic on the road than previously too given the speed of the cab as it squired Tia west back towards the City.

I listed options as Tia drove on. Most of the people who worked with her lived in Central London. Some had decamped outside Zone 1, but they tended to be junior staff attracted by the deals proffered by desperate developers, hungry to fill their burgeoning list of empty lets in the wake of the banking crisis they thought would end all banking crises, a hope that – and as with so many when it came to all-matters financial – proved all too fond.

So where was Tia heading? Joseph had a house near the Embankment. Tia had attended a party there once along with the rest of her colleagues from the company, a night that started with drinks served on a roof terrace looking out over a skyline of similar terraces. From Tia's description I could appreciate the understated opulence with which it was furnished. So was she about to make acquaintance again with Joseph and his house and all that understated opulence? Was Natsuo there with him – or Nikki, another of his apparently casual partners – or was this to be a strictly private encounter? Was I about to discover that the simple nod I'd seen exchanged outside that airport car park, that apparent caress in the balcony doorway hadn't been magnified by my over-active imagination after all? Had those simple gestures indeed lifted a lid on a life lived very much apart from the one I assumed we shared in its each and every important detail?

I frowned as the cab suddenly took a left, crossed the river. My eye strayed to the icon blinking at the bottom of the screen checking the software wasn't malfunctioning. But the light was steady and the progress on the screen was steady too. Tia was now heading back to the station she'd hurriedly quit just an hour or so before.

So why, what was the point? She'd found out all she could on her last visit, she'd found the car park, she'd seen the parking ticket on the Duke, she'd checked the time, she'd done the necessary mental arithmetic; then I paused.

The Duke.

She was fetching the Duke.

And suddenly I had the feeling of being enveloped in some way. Of being cared for. Protected. Tia had no idea where I was right now, what state I might be in, but she knew where my precious bike was and she was not going to leave it there in that car park, she was bringing it home, returning one part of our world to normality at least.

Sure enough on the screen her progress halted at the station before that progress resumed once more, significantly faster this time, as she fired the Duke into life and rode it back across the bridge before taking a right back along the Highway towards the loft.

I stared at the screen, letting a warm feeling spread through me from the top of my head to the tip of my toes.

2 4 .

TIA PARKED THE Duke in the underground car park of the loft roughly ten minutes after she'd left London Bridge.

I was impressed. I timed myself on various runs and I'd tried the relatively short run from London Bridge once on a weekday night – late on, after the rush hour – and hadn't managed it in much less than fifteen. Either the roads in that part of London – again unlike the rest of the capital – really were particularly quiet that night or Tia had very definitely been hiding her prowess as a biker.

I stared at the screen evermore intent as Tia locked the Duke and headed up the stairs to the loft. Before she went inside she paused outside the door of the neighbour who'd complained, albeit mildly, about the impact of the bike on the sleep patterns of his child. Was she looking for companionship? To unburden herself? To continue the confessional-type conversation she'd endured/enjoyed with the respondent manning the emergency number? But if she was even briefly tempted the impulse passed and Tia moved on into the loft.

I activated all the bugs as she came in through the door. I heard her first moving into the open-plan sitting room, the picture frame picking up a step that – to my straining ears – already sounded heavier than I remembered. She made to put the Duke keys down on the table by the door, then – some memory clicking into place – gave a gasp and then moved into my line of vision, keys still in hand, placed them instead on another table, just under the picture frame, well out of sight of the door and the reach of any potential thief who might try to hook them from the vantage point of the letterbox.

My first reaction was almost of amusement. It might have taken my possible death to finally bring home to Tia the importance of household security. My second reaction, tinged with absolutely no amusement at all, was amazement at how a human face can change in just a couple of hours.

Tia looked – I searched in my mind for the word – haunted. There was no other word for it. She looked to be carrying some invisible burden, impossible to divest which ushered in my third reaction – and who wouldn't feel this way? – which was gratification, pride almost that I clearly counted to such an obvious and visible extent. If I'd entertained doubts about her they were already beginning to vanish and if I didn't have a cover story to maintain – my temporary amnesia – I might have ended all this there and then. Surely Tia couldn't be that good an actress? And anyway why maintain any sort of fiction now? What was the point in continuing to wear a public face of grief in private?

Tia dialled a number on her mobile. Within seconds she was contacted to the staff maintaining the emergency number. Now – sounding more crushed than desperate – Tia explained who she was, her reasons for believing her partner might be on one of the trains involved in the multiple crash, gave my name, waited only a second or two before being told that name was not on the list of people – alive, injured or dead – who'd been discovered at or near the crash site as yet, before being advised to call back at regular intervals over the next few hours.

Which Tia did. On the half-hour, every hour. Regular as clockwork and the rest of the time she just remained seated, staring at the loft phone and her mobile beside it. She didn't move, didn't fix herself anything to drink or eat. She just remained in some sort of temporary suspension, only moving to reach out a hand and press a redial key.

Around dawn her body finally gave up the increasingly

unequal battle with her resolve. I watched her head droop, jerk up, then droop again. She rested her head on the small table, closed her eyes and was gone. Within seconds I'd done the same, the efforts of the night, not to mention the previous day, now taking their toll on me too.

I woke about an hour or so later. Tia must have woken moments before because when I blinked my way back to consciousness it was to hear the sound of her crying for the first time, great, rasping sobs filling the room, amplified through the speakers of the laptop.

I stared at the screen and at Tia, her head still on the table, unable to move in what appeared to be the extremes of abandonment and grief.

2 5 .

Tia slept for just a couple more hours that night. I couldn't sleep at all, found myself patrolling the corridors of the hotel much to the bemusement of a solitary security guard who seemed to double as the night-time receptionist, although I was to later discover he multitasked as the leisure club attendant too. In his latter role he opened the door to the hotel pool at 8 a.m., checked the security cameras connected to reception were working and whether any hotel guests had fallen in during the night. He also let me in to use the pool an hour before it officially opened after I explained I'd just endured a long flight in from Central America and was severely jet-lagged.

I had once been genuinely jet-lagged on a flight back from Venezuela. I was hoping, should anyone be inclined to check on this stay at any time in the future, then such a detail would be taken as a clear indication that in my confused state I was mixing up timescales and dates. I'd read enough of the experiences of souls caught up in the aftermath of disasters to know that at least part of the fantasies they subsequently invented to deal with the horrors they'd experienced would always be based, in some loose part, on fact.

Myself and Tia had once met a police officer who'd been invalided out of her specialist section which dealt with witness protection. Her job was to coach witnesses who faced relocation in their legend – defined as the story they had to tell the world from that point on to explain their presence in a new community. The best legends, so she'd told us, were always those that were based in some measure on truth. The more fantastic and outlandish the back story, the more likely the witness would stumble. So

I made sure that everything I told the solitary security guard, the receptionist and the waitress who served me coffee in the bar was, in some way at least, based on the facts of a life I'd seemingly just abandoned.

The pool was tiny and the changing rooms cramped. I managed a couple of laps before tiring of the constant turns that had to be negotiated to complete the next. I dried myself, headed back to my room and turned on the laptop to find Tia sleeping again.

I stared at the screen with something approaching irritation. It was unreasonable I knew, but this seemed insensitive somehow. The events of the previous day had left me wired beyond anything I'd experienced before even in those days in the past when I'd have popped all sorts and variety of pills to keep me awake on some assignment or other. I was desperate to see what was going to happen next but perhaps Tia was the opposite. Perhaps her extended sleep was a way of trying to protect herself from the sort of news she really did not want to hear.

When Tia did wake it wasn't with any sort of drama or sudden shock as she realised just why she'd lain down to sleep with her head on that table rather than the upmarket pillows we'd invested in following a stay one New Year at an exclusive island resort in Thailand. She seemed to know instantly where she was and what she was doing, but perhaps she'd been awake for some time without my realising it, not wanting to move, psyching herself for what was undoubtedly going to be another series of trials ahead.

Tia reached out and checked her mobile. Nothing. She dialled the emergency number, repeating in even more of a monotone than the previous night the information regarding my name, address and the reasons she had for suspecting I might be on one of those fateful trains. A different but no less sympathetic voice checked a list, a process that took longer this time – clearly the number of dead and injured was rising all the time – before telling Tia that my name had not as yet appeared on any official record and advising her to keep trying which Tia assured him, in the same monotone, she would.

Then Tia went into the bedroom, sat down on the bed and stared, unblinking, at the radio alarm clock that, unbeknown to her, was recording her every move right now, meaning that for those few moments Tia was staring straight at me as I watched her on the monitor on my laptop.

She couldn't have known what was happening and yet she seemed to be looking deep into my eyes, holding my stare, daring me, challenging me almost, as if she was asking, what are you doing, why are you doing this?

But of course she wasn't and after a period of maintaining that more-than-unsettling silent stare she stood, went out onto the balcony. I couldn't see her – she was now out of range of the camera – but I could hear her as she again burst into tears.

And now I had to think and think quickly. All this had to be now quite finely judged because I'd already had the answer to the question that had sent me aboard this ship of fools in the first place.

But then, suddenly, an unsettling thought flashed through my mind.

Tia could still care for me of course – love me indeed – and could still be having an affair. But then I dismissed that. Her responses had been too visceral, too raw. So the issue, now, wasn't one of fidelity, loyalty, call it what you will, the matter of the moment was that of timing. How long did I now stay away? How much of a gap should I leave between enduring what was still being called the incident and apparently coming to my senses in some strange, crumbling, country hotel a full hour or so away from the crash site?

I racked my brains trying to remember details of the Parisian bus driver and his extraordinary walk away from his blazing vehicle. From the little I could recall that was only a few hours which would hardly have been fit for the purpose I had in mind. But I did recall reading other tales where victims of temporary amnesia stayed away for days, if not months. And there was always the template of course – Wakefield – and his absence for something over twenty years. But that was more down to the nineteenth-century setting than anything else. If Wakefield had managed to get hold of even one of the bugs I'd installed in and around the loft he'd probably have been back with his long-suffering wife by the weekend.

I stared at the screen, my mind computing possibilities. One day was the absolute minimum, but I'd stayed away almost that already. If I was Tia I could just about buy a partner being so traumatised that they'd simply closed down, retreated somewhere, their mind refusing to engage or deal with an experience it simply couldn't process.

But two days? Three days? To go to sleep, to wake, to function apparently normally, to eat meals, drink coffee, surely that partner would have to come face to face with it all sometime during that period – catch a TV report – see a headline in a paper – surely something would penetrate the self-protective fog that had apparently descended?

And then there was simple humanity. Tia was suffering, of that there was no doubt. How long did I keep her in limbo? If I'd already had my answer then surely it was simply cruel to perpetuate the question. The clear secondary danger was there in the original story too, where there was more than a hint that Wakefield began to enjoy the torment he was inflicting. I had no wish to do that. Up to now this had been an experiment that could be justified in terms of the greater good. If Tia failed the test, failed to respond in the way she so clearly had responded, then I was saving us both years of pain, frustration, doubt and deceit. In one sense – and while I accepted it might look the opposite to some eyes – my actions up to that point had almost been altruistic.

I stood, went to the small balcony and looked out again at the bank of trees, watched the peacocks as they moved round the car park, dodging the shrieking attentions of a couple of small children who'd just arrived and who wanted – to the clear alarm of their parents and perhaps the peacocks – to make friends. All the time I computed options, assessed strategies but I knew the answer already.

I couldn't stay away another night. I was going to head down to reception, settle the bill – in cash, not via my card, I didn't want anything alerting the authorities before I was well and truly ready. I wanted to choose the moment I lifted the cloud. I wanted Tia to realise I was alive and well when she saw me standing before her. I wanted to see the look in her eyes, wanted that imprinted on my memory forever so if I was ever tempted to subject her to any similar tests in the future, I'd have before me all the evidence any reasonable person should ever need that anything I'd previously imagined was just that; pure imagination and nothing else.

Besides, how long could I maintain the pretence of the jet-lagged traveller aside from anything else? I didn't want to go for some kind of world record here. The longest period of incapacity suffered by a passenger at the hands of British Airways.

Then, from inside the room, came the sound of a ringing phone. For a moment I tensed, unwilling to even look back inside. Who'd be calling, why would they be calling? No-one – quite clearly – knew I was here. Then I calmed as I realised I was listening to Tia's mobile, filtered through the bugs, captured by the software on the laptop.

I headed back inside, quickly. Up to now all I'd heard were conversations that Tia had instigated, what would she be like when someone called her, some friend perhaps, what would she say, would they already know, had she told anyone?

Tia answered the phone, the voice on the other end not waiting for a greeting.

'Tia.'

It was Joseph. The man of the conspiratorial nod in airport car parks. The man who, partly at least, had kick-started all this.

Silence from Tia. At the same time I realised that in the last few moments, while I was out on the balcony, Tia had sent an email to the office, informing them of her upcoming absence and explaining – briefly, almost curtly – the reason. As I was reading it, Joseph cut across again.

'Let me come round. I can be there in half an hour, less. I can't imagine – .'

Joseph tailed off. Tia hadn't said a single word so far. Then he spoke again.

'Please.'

Then Tia spoke. One word. Low. Almost a whisper.

'OK.'

Then Tia cut the call.

26.

I COULDN'T GO back yet. Well, could I? OK, everything I'd previously vowed still stood. I would not become Wakefield. I would not let even a hint of the twisted intoxication that informed the actions of that fictional creation inform my own.

But I simply had to see this meeting between Tia and Joseph. Neither could have the slightest idea that I'd be watching. Neither could have the faintest clue that every word they said, every gesture, would be monitored and not only monitored but recorded so I could replay the encounter again – and, if need be, again and again – just to make sure there was nothing I'd missed. Or maybe just to watch the confirmation of all I'd previously feared played out before my eyes. So I could stiffen my resolve for the then-inevitable confrontation to come.

I turned back to the laptop. I'd left Tia sitting by her phone and that was where she remained, silent, immobile, staring into a distance that seemed unpopulated by anything or anyone. She didn't look like a woman about to receive the ministering attentions of a lover in her hour of need. She looked wracked. Tortured.

Or guilty of course. That would also explain the numbed fragility that seemed to have claimed her. Frantic with worry or desperate with guilt? Time – and only a short period of time – would now tell.

Behind me, a knock on the door suddenly sounded. I wheeled round, then – instinctively – looked back, fearful, at the screen. Even now I still couldn't get used to the idea that I could see all, hear all, but Tia could see and hear nothing. Even now some irrational panic still seized me that she could somehow hear the sounds that I could hear.

But Tia was still immobile, still just staring into a middle distance that might promise salvation or deliver yet more horrors to come. I turned the laptop screen to one side so it wouldn't be visible from the door. It was probably the maid come to clean the room. I couldn't actually remember if I'd done what I intended to do on returning to the room from my swim and placed the DND sign on the door handle.

I opened the door to find a frock-coated waiter wearing a practised smile and carrying a tray.

'Room service.'

I stared at him stupidly, not moving in the doorway, not allowing him in and his practised smile began to fade.

'Nine-thirty.'

I kept staring at him as he prompted me.

'Your breakfast order?'

I looked at the tray. On top of a metal dome covering a plate was a copy of a room service order. The room number was filled in – my own – a selection of items were ticked, a time was noted and a signature was scrawled at the bottom. Even at a first glance I could see that the signature was mine. I stared at it, thrown. I had absolutely no recollection of filling in that card.

'Yes. Of course.'

I stood to one side and let the waiter into the room. With a well-rehearsed manoeuvre he swung the tray around the edge of the bed and made for a small table by the balcony, the table currently occupied by my laptop. I sprang forward, quickly.

'I'll move that.'

'No need, sir.'

The cheerful waiter whipped out a chair with one hand while keeping hold of the room service tray with the other, placing the tray down on the chair with a flourish. I had the impression it was something of a party trick. Then he handed me a room service receipt to sign.

Once again I stared at items that apparently I'd ordered. I'd obviously simply forgotten but it was throwing me rather more than was warranted by a simple lapse of memory. Perhaps having become so used to being in control of all around me over the last day or so it was more than a little disconcerting to find myself not as totally in charge as I thought. But as I signed the room service receipt I gave myself a mental note to get a grip. This was only breakfast after all and any confusion reported by my smiling waiter to his colleagues would be taken as yet more evidence of my jet-lagged state so in the end this could all work to my advantage.

I moved back to the laptop. There didn't seem to be any change in Tia in the short time I'd moved to the door and collected a breakfast I couldn't remember ordering and certainly didn't want. Steam wafted from a chipped coffee jug, floated towards the open balcony window. On screen, Tia remained seated; then suddenly she stood.

For a moment I thought one of the bugs had failed, that there'd been a ring on the loft doorbell that I'd missed somehow, but Tia didn't make for the door. She picked up her phone, made a last-minute check – presumably before Joseph arrived – as to whether there'd been any news, finding out whether at this late stage she could forestall his visit perhaps – but of course there was still no news, still no record of my name among the ever lengthening list of dead and injured still being excavated from beneath the twisted carriages at the crash site.

As Tia came off the phone the buzzer sounded from outside. She checked the image on the video link, pressed the entry button, then stood for a moment, composing herself it seemed; but for what? Then she moved to the door as the bell sounded. From the bedroom the camera in the radio alarm clock recorded her pasting on the semblance of a welcoming smile, that smile then wiping as Joseph stood in the doorway, as he held out his arms and she moved into his embrace.

I leant forward, my face almost touching the screen. Tia was resting her head on his shoulder. He had both arms circled around her back. In one sense it was intimate – how could it not be, they were in each other's arms, holding each other, her body pressed against his? But there was also something about the unspoken language of this embrace that was oddly formal. He held her as you might hold a delicate object, there was a lack of familiarity that I wouldn't have expected had this been a rerun of many similar previous embraces in different situations in the past.

After a moment, Tia drew back but Joseph still didn't speak, just looked at her and Tia shook her head, answering a question he hadn't asked and hadn't needed to.

No.

Still no news.

For a moment I felt a stab of unease. Now there was a degree of intimacy in that unspoken answer and question, some hint at a relationship that went beyond simply that of office colleagues. But these were extraordinary circumstances and again I'd read enough accounts from the journals of survivors to know that the most intense of relationships could flare in the immediate aftermath of some tragedy, most of which weren't relationships at all, just humans reaching out to each other, not exposing to public view an affair they'd gone to considerable lengths, up to that point, to keep private.

Then Tia moved out of range of the camera, leading Joseph towards our open-plan kitchen, the next stage of their encounter now to be captured only aurally. But the bugs were well placed and would pick up every word, every intonation.

Initially the conversation was strictly practical with Tia – in another seemingly-cathartic burst of explanation – reviewing all she'd done so far, the steps she'd taken to trace the Duke, the implications of finding it in that particular car park with that particular ticket attached to the grip, the calls she'd been making to the emergency number ever since, the lack of any information they in turn had been able to supply.

All the time Joseph stayed largely silent. At first the silence unsettled me, was he holding her again, was she saying all this while all the time she was in his arms? But then Tia started pacing and the camera in the bedroom picked her up once more through the open door and I could see her as she came into vision, turning, wheeling as she continued with a résumé of events she could hardly bear to recall. And all the time Joseph simply listened, didn't make any move towards the pacing Tia, just let her talk herself out.

Then, suddenly, the bedside phone rang behind me. Another instinctive reaction, I wheeled, then stared back at the screen, again half-expecting the sudden intrusion to stop Tia, to alert Joseph, but on screen Tia just continued pacing of course, kept on talking.

Now in something of an agony of frustration, I moved to the bedside phone and picked it up.

'Hello.'

For a moment there was silence on the other end of the line. Then a well-modulated voice returned my greeting.

'I'm terribly sorry.'

'What?'

'This is Reception.'

There was a pause as the well-modulated voice checked some papers before him, a rustling sound now heard.

'I called you by mistake, sir, my apologies again for disturbing your rest.'

I swallowed, choked back a sudden instinct to scream back

at the ham-fisted receptionist who had presumably misplaced a digit in making a wake-up call. But I didn't, I simply mumbled something about that being fine before slamming down the handset and turning back to the screen.

Now the background acoustic had changed. Now Tia and Joseph had moved out onto the balcony but I could still hear every word. Now Joseph was talking and he was saying all the things you'd expect anyone to say in the circumstances. He wasn't insulting her intelligence with platitudes, he acknowledged the overpowering – if still-circumstantial – evidence that I had been caught up in the crash and he further acknowledged the likelihood that I'd been injured or worse, otherwise, why hadn't I been in touch? He acknowledged also the increasingly probability that with my name still absent from any official records, I must still be at the crash scene, meaning I was either too badly injured to move or, of course, that I was dead. If that sounds harsh that's probably due more to my perhaps overly-brutal summary than his rather more diplomatic phrasing. But the essence of what he was saying was the same.

But it was all leavened with practical suggestions too. Joseph offered to take over the calls to the emergency services and he also mentioned a couple of people he knew who were helping coordinate the whole thing – apparently several of the out-of-work actors the agency used for their promotions were also pressed into service by the authorities at times like these. He couldn't guarantee any sort of fast track to new information but he could at least ensure my details were given added prominence as any further names came in.

Joseph also offered the services of several other people from the agency – mutual friends who could keep Tia company, provide help, a rota system of care and support.

It was all as I'd have expected. It was warm, it was supportive and there was genuine concern in his voice and in his offers of help. But it was the care and concern of a friend. Not once did it stray into anything that could remotely be called inappropriate. It was the sort of conversation Tia and myself might have had ourselves with a friend going through a similar torment. It was the sort of conversation countless friends were probably having all over the capital and beyond right at that very moment in time as anguished relatives, lovers, wives, husbands and partners haunted the phone lines, waiting in a similar limbo for news.

It all added up to the same thing. Tia and her conversation with Joseph – Tia and her reaction, first to my apparent disappearance, and then to my possible involvement in a larger tragedy – all told me the same thing. Tia loved me. It wasn't just the fact she told Joseph this – although she did – time and again – recounting small details of the times we'd spent together – telling him how she couldn't bear the thought I could now be lost to her – it was all that lay behind her words, all I could see in her eyes and hear in her voice.

She truly loved me. In this, her hour of need, that simple fact was inescapable. In this, that hour of need, she hadn't turned to anyone else, to any lover for comfort or support. Her whole being was focused on one thing and one thing only and that was her missing partner and every tremor in her voice, every movement of her body told me that she wanted, more than anything and in more ways than she could even begin to express, for me to walk back through that door, unharmed and restored to her, spared where so many others had not been.

I stood up from the laptop and crossed to the bedside phone. Now I really had seen and heard enough and I now wanted some semblance of sanity to be restored, for the endgame in this charade to be played. In the loft Tia was saying goodbye to the departing Joseph and I kept one eye on them as I dialled Reception. But again all was as it should be – a hug, a peck on the cheek, a few last comforting words and then Joseph was gone.

Then the well-modulated voice from a few moments before floated once again down the line.

'Reception.'

'I'd like to order a taxi.'

'For what time, sir?'

'Say, an hour. And could you prepare my bill, I'll be checking out too.'

'Would you like assistance with your luggage?'

'I only have a small bag.'

A professional smile infused the voice.

'Travelling light.'

If only he knew.

'And where will you be going?'

'I'm sorry?'

'I'll need to tell the driver.'

For a moment I had an irresistible urge to say, 'Home'. There was something so seductive about the simplicity of that one single word. I turned back to the laptop to stare at the world I'd be rejoining in just a short time, then paused as I saw Tia, the loft phone now in her hand, pressing numbers on the display.

I turned back to the hotel phone.

'Could you just hang on a minute?'

'Of course.'

My hand over the receiver, I continued to stare at Tia who was now pressing a different, longer, number to the emergency number she'd accessed earlier. Then Tia waited, rather more impatient than I'd seen her before too and as I kept waiting I now noticed her mobile, discarded on the table; which was odd.

It was a running joke that Tia always used her mobile even when there was a landline close to hand. She could never explain why, it was just a tactile thing, something about the design of even the most primitive mobile winning every time in the aesthetic stakes. But now she'd chosen the landline which was curious but nothing – in the curiosity stakes – to what was to follow.

Tia leant forward, her call clearly having been answered and she plunged straight in.

'I need to see you.'

Tia paused, presumably as the voice on the other end of the line responded.

'No, now, this can't wait.'

Tia paused again as, across the room, the hotel phone still in my hand, the receptionist hanging on the other end of the line, I stared at her. Then Tia nodded as, presumably, her respondent agreed to her sudden and insistent demand.

'Yes, the usual place.'

Then Tia put down the phone, stood still for a moment, then headed on into the bathroom where she began to throw up.

On the other end of the hotel phone line a cautious voice sounded.

'Sir?'

I didn't reply.

'The taxi? Where shall I tell the driver you want to go?'

I still didn't reply, just kept staring across the room at my laptop, the sound of Tia throwing up continuing over from the bathroom.

27.

I'M NOT SURE how long I stood by that bed staring at the laptop. I remember telling the receptionist that I'd changed my mind, that I wasn't checking out after all, but that aside, not a great deal more. I replaced the handset, I must have done, it was back in place when I next recalled looking at it, when my brain began to process all that had happened at least half-coherently once again. But for the rest of the time I seemed to have been in some state of shock.

Partly it was the switch in Tia. It was as if a button had been pressed. All of a sudden she seemed to have gone from a woman who was totally dissolving to a woman in complete control; brisk, business-like, efficient.

That was unsettling enough. I couldn't believe Tia could have acted all the emotion I'd seen displayed in her encounter with Joseph but that was a secondary issue compared to the hammerblow thought pulsing through my head right now.

Who did Tia simply have to meet?

Why did she have to meet them – him? – her? – straightaway?

And where the hell was 'the usual place'?

It was probably the latter issue that really stopped me in my tracks. Leaving aside the sudden switch in her personality – or what seemed to be the sudden switch in her personality – it was the fact that Tia had some place unknown to me which was quite clearly the scene of some previous liaison or rendezvous. Her call could have been to some friend – male or female – some confidant – someone she trusted – someone she needed to share everything with right now. There were a number of possibilities among her wide circle of friends and acquaintances – she even had a sister who lived a couple of hundred miles away but who could quite reasonably be called on at a time like this. But none of those friends, acquaintances or family members would have a usual place in which they and Tia met.

A usual place was the stuff of clandestine meetings of romantic fiction, a setting known only to the people most intimately involved in those encounters, a place chosen to include just themselves and exclude others; a secret, in fact.

Which was why I stood there for what seemed to be an instant but was, in fact, several minutes. I was trying to take in that simple fact and largely failing. After wondering for so long, after going to such elaborate lengths to reassure myself about my partner, after being on the very brink of abandoning the whole exercise as redundant I'd uncovered, at the eleventh hour, something hidden.

I moved back to the laptop, watched as Tia came out of the bathroom, her hair now wet, kept watching as Tia, towelling herself down all the while, discarded her vomit-spattered clothes and selected a new outfit for her upcoming meeting with... who?

I still wasn't thinking all that rationally or coherently but I did have the presence of mind to check out the outfit she selected and the image it might present. Was it the sort of outfit you'd choose for a rendezvous with a business acquaintance, the sort you'd select for a meeting with a close friend – or the sort of outfit to which you'd incline, even unconsciously, for a liaison with a lover? The choice gave little away. There were no killer heels. But the outfit was among the newest and sleekest she'd acquired over the previous couple of months, the type she might have selected to attend some upmarket launch or party.

I watched in a mounting agony of anticipation as she removed the last vestiges of her previous make-up and reapplied a new layer. All the time I was desperate for some other phone call to come through, some confirmation text on her mobile, perhaps from the caller she'd just contacted on the loft landline. Failing that, I just wanted a clue – a call to a taxi service, giving me some idea where she might be heading, some geographical fix so I might start narrowing down the list of possible options. But there was nothing. Tia simply finished applying her make-up, dressed, then picked up her mobile and headed for the door.

I closed down all the bugs in the loft. I was now just monitoring the bug in her phone. I followed Tia remotely as she headed out onto the communal corridor, endured a few moments characteristic panic as the signal wavered on the stairs, then breathed a sigh of relief as she moved out into the courtyard and the signal re-established itself again.

All the time I computed possibilities. Tia hadn't called for a taxi so did that mean the usual place – and how that phrase kept resonating inside my head – was somewhere local, was perhaps within walking distance, was the answer to the question that had sent me away to be found somewhere on our very own home patch?

Or was she intending to take the Duke? But the moment that thought flashed across my mind I discounted it. She was hardly dressed for a burn-up on a bike.

Still tracking her via the bug in the mobile, I kept watching as Tia cut across a small bridge over the Limehouse Basin, moved between two new developments including one housing an extended water garden which, we'd both agreed, would have driven us insane with its endless succession of extended mini-waterfalls sounding all day and night. Then she cut across a busy street and headed into the nearby station.

All of a sudden a chill feeling claimed me. If Tia was taking the shuttle east then I could continue tracking her with few problems. That part of the track was almost exclusively overland.

If she was heading west then I'd be fine for the early part of the journey but if she continued by Tube I'd lose her.

Tia bought her ticket and stood on the station. I couldn't tell which platform, all the bug showed was an indistinct blob at a general location, it would only be when she started moving again that I'd know for sure.

After a few moments Tia started moving west.

I got up from the laptop and paced the room. Outside, one of the male peacocks had hoisted itself onto a small wall below my balcony and was just sitting there, feathers curled in on themselves. He stirred and looked up at me lazily. Below, another of the peacocks was crying out again but the resting peacock took no notice, just kept staring up at me. I walked back into the room, closing the patio windows.

On screen, Tia was approaching the terminus. She hadn't alighted at any of the intermediate stations and I watched, ever more tense, as Tia moved from the overland shuttle towards the exit that could have taken her out onto the street, but then she turned and headed instead for the Tube. For a few moments the signal flickered as the bug tried to keep in contact with Tia's fast-failing mobile but then all activity ceased on the laptop as the signal died completely.

I opened up a new window, summoned up a map of the Underground. Direct services from Bank, the station Tia had just entered, included the Central, District, Circle and the Northern lines. As sheer bad luck would have it, that station was blessed with a choice of different services. Tia could be going north-east to Epping, west past Ealing, north to the outer reaches of Finchley, south down to Wimbledon, or out past Barking and beyond. Her journey time was a complete unknown as well. If she was staying on whichever Tube she'd taken for the majority – or all – of the stations that would be visited en route then she could be on the train for at least another hour – perhaps longer in the case of some of the choices on offer – which meant a fruitless wait of exactly the same time for me.

And the fact Tia had chosen the Tube did suggest there was a fairly extended journey involved. Tia had a phobia about the Underground. If there was any other way of getting around – taxi, the Duke – that would be her strong preference. The Tube was for those journeys out to far-flung parts of the city where a taxi would either be prohibitively expensive or simply more trouble than it was worth, turning a one-hour endurance ride underground into something a great deal more onerous up on the exhaust-raddled streets.

Or perhaps other considerations had eclipsed her usual concerns. Maybe Tia simply had an overpowering desire to be somewhere with someone right now and everything else was simply too inconsequential to get in the way.

The minutes ticked by. The software on the laptop monitored no activity from her phone meaning Tia was still travelling. I paced the floor, went out onto the balcony again, then paced the floor some more. Still nothing from the laptop. Still no activity being recorded via the phone. Tia was still out of range.

Almost for the sake of something to do I turned on the TV and came across a special programme on the train crash. They were still a long way from determining the cause, although a union leader was waxing loquaciously about under-investment and the implications for safety, but the programme was much more concerned with what might be called human interest. Time and again, relatives of victims and relatives of those still missing were paraded before the camera, the interviewers probing all the time, mainly with variations on just one question, redundant in one sense, eerily compelling in another: How do you feel?

Time and again variations on the same grief-stricken response filled the screen. For a few moments I watched, finding it impossible not to be caught up in it all, unable to stop myself responding to the real-life tragedies unfolding before my eyes.

Then, at the end, a roll-call came up, a list of those people who were confirmed as having been killed and then – totally unexpected – a list of those people believed to be still missing or otherwise unaccounted for. It had never occurred to me that my name might be included on that list, even now. The fact I knew it was a charade made the possibility absurd, but all of a sudden there it was, my own name, among the other names scrolling down the screen.

I stared at it, unable to tear my eyes away. And for a moment I couldn't help delight surging through me, delight in a deception so comprehensive it seemed to have already become part of some official record. A crazy, half-formed, completely instinctive response to sudden and total chaos had solidified into something else; fiction being translated, apparently, into fact.

Then, a sobering blast, came the second reaction. If I was watching this then who else was watching at the same time? Would anyone recognise my name? I'd had to give a name to the female receptionist when I arrived and I didn't want to invent one, that really would seem curious to anyone who might later check on my movements.

Was that receptionist watching the same programme right now, was she – even as I was standing there – double-checking the register, matching the name on the screen with the name of the strange, seemingly jet-lagged figure who'd checked in just a couple of hours after the train crash, carrying precious little in the way of luggage and now – watching that same TV programme – had she just realised why?

On screen the software beeped. Tia seemed to be in range again. I crossed to the screen quickly, but as I got there the signal vanished.

I stood for a few moments expecting contact to be re-established within moments, but it wasn't.

Again I computed possibilities. Tia had briefly, very briefly, surfaced for some item or other – a coffee – to check messages – to pick up a paper – and was now resuming her journey. But I discounted that notion pretty well immediately. She'd now been underground for the best part of an hour. Wherever she'd been heading, surely she had to have reached the end of her journey by now.

The second possibility was that she'd hit a blackspot, a reception-free part of the capital, which again was unlikely. Mobile blackspots existed in far-flung reaches of the countryside, but the capital wasn't exactly short of phone masts. On another crime reconstruction programme I'd watched recently a prominent police officer had made the vaguely threatening point that there was nowhere in London that wasn't covered by satellite technology and the implication was crystal clear. Wherever you are, if you're up to no good, we will find you.

The third – and most overwhelmingly likely possibility – particularly in the light of the way her mobile had briefly flared into life and then died again – was that Tia had simply turned it off.

Meaning she didn't want to be disturbed. Meaning her meeting – wherever that might be and whoever that might be with – was very definitely a private matter. Meaning also that I had no way of tracing where that might be and who that might be with. I was probably still only about thirty miles away from her but I may as well have been on a different planet.

I sank slowly onto a small sofa. I stared at the TV screen, now blank, my own face reflected on the monitor. There was only one thing I could now do and I was going to have to do it pretty well immediately. I had to get back into the loft – while Tia was still away – and find out just whose number she'd dialled and just who she had to see.

28

I DOWNLOADED THE software tracking Tia's mobile phone from the laptop into my own mobile. The smaller screen wouldn't provide anything like the detail I could access before, but that wasn't the point. The point was to tell me when Tia had turned her mobile back on. That meant she was probably on her way back to the loft, her mission of the moment accomplished, her meeting – with whoever – wherever – concluded.

Of course it was possible that she wouldn't turn her phone back on at all, that it would slip her mind or she'd keep it off for some reason. In which case I'd have no advance warning. The first I'd know of her approach would be hearing her key in the lock as I patrolled around inside the loft, searching for clues as to who she'd been to visit. In which case I could pretend I'd suddenly regained my memory and had returned home in her absence, citing the lack of response from her mobile as a reason why I hadn't alerted her in advance.

It was hardly ideal. Aside from anything else, should she decide to check the log on her mobile my number would be spectacularly absent, meaning I'd have to somehow get hold of her phone and reprogram the menu before she had time to check.

And there was the fact that I'd be caught on the hop. I was going to have to trust to some fairly rusty acting skills anyway with my original plan, but I would at least have been in control of the circumstances. Now I was at their mercy and the chances of carrying it all off with anything like my previous assurance was now severely compromised. I just had to hope that either I received sufficient advance warning of her approach or that Tia would decide to stay away from home for the whole of the time I was there.

That meant her meeting – with whoever – wherever – would have assumed an even more pressing importance – making it even more important in turn that I find out what it was all about. I felt now as if I was on the verge of some kind of breakthrough, on the edge indeed of justifying the whole extraordinary exercise that had so consumed both of us this last day or so and it would have been total folly not to see it through to its conclusion. Having come this far, to fall short now would be unthinkable.

I asked the hotel again to call a taxi for me. I gave the nearby station as the destination. The taxi arrived around ten minutes later. I watched it pull round the car park but waited till the receptionist buzzed me to tell me it was here. I didn't want anything to stand out about my request and my hovering outside in a clear state of impatience would certainly have done that. I wanted it to meld into the hundred and one similar requests received by herself and her colleagues every day.

It was as the taxi was pulling away that I told the driver of the change of plan but that was hardly any sort of problem so far as he was concerned. A round trip into the capital would be worth roughly ten times the fare of the short journey from the hotel to the local station if not more. Something like that didn't come along every day. Which was precisely why I'd waited till he'd pulled away from the hotel before broaching the matter. Again, I didn't want any curious receptionist thinking the same.

The driver had the radio on all the way. Some middle-of-the-road station playing popular hits mainly from years before, punctuated by regular news bulletins. Inevitably the train crash provided the lead story for every one of them. Relatives of those waiting for news were interviewed and most recalled reports of similar disasters in which victims had emerged alive and more or less well sometimes days after being incarcerated in wreckage or under rubble.

The driver tried to engage me in conversation about it all but gave up as he saw me concentrating on my mobile. All the way back to the loft no warning signal appeared. Tia was still out of mobile range for whatever reason.

I asked the driver to stop as close to the loft as possible so I'd only be on view on the street for the shortest possible period and to wait half an hour – ample time to accomplish what I now needed to achieve. I paid him in advance not only for the fare from the hotel but for the time he would also have to wait. He asked for a number to contact me in case of any problems such as the police moving him on. I debated whether to refuse then realised how strange that would sound and gave him an invented number instead, the loft landline but with a couple of digits transposed. Then I took a deep breath, exited the cab and headed down the street.

It was the strangest sensation, but one I had experienced before. When I was in my late teens my parents had left a house we'd lived in for years. They were moving to a smaller place and I was moving into an even smaller flat of my own. They left first – having further to travel – and I was deputed to hand over the keys to the estate agent who was coming to prepare the property for sale. The thought of missing the place hadn't occurred to me – the prospect of my own accommodation was too heady a prospect to be distracted by considerations such as those – and so it wasn't until I was actually outside the house, keys duly transferred, looking back at a door I used to walk through at will, that the oddest sensation engulfed me.

It was all so familiar and yet not familiar at all. It was a place that was mine and now – suddenly – was not. I stared at the front door, half-expecting it to change shape in some way, something to mark what suddenly felt like the most extreme of transitions, from a house that was a home to one that would from now on be locked and barred so far as I was concerned.

I had the same sensation as I approached the loft, a place that was mine, a home Tia and myself had made together, still there, unchanged externally and internally; yet it still felt like some threshold had been crossed, some border traversed. In the case of my previous family home that journey had become irreversible. The next half-hour would play some part in assessing whether the same applied here too.

I checked the alarm system which had been armed by Tia on her exit and made a mental note to adjust the log on the keypad on my way out. It was hardly likely that Tia would check the entry and exit log – it was hardly likely she'd even know such a facility existed – but, and as with everything at the moment, I wasn't taking any chances.

Inside the loft, all was as I'd viewed it via the various bugs on my laptop. For a moment I paused as I realised that waiting for me back in that ramshackle country hotel would now be footage of my own time there, ready to be played back on my return. I glanced, involuntarily, across at the radio alarm clock wondering – unable to help it – how I'd come across? Then I crossed to the phone and picked up the receiver.

The obvious button to press was LNR – the touchpad abbreviation for Last Number Redial. No-one else had been in the loft since Tia left so her mystery respondent – the man, woman, she simply had to meet – would have been the last number dialled. The problem being what would I say? How would I react when I heard that voice on the other end of the line? Would I recognise him or her immediately and would everything instantly fall into place for better or worse? Or would I be left on the other end of the line as puzzled as ever, totally unable to place the voice I'd just heard, completely unable to begin anything like a conversation; as much in the dark as I was right now in fact?

But what choice had Tia left me? She hadn't provided any other clue. She'd uttered no name as she greeted the voice on the other end of the line, gave no hint as to the location of the usual place. Also, while our landline phone boasted caller display it didn't sport an on-screen call log. I did have the option of calling our telecom provider and requesting a print-out of the last few numbers but I knew that while they were contractually bound to provide the information it wasn't the sort of detail they'd provide on the spot over the phone. They'd mail the log to the home address of the bill holder which might have made perfect sense from the point of view of confidentiality and security – a voice on the other end of a line requesting a specific number could be any sort of oddball with all sorts of dubious motives after all – but was precious little help to me in my current quest.

So I took a deep breath, tried to control the shake in my fingers as I picked up the handset, then pressed LNR.

For a moment, as I listened to the number, I stilled, unable to take in what I was hearing. Or more accurately, the implication of what I was hearing.

I kept staring as the same number was repeated again and again, but no matter how many times I pressed that redial button it was the same result.

The same number was coming up.

1471.

Which meant Tia, unseen by myself, had pressed those same four numbers herself – 1471 – just before she'd walked out. She'd clearly done it to erase from the log the immediate record of her last, actual, call.

But why? Tia couldn't have expected me to walk back in and check that number. So why was she attempting to hide it?

Or had it simply become second nature by now? Had she

become so used to subterfuge and deceit over the previous few months that she automatically erased all record of that number the moment she replaced the receiver? Was it by now a reflex action of some sort, the instant she stopped talking to whoever she had been talking to on the other end of the line, she made sure no-one – meaning, presumably, myself – could access that same number?

Then, from behind me, came a knock.

I wheeled round staring at the door. My caller was in the complex, meaning this wasn't some visitor dropping in, this was someone who either lived in one of the adjoining lofts or – and I was already starting to grow cold as the possibility occurred to me – someone who'd followed me inside, perhaps because in my understandable distraction I hadn't secured the exterior doors properly.

In which case the game was well and truly up. If I'd been spotted by someone who knew me well enough to actually follow me home, then that was that. It wouldn't matter if I did or didn't open the door. Even if they went away they'd still make it their business to contact Tia, to report the strange sighting, to tell her that during her absence a partner believed to be missing in tragic circumstances had coolly and calmly walked back into their home while the witness – whoever that might be – stared, presumably in blank incredulity, from across the street or from inside a nearby parked car. Either way, it was a story that was unlikely to be dismissed as fantasy or mistaken identity.

So did I cut my losses right there and then and abandon this charade? I'd intended to present myself restored to health and sanity and back in the land of the living to Tia and to Tia only. A third party hadn't come into the equation but now it seemed as if a third party might have to do so. No time to lose, acting on my sudden and enforced decision, I made for the door only for the letterbox to open and for a card to appear, pushed through from outside, falling down onto the wooden floor. Then I heard footsteps moving away from the door back down the communal corridor, heading for the stairway.

I moved cautiously to the door. I must already have become so used to living in a world of shadows and tricks that I was imagining some trick was about to be played now too. But nothing happened as I bent down to pick up the card. No voice sounded behind me. No presence suddenly announced itself.

I looked at the card. It was glued down loosely and a name was scrawled on the front. *Tia*. For another moment I wondered what to do but only for a moment. I couldn't have walked out of that loft without knowing what was inside that card and who had sent it. If I could open the card without damaging the seal too much I could leave it back on the mat for Tia to discover on her return. If I couldn't – if the evidence of my tampering was only too obvious – I'd have to take it with me and risk Tia finding out at some later stage that a card pushed through our internal letterbox had somehow vanished into thin air.

I pushed my finger carefully under an open part of the seal and slid across. The seal gave quite easily, there was just a small section at the corner that remained stuck for a moment but that then gave too. I slid out the enclosure and stared at a blank card on which a neighbour – identified by their name inside – had scrawled a simple message.

Thinking of you.

I exhaled a sigh of relief at the simple message of sympathy. I even felt a stab of gratitude at the kindness behind the gesture. In similar circumstances I was unsure whether it would have occurred to myself or Tia to do the same. We might have discussed the misfortune of a neighbour but whether we'd have acted on it in a similar way I couldn't say.

I smoothed down the flap. The envelope was now rather more dog-eared than before but as Tia wouldn't have seen it in its previous state she'd be unlikely to notice. Then I placed it back on the mat. I checked my watch – the half-hour I'd told the mini-cab driver to wait was almost up – took one last look round the loft, then made for the door.

Then, out of the corner of my eye, I saw a pile of papers open on one of the kitchen worktops, an area of the loft out of range of the camera from the bedroom. I glanced at my watch again. It was now getting dangerously close to the time the driver might decide I wasn't coming back and head away. Then again, returning with a fare on board was always going to be preferable to returning alone and the prospect of a healthy tip would also probably make him linger a little longer at least.

I crossed to the kitchen worktop and looked down at the papers face up on the surface.

Tia had searched out our life insurance policies. Mine and hers, although it was mine that was uppermost on the pile. We'd taken the policies out when we'd moved into the loft – a sensible precaution given the mortgage then involved. If anything happened to either of us it made sense that the survivor wasn't faced with financial problems as well. We hadn't thought a great deal about it at the time, had just signed the forms and put away the policies when they came through a few weeks later. I don't think either of us had looked at them since. They'd been buried in the bottom of some drawer somewhere along with a warranty on the Duke, documents we didn't really expect to have to retrieve.

Only Tia had retrieved them.

And she'd quite obviously been studying them before she went out too.

29.

O N THE WAY back in the taxi – and after first making sure the privacy light was on and the middle-of-the-road radio station was filling all available audio space in the front of the cab – I called Dom.

The phone was answered after two rings. Maybe it was a quiet day. His always-upbeat voice gave the name of the shop and wanted to know how he could help.

I plunged straight in, told him I'd made a couple of purchases from the store lately and now wanted to know if he sold any software to monitor a landline as well as a mobile.

As I expected, Dom replied immediately in the affirmative, no problem. Then I paused, well aware that the next request might sound rather more strange, even to the likes of Dom.

'Could this monitoring work retrospectively?'

'Retrospectively, as in?'

His voice was already growing cautious.

'As in providing a list of previously-dialled numbers.'

'As in dialled previously to the installation of the software?'

I paused again, aware how dubious all this must already sound.

'And where the caller has already taken steps to hide the identity of the call.'

And now it was the turn of the man with the shock of black hair to pause.

'There might be something. It's not the sort of software we'd normally stock but I can make enquiries.'

I heard the rustling of paper as Dom hunted out a notepad and pen.

'Can I call you?'

Something in his tone of voice told me he really didn't expect an affirmative and there was something else in his voice now too – some new note of intrigue almost – and I was soon to find out why.

'I'll call you.'

'No problem.'

'Have you any idea how long it'll take?'

And all of a sudden, right out of the blue, Dom came straight out with it.

'Is that Mr Connolly?'

I felt my breath catch in my throat.

'Is that Jack?'

I didn't respond for a few moments, my silence answering that sudden question only too eloquently of course.

Dom dipped his voice, becoming almost conspiratorial now as he hunched ever closer to the mouthpiece.

'Look, tell me to get lost, OK, it's just I do recognise the voice.'

Dom paused again.

'I guess I've special reason to remember you right now, yes?'

Now it was his turn to let the silence stretch but when he finally spoke there was a mixture of amusement and something else – admiration, respect indeed – in his voice.

'I've got to be honest, Jack, some of the losers we get in here, you wouldn't believe.'

Dom paused once more.

'I really like the interesting ones.'

TIA DIDN'T RETURN to the loft that night. I monitored her mobile and all the bugs in the loft from my laptop back in the country hotel, but there was no activity. Tia simply couldn't have been out of mobile range for the whole of that time.

As a precaution I called her service provider. I assumed the role of a careful user checking the coverage of various networks. I'd been let down badly in the past by one of their competitors, I told the sales agent, and didn't want to be abandoned in a similar fashion if I changed to them. The sales agent not only provided a reassurance as to their service but emailed – to a different account on my laptop – graphs detailing the extent and effectiveness of their coverage.

I studied the graphs. Wherever Tia might be – and I had to assume she was still somewhere in the capital – she wouldn't have been further than a few hundred metres from a transmitter.

Which meant that in addition to the landline bug Dom was currently researching, I needed some other device that wasn't going to place me at a similar disadvantage again when it came to monitoring mobile activity, something that would continue to operate irrespective of the operator. All of which made it something of an advantage that I was now one of his more interesting clients, to use Dom's own description. Other – perhaps more balanced – souls might have seen that as saying more about Dom than anything else, but I didn't care. At this stage I needed to grasp every opportunity with both hands.

One phone call later and we'd arranged to meet in the foyer of another, rather more anonymous, hotel a few miles down the road from my current bolthole. I'd spent a night there once years before. It was a favourite haunt for conferences and the foyer was always thronged with businessmen holding meetings. It was corporate and soulless and totally ideal for the purpose I had in mind right now.

That left the matter of the hotel I was staying in at present, home to myself and sundry assorted peacocks and that matter was decided fairly speedily too. The longer I stayed in the one location the easier it would be for any member of staff to remember me and to recall how I behaved during the time I was there. It was easier, less complicated, to keep moving. Maybe I'd even check into the businessmen's haven where I was to meet Dom. Questions of personal comfort didn't really come into the equation right now although the hotel in question was perfectly adequate on that score. All I needed was reliable and high-quality broadband access and the hotel scored more than adequately on that count too.

I went out into the gardens of the hotel to debate the next issue; that of transport. I was becoming increasingly uneasy using a taxi service all the time. The small town on whose boundary the hotel squatted had more than one company, but I'd seen drivers from the different companies chatting on the hotel forecourt as they waited for customers, swapping tales, chewing over the experiences of their respective working days. It was probably paranoia on my part but I wanted something more anonymous. I also wanted to be in control of any movements myself rather than at the whim of a hotel and a dispatch service. I needed, in short, transport of my own which was a relatively simple decision. How to secure that transport took rather more thought.

From the start I knew the kind of transport I needed. It had to be a bike of some description. Aside from any other consideration it has to be the most anonymous form of locomotion known to modern man. Underneath the protective leathers and helmet literally anyone could be riding that machine. I could ride down my own street in total confidence, secure in the knowledge that even if I were to pass Tia herself she probably wouldn't give me a second glance amongst all the dozens, sometimes hundreds, of riders weaving in and out of the usually-stationary traffic.

Not that I was planning to head home or anywhere near it. But no matter where I was planning to go I could travel anywhere at any time to meet anyone and not even begin to worry about being recognised. I could even walk into the lobby of that anonymous hotel making to remove my helmet as I did so, thereby checking out each and every soul in there before I removed it completely just to be on the safe side. Just to be sure that no-one would look up with a sudden light of recognition in their eyes.

But how to acquire a bike? I couldn't simply buy one – I'd taken the precaution of bringing some cash with me but it wouldn't stretch to a purchase of that type, and besides, a cash purchase – even if it was within budget – would still raise eyebrows, provoke the kind of interest and questions I very much wanted to avoid. And to purchase such an item on one of my credit cards was equally out of the question. If they weren't being monitored already, with my name now on a nationwide missing persons' list, they soon would be. One incautious purchase in an unlikely location and this whole fragile edifice really would come crashing down.

I had a similar problem with the second option. There was a hire company in the town – a quick trawl of a Yellow Pages left in one of the bedroom drawers established as much. But even the most casual of hire companies would insist on a check of the hirer's licence at least, even if they could be persuaded to dispense with a debit or credit card deposit. I had no way of knowing if my licence was being monitored along with my credit cards but once again it would have been total folly to take the risk.

Which meant – if I was serious about the bike option and the more I thought about it the more perfect an option it was – there was really only one course of action left.

I returned to my room to hear a beep sounding on my laptop.

Sometime in the last few minutes, while I'd been outside, Tia had arrived back in the loft.

Quickly, I moved across to the monitor, hit the space bar, a picture flashing up on screen a moment later. For a moment I blinked, stupidly, unable to take in what I was seeing. Tia was standing in the middle of our sitting room, something at her feet. It took another moment or two to realise just what that was, but maybe that was my brain crashing into denial mode, not allowing my mind to take in what I knew even then to be the incontrovertible evidence of my eyes.

Eddie – the venal pawnbroker from a few months before – was with her. And was not with her. That didn't exactly make a lot of sense I know, but then none of what I was currently seeing made any sort of sense either.

Eddie was stretched out on the floor at Tia's feet. Blood was seeping from underneath him. His eyes were open and his lips were already turning white. Tia was just standing over him, looking down, her eyes open too, staring, fixed.

As I watched, in dumb stupefaction, Tia knelt down and touched his cheek, but she really didn't need to.

It was all too obvious that Eddie was dead.

3 1 .

THIRTY MINUTES LATER I'd caught up on what had obviously been some quite momentous few moments in the loft.

Tia had moved away from Eddie and had gone out onto the balcony, presumably recovering – or attempting to recover – from all that had happened while I'd been out in the hotel gardens debating modes and methods of transport. But by the time she returned to the sitting room, white-faced but just about in control, I'd discovered exactly what had happened while I'd been away.

Replaying the surveillance feed, I watched as Tia had let herself back into the loft, bending to retrieve the well-wisher's card, only for a flicker of something – irritation perhaps – to furrow her brow less than a minute later as the internal doorbell sounded. Later, thinking more clearly, it was pretty obvious that her caller had been watching as she returned home, the proximity of Tia's return and the doorbell sounding was just too much of a coincidence otherwise. Tia crossed to the door, possibly expecting some concerned neighbour, maybe the one who'd left that card.

But it was Eddie who was standing in the doorway.

Tia stared for a moment, genuinely rocked by the apparition. Which wasn't much, but it was all he needed. Stepping inside the loft, he flipped the door back behind him, the deadlock crashing in as he did so, locking Tia and himself inside.

And I could now see the expression on Eddie's face and what I was seeing right now was all too predictable in a sense given Eddie's previous dealings, not only with the two of us but with most souls who strayed into his path.

What I was seeing was triumph. What I was witnessing was the most ultimate expression of gratification. If Eddie, right at that moment, could have offered up a silent prayer to the gods then he would have done so. He might have sought to put the two of us – and Tia in particular – at some sort of disadvantage in the recent past but that search was over. He truly had no need to do so any more, courtesy of a random act of mass misfortune. That had done it for him. Now, so far as he was concerned and with his quarry in a disadvantaged if not positively stricken state, she was well and truly at his mercy and he could do with her as he wished.

Eddie – being Eddie – didn't say any of that, of course. He didn't need to. All that flashed across the room from persecutor to persecuted was an inclination of the head from the former to tell the latter all she needed to know. But Eddie – being Eddie – needed to make some immediate gesture too, some concrete demonstration of the new order, some silent exercise of what he clearly felt to be his new-found power. And Eddie – being Eddie – did that in the single most effective way he could think of right at that moment in time and the single most effective way he could have thought of at any moment in time probably.

Tia had retreated back towards the window, but Eddie crossed the floor of the sitting room quicker than either Tia or myself might have expected for such a large and shambling man. He stopped a short – too-short – distance away, stared at Tia for a moment as if drinking in the prize before him, his fleshy lips already twitching in anticipation of the pleasures he might now sample.

Then his hand snaked out.

Tia didn't seem to register what he was doing for a moment. She moved away but her back was against the wall and now Eddie had her trapped and he reorientated himself, some sudden rush of blood to the head – or more likely other regions – temporarily ambushing him. But he now had his quarry in his sights or, more accurately, between his sweating fingers.

Tia shuddered as she felt the ball of his hand jam hard against the bone of her crotch. Before she could absorb that shock there was another, his fingers tightening underneath her, digging through the fabric of her clothes, his breath quickening all the while as Eddie dug deeper trying to force one or more of his scrabbling fingers up inside her; a doomed manoeuvre but that wasn't the point. The point wasn't the attempted intrusion. It was the fact Eddie felt he could even try.

In any terms it was assault of the most serious kind but in his mind it was quite obviously justified because he'd suffered a similar assault of his own. His property had been violated. Now it was his turn to mete out to one of the perpetrators a taste of her own medicine. Let her see how it felt. And it was more than that too, of course, much more. It was a promise of even more serious violations to come.

Only Eddie didn't get that far. He should have realised from his last attempt at a much more innocuous physical approach that Tia was never the type to let such advances pass lightly. He'd been felled to the floor by the brushing of a fingertip on a breast, had he been thinking even remotely clearly he must have expected something rather more extreme. And he got it. Tia twisted out of the grasp of those scrabbling fingers, reached out and closed her fingers around a large glass ashtray on a shoulder-high shelf only for Eddie to smash it, almost contemptuously, out of her hand, the ashtray shattering into glass shards as it fell on the floor.

Then Eddie reached out in turn, snatched up a large knife from one of the open-plan kitchen worktops. Tia stared at it, frozen, as Eddie brought it ever closer to her before – swiftly, almost expertly – slicing it through the waistband of her new, sleek, dress, now exposing her crotch before jamming his hand up against her pelvic bone once again, his fingers this time penetrating inside her.

Tia tried yelling but Eddie's other hand was now clamped across her mouth, his fingers forcing themselves ever deeper inside her at the same time. Tia tried pushing him away again but his grip remained iron-tight, his breath coming now in great excited gasps. So Tia did the only thing any other street kid from the Island would do in similar circumstances. She leant back a fraction before cannoning her forehead into the bridge of his nose.

Eddie crashed down onto the floor, his fingers slipping from inside her. As he fell, the back of his head smashed into one of the large shards of glass from the ashtray, the jagged sliver forcing its way into the rear of his neck where it severed one of his main arteries, killing him virtually instantly.

Then Tia had stared at Eddie, now at her feet, and at the blood beginning to coil underneath him.

Half an hour later, hardly knowing what I was doing, I'd checked out, said goodbye to the peacocks and had negotiated the few minutes' walk to the local station. The whole place was quiet, the town was just forty minutes away by train from central London making it commuter territory, meaning the platforms and small café area of that station would be packed from roughly seven in the morning till about eight-thirty and would once again be thronged with returning office workers in the early evening but for the rest of the time it would be graced only by the occasional shopper. Or, today, by a single male intent on theft.

Still on autopilot, I checked round the station car park as casually as I could manage right now. There was the usual collection of commuter cars, mainly gleaming off-roaders whose only off-road excursions were likely to be an occasional foray over the kerb of a local pavement, but at the bottom of a small slope was a section reserved for bikes.

For a second time, I checked the pay and display tickets tucked into the grips. Most were for one day only and if I had to opt for one of those then I would. But then, on one of the bikes, just out of sight of the ticket office but within sight, unfortunately, of the small station café, I came across the bike of my dreams and that wasn't down to the spec, although that was pretty impressive.

It was a BMW, F800ST. A quick check on the manufacturer's website, via my phone, told me it had a displacement 798cc engine, parallel twin horse power with a petrol tank that would hold just over 16 litres of fuel. Other features included heated grips and ABS, all of which was neat enough but what made it even more attractive was the pre-paid ticket tucked into the grip telling me its owner was going to be away for the next three days.

Next, I took a taxi into the town, approaching the rank from the direction of the platform, coinciding my approach with a train recently arrived from London so as to mingle in with a sprinkling of newly-arrived passengers. The driver in question was one of the – presumably dwindling – number I'd not used before. I alighted at the top of the main street and headed for a small Motor Factors I'd also found in the Yellow Pages. I kitted myself out quickly in the correct size helmet and totally anonymous leathers, paying by cash. I also bought a small budget range of tools. I took the items from the carrier bag provided, complete with the Motor Factors logo, transferred them to my small holdall, then disposed of the carrier bag complete with logo in a nearby bin.

Then I headed for another car park a short distance from the High Street, found another area reserved for bikes and using a screwdriver from the tools I'd just bought, removed a number plate of the same dimensions from a bike roughly the same age as the BMW back at the station. Then I took a taxi back to the station, checked the bike was still in place, that my eyes or memory hadn't played tricks on me. The incident with the breakfast card back in the crumbling country hotel was still niggling away at the back of my mind. But the bike, complete with ticket, was where I'd left it some hour or so before.

I went into the station café and ordered a coffee, bought a paper. The headlines still reported the train crash. After a short time I picked up my bag and went into the station toilet. There I changed into my leathers and headed back down the small slope to the Beemer.

This was another tricky moment. It wasn't the taking of the bike that bothered me. As any petrolhead will tell you, it's actually relatively easy to ride away on any machine. The classic technique is to use a pair of vice grips, clamping them as tight as possible to a flat head screwdriver for leverage. The screwdriver and vice grips were among the range of tools I'd purchased from the Motor Factors. You place the screwdriver into the ignition, holding the vice grips as you do so. Then – trying not to make any more noise than absolutely necessary – it's simply a case of hitting the screwdriver with a hammer, or anything with a flat surface if a hammer isn't available, turning the screwdriver with the vice grips at the same time and that's it. All the lights illuminate, meaning you simply then hit the start button and off you go.

That was all straightforward enough but the main matter of the moment was the owner of the bike itself. Was that owner known to the station or café staff? If the owner was a regular traveller there was always the possibility some member of staff might spot me taking his machine away. I'd made sure to pick a time when there were no customers in the café, but that still left the woman behind the counter and I'd seen a man from the ticket office coming out at what seemed fairly regular intervals for a cigarette break. Unfortunately there was no way of checking out this unwelcome possibility in advance. In this instance – and much as I hated doing so – I simply had to trust to luck.

A few moments later I sauntered up to the bike, fixing my helmet in place as I did so. It meant I'd have restricted vision for the actual theft but it also meant I could be on the bike and away in moments. The last thing I wanted was the sound of the engine firing up attracting the wrong sort of attention and then having to hang around by the idling bike trying, with fumbling fingers, to fix an unfamiliar helmet in place.

I took out the screwdriver, grips and small hammer making sure my body was between the bike and the windows of the station café. It took only a few seconds to fix the screwdriver with the grips and steady the hammer. Then – one blow later – the lights on the dash had illuminated. I stashed the screwdriver, grips and hammer back in the small holdall, swung myself onto the seat, pressed the button, selecting a gear at virtually the same time, let out the clutch and rode up the small slope, turning left out of the station, heading out of town along a winding country lane.

Nothing. No shout from the station café. No inquisitive member of the station staff coming out to challenge me as I rode away. I was just another traveller taking away his transport for the final leg of his journey home.

One stop in a lay-by a few moments later and the rogue number plate was fixed to the rear of the Beemer. The chances of the bike being reported stolen for another couple of days were remote, barring an unforeseen circumstance such as the owner returning earlier than planned. But even if the theft was now reported, the bike might be the correct make and model but the number plate wouldn't check out. It wouldn't prevent the bike being correctly identified if a police officer decided to check the chassis number. But that would mean actually stopping bike and rider to investigate further and there was no reason to do that and I didn't intend to give anyone such a reason either. There'd be no burn-ups on the ever-so-inviting dual carriageway that wound from the hotel back to the capital. For the next day or so this was one rider – perhaps the only rider in a large radius – who was going to observe, to the letter, the Highway Code.

And then – and only then – I finally allowed my mind to return to what had happened with Tia and Eddie. And its sequel which I'd also just witnessed a few moments before I quit the hotel.

Tia hadn't wasted any more time. She'd come back into the loft, picked up her mobile and made a call. I didn't hear the conversation as she went back outside to conduct it, standing on the balcony just as a jet flew past, low, heading for City Airport. But something told me she wasn't calling the police.

Sure enough, within ten minutes, a buzzer sounded on the entryphone. Tia checked the identity of the caller, quickly, and buzzed him in. Thirty seconds later a figure I vaguely recognised was standing next to Tia, staring down at the prone figure on the floor; and from the way Tia's visitor's nose wrinkled as he came in I could see that the loft was already beginning to smell of something decayed and evil which, I hoped, was just to do with the body that was already beginning to putrefy in its own congealing blood on our wooden floor. Then I placed him.

I'd come across Tia's caller some time before when he provided security at a shoot for a rock video that her company was overseeing. The producers expected all sorts of hassle from fans of the band, a weird collection of more than usually lunatic oddballs who veered from hero worship of their favourite act to making death threats against them, sometimes in the course of the same evening. I'd been contracted to take some stills which I already knew were destined never to be used. Moving image can be manipulated, it was less easy to do so with stills, and anyway in most of the images I'd captured the band looked, frankly, ordinary. The whole thing was further damned by the fact that the few fans who had managed to penetrate the security cordon spent the whole session listening in what used to be called respectful silence.

All in all, as Gene pointed out – Gene being the individual now standing next to Tia – the whole thing was more like a vicar's tea party than the red-hot riot he'd been led to expect. And he proceeded to spend the rest of the night detailing some of the exploits of the wilder individuals he'd looked after over the previous couple of years and some of the more excessive demands he'd attempted to service.

I'd written it off at the time as just so much hot air. Clearly I was wrong because Gene wasn't even remotely fazed by the sight that had just greeted him and was wasting little time in now engaging in an urgent debate as to what should be done about it too.

As was Tia. One thing and one thing only was quite clearly in her mind and that wasn't informing any authorities. She could easily have pleaded self-defence, but she didn't seem to have entertained the possibility even for a moment.

Swiftly, Tia updated Gene on who exactly Eddie was and what he did. Or used to do, at least. She also updated Gene on where he lived. She further confided her not-so-shrewd suspicion that Eddie wasn't exactly blessed with a large circle of friends or a wide and caring family.

So his closed shop would probably excite little comment or interest. Eddie was its sole proprietor. He had no business partner to account to, no employer or employees to consider. If he decided he wasn't going to open up one day that was his decision and his alone. If he decided not to open up for a good few days – even a week or so – then that was his business too. Everyone, after all, was entitled to a holiday.

And his silent flat would be unlikely to attract any undue interest either. Which, it was fast becoming clear, was why Gene was there. Gene was being deputed with the task of getting Eddie's body back there. Via the monitor, I stared at Tia in mounting disbelief. Tia didn't bat an eyelid.

'And then what?'

'What do you mean?'

'He's going to be found sometime.'

'It may not be for weeks, months maybe.'

Gene persisted.

'Then?'

'And if it is weeks or months then maybe it won't be any sort of issue anyway. After all that time maybe no-one's going to be able to say for certain how he died. He could have dropped that ashtray himself, maybe fallen on the splintered glass, maybe after he suffered a heart attack or something.'

I kept staring at Tia as if she was a stranger. Maybe she was. I'd seen examples of her ice-cold nature in the past as well as her talent to dissemble and deceive – take the Bristol house stunt for example. But this was on a whole different plane.

But then, as I kept listening in my mind strayed, a defence mechanism perhaps, displacement activity while I tried to absorb all I was hearing and seeing. All of a sudden a story I'd been told years before by Natsuo came into my head about this boy from a good, loving, family. She'd told me so many stories in the time we were together. All involved exiles from normal life, those who'd fallen through the cracks somehow and this story was no exception.

The boy had been adopted when he was an infant but there'd never been any issue or mystery about that, he'd been told about it from an early age. And from that early age he'd had all the love and attention anyone could wish for according to most independent witnesses as well as members of what was to become his grieving family.

As well as being blessed in the love and affection stakes, the family were comfortably off too. Not wealthy as such, but wealthy enough to afford a house in stockbroker commuter country in Surrey and to provide him with everything he desired to indulge his whims. So when he began to display an early talent for golf they enrolled him in their local club and arranged private lessons with one of the professionals.

The general opinion was that he was good. The general opinion also was that he was not great and you really needed to be to even contemplate making any real impact in that field. So all in all it was something of a surprise when he told his girlfriend – the boy was now seventeen – that he'd been accepted into a prestigious tournament in Florida. The invitation came complete with accommodation for himself and a companion as well as two club-class tickets and did she want to go with him?

What would any seventeen-year-old girl say to an offer like that? She said yes. Her parents required a little persuasion but a reassuring phone call from the father of the boy put their minds at rest. The boy and his girlfriend flew to Florida, the girlfriend visited Disneyland while the boy met up with the rest of the competitors in the tournament and played his matches. On the fourth night the boy returned to their hotel with the news that he hadn't actually won the tournament but had been sufficiently highly placed to earn an invitation to another tournament beginning in Dubai in eight days' time. Once again the same deal was on offer – accommodation for two plus two club-class flights from the UK and, once again, did she want to go with him?

The girlfriend felt like she was living inside the pages of some celeb magazine. She was being flown around the world at someone else's expense in the company of a sportsman boyfriend. Life simply didn't get much better at that age. The couple returned to the UK, the boyfriend showed his girlfriend's parents a plaque he'd received for his placing in the US tournament plus the invitation from the tournament in Dubai. The girlfriend went off to tell all her friends about her adventures. The boy returned to his proud and doting parents.

In fact the boy let himself into the family house and moved carefully past their bodies on the hall floor. He retrieved again the credit cards belonging to those dead parents which he'd used to finance his Stateside trip. And he then used their cards to withdraw a similar amount to finance his next trip to Dubai accompanied again by his completely unaware girlfriend.

I kept watching Tia and Gene as they now moved outside again, onto the balcony, Eddie's body still lying on the loft floor.

The phone call from the parent was later revealed to be from the boy himself. He was, if nothing else, something of a consummate actor. The plaques were purchased in a store devoted to sporting memorabilia with an inscription added later by a sign writer. The invitations were mocked up on a home computer and could have been done by a seven year old let alone a clearly ruthless and highly motivated teen killer.

Why had he killed? The police never found out and the boy, while not denying the crime, never said. Family members recalled tension over a different trip he wanted to make and which the parents, mindful of his upcoming school exams, were reluctant to finance. They could only speculate that the tension had escalated into a row which had further escalated into a full-blown attack. All that was relatively easy to explain if not to understand. What was inexplicable was the mindset that allowed a young man to not only murder his elderly parents but then take off on a succession of overseas trips, squiring his girlfriend to the fringes of tournaments that had never heard of him before returning to the family home, ignoring the bodies of the father and mother he'd murdered, to steal more money to finance yet another pleasure jaunt to some far-flung clime on some other totally fictional pretext.

By the time the police realised what had happened he'd been on two further trips. His girlfriend thought she'd died and gone to Heaven. When she found out the truth behind her recent holidays – and who they'd actually been financed by and in what circumstances – she thought she'd entered Hell. She had a breakdown from which she took the next year to recover.

How the police realised what had happened was a macabre little tableau all of its own. The parents hadn't been seen for a while but there were frequent sightings of the son as he popped back and forth, mowed the family lawn, put out the bins. One neighbour did enquire after the parents at one point, only to be told by the cheerful boy that they'd gone away on holiday before showing the same neighbour a postcard that had arrived from them that very morning from the Seychelles.

It was a week or so later that the neighbour first noticed it although even then he didn't act immediately. He knew the parents were still away and he assumed the son must have put some dark material up over the windows, perhaps to protect the furniture inside from the effects of the sun. It was now mid-summer and the light was strong. For a day or so he didn't think too much about it but then one afternoon, mowing his own lawn, he stopped, puzzled, as he saw the dark material apparently move. He decided it must be a trick of the light but when he was cleaning down his machine the same thing happened again. The sunlight was now full on the window and the dark material was definitely moving. The neighbour hesitated a moment, then opened the gate and went up the drive. As he drew closer he could see that his eyes hadn't been deceiving him and this was no trick of the light either. It was as if the whole window was moving which, in a sense, it was. It took him a while to realise just what he was looking at.

Flies. Thousands and thousands of flies, packed around the window so tightly they looked, from a distance, like a giant black shroud. Even from a good few metres away he could hear the sound of their angry buzzing as the insects attempted to get out into the sunlight, presumably to attempt to feast on more of the same treats they'd gorged on inside. Half an hour later a specialist police team forced their way into the house to discover two bodies submerged beneath another black shroud of milling insects, unrecognisable even as human beings by then, just a decayed mass of exposed tissue and blood.

I replayed the story in my head, transposing the scene to Eddie and his flat. In Natsuo's story it was initially impossible to determine exactly how the father and mother had died. But the guilt of the son was clear, not just because he'd been seen by several independent witnesses entering and leaving the house over the period his parents were quite clearly lying dead inside; but also because he offered no defence. He simply nodded as the facts of the matter were put to him and only spoke once, to ask if he could keep the plaques he'd had engraved with the record of achievements he'd not earned.

So if Eddie's body was left undiscovered for a similar period then the same process would occur. The same problem over determining how he'd met his death would arise. And – assuming no-one saw Gene entering or leaving Eddie's flat as he deposited his inconvenient cargo – then the police would have little option but to consign this case to the rear of whatever filing cabinet housed similarly hopeless investigations.

3 2 .

STILL ON A strange kind of autopilot, I swung back past the hotel taking care to avoid the vicinity of the station, although – and still desperate to fill my mind with anything save all I'd just witnessed – I'd decided that the chances of the owner of the Beemer being a regular commuter were on the slim side now I paused to think about it at least half-rationally.

If he was local, why abandon an upmarket bike in a station car park for three whole days? Why not tuck it up safely back at home? Then again, the thief who'd taken it had done so for the express purpose of perpetrating a gigantic confidence trick on his partner and was now about to embark on a further refinement of the same. All of which only went to prove that sometimes people did things for reasons other than the strictly rational, so I still avoided the station like the plague.

There was the same long straight past the hotel before it ended in a T-junction and just for a moment and despite everything that had happened in the last hour or so – or maybe even because of it – an all-too familiar urge came over me to floor the throttle, to watch the nose of the bike rise, feel the wheels dig into the tarmac as they scrabbled for grip before rocketing, bullet-like, along the road, adrenalin coursing through me like an electric charge as it did so.

Which would have been lunacy. It also meant I'd have broken the solemn promise I made myself regarding the rules of the road within roughly thirty seconds of setting off. My hand hovered over the throttle but I didn't press down. For one second – two – three – I stayed in that excruciating limbo. Maybe, having spent so long simply waiting and watching, I was desperate now for something to happen, something to actually do, where I could take charge, direct my own destiny and not wait for it to be decided by persons viewed from the other side of a laptop, living by some sort of remote control. Or maybe I just wanted to indulge in the automotive equivalent of a giant, tension-releasing, scream.

For those few moments, nature battled nurture. Instinct went head-to-head with reason. For those few moments the laws of evolution laboured to impose themselves. Primitive cavemen might have given in to baser impulses, modern-day city dwellers were expected to exercise rather more self-control.

As I did.

For the first three of those four seconds anyway.

Then I jammed down the throttle, the nose rose, the back wheels squealed and the bike shot towards the T-junction where the high-performance brakes stopped it on what used to be called a sixpence.

I took a right onto the main road, a huge grin illuminating my face, wiping everything else for that one, single, blessed, diversionary moment.

One second later that smile wiped in turn as through the mirrors I caught a glimpse of a uniformed traffic cop sitting astride a bike that would easily catch, if not outstrip, the Beemer, watching me as I drove away.

Quickly, I contemplated my options. There were four exits off the next roundabout and three of them would take me onto country roads with any number of options after that. The fourth – my preferred route – would take me onto a dual carriageway with the first exit not presenting itself for at least three miles. Plenty of time for the uniformed cop to do a quick check on the number plate of the bike that had just screamed past him before setting off in close pursuit. The front wheels of the Beemer wobbled slightly as I banked to take the roundabout as if sensing the indecision in its rider. Then I pressed the throttle again – the thought of skulking round those country lanes for the next hour or so just too much to bear – and I took the exit that would sweep me down the dual carriageway before cutting through two more commuter towns to the anonymous hotel and Dom.

For the whole of those three miles I kept my eyes glued to the rear view mirrors expecting at any moment to see a telltale flash of light as a bike began to approach behind. A glint of sunlight reflected off a passing lorry convinced me briefly that the vision had just assumed concrete shape. But nothing happened. No police rider appeared. Maybe he'd done the calculations regarding the roundabout and decided the odds were stacked just that little too much against him. Or maybe he just didn't care.

I didn't replicate that moment of madness for the whole of the ride down through the two commuter towns, crawling past schools and arcades of shops at the regulatory speed, slowing for pedestrian crossings, pausing for gaps in the traffic at the various roundabouts rather than, as was more usual, powering through any and every fleeting opening in the oncoming traffic. Nurture finally triumphed over nature.

I joined the motorway for a short hop down two further junctions which was when I saw it. A flash of light in the rear view mirror. I slowed, peering into the mirror and there it was again. Another flash, only the lights were too wide apart to be a bike, the police rider hadn't been playing me all the way down through commuter-land, lulling me into a false sense of security before he finally pounced. I relaxed, powering up the Beemer, only the lights stayed steady behind. They didn't fade into the distance, meaning the driver had increased his speed to match. Or maybe he'd just increased his speed. For a moment the extent of my occasional self-absorption – which now extended to other motorists deliberately keeping pace with me as if I was pulling them along on some sort of invisible string – rocked even myself. Then, before I even realised it was there, the car with the illuminated headlights screamed past, close, too close, the draught churning the air in front of me, the sudden turbulence rocking the front wheel of the bike as I fought to keep control.

I looked ahead, immediate drama over, to see the car, a mid-range Jag, slowing now, the driver throttling back, almost idling compared to the speed he'd just reached racing past me.

It happened of course. Every biker had a million similar war stories. It wasn't just the drivers at intersections who drove straight at you or the ones who pulled out to overtake just as you were overtaking in turn, sending you straight into a close encounter with a horn-blaring, brake-squealing lorry. There were also the ones who'd never seemed to have heard of the laws of physics, who swept past so close the hapless biker could have hitched a tow in the slipstream although he'd be more likely to take a nosedive into the nearest ditch.

But those drivers were usually either stupid or unaware. This one seemed neither and this wasn't me decoding the actions of a man I still couldn't even properly see in a car I'd never seen before. There was something almost deliberate in the way he was slowing now as if he was waiting for me to catch up, as if the sport of the day wasn't entirely over. I could have been wrong but I really didn't think so and decided to test the waters by checking the mirrors, then hitting the throttle, driving up almost to the boot of the car in question, before sweeping down a long, gentle slope and up the other side. Then I throttled back, checking the mirrors again for the telltale flash of light that would tell me he'd responded in kind.

Nothing. No approaching lights, no wailing engine fighting the upper reaches of its rev limit. I slackened off, keeping a wary eye on the mirrors but as I pulled off the motorway a short time later, idled up to the traffic lights on the roundabout, I began to concentrate again on another of the real matters of the moment, the upcoming meeting with Dom.

Which was when the Jag driver pulled alongside. Actually he pulled a short distance ahead as he wasn't taking the same river-bound exit that I was taking, but was heading instead for the local town. I looked across at him but all I could see was the back of a head as he stared straight ahead. Both sets of lights changed at the same time and he moved on, taking a right around the roundabout as I eased out the clutch and went left. From there it was a short run down the hill to another exit, over another roundabout, then down the road that would take me, somewhat improbably for a relatively upmarket hotel, through an industrial estate to its front door.

Once again my mind drifted to Dom, working out what I wanted to say, what I wanted from him, how he might help me break the unexpected deadlock.

I felt it rather than saw it. A rush of approaching air that spelt danger, sudden and acute and then, before I could react, it was upon me. The mid-range Jag, which had obviously completed a full circle around the roundabout before following me down the hill, was now alongside me again and this time there was a screech of brakes, the wheels locking as the driver hit the pedal, drifting the car across the carriageway, coming at me sideways now, turning his vehicle into the widest possible weapon, leaving me virtually no opportunity to evade what seemed in that moment to be an inevitable collision.

In that split second I had two choices, brake or accelerate. Neither was anywhere near guaranteed to avoid an impact but to do neither really was to invite disaster with open arms. So I accelerated. For a moment, the Jag closed in on the rear wheel of the bike as I rocketed ahead. Then, inches to spare, it missed, clipping the verge instead, the driver keeping the throttle down himself meaning he very much knew how to handle that machine, before opposite-locking it back onto the carriageway, shooting past the exit I'd just taken up onto another roundabout, the driver disappearing under a bridge below.

Dom was bent over his laptop as I walked into the hotel lobby. He'd tucked himself into a quiet corner where no-one could see what he was looking at on his screen and didn't look up the whole time I was approaching. But he still seemed to know I was there. Maybe he was already demonstrating some new toy he wanted to show me. Or maybe the man really did have some sort of sixth sense.

I kept the conversation short and business-like. For now anyway I didn't want to think about anything other than the immediate problem of tracking the movements of my partner.

'No problem.'

I looked at him.

'Really?'

'Which is what I could have told you over the phone, there was no need to meet up in some shitty hotel, miles from anywhere.'

Dom smiled at me.

'Maybe you should open up a little. Learn to trust a touch more.'

It was already inappropriate. He was playing with me and enjoying it. In a different world and time, I might have enjoyed it too although I severely doubted it. For now I just wanted to get my hands on whatever gizmo he'd spirited away from the store and be on my way to somewhere else, anywhere else, somewhere, preferably, without roads.

Dom handed me a small, unmarked, box.

'This should do the trick. Logs into the signal beamed to the mobile even if the mobile isn't turned on. The police use it all the time to track the kind of people who don't want to be traced. A couple of companies – mainly of the outlaw variety – have found a way to block it but from what you were telling me this partner of yours isn't exactly rubbing shoulders day-in day-out with organised crime, right?'

I didn't reply. I didn't know who the hell Tia was rubbing shoulders with right now. Which was sort of the point.

'And the best thing of all is you don't need to get hold of her phone to set it all up.'

'How does that work?'

'So long as she turns her mobile on once she's back home, we can use one of the other bugs to provide a frequency match. Doesn't matter where the little lady goes after that, you'll be able to track her.'

I took my laptop out of the small bag I'd stashed in the pannier of the Beemer, held it out to him.

'Show me.'

Dom fired up my laptop.

'And the other device, the one that can log retrospective calls?'

But Dom ignored that for now, nodded down at his laptop instead.

'I came across this just before you came in too.'

He pushed his machine across to me while mine was still wheezing into what, in computer-land, passed for life. For a moment I stared at the screen, couldn't really take in what I was seeing.

Faces. Dozens and dozens of faces. Smiling faces, sad faces, serious faces, haunted faces. All of them posed individually but combined into some strange kind of montage. A Sgt. Pepper tableau with, so far as I could see, no odd costumes. Almost all the faces were complete strangers to me aside from one to the left of the frame. That was my face staring out at the camera. I had problems identifying the provenance of the shot for a moment – it was from some years before without doubt. But where had it been taken and more to the point who had supplied the picture and why? Then I realised. It was a staff shot from a magazine I'd once worked for briefly on a freelance basis. Which cleared up one mystery and another was about to be cleared up now too courtesy of Dom.

'The committee coordinating the rescue efforts put it online a few hours ago. They were going to be put up on a few billboards too but that's such a bad idea, right? Any one of these faces could suddenly appear – or not – any time at all and imagine the fuss there'd be having to paste up new posters all the time.'

Dom nodded back at the screen.

'This is much better. Just one stroke of a key.'

Dom demonstrated, briefly removing my face from the montage, shading the faces immediately around my own to fill the gap.

Dom hit another key and my face reappeared once again.

I looked at him, still blank.

'These are all the people still missing – or presumed to be still missing – at the crash site.'

'And they've put them all together for?'

'Process of elimination. Some of these people may be somewhere else entirely. Some of them might have been nowhere near the crash site at all, just presumed to be by panicky relatives. The idea is that a few of those people might see this, realise that some other people somewhere are worrying about them, so then they get in touch and, hey presto.'

Dom hit the first key again and once again my face disappeared from the tableau.

'They rejoin the land of the living again.'

Then Dom looked up. For a moment I thought I was going to get some sort of admonishment for putting those nearest and dearest to me through this sort of ordeal. But that didn't explain the frown that had suddenly furrowed his brow or the new hesitation in his manner. Dom, it seemed, had more pressing matters on his mind right now than simple matters of morality.

'What's happened?'

'What do you mean?'

Dom turned my laptop round so the screen was now facing us both. For a moment – one awful moment – I thought he was somehow seeing the pictures I'd seen just a short time before, Tia and Eddie, impossible I knew, but so much had happened in the last few hours it was no wonder demons were starting to multiply within.

But the screen was blank.

'You need to activate the software.'

'I have.'

I stared at him again, then took the laptop from him, retraced the steps I knew already he'd have taken just moments before, clicking on the icons that accessed the various bugs in and around the loft.

Still nothing.

The screen remained blank.

'Problem with the laptop?'

Dom took it from me again, didn't say a word. It was the only reasonable explanation and we both knew it. The bugs came with their own individual software and were installed into different folders on my hard drive. It was inconceivable that every single one should have failed at exactly the same time – and in the short time that had elapsed between my signing on back in that peacock-infested country hotel and now.

So why had both Dom and myself fallen silent?

Dom took out a cable, fed it from a port on my laptop to his own, waited a few seconds, then disconnected. Then he hunched forward, hit a couple of keys and waited. I didn't need him to turn the screen round again to tell me what I already knew.

My laptop was working perfectly. His laptop was working

perfectly as well. So were the individual pieces of software that governed the various bugs. But nothing was coming through to either my laptop or his.

Which meant that every bug in the loft had indeed gone down at exactly the same time.

A thought struck me.

'Tia's computer.'

Dom nodded, way ahead of me.

'Her last session's stored from a few minutes ago.'

'Nothing since?'

'And there won't be either.'

Dom turned the laptop screen towards me again.

'The USB stick's been removed.'

'Removed?'

'Taken out of the port. Has to have been, it's not registering on the software either.'

Across the lobby a small group of businessmen milling by the door laughed at some anecdote told by one of their number. A sole girl, uncomfortable and out of place, affected a strained smile.

Dom was looking at me, curious.

'Explanation?'

I kept staring at the screen.

'I don't know.'

'Could your partner have worked it out, come home, taken everything down?'

'No chance.'

'So what's happened?'

I paused again. Across the lobby the girl smiled again, ever more tense, as more raucous laughter sounded. She didn't understand a single word her colleagues were saying and obviously didn't want to.

I stared beyond Dom out at a man-made lake behind the

hotel and at a fountain – little more than an underwater jet in truth – spouting water a few feet into the air. I knew exactly how she felt.

'I don't know.'

I didn't stay in the anonymous hotel. I was already coming to the conclusion that hotels weren't exactly the best kind of hiding places right now and that was before Dom had shown me the billboard-type montage of faces missing or presumed still missing from the train crash. The crash itself was still big news. All across that lobby sundry assorted business types were accessing their own laptops, checking emails. Any of them in an idle moment could easily click on the same image, look up from the screen to see a face remarkably similar to the one they'd just seen staring out at them from among so many others. I was just too visible and now, with the publication of my image online, I was becoming – ridiculous thought but true nevertheless – too high profile as well.

I'd come across an agency that specialised in short-term apartment rentals some time before. Myself and Tia had used them a couple of times when we were planning on staying more than a few days somewhere. After a while, no matter how fine the dining in some luxury hotel, it was simple pleasures we wanted and an apartment fitted the bill perfectly. I couldn't use my credit card to secure the booking but I did manage to persuade Dom to use his card to do so, after receiving strict assurances that it was simply a guarantee and that I'd be settling the bill myself on departure. The transfer of the relevant amount of cash for the deposit in question helped in persuading him and half an hour later I was steering the Beemer out of the hotel car park and heading for a town some four or five miles distant.

The agency had sourced a two-bedroomed apartment on the outskirts, but with easy access to the rail station, I was assured. It was hardly a selling point at present but I didn't bother pointing that out. I just took a note of the address on a hotel notepad lying on a nearby table, jotted down the access codes for the building and the emergency number in case the codes failed to operate properly. There was no full-time receptionist on site, the hard-pressed duty manager oversaw several such apartment complexes in the town as well as surrounding towns but she was always within a few miles drive of any of her customers, I was also advised.

On the short drive down I allowed myself to do what I hadn't done up to then. Little matters like my fake disappearance, previously so all-consuming, had now very much taken a back seat in my mind. For those few moments the unintended consequence of it all, Eddie's attack and Tia's retaliation, was also – momentarily at least – relegated in the priority stakes. Now I allowed myself to think about my companion on that equally short hop down the motorway and his two attempts on that journey to seriously injure, if not kill me.

Because if that's not what that driver was trying to do – seriously injure or kill me – then what was behind all that? What other game was he playing? And if that was the game, then why? What possible reason could he have for acting like that?

It could have been a simple lunatic of course, one with a hatred of motorbikes, Beemers in particular. Maybe his wife or girlfriend had dumped him for a biker and something inside him just snapped.

Twice.

That was the seriously spooky part. A sudden explosion of fury was possible. Immediate help, if not even more immediate incarceration, should be sought for the perpetrator. But twice? That was no explosion of fury. That was cold. Controlled. And the way he'd distracted me by taking the right turn at the roundabout when I was going left was very much a cool and controlled manoeuvre too. So it was deliberate. Premeditated.

It was all too big, too strange to take in, especially right now. Perhaps if Dom hadn't shown me the montage, if we hadn't discovered all the bugs in the loft had suddenly been rendered inactive, I might – cautiously – have said something, used him as some sort of sounding board, rehearsed with my new companion the options and possibilities that were reverberating inside my helmet-clad head right now.

But all that had to take its place in a world that had suddenly turned strange and cold in more ways than that. And perhaps it said something about my current priorities that it was the bugs in the loft suddenly becoming inactive that was once more soon dominating my thoughts even more than some apparent attempt to rid the earth of the person who'd planted them.

I pulled up outside the apartment half an hour later. There'd been no further attempts to force me from the road in that time for which small relief I muttered heartfelt thanks as I stashed my helmet in the pannier, retrieved the hotel notepad on which I'd jotted down the access codes and emergency number.

For a moment I half-expected to stare at a totally blank sheet of paper. No access code, no emergency number, no indentations on the page beneath that might bear testimony to that access code and number ever existing. Perhaps even no hotel notepad at all. But the world hadn't turned quite that strange yet. The code and number were there. The address matched the apartment. Some small part of the universe at least was still in some sort of balance.

As I opened the door of the apartment, the access codes working exactly as the agency promised, the phone on the table in front of me started to ring.

I DIDN'T KNOW what to do for a moment. I just stood in the doorway staring at the ringing phone.

Then I took a deep breath, composed myself. There were two possibilities now I started to think all this through and neither presented any sort of problem.

Possibility number one; it was the agency checking everything was OK, the kind of common courtesy I probably should have expected. I'd have to field a solicitous-sounding voice assuring me of their best attentions and reassuring me that should I have any sort of problem during my stay they would be on hand.

Possibility number two; it was a call for the previous tenant and an even shorter conversation would clear up the confusion and ensure I wasn't disturbed in the same way again.

I picked up the phone and spoke, cautiously.

'Hello.'

There was a momentary pause which, I was to realise when the caller finally spoke, was a man relishing a moment.

'Hey.'

It was neither the agency nor some mistaken caller seeking a previous tenant. It was Dom.

I all-but exploded.

'How the hell did you get this number?'

'You're asking a guy who spends his life tracking people how he traced you?'

'Don't be so fucking stupid.'

'Oh, relax will you.'

'You haven't answered my question.'

'The agency called me. You guaranteed the reservation on my card, remember?'

I paused.

'And I couldn't call your mobile, could I, seeing as how you've had it turned off for – .'

Dom paused.

'Two days, four hours and eighteen minutes.'

I frowned, still not thinking clearly, still a few seconds behind even the simplest conversation right now.

'What are you talking about?'

'That's how long it's been. Since the train crash. It says so on the website, the one I showed you.'

I cut across.

'What do you want?'

Dom paused again.

'Just a thought, that's all. Tell me if this is none of my business.'

'Go on.'

'That insurance policy.'

'What?'

'The one your partner was looking at.'

I'd mentioned that to Dom too. I didn't really know why. Maybe it was an attempt to justify the unjustifiable. Who knows?

'It was in a pile of other papers.'

'All to do with insurance, right?'

Why had I told him all that? He hadn't seemed surprised that I had, had even seemed to accept it as somehow his due and maybe it was. In his line of work Dom had clearly become used to the outpourings of seriously stranger characters than even the occasionally deranged figure I'd turned into right now. Plenty of callers to his shop seemed to have treated the whole exercise as something of a confessional.

I conceded the point.

'All to do with insurance.'

'Then you need to take care, my friend.'

'I don't understand.'

'If that partner of yours – .'

'Tia. Her name's Tia.'

'Right. If she's already acted on the claim – .'

'I don't know that, all I saw was the policy.'

'But if she has and then all of a sudden you're found or you turn up – .'

Dom hesitated and I stepped in again, now growing evermore impatient.

'If I'm found, if I turn up, I'm not dead, meaning the insurance company don't pay out, meaning no problem.'

'Or they might think this is a scam that's gone wrong. That the two of you had cooked up some crazy con to score some cash and maybe you'd had some big row or something or you'd found out she was planning to cheat on you in some way.'

'But we haven't had any big row and I haven't found out she is planning to cheat on me.'

I stopped. That wasn't strictly true of course. Tia was doing something behind my back. It might not be anything to do with a fraudulent insurance claim but there was some subterfuge involved here otherwise I'd have been back in the loft right now consigning all this to history.

'I'm trying to look at this from their point of view. When this sort of accident happens they get it all the time. Someone always tries to score an easy payout. I was reading about it the other day, they're taking a really hard line on it all.'

'Tia won't have put any sort of claim in yet.'

'She'd just pulled out those policies because she fancied a little light reading?'

I paused.

'I don't know.'

Dom paused too.

'Just a word to the wise.'

A few minutes later, Dom cut the call leaving me in the small hall staring at a brochure detailing some local attractions. There was also a guide to nearby restaurants and a small map showing the location of some local shops. Someone had scrawled a number at the bottom of the flyer. Later, in an idle moment – and double-checking there was nothing sinister about that seemingly innocent annotation – I'd discover it was the number of a local massage parlour.

I checked out the rest of the apartment which was pretty standard. There was a lounge area off the open-plan kitchen, a bathroom at the end of a hall, a bedroom along the hallway from the bathroom and a smaller second bedroom beyond that. There was also a small garden area outside the lounge fenced off from the next apartment, but something about the mildew on the wooden furniture told me it didn't see much sun. Which was fine as I didn't intend to see too much of the small garden either. For now, all I wanted to do was check out, via the record facility on the now non-live software, if anything had happened with Tia before the driver of that mid-range Jag had attempted to turn me into roadkill.

I fired up the laptop and accessed the memory bank. I hadn't dared do that while Dom was around.

Tia was now alone in the loft, Gene was gone, Eddie's body was removed. There was about half an hour of material on there before the bugs mysteriously failed or were disabled in some way, it was still impossible to tell.

Two matters quite clearly now dominated for Tia. Regular, again almost metronome-like, calls to the dedicated emergency line established there was still no news regarding my current status.

For the second of those matters, Tia was now in front of her desktop affording me an unwitting grandstand view of all she was doing. Which was researching the grisly subject of human decomposition.

I knew why she was doing it. I could almost hear her voice justifying it all. If she'd been able to talk to me right now she'd be telling me that she needed to know just when a body might have decomposed to the point when – courtesy of smell or whatever – it would inevitably be discovered. She'd want to prepare herself, so she'd claim, for the intense police inquiry that would also inevitably follow. If she really was going to front this out she had to be ultra-prepared.

I think both of us would have known that there was something else at work here. Some innate fascination with the effects of her actions over and above the understandable desire to escape their consequences perhaps. But neither of us would have dragged that somewhat disturbing notion out into the open.

From Tia's on-screen researches I discovered, along with my partner, that once death occurs human decomposition takes place in stages. The actual process of tissue breakdown may take from several days up to – incredibly enough – a few years although the first, fresh stage of decomposition occurs during the very first few hours.

There's no physical signs of decomposition during this time, but cellular and soft tissue changes would be occurring because of a process called autolysis which is the slow destruction of cells and organs. At this point the body enters what the medical profession calls algor mortis, which is the cooling of the body temperature to that of its surroundings.

When the body cells reach the final stage of autolysis an anaerobic environment is created, literally an environment where oxygen is not present. This allows the normal bacteria of the body to break down any remaining carbohydrates, proteins

282

and lipids, the products from the breakdown creating acids and gases.

Which is when the visitors are attracted, beginning with diptera – or flies to the layman – which first begin to lay their eggs on the body. Then putrefaction causes colour changes and bloating of the body with the lower part of the abdomen turning green due to bacteria activity in the cecum. Bacteria breaking down haemoglobin into sulfhaemoglobin apparently causes the green colour. A formation of gases then enters the abdomen which forces liquids and faeces out. The gases also enter the neck and face causing swelling of the mouth, lips, and tongue. Due to this swelling and misconfiguration of the face, identification of the body can be difficult although Tia clearly couldn't rely on that in the case of Eddie. It was still going to be pretty obvious just who was concealed beneath all that.

Bacteria also leads to the formation of red streaks along the veins but this soon changes to green through a process known as marbelisation, a process first seen on the shoulders, chest and shoulder area, and thighs. The skin then develops blisters and becomes fragile leading to skin slippage, making it difficult to move. Body hair will also now come away easily. The discolouration from green to brown then marks the transition of the early stage of putrefaction to the more advanced.

After the body goes through the bloating stage it begins to further putrefy and blacken. At this point the body cavity ruptures and the abdominal gases escape allowing for a greater invasion of scavengers, meaning insect activity increases. This stage ends as the bones become visible, which can take anywhere from ten to twenty days after death.

After the early putrefaction phases have taken place, mummification begins and the body begins to dry out. Body odour now actually reduces and there's the formation of what appears to be almost a cheesy appearance on the cadaver. At this stage most of the internal organs would have been lost due to the attentions of the insects.

When the last of the soft tissue has been cleared from the body, the final stage of decomposition, called skeletonisation, occurs. This stage encompasses the deterioration of skeletal remains and is the longest of all the decomposition processes.

Then I saw the sketches by the side of Tia's screen. They were difficult to work out at first, just seemed strange doodlings. But then I realised that Tia was sketching the different stages of decay. She was actually placing herself in Eddie's flat, alongside his body, imagining the physical deterioration. Again, if challenged, she'd have defended it, I could almost hear her again. When the body was finally discovered, when the police – as they must – began those inquiries, she'd need to understand exactly what had happened, couldn't risk any stray detail dropped apparently innocently by the police in the course of any subsequent interrogation that might shock her into any sort of inappropriate response. The more she knew the better she would be able to guard her reactions.

And as I kept looking at her, the same question hammered inside my head.

Who are you?

Who – the fuck – are you?

Then the recording ended as the bugs, unaccountably, all went down.

I stood, paced the small apartment. At that moment, and so far as my apparent disappearance was concerned, I was naked. With the bugs in the loft all down I had no clear way forward. I couldn't access Tia's mobile even indirectly to plant Dom's super bug. I certainly couldn't go back again to plant the device necessary to retrospectively access all calls on the landline either, as Dom had also explained I'd have to do. All I could do, it seemed, was wait and hope that some glitch somehow – although Dom really didn't understand how it could have happened – had knocked out all those different bugs at the same time and that somehow – although Dom again didn't see how such a thing was possible – they'd all suddenly be restored back to life again.

In the meantime I waited and wondered and speculated, tearing myself into ever smaller pieces all the while. I felt as if was going mad with frustration. I had to do something, had to take action, any sort of action, it didn't matter what so long as I could cling onto the illusion at least of purposeful activity, lest those inner demons began to multiply again.

Early the next morning I rose from a sporadic sleep, moved down the hall and walked out of the apartment. All of a sudden I knew where to go and what I had to do.

34.

FIVE MINUTES LATER I was back on the Beemer. Ten minutes after that I'd negotiated the last of the roundabouts that would take me onto the motorway back to London. Each one had been taken smoothly and with no heroics, even when a Harley cut in ahead of me with a clear if unspoken invitation to have a little fun. I kept the throttle barely open, didn't even offer the ghost of a response and the Harley soon got bored. All the time I watched every road-mounted camera, checked the mirrors. But the police were conspicuous only by their absence. I swung down onto the motorway, observing the same statutory limit and settled into the ride.

The traffic was lighter than normal. With massive disruption inside the city still, many had chosen to work from home. With the local transport links in chaos, schools in the immediate vicinity of the accident had also closed adding to the uncharacteristic calm on the normal highways from hell. It was unwelcome of course. I wanted, indeed needed, traffic piled high along every road. With everyone else keeping away I was all the more visible. But I had to put that to the back of my mind. For now I just kept travelling.

I was heading for Joseph's house. I'd been reassured by the seemingly-clear display of friendship and nothing else that I'd witnessed during his visit to Tia, but the sudden failure of all the bugs was now making me question everything. In my eagerness to believe the best of my partner I might have put too generous a gloss on all that, might have been too inclined to dismiss as simple affection, gestures and embraces that were anything but.

Had it all been some sort of act? Was Tia – ridiculous

thought, I knew – already aware she was being watched? Had every move of that encounter from arrival to departure been choreographed in some way, agreed in advance somehow? Had I watched a rehearsed exchange as opposed to the spontaneous demonstration of care and concern I'd previously believed I'd been witnessing?

Again it was madness – and again I already knew it. But at least by travelling to his house and seeing who went in and out, I'd be able to eliminate one potential bolthole to which Tia might have decamped either by way of seeking sanctuary or something else.

I parked a short distance from the house about half an hour later. It was in a small street that ran down to a park which fronted onto the Embankment. The house itself was six storeys high, each storey containing just one or two rooms. From Tia, after she'd returned from Joseph's party, I'd learnt, firstly, that the house dated from the year after the Great Fire of London and, secondly, that there was a large metal stanchion that ran from the basement to the roof which had baffled just about every mechanical or structural engineer who'd been brought in to examine it. No-one seemed to know what precise function it served. In the absence of any sort of explanation it had remained where it was where it continued to baffle subsequent generations of surveyors.

It was, in short, a mystery. So what other mysteries did that house contain right now?

From the park at the bottom of the street I could keep watch on the front door. I kept my helmet on as I read one of the free papers that had been thrust into my hand as I turned the corner. I didn't know how long I'd have to wait or what I'd achieve if, by some miracle, my vigil coincided with the sudden appearance of my partner.

By sheer bad luck I also noticed – via a sign on the entrance to the park – that it closed that afternoon at 2 p.m. Which meant that I had just a few more hours before I'd need to find another vantage point. Few opportunities presented themselves, I could hardly huddle down for the rest of the afternoon in one of the adjoining doorways. It wouldn't take long for one of the occupants to spot a helmet-clad biker lurking with what would most definitely look like some sort of sinister intent and summon the police to do something about it.

As it happened, I didn't need those few more hours until the park closed up. I only needed a few more minutes.

A taxi pulled into the street, stopped outside the house, beeped its horn. A few moments later the front door opened and Joseph emerged, suitcase in hand. A girl – mid-twenties and brunette – came out carrying a small holdall. The girl settled herself in the cab as Joseph set the alarm on a control panel just inside the front door. By that time I was moving up the street towards them, secure in the knowledge I was hardly going to be recognised behind the full-face helmet. I passed the taxi just in time to hear Joseph confirm the airport terminal to which they were bound before he slammed the door shut and the taxi did a U-turn in the narrow street before heading for the junction at the top and taking a left.

I retraced my steps, headed back to the Beemer. Wherever Tia might be right now it was a reasonable bet she wasn't inside the house. The security preparations taken by Joseph on his exit was ample proof of that. The brunette with the holdall also more than hinted at other priorities in the relationship stakes too. Maybe his dalliance with Natsuo was over now as well.

But I didn't waste time thinking about that. Tia might have been on his radar as a friend and colleague in distress but my first instincts were right. Everything I sensed as I watched the pair of them together, alone in the loft, unaware that anyone was watching, had been correct. There really was nothing going on between them.

Which still left the question of where Tia might be right now and who she might be with, but at least I'd felt I'd achieved something in eliminating, once and for all, one stark and unwelcome possibility. It had also, and for a short time, sideswiped all thoughts of Eddie. I fired up the Beemer, pointed it up the short steep hill, then swung through a service alley onto the Strand. I eased the bike into the traffic, then pointed it towards Charing Cross intending to cut down to the Embankment, hugging the river all the way to Chelsea before cutting up again for the motorway link to the west and the rented apartment where I could do some – hopefully rather more collected – thinking. About everything.

I'd travelled about fifty metres, no more. There was some sort of demonstration taking place in Trafalgar Square and traffic, while definitely lighter than normal, was still becoming rammed. Cabbies were shooting off in all directions, exploiting rat-runs to circumnavigate the developing mayhem. I knew the area well and could have done the same, could even have followed Joseph's taxi which I could see some distance ahead, now swinging up towards Covent Garden to find another route out to the west. But I was in no particular rush. Encased inside the full-face helmet, I was welcoming the chance to pause, take stock.

Which is when I saw her. For a moment I thought it was a trick of the light or perhaps my mind playing some sort of trick on me. But as I kept staring out of the sun-dimmed visor the sudden apparition didn't vanish or change shape or mutate into someone else.

Tia.

Walking along the street. Hand-in-hand with a friend, not a man, a woman, looking for all the world as if she was out for a simple stroll. OK, she wasn't laughing or joking and she was deep in what appeared to be fairly intense conversation with her companion but she still wasn't the tormented figure she'd presented in the loft.

After all that speculation, to suddenly come across Tia, passing now no more than a few metres away on the pavement while I waited in a line of traffic on the road, was surreal. But it wasn't just the sight of Tia that stopped me literally and metaphorically in my tracks. It was the sight of her companion and now I really was wondering about tricks of the light. It seemed impossible, inconceivable even, but no matter how many times I stared across the road the same sight revealed itself.

I had absolutely no idea why Tia, my partner, should have been walking along, hand-in-hand, locked in what was obviously a fairly intimate conversation with my ex-girlfriend but she was, of that there was absolutely no doubt. And as Tia and Natsuo moved on, as they were engulfed in the crowds heading for Trafalgar Square, I knew that any attempt to do that hopefully rather more collected thinking had just been placed in some serious jeopardy.

I drove down to the Embankment in a daze, taking a left onto the wide expanse of Northumberland Avenue before turning at the bottom and heading towards Parliament Square. Still in the same daze I took the dogleg around the Palace of Westminster before crossing the small roundabout to Millbank. By the Tower I pulled up, the traffic now flowing freely around me. I removed my helmet relishing briefly the sensation of fresh air on my face, then looked out over the river and tried to absorb all I'd seen just a few moments before.

Tia and Natsuo, to the best of my knowledge, had never met. Tia knew of Natsuo of course. There'd never been any mystery about any of my previous relationships and no reason to hide them either. Similarly, Tia had always told me of past boyfriends, ranging from the serious to the regrettable. Again, there'd been no reason not to do so. It might sound strange in the light of present circumstances and my recent actions, but neither of us had ever had any reason to feel threatened in any way by anything that might have taken place in either of our lives prior to meeting the other.

But while I hadn't attempted to hide anyone from Tia – Natsuo included – I hadn't gone out of my way to introduce her to anyone – Natsuo included – either. What would have been the point? So why had I just seen my current partner walking hand-in-hand with an ex-partner on a busy London street after she'd called some mystery respondent saying she had to meet them? As in right now, no delay and in the usual place?

Was it Natsuo she'd been meeting? But how could it be? And why would Tia have hidden those meetings from me? Leaving aside the question of why they would have been meeting up in the first place.

Of course Natsuo, as I already knew only too well, was a player. A woman who loved – no, that was understating her dedication to the cause – who positively lived for the game. A woman addicted to the unpredictable, who spent most of her days ensuring that those around her should never feel on sure ground. To feel safe, cocooned, cosseted, was associated in Natsuo's mind with the grave. The end of everything.

And now Tia was apparently – if that holding of hands was anything to go by – on the warmest of terms with a woman who saw life as a giant trick at the same time as she herself was at the mercy of one of the cruellest tricks imaginable as her lover sought to stand her world on its head, attempted to turn her emotions inside out so he could examine and dissect them, pore over them in their every exposed detail much as Natsuo had done right at the start of our own relationship.

I didn't think for a moment that the relationship was sexual, although if challenged I couldn't have said why. Perhaps it was something in their easy familiarity. They didn't seem intimate in the way you'd expect with lovers. They acted the way friends behaved around each other, expecting nothing, taking nothing, content in each other's company, anticipating and desiring no more.

But, in a way, that was even more unsettling of course. It wasn't then some immediate attraction that couldn't be denied. If this was a friendship of that sort then that took time to build, needed space to grow. So how long had it taken for Tia and Natsuo to get to the sort of close companionship where they'd walk hand-in-hand down a London street uncaring of who saw them?

I turned back to the Beemer, took my helmet from the seat where I'd placed it, prepared to put it on.

Which is when I heard the shout.

'Hey!'

For a moment I didn't respond. The figure who'd called from across the road was on the opposite pavement and could have been calling out to anyone. Then he said it.

'Jack!'

My head jerked up, helmet still in hand and I stared across two lines of traffic, either accelerating out of a roundabout or slowing to enter it as Toby – an open-mouthed Toby – the man I'd least like to see at any moment and a man I very definitely did not want to see at that moment – stood rooted across those two lines of traffic staring straight at me.

I saw his mouth begin to form around my name again. But that's as far as he got. Within a second, less, my head was encased once again inside the helmet, my fingers, strangely fumble-free, had pressed the starter, I'd swung my body onto the Beemer and was smoothly accelerating away, making for Dolphin Square and onwards out of the city.

Toby couldn't have managed more than a fleeting glance I assured myself as I rode on. He was on the other side of a busy road and I was definitely facing away from him as I looked out across the river.

Then again if he'd come out of Millbank, if he'd been in the Tower recording some interview or other he could have been studying me for a good few moments as he turned left out of the main door, made to head along towards Parliament Square. He could have paused a few times on that short journey, taking in the figure on the bank across the road, wondering, checking, wondering again, before finally making his mind up and calling out to me.

I rode on, powering up through Earls Court. There was real shock in his voice though. Toby seemed to have been genuinely rocked by the sight he must have believed he was witnessing – a man feared lost, now not only restored to life but standing on the banks of the Thames as if he was just some ordinary sightseer, looking out over the water, seemingly unaware of the frenzy that surrounded him.

I yanked the throttle savagely, accelerated up onto the elevated section above Hammersmith, cursed myself for the lapse of concentration that had allowed me to remove my helmet for even those few moments.

It was, of course, all down to that sighting on the Strand, Tia and Natsuo, together, walking along, hand-in-hand. I was too distracted trying to absorb all that to even begin to register the new danger just a mile or so away. I'd taken such care up to that point, such pains. Would it all now count for nothing? Was the whole thing about to come crumbling down for the sake of one unguarded moment and a chance sighting on a busy street?

I rode on, coming down from the elevated section, heading for the roundabout that would take me either down the M3 to the south coast or along to the nearby M4 corridor.

Maybe I really was now into damage limitation. Toby must still be reeling from the sight he'd just witnessed, had probably not had time to act upon it in any way – although there was always the option he wasn't going to act on it at all of course. He might mention it to a couple of colleagues, he might not even do that if there was any vestige of doubt in his mind as to what he'd witnessed. He might not, in either scenario, go within a million miles of Tia. He'd never been exactly close to either of us, so why should he bother?

But there was still that risk. So should I anticipate it? Should I seize the initiative, turn the Beemer round, head back to London, park it up somewhere, then head for the loft, play the temporary amnesia card I'd always planned to play anyway, end this whole thing here and now? That way, if Toby did appear at some later point in the proceedings, anything he had to say would already be old news. That sighting on the Embankment would then be totally consistent with the apparent facts – that I'd stumbled around for a couple of days, unable to remember exactly where I'd been, where I'd been staying. Over the last few hours I'd felt the mist lifting, my mind clearing, memory returning. Which is when I'd returned.

I throttled back, hesitating.

'Then there's the second problem.'

Maybe it was that sighting of Tia and Natsuo again. But now it forced back into my mind the second half of my previous phone conversation with Dom. I rode back along the motorway, seeing not only my current and past partners but my current companion too as I heard his voice once again waft down the line.

'OK, there's the insurance angle. They're going to be watching for this sort of thing like hawks, but leave that aside, let's assume that partner of yours was just reading those policies out of simple curiosity, she had an idle moment and thought, let's check, just in case, just how much he might be worth.'

I'd cut across. He sounded like he was luxuriating in all this just that little bit too much.

'Your point?'

'So she hasn't put in any call, hasn't set any balls rolling, there'll be no reason for an insurance assessor to even call, but that still leaves what you might call the bigger question.'

Dom paused.

'The question that kick-started all this in the first place, right?'

The question that was pounding inside my head, right now as I was riding down the motorway, the question that, even now, wouldn't go away.

What's she like when I'm not watching?

If I returned now what would happen to the question that had sent me away in the first place? How then would that ever be resolved?

Of course it wouldn't. It couldn't. And even if I managed to carry off my return from the dead, even if all that was successfully negotiated there was still the matter of the unfinished quest, destined then to remain unfinished forever; which was an intolerable thought. I knew exactly how I'd feel if I simply and meekly now returned home giving up all chance to follow this journey through to its end. It had cost so much already. Just ask the unfortunate Eddie.

I put my hand back on the throttle, twisted the grip, moved into the outside lane and propelled the Beemer back along the motorway to the rented apartment.

I LET MYSELF back in half an hour or so later. For a moment I stood still, knowing something had changed, unsure what. Then I realised. Someone had been inside the apartment.

The small pile of brochures detailing local attractions had been restacked neatly on a small table in the hall. I knew I'd deposited the whole lot in a drawer before I left. It had become a reflex action on entering any hotel room or rented apartment; maybe part of a desire to rid the room of any impression of transience, an attempt to make my surroundings my own even if I was only there for a night or so.

Then, through the open doorway, on the kitchen unit, I saw another item not there when I was last inside. A bowl full of fruit, some apples, oranges, bananas and a small card wishing me a pleasant stay, offering this gift with the compliments of the manager of the residence.

I moved into the bedroom, dumped my helmet on the bed, stripped off my leathers and walked down the small hallway to the bathroom. There I stood under the shower for a good ten minutes, my mind full now – not of Toby and close encounters on London streets – not of Eddie and violence witnessed at one remove – but close and violent encounters of a rather more immediately threatening kind.

I still couldn't get the road rage driver out of my mind. For some reason I kept replaying that first moment I saw him in the mirrors, that distant flash of light, followed only a short time later by that sudden rush of air buffeting me from his close, too-close, attentions, followed next by that blatant attempt – it could be nothing else – to force me from the road.

Accident or design? Coincidence or just circumstance occasioned by an unfortunate combination of a psychopathic driver and an overly-paranoid biker? All logic told me it was just bad luck, the sort of encounter that could happen anywhere at any time, a modern-day gladiatorial contest played out with the twenty-first century equivalent of chariots; nasty, but nothing more.

I stepped out of the shower, fell onto the bed, tried to forget all about road rage drivers, Dom, Eddie, Natsuo and sworn enemies who shout open-mouthed from across busy city streets. And I did. By rights I should have tossed and turned all night but in fact I slept the sleep of the untroubled and untormented.

Or, of course, the dead.

I woke the next morning to see Tia staring at me just a metre of so from the end of my bed.

3 6 .

F OR A MOMENT that seemed to stretch all infinity, I stared
at the apparition. For that same moment a million and one
thoughts assailed me, each making less sense than the last. Then
the face of my partner dissolved into a wider shot of a sofa and
a TV presenter staring sympathetically at her. Behind, on a wall,
was the same montage Dom had shown me, face upon face all
staring out at the camera, some smiling, some not, a banner
headline above and below the sea of faces with a single word in
black type.

Missing.

Only one of those faces – the face currently picked out
by a red circle – might not be missing after all. The presenter
turned to look at the face, my face – and the camera went in
close. Now I was lying in bed in a rented apartment miles from
home staring at a picture of my own face staring back at me on
national television. As starts to a day were concerned they hadn't
often begun in a much more surreal fashion.

Then the camera cut back to Tia again, her face filled the
screen once more and, prompted by the honeyed tones of the
presenter, she began to tell the tale of the last twelve hours,
setting it in the context of the previous few days or so, taking in
her trawl around the various car parks of Victoria and London
Bridge, her calls to the emergency service, her alternating
feelings of despair, numbness, grief – and then, suddenly, the
wild, dizzying hope occasioned by a simple phone call she'd
taken the previous evening.

The call was, of course, from Toby. I should have known that even had he been in two, three or four minds about the sighting he wouldn't have been able to resist acting on it. Toby always did believe he was the sort of man born with weighty news to impart.

Not that he believed himself to be in anything other than the one totally convinced, totally resolute mind so far as this particular piece of news was concerned. He was in no doubt as to the seeming miracle he'd witnessed. And now the picture on the screen dissolved again, now we were outside Millbank, commuter traffic clogging the route towards Parliament Square with Toby himself being interviewed outside the Tower.

His old colleague and companion – and even in my shocked state something inside me jarred at the somewhat-glossed description – had risen, Lazarus-like, before his eyes. Toby, it seemed, had emerged from Millbank and had then simply stood in stunned astonishment as he drank in the sight on the opposite pavement. And now the camera duly panned across the road, focusing on a spot, now empty, where Toby had apparently seen me. Then it was back to the man himself and his deep regret in actually shouting out my name like that. If only he'd kept his composure, hadn't done anything to alert me, had crossed the road and come up to me then maybe the outcome would have been different. Maybe I wouldn't have simply taken off like that. I was obviously still too fragile to absorb a direct challenge of that kind. Faced with reality intruding on whatever fantasy I'd constructed in order to deal with the horrors I'd witnessed, I'd retreated.

The last sentiment was pure Toby. Cod psychology wrapped up for a daytime TV audience. And to her credit, Tia didn't indulge in any of the same. Once the Toby sound bite had finished, once we were back in the studio, she introduced a note of caution into it all which was all the more affecting for its sincerity and its understandable confusion.

Tia hadn't been there. She hadn't been standing on that pavement looking out at the figure on the opposite side of the road. So, and while being careful not to contradict Toby directly, she couldn't be one hundred per cent sure that the man he'd seen across two lanes of busy traffic, a man who – by Toby's own admission – was staring out across the river and was therefore facing away from him for much of the time, was definitely her partner.

But it was the first positive piece of news that Tia had received since the day of the crash. I'd still not appeared in any official record of the dead or injured. And there had been instances of casualties walking away from similar disasters in the past in similar dazed states to the one I was perhaps currently inhabiting. If that was the case then it was possible I didn't even register the shouted challenge, that I simply got back onto a bike I seemed to have acquired – from somewhere – somehow – and rode away. Which meant that I was still locked inside some bubble in which I'd cocooned myself.

And that was why Tia was appearing on that breakfast TV show. She was making a direct appeal, not just to her missing partner but to anyone who may see me. Like myself, if that chance sighting on a London street was accurate, Tia wanted help.

And if I was watching this, Tia now begged, then please keep watching, please look at these pictures, please see if they make any sort of connection – and then, on screen, images appeared of myself and Tia. Then there were moving images of the street on which we lived, some of the local landmarks we passed each and every day, the exterior of the loft and the interior too. They'd obviously dispatched a small crew to record it all that very morning.

I was already sitting bolt upright staring at the screen as the camera picked up the picture frame – still there – the radio alarm clock – still visible on the bedside table. The bugs were very obviously still in place. They hadn't been removed. Then the camera moved outside onto the balcony taking in the view I'd have seen every morning up and down the river, even taking in one of the commuter clippers as it headed from Canary Wharf up to the City.

The camera held on the river for a few moments as if it was some sort of talisman, then faded, cutting back to the studio. There was just time for Tia to make one last appeal for information. I was only one person in a tragedy that had engulfed so many and she knew that, but if that sighting was correct then perhaps this might be one story at least that might end rather more happily than most.

Then the picture dissolved again to a garden somewhere and to a girl in a coat and hat detailing the general weather forecast for the day ahead. I turned, found the remote control by the side of the bed where I'd dropped it when I'd fallen asleep the previous night, knocked off the TV and sank back on the thin pillows.

For a moment my mind went blank at this fresh evidence that I was now very much at the mercy of a game I myself had instigated.

But it wasn't just shock I was experiencing. There was something else too and as my mind replayed all I'd just seen, replayed the face on the screen, replayed all Tia had said which I seemed to be able to recall in almost forensic detail, another response, a different emotion indeed, began once again to claim me.

I once again replayed in my mind all the key events of the past few weeks. I replayed once more all my different responses and reactions. I moved myself almost physically through different degrees of separation from it all.

I'd read this article once, written by some screenwriter. The article was long gone along with the name of the screenwriter but the main thrust of his argument had stayed with me.

The article was all about the angle you adopt – consciously or unconsciously – when you first happen upon an idea or a story. With most ideas or stories, so the screenwriter averred, it was possible to almost physically place the idea down as if in the centre of a room and then – again almost physically – walk around it.

Say the idea or the story is about a man and a woman in their thirties. Walk round it. What if the man is twenty and the woman fifty? Say the idea or story is set in the modern day. Walk around it. What if it's set in the fifth century AD? If the idea or story is a romance, walk around it again. Take the same protagonists, use the same characters. What if it's a horror movie instead?

The point was simple. Any idea or any story is always susceptible to a dozen different interpretations depending on the perspective or prejudices of the person viewing that idea or story. Shift perspective and the story shifts. It no longer becomes what one might have imagined it to be.

Which was exactly what was happening now with the Tia story.

So Tia had exchanged a seemingly significant nod with a work colleague in an airport car park. A few days later that same man was escorting a brunette into a taxi for a trip somewhere, having previously behaved himself impeccably while alone with her.

So Tia had called someone I didn't know, insisted she had to meet them somewhere I couldn't access. Previously I'd boiled inside with frustration at that. Shift perspective, move around the story. Wasn't Tia entitled to the odd secret in her life? An old friend perhaps who was kept in the background most of the time but to whom she turned in times of trouble? Maybe I'd even met them but they simply hadn't registered all that strongly.

It all added up to the same, simple, truth. For every potentially sinister development there was a potentially innocent explanation. And what was shifting my perspective, altering my viewpoint, changing my emotions all the time now were Tia's eyes, the eyes I'd just seen staring out at me from the TV screen that metre or so from the foot of my bed.

There was a look illuminating those eyes. There was a joy inside them which Tia was terrified to allow full rein but which was there nonetheless and which touched even the hardened presenter charged with coaxing her responses. Tia looked like a woman who'd been granted hope once more, a woman who was just beginning to allow herself to believe that fairy tales could, somehow, come true.

There wasn't the slightest hint of doubt about my motives. Tia believed totally that I must be suffering from some deep shock and that if only she could get to me, could reach me, then everything would flow from that.

So I'd misinterpreted everything. I'd espied ogres where none existed. I'd allowed demons that flourished only inside my own mind to turn others into demons too, recognisable only in a twisted version of reality that I myself had created.

I'd felt this way before of course. Spying on Tia in the loft, listening to her begging the emergency number for news, talking to Joseph about our lives together, I'd felt this way then. I should have trusted my instincts, I had the answer I was searching for already, why did I allow those doubts to multiply, to capture – again – all that was healthy and turn it into something that was anything but?

I stood up, threw open the wardrobe, started to take out the few clothes I'd brought with me, starting to think, quickly, rationally, planning the steps I knew I had to now take.

Nothing connected me to this apartment. Nothing connected me to the Beemer parked in the rear yard. I could just walk out, abandon both, walk to the nearest police station and effectively turn myself in. I could play the troubled accident victim for a while, wait for them to make some checks and then wait for Tia to come and claim me.

Or I could simply call home. Find a public phone box and pretend that I'd seen the broadcast somewhere – maybe in some café – and that all of a sudden it was like a shaft of light breaking in.

Then the phone started ringing from the hall. For a moment I stilled, but then relaxed once more – more evidence, if any was needed, that I was beginning to conquer all that had previously claimed me.

It had to be Dom. There was no-one else who knew I was here. And no-one was going to win any prizes for guessing just why he was phoning right now, less than a minute after that broadcast had ended.

I was right and I was wrong. It was Dom. But it had nothing to do with the broadcast which he hadn't even seen.

I'D NEVER HEARD Dom so excited. He was back in the shop in Covent Garden and one of his regular suppliers had just come in. He'd brought Dom something special, something that took the usual world of surveillance and spy gadgets and blasted it into orbit. Compared with what else was out there on the market, this was on the other side of the universe apparently.

The problem being that this particular little beauty hadn't exactly been road-tested yet. Which was on account of the fact that it really couldn't be road-tested in any conventional sense. This was more aimed at the underground part of his trade, at clients who were guaranteed to remain discreet whatever they did and whoever they encountered along the way. It was also aimed at a very specific part of the market, domestic as opposed to corporate, for those dealing or attempting to deal with matters of the heart as opposed to matters of the balance sheet. Which was why Dom had thought of me.

He hadn't let me get a word in edgeways. All I'd had since I'd picked up the phone was a torrent of excited chatter. I'd only caught about half what he'd said to me and the half I caught didn't seem to make a whole lot of sense. No doubt it would have made more sense if I'd been in any other frame of mind, but I already felt as if the person who might have found this so equally and obviously fascinating inhabited some other planet, one I no longer recognised and, now, had no wish to visit.

'OK, it's weird. Well, more than weird. And all right, there is an element of danger involved, because it's unpredictable; it's been tried out a couple of times but everyone's different so this comes with no – and I mean absolutely no – guarantee but for the kind of thing you've got in mind, Jack, the particular problem you want resolved, this, believe me, is the answer, one hundred per cent; this is the baby that is well and truly going to deliver.'

Finally, I cut across.

'Have you seen the news?'

'No.'

'Is your laptop on?'

'Does the Pope reside in the Vatican?'

I gave Dom the name of the TV programme I'd just watched, told him to watch it via any one of the current players that allowed access. I didn't say anything else, didn't bother explaining any further. Once Dom had caught even a few moments of the broadcast, once he'd seen Tia, he'd understand.

I hung up and spent the next ten minutes further debating my options, deciding in the end that I should simply turn up at the loft as I'd always intended. Everything else seemed too premeditated, too stage-managed. If I'd been totally on the level, if I'd begun to remember key facts about myself, my life, who I was, where I lived, wouldn't I simply go there, would I really bother with telephone calls or police stations? It just felt more real to walk in, to see Tia alone, just the two of us with no outside bodies watching and spoiling the moment.

That meant the Beemer had one last journey to make. Riding that, encased inside the leathers and helmet, I could park as close to the loft as I dared, meaning I only had the shortest of distances to walk. There was always the chance that I'd be spotted by some neighbour or other but I didn't need to actually stop even if directly challenged.

I was recovering from deep shock. So I came across as odd.

No shit, Sherlock.

I did a final check on the rented apartment and made for the door. As I reached it the phone began to ring again.

I knew it was Dom and of course it was. I guessed he'd seen the TV show and he had. And he definitely sounded different now, there was none of the excited hard sell in his voice, in fact he didn't even refer to the new product to which he'd just been introduced, whatever that might be. He sounded almost troubled in fact.

Dom had seen the programme. He'd seen Tia. He'd also been impressed by the apparently genuine show of emotion she'd displayed. But that wasn't the reason for the hesitation in his voice, the unsure timbre in his tone.

'Is your laptop on?'

For a moment I thought there must be an echo on the line or something. Why was Dom repeating my own question back to me?

'Why?'

'Put it on.'

'What for?'

'That programme.'

'I've seen that programme.'

'There was an update. Right at the end.'

Dom paused.

'I think you should see it too.'

Then the phone went dead.

For a good few moments I didn't do anything. Some instinct seemed to be at work – self-preservation perhaps – a desire to protect myself from one more shock at a time when there'd been too many already, not helped by the fact that the vast majority of them had been, as I would have to concede, self-inflicted.

I looked over at the table, at the small amount of cash I'd left to cover any extras or incidentals – phone calls, electricity and the like. I didn't want anyone from this life which already, in my mind, was in the past, disturbing the new life I was about to embrace. I'd even traced out a route that would take me away from most of the CCTV cameras that covered the major routes into the city. I'd left nothing to chance and now just wanted out, of everything.

But there was obviously a complication. And a complication was the last thing I needed right now so I knew I had no choice but to do as Dom said. The success or otherwise of the next few hours depended absolutely on my ability to carry off an act, play out a story much as Tia obviously planned to do with Eddie and I also had to feel I was on a similarly secure foundation. If there was a development of which I was unaware and I walked back into the loft and saw Tia, only to be confronted by that development, whatever that might be, the risk to my composure, understandably fragile already, might be too great.

I opened my laptop, connected to the wireless provider. For a few moments, while I waited to be redirected to the relevant website, I studied a few headlines that scrolled down the side of the page, a feed from an online news service. The train crash had now been relegated from lead story. The world it seemed had moved on. So what was Dom talking about, what development was so important and urgent I just had to see it for myself?

The programme came up on the screen and I clicked on the play icon. The opening titles began and I accessed the fast-forward facility, jumping to the last few minutes.

I slowed the replay down to normal speed but still couldn't understand what he was talking about for a few moments. The presenter was giving a rundown of the anticipated highlights of the next day, including interviews with a Hollywood A-lister over for an awards' ceremony and then there was another résumé of the weather forecast for the day ahead too. Behind, some music started, signalling the closing titles were about to begin.

But then the presenter paused, something obviously having been communicated to her via her earpiece from the producer in the control box. The presenter advised the audience she was getting some late breaking news in connection with one of the main stories of the day as more detail was fed via her earpiece from the control box. Then the presenter paused again, ordering the new information into what I'd already realised to be her usual pithy sound bite style and turned to the camera.

But despite that pithy sound bite style she gave it her all. There'd been a heart-rending turn of events it seemed, a shattering piece of news for the young woman who'd so bravely and eloquently told her story earlier, concerning her partner presumed missing in the recent train crash but spotted, apparently, on the banks of the Thames the previous day.

Only it seemed I hadn't been spotted on the banks of the Thames the previous day at all. Whoever it was that had been spotted, it had just been proved in the very last few minutes and without a shadow of a doubt, that it was not Jack Connolly. It was a false hope, in fact. Because the emergency services had just been in touch with the woman in question, the woman who'd so touched the hearts of so many that day to tell her that her partner's DNA had now been positively identified at the crash site.

Tia finally had the proof she really did not want that I was dead.

38.

O NE HOUR LATER I was on the bank of another river.
On the other side of the water a rowing team was preparing a boat for a practice run. Traffic crossed a centuries-old bridge a couple of hundred metres further upstream again. An old coaching inn, now an upmarket hotel owned by a celebrity chef, was opening for the lunchtime service. It was a totally ordinary, totally familiar scene but that didn't change a thing so far as I was concerned. I still felt as if I'd just landed on Mars. In a world that had made little sense for some time now, this latest development had just turned the inexplicable into the insane.

It hadn't been helped by the phone call that had come through from Dom roughly thirty seconds after I'd watched the update. He'd obviously calculated with characteristic accuracy just how long I'd take to access and watch the relevant section of the programme.

'You saw it?'

'I saw it.'

Dom paused and I didn't fill the silence. My brain was too occupied trying to take in the implications of all I'd just seen to try and multitask with conversation at the same time.

'What are they talking about?'

'I don't know.'

'You've never been near that crash site, have you?'

I didn't reply, didn't need to, couldn't anyway. My mind was too busy racing, computing possibilities, rehearsing options, failing totally, falling now.

'But if they've found your DNA somewhere at that site that means someone must have.'

'What do they mean, DNA?'

'Could be anything. Skin tissue – unlikely in your case – you'd have sort of noticed if someone took a swab sometime in the last couple of days, right?'

I cut across, closing him down.

'What else?'

'I don't know.'

Dom paused.

'Maybe hair.'

'What?'

'Leave a few strands around, wait for it to be picked up in the next sweep of the site, wait a little longer for it to be crossmatched with the bank of DNA they've collected.'

'Collected how?'

'If it was hair, it could have been lifted from a brush. Even a comb.'

Dom paused again.

'There's always plenty of hairs left on the average comb. Use some to provide the crossmatch. Use some more to plant at the scene.'

I stared at the phone as if I was staring directly at him.

'You're saying someone lifted some of my hair from a comb, travelled down to the crash site and planted it?'

'Someone?'

I knew what Dom was getting at and didn't reply again. If the DNA had come from a hair sample, if the sample had come from anything in the loft then there was only one person who could have provided that and I knew it.

Tia.

Which made no sense. Absolutely none at all. It made about as little sense, in fact, as sitting in a rented apartment having let the rest of the world believe you're dead only to find that apparently you are.

Then Dom spoke again.

'There's something else.'

'What?'

'The bugs, the ones you planted.'

'What about them?'

'They're working again.'

'I don't understand.'

'Every single one.'

I tried working it through.

'So they can't all have failed at the same time?'

'Correct.'

'And they can't all have suddenly started working at the same time either?'

'No.'

'Unless someone turned them off – .'

I could almost see Dom nodding down the phone.

'And then turned them back on again.'

Five minutes later I was staring at the laptop. I'd accessed each individual piece of software for each bug dotted around the loft. The spy camera in the radio alarm clock, the audio bug in the picture frame, all were working as perfectly as on the day I first installed them. A sudden thought struck me and I checked the USB drive on Tia's desktop. That was now active too. If it had been removed at anytime in the last day or so it had been replaced. I could now hear and see everything that was taking place in the loft again. I could see Tia again and could watch everything she was doing.

And Tia was doing a lot right now. She was fielding an avalanche of phone calls from just about everyone we knew for one thing. The fact of my disappearance had been disseminated far and wide thanks to her TV appearance and its extraordinary postscript. The crushing news from the crash site just moments after her emotional appeal had guaranteed that those few friends or acquaintances who'd remained unaware of all that had happened in our lives these last few days were now very definitely in the loop.

Tia was dignified with each and every caller. She reiterated largely the same sentiments, expressing her thanks for their call and the obvious sympathies expressed. She maintained an equally dignified silence as every caller remarked on the cruelty of the timing of the devastating bombshell from the crash site. To be robbed of all hope so soon after Tia had allowed that hope to flare into life was beyond belief.

At the same time there was a steady stream of callers – the neighbour who'd delivered the card while I was checking out the loft – another neighbour who'd occasionally taken in deliveries for us in our absence, even – extraordinarily – the local shopkeeper from the convenience store down the road, tears already flowing down his face as Tia opened the door to him before he enveloped her in a giant bear hug, repeating all the time – almost word for word – her interview that morning which he'd obviously watched over and over since its broadcast.

All the time Tia maintained the same dignified composure. A couple of callers remarked on it and wondered whether she was in shock, before they corrected themselves, acknowledging the ridiculousness of the observation. Of course she was in shock. How could she not be? How could anyone not be in these extraordinary circumstances? Tia simply acquiesced with a simple incline of the head.

And all the time I watched her intently. All the time I strained my ears when she moved out of video range and I had to rely on the audio bugs alone. I knew Tia inside out. Or thought I did. I knew – or thought I knew – every inflexion in her voice, every expression that might steal across her face. She had to be under the most intense pressure right now, not just in dealing with all that had happened with Eddie but in dealing with all that had apparently happened to me too. But watching her now, listening to her, was like watching and listening to a total stranger.

Back on the river bank I watched as the rowing team put their boat in the water and then set off, their every move in unison, every member of the team working in complete harmony, acting as one.

3 9.

THE NEXT MORNING, Tia had another unexpected visitor – unexpected that is so far as I was concerned. The way events had been unfolding lately maybe I was going to find Toby had been a regular caller over the last couple of years and that Tia was bosom buddies with a man I'd always seen as a grade one pain in the arse.

But her expression on opening the door reassured me on that score at least. I could almost feel the temperature dip several degrees as she took in the apparition on the doorstep.

Tia stood aside and let in her second unwelcome guest. First Eddie, now Toby. For a fleeting moment I entertained the not-entirely-unappealing fantasy of this second guest being dispatched in a similar fashion to the first.

Toby seemed to have second-guessed her response, although he obviously believed this to be due to the misleading call he'd made to Tia those couple of nights before. The truth was that Toby would have received the same reception irrespective of the circumstances. The woman I once knew as Tia hadn't changed that much. She clearly still loathed the slimy little shit.

Toby had arrived on a mission, part-apology, part-expiation, part-exploration. He wanted to apologise for raising her hopes like that. He wanted forgiveness from a woman he appeared to have wronged. But being Toby, he wanted to leave a sting in the tail behind as well.

For the first few moments it was all pretty one-sided stuff. Toby, it seemed, had been tormented by the way he appeared to have made this difficult situation worse; raising hopes like that only to have them crushed so quickly and in such a public way too. So it was I learnt that Tia was still actually in the television studio when the news came through. She did learn of the discovery before the presenter announced it to the rest of the nation but it was, apparently, a pretty close-run thing.

Tia listened to and accepted the florid attempts at apology in largely polite silence. Having completed the matter of the moment, Toby really should have done as most of the other callers had done, and simply left. But Toby, again being Toby, wasn't quite finished yet.

'Do you mind my asking exactly what they found at the crash site?'

'I don't understand.'

Neither did I. Or, at least, I really hadn't credited him with such crass insensitivity as to ask. But Toby never did anything without a careful consideration of their effects and implications.

'I'm not asking for details of body parts, whether it was an arm or a leg, anything like that.'

Even with the camera some distance away and with the image on my laptop only affording a side view of Tia, I could see her skin mottle.

'I think perhaps you should go.'

But Toby didn't move. He'd done what he'd set out to do, he'd burrowed under her defences. Now it was a case of seeing just how much further he could creep inside.

'I just wondered – .'

Toby tailed off. In a different world and time I wouldn't have given him the ghost of a chance of finishing even his next sentence. In this new world and time, Tia actually invited him to do so.

'What?'

'Whether there was any possibility of a mistake?'

Toby looked beyond Tia, out to the balcony, but from my

viewpoint it looked as if he was looking straight at the camera, straight at me.

'I've been going back over it – again and again – I've replayed it all – coming out of Millbank – looking across the street – .'

Toby paused.

'You were mistaken. Accept it. I've had to.'

'There was one other detail I didn't tell you. I didn't want to hurt your feelings I suppose.'

Tia had been on the point of opening the door, of signalling that this encounter was at an end but now she paused.

I leant closer to the screen. What was this all about now? What not-so-little bombshell was Toby now about to drop – the real reason, I realised too late – for his trip? Tia had probably realised that by now too but, like the third party listening in to this conversation from his remote location, Tia also now really needed to know what he was talking about.

'When I called – when he turned – when he saw me – it wasn't the look of a stranger, puzzled at being accosted by another stranger from across a street.'

Toby hunched forward too.

'Jack was shocked. Shocked at my calling out, shocked at being spotted and there was something else too – fear – guilt almost – that was the overriding impression I got. He seemed to know that if he didn't put on his helmet, get on that bike and get away in the very next few seconds then the game was up.'

Tia studied him coolly.

'What game?'

Toby, to his credit, held her stare.

'I was hoping you could tell me.'

O NE OF THE swords currently suspended over Tia's head descended a couple of days later.

She'd taken in a special delivery that required a signature, a large bunch of flowers from a sympathetic well-wisher whose name I couldn't see on the accompanying card. The delivery came courtesy of a local postman who'd actually become a friend, of sorts anyway.

A few months before he'd delivered, along with the usual circulars, bills and occasional party invitations, a Christmas card. We'd taken it at first as a simple compliment of the season. We bought him a Christmas card in turn, intending to give it to him the next time he buzzed on the intercom with some parcel or other. Talking to a neighbour later that same day, Tia discovered this was something of a ritual which contained within it a gentle hint. In exchange for his good service over the previous year, not to mention his habitual determinedly-cheery stream of banter, a little consideration was considered appropriate. In other words he was soliciting quite blatantly for a tip and a Christmas card by itself without any sort of enclosure would not really be considered any sort of reciprocal gesture on our part.

Point made, we duly enclosed a couple of banknotes guaranteeing us another year of upbeat greetings.

Only this morning that usual smiling face was clouded, his tone almost hushed. Partly that was out of natural respect. Very few people bounded into our loft full of the joys of spring right now. But partly it was because of something else, something that had just happened out on his round.

It was ironic in a sense. Tia must have rehearsed in her head a number of ways in which the news about Eddie might break. She'd probably imagined knocks on the door in the middle of the night or screams cutting through her fitful sleep as a neighbour or friend finally forced themselves into his flat and made the grimmest of discoveries. She really couldn't have expected it to be dropped, almost casually, into a doorstep conversation by the local postie, especially as it came in the wake of a rehash of his latest workday drama which involved striking a local dog with his van as he turned from a busy main street onto a nearby small estate.

'All the bloke was going on about was how long they'd had it and how much his kids loved it and how was he going to explain it to them when they got home and did my lot offer any sort of compensation for things like this because if they didn't they should.'

Tia had nodded, barely listening although her attention was rather more grabbed by the next part of his rant.

'So I tried telling him that he really should have been on a lead, especially if his kids loved him that much, anyway it wasn't much of an accident, a quick check-up down the vet's would probably see him right as rain and worse things happen at sea, in fact worse things happen right under our noses, just look at poor old Eddie.'

I focused in on Tia, who was now staring at him.

'Didn't cut no ice though, he kept going on and on about it and between me and you I reckon he's sniffing the chance of some sort of payout.'

The man from the Royal Mail leant closer, almost conspiratorial.

'In fact, I wouldn't put it past him to have staged it in some way – you know, get the dog to run out in front of me like that, knowing I couldn't stop in time, bit like them insurance scams you read about when some punter brakes hard in front of you,

you smash into the back of him and he cops a payout from one of them personal insurance merchants.'

For me, everything seemed magnified in those few moments, sharper, clearer than ever before. But had I been called upon to respond I'm not sure if I'd have been able to actually speak. Tia was rather more self-possessed even if her voice, when she finally responded, sounded slightly higher in pitch than normal.

'What about Eddie?'

Still ruminating on his conspiracy theory, he stared at her for a moment, blank.

Tia prompted.

'Poor old Eddie?'

His brow cleared and he nodded.

'Oh yeah.'

'Has something happened to him?'

Tia's researches into the macabre subject of decomposition had proved prophetic, that indeed being the means whereby Eddie – or what was left of Eddie – had been discovered.

Eddie himself hadn't been missed, it seemed, by anybody. No family – if he had any – had called to see how he was, puzzled by an extended absence. And no friends – if, again he had any – had called on the same mission. So far as the wider world was concerned Eddie could have stayed in that flat from the moment he died till the day Hell froze over.

But he still attracted some kind of attention. The natural world had very much come calling. In life Eddie might well have spent most of his waking hours unvisited and unloved. In death he might have remained unloved, but he very definitely had not remained unvisited.

The problem had arisen as a result of that very multiplication of visitors. His decaying body provided rich pickings for a time but the law of diminishing returns was always going to kick in at some point. At some stage in the gorgefest there was always going to come a time when those wishing to be fed were going to have to look elsewhere for fresh supplies. That meant the trail of scavengers started to move away from the body, taking in any stray foodstuffs that might have been left out on various surfaces and in any bins. Once that was exhausted the voracious army moved even further afield, exploring each and every nook and cranny they could find which was how the residents of the flat below Eddie had become alerted to something not quite right as small creatures suddenly started to drop through their basement ceiling via small cracks in the plasterboard.

Initially they thought they simply had some kind of infestation in the space between the two dwellings and called in the council to investigate. The council had long ago disbanded their in-house team of pest control officers and had farmed the whole operation out to private contractors. The private contractors, in turn, had subcontracted this side of their operation to another company who didn't exactly commit anything like the required resources to investigate the outbreak. A quick spray of a general-purpose fungicide in the space between the ceiling of one flat and the floor of the other represented the sum total of their initial efforts. It killed some of the multiplying wildlife that were occupying the space at that time, but that only provoked another feeding frenzy as their less adventurous companions back in the flat suddenly discovered a new source of sustenance and poured into that same gap.

That led in turn to even more bloated visitors dropping down into the flat below leading to yet more calls to the council leading to yet more visits and leading in turn to the inescapable conclusion that perhaps this really couldn't be put down to the warm weather the capital had been enduring lately and that some more intensive investigation was merited.

Once that more intensive investigation had commenced it

didn't take long for the council to discover the real problem. They couldn't gain access to the flat above for one thing and the stench, as the first visitor raised the letterbox and peered inside the hallway, told them all they really needed to know. The council employee immediately called the police and the rest of the story followed a well-worn course. Yet another murder victim had been discovered in yet another London dwelling.

Tia went straight out and bought all the early editions of the local papers, poring over every detail of the discovery. Not that there was a great deal to report at that stage. The facts were fairly clear, Eddie had certainly been killed by a person or persons unknown but the motive and the identity of that person or persons unknown remained unclear. For now the papers concentrated more on the gory aspects of the discovery than anything else. It was all pretty standard stuff – aside from the gruesome description of the infested flat – but it still didn't stop Tia drinking it all in, reading and rereading every word.

She was filling a void of course. Unable to move forward and finding it impossible not to look back, she was simply turning round and round in the same circle and would do so until something or someone stopped her.

The next development happened the very next day. The police had wasted no time in calling a specialist team to clean the flat. It had been a fairly painstaking process, as they had to do so without disturbing what little evidence hadn't been devoured by the parasites that had made the dead body and that flat their own little kingdom.

The police had also been open about the difficulty of their task from the start, hoping perhaps to enlist some local sympathy and support. They also played on local fears as regards safety and security. If this could happen to a totally ordinary businessman in a totally nondescript and unremarkable flat – and for no good reason that the police at this stage could establish – then it could presumably happen to anyone. And if they remained in the dark as to any motive and the identity of the killer or killers then there was nothing to stop he – or she – or them – striking again.

It was all part of the softening-up process of course. They'd already established that little of value had been taken from Eddie's flat, meaning either the murderer or murderers had been discovered before they could do so or robbery wasn't the motive. That left the obvious possibility of revenge. Eddie's profession was one that brought him into contact with some desperate people. Even from the few inquiries they'd conducted thus far, it was fairly obvious he would never have won any popularity contests. Eddie had made many enemies in the course of his work and seemed to have no compunction in taking advantage of people who'd already fallen further than most. One of them could well have decided enough was enough and that their world would be much better off with one less persecutor pulling their strings.

If that all-too plausible scenario was correct then the chances were that his murderer or murderers were to be found amongst his clients. Meaning that somewhere in that fairly extensive but not impossibly long list was a name or names who were really beginning to sweat. And the police had already decided how they might be smoked out into the open.

They presented the appeal as a necessary evil. Despite the attentions of the parasites, they did still have some leads to pursue, principally some evidence of human occupation of that flat in the last couple of weeks in addition to the non-human residents.

Eddie sometimes conducted business in there as well as in the shop it seemed, and if the police suspected the vast majority of those flat-based visitors were young, female, frightened and at their wits' end as to what to do and who to turn to in order to seek help they kept that, diplomatically, to themselves.

Whatever else he was, Eddie was a meticulous businessman. He kept immaculate records, detailing all his transactions, dates, times as well as names and addresses. And so the police put out an appeal to anyone and everyone whose name appeared on those records. In order to eliminate the customers of the deceased from any hint of suspicion, everyone was being invited to submit to a DNA test. The results would be crossmatched with the DNA found in the flat. In the vast majority of those cases the volunteers would hear no more as there'd be nothing to report. In a tiny minority of cases there might be a match but there'd no doubt be a perfectly reasonable explanation for that. The police didn't go into what would happen if they found a match for which there was no reasonable explanation.

Tia stared at the reports of the appeal in the local paper, the realisation clear on her face. She'd come into the closest possible contact with Eddie during his attack. How could some of her DNA not be present in his flat?

The test was entirely voluntary of course, but that didn't mean a thing. In a fairly short period of time the police were going to have a list of names who'd provided DNA samples and who'd been eliminated from the inquiry.

In that same fairly short period of time they were going to have a list of names who hadn't and thus were very much not eliminated from any future inquiry.

And among that number would be Tia.

TIA WASN'T WASTING any time over the other not-so-small matter in her life right now though.

I was still living in the rented apartment although in truth I was existing inside a self-inflicted prison, afraid to go out, to answer the phone even when I knew – we'd set up a prearranged call signal – that it would be Dom. Her appearance on the breakfast TV show had turned Tia into something of a minor celebrity. The audience hadn't just listened to a story, they'd watched hope extinguish virtually before their eyes. As water-cooler moments go it may be destined to rank among the more minor that year but it still earned Tia her brief spot in the sun. She'd neither sought that nor – now – did she run from it. She had other matters in mind instead.

But it made any excursions into the outside world more than a little tricky so far as I was concerned. My face had been splashed over every news bulletin. A couple of the tackier tabloids were still milking the story. A couple of the broadsheets had reprised my photographic career, short-lived as it was, glossing over the circumstances behind my premature retirement. This was a human interest story. Feet of clay were very definitely not on the agenda for either tabloid or broadsheet right now. When it came to the facts or the legend then print the legend, as a wise man – James Stewart, I think – once said. And it remained as true in twenty-first-century London as it was in twentieth-century Tinseltown.

So for now I stayed indoors, my only link to the wider world via my laptop, my only focus the loft and Tia. Like myself – and apart from retrieving that stack of local papers – she hadn't set foot outside since her return. Unlike myself, every minute of her every waking hour was filled with activity, all to do with her partner who was now confirmed as deceased.

There were various formalities to complete of course, documents to forward to various officials and companies, all of whom were solicitous and courteous in the extreme. Her short burst of fame was opening every door it seemed. There was family – distant and long-lost – to contact, yet more friends – some long fallen by the wayside – to entertain as they either phoned or called round in person. As Tia said, on more than one occasion to more than one caller, she had no idea before of the width and depth of our circle of family, friends, even acquaintances. An extraordinary number and range of people were calling almost hour by hour.

At first it seemed to ambush her, pierce her emotionally in some way, but after a short while it seemed to give her a fresh burst of energy and become a source of new strength. And out of all that came a decision.

Tia decided she wanted to host a memorial service. My funeral, such as it was, would be a different affair, quieter, more low-key. There was always going to be something undeniably strange about a funeral with no body to bury or cremate. The authorities would be able to supply the few fragments of DNA they'd recovered from the site but that would hardly disguise the fact there'd be no physical presence inside the coffin. It didn't seem right somehow to turn that occasion into the celebration of my life that Tia obviously had in mind. So she hit on the notion of the memorial service instead.

Once started, the idea snowballed. Partly that was due to that extraordinary burst of energy that seemed to explode inside her. Maybe – and this I could well understand – after spending so many days in limbo, simply waiting, unable to move forward in any way, there was blessed relief in being able to take charge of events once more.

But partly that was also due to the extraordinary response from the various people she began to contact. Right from the start, acceptances flooded in even from those we'd lost touch with years before. No-one, it seemed, had a prior or pressing appointment that day, would be out of the country or required elsewhere. Not only that, but Tia was contacted by many others, some of whom we'd met only briefly, who also requested permission to attend. Already Tia was wondering, as her phone calls made clear, whether to shift the venue, whether she was going to need somewhere larger with possibly some kind of on-site catering. Because if that number of people were going to attend it seemed a shame that they'd just do so and then leave, surely there should be something laid on afterwards so everyone could congregate, raise a glass to a memory, extend the shared experience in some way.

I was under few illusions from the start. This outpouring of affection wasn't directed particularly at myself. What had really touched the hearts of those now eager to attend was Tia. She was always – courtesy of her work as well as her personality – at the heart of any hub she chose to frequent, forever at the centre of a thousand spinning wheels. And Tia had also touched their sympathies and affections. As with most events of this kind, the fellow-feeling was always going to be directed not at those who'd been lost but towards those who remained.

But it was still a heady and a quite remarkable experience. I'd begun by observing the actions and reactions of just one person. Now those actions and reactions were multiplied over and over. Stories were told about me by callers, stories that I knew bore some fleeting resemblance to truth but fleeting was perhaps the most charitable description. Already my life was being rewritten, reworked, filtered and modified in the light of its ending.

Dom called into my rented apartment a night or so later. I'd rigged up a feed to his laptop just in case mine, which was working overtime right now, went down for some reason, innocent or otherwise. I still couldn't even begin to work out how all those individual items of software had suddenly crashed all at the same time only to fire back into life at apparently the same moment and still wondered about some unseen and, as yet, unidentifiable hand behind all that. But that was then and this was very definitely now and the matter of the moment wasn't to do with computer malfunctions, sinister or otherwise. All that was on my mind and the mind of my increasingly absorbed companion and confidant was how this latest development affected what was supposed to be some kind of master plan but which, as that same companion and confidant was already beginning to point out, was resembling less a coherent and seamless strategy than a total fuck-up.

Or at least it was. For the first ten minutes of our latest exchange anyway, which was taking place against the backcloth of not just one, but two laptops now recording Tia and her near-ceaseless activities in the loft. For those first few moments it seemed that all the events I'd set in motion, all the circumstances I myself had initiated really had turned back on its originator with the remorseless vengeance of a thousand furies. From directing all that was taking place in my own small world I was now totally at the mercy of an event so large it was threatening at any moment to engulf me.

Which was when everything changed, when the axis shifted, perhaps only slightly, but still significantly, back in my favour. Because among the thousand and one phone calls that Tia was fielding right now, one – on the landline – seemed to stop her in her tracks. There was an odd pause before Tia greeted her respondent, a pause that cut across the ongoing inquest currently taking place between Dom and myself and which alerted us both to something very definitely out of the ordinary as regards this particular call. And it wasn't just the new hesitation in Tia's manner, there was something else too, a certain and intimate lowering of her voice.

Dom looked over at the two laptop screens. As chance would have it, Tia was looking into the bedroom, looking at nothing again, but she still appeared to be staring straight into the camera.

Once again I cursed my lack of foresight in only bugging her mobile. If I'd extended the surveillance to the landline too I wouldn't be in this position and wouldn't have had to endure the situation I'd also chafed through all those days before. I hadn't dared journey back to the loft again to put in place the new bug, but if I'd done it at the start then at least I'd have heard the voice of that mystery caller, the caller that Tia simply had to meet in the usual place wherever that was. I might or might not have recognised the voice but at least I would have been able to narrow down the field of suspects. I still, in my heart of hearts, didn't believe it was Natsuo.

And I also wouldn't be in the position I was in right now too, yet again that of the hapless observer, the impotent onlooker; because whoever it was Tia had been talking to then, she was very definitely talking to that same person right now too.

What was said wasn't really the issue. Tia was simply mumbling stock responses to what sounded like equally stock questions – how she was – how she was bearing up – how the arrangements were coming along. It wasn't the fact or the detail of the conversation that mattered, it was more the tone that had crept into her voice, the clear emotion that now softened her face and that wasn't just my paranoid interpretation of it all. Dom was also staring, rapt, at the screen, entranced by a picture of a woman who herself seemed rapt and entranced.

'That's him.'

'Or her.'

'Whoever.'

'I'm just saying.'

Then I stopped. Tia was struggling now, what her mystery caller had just said was obviously causing her considerable problems – distress even.

Then Tia spoke.

'I don't know.'

Tia listened as her respondent presumably – in the light of how this conversation was to end – argued their case.

'It just doesn't seem right.'

Tia listened again and I could see the muscles around her eyes relax, the lines around her mouth settle, could almost sense her will bending to that of another.

'No. I don't suppose it does make much difference now.'

Then Tia nodded and it was almost like a cloud being lifted and that wasn't just down to some decision being made, it was as if some line had just been crossed, some membrane pierced.

'OK. Come here.'

Tia listened.

'No, later. Make it after six.'

Then Tia put down the phone.

I looked at Dom who looked back at me.

'Wow.'

That was Dom. I didn't speak for a moment, couldn't speak, was still trying to take all that in.

'I think you just hit pay dirt, buddy.'

I nodded.

Whoever Tia had called, whoever she'd previously travelled to meet, wherever she'd travelled to meet him – or her – they were coming to the loft. All I had to do now was sit and wait. I even knew when her caller was to arrive.

Six o'clock.

Four hours' time. In four short hours the mystery that had kept me away up to that point was about to be solved.

'That surveillance technique.'

'What surveillance technique?'

'The one I told you about.'

'You haven't told me about any surveillance technique.'

'OK, the one I tried to tell you about. The new one that hasn't been put on trial yet.'

'The sensitive one, yeah?'

'That's one word for it. Want to hear about it?'

'What's the point? All I've got to do is sit down, watch my laptop and that's it, I'm going to find out everything I need to know.'

We were in a small café just down the street from the rented apartment. It was still a risk going out in my view, but a healthy dose of debunking common sense from Dom persuaded me. As he pointed out, as a news story mine was hardly up there with the exploits of movie stars or highly-paid footballers. To most people in the world this was always going to be the smallest of small-scale fillers and in any event there was only one face they were likely to remember from it all and that was much more likely to be the face that made the actual emotional impact, meaning Tia, rather than the face that had been seen only fleetingly among so many others on that poster.

'And what if you don't?'

'What?'

'What if there's a change of plan? What if she goes out instead?'

'Whoever called seemed pretty determined to meet at the loft.'

'What if that partner of yours has second thoughts? Or what if she does meet the person – and you watch and you listen – and you haven't the faintest clue who it is?'

'So I'll still hear what Tia says, I'll see how she is with them, I'll know.'

'For sure?'

'Maybe.'

Dom nodded, in that point-made way I'd come to know so well and, increasingly, was coming to dislike.

'Maybe's right. With this little sucker you'll know. No ifs or buts. You'll one hundred per cent, absolutely without question, money-back-guarantee, once and for all, know.'

Dom stood, handing me a small brochure, largely blank on the outside for reasons I was soon to understand only too clearly, some text on the inside.

'Just take a look, that's all I'm saying. See what you think.'

I still had no idea what it was all about but one thing was already puzzling me.

'So have you tried this? Is that why you're such a convert to the cause?'

Dom shook his head.

'Haven't the nerve.'

I stared back at him.

'Will never have the nerve.'

Dom nodded at me.

'But you have. You're probably the only person I know who has. Look at all this.'

Dom nodded at me – point proved again – then headed for the door.

'I'll call later. See what happened.'

I watched him go, then looked back at the brochure. I opened it, read the first few lines. Then I looked up, towards the door again, half-expecting to see him standing in the doorway, looking back at me, checking my reaction.

But he wasn't.

Natsuo was staring at me instead.

42.

TIA WOKE THE next morning to a letter pushed through the door, hand-delivered – presumably – by a police officer on his beat. It wasn't personalised in any way meaning a number, albeit a dwindling number, of local residents must have received the same. It contained an update on the search for Eddie's killer and professed some fine-sounding sentiments about the progress that had been made thus far.

But progress wasn't the same as an actual result of course. The letter noted that no-one from this address had yet attended the previously-announced screenings for DNA and invited them along to the next session which was to be held in a local school that coming weekend.

I knew the school. It was a large Victorian building, four storeys high, crumbling on the outside, one of the best run in the borough on the inside according to a number of local mothers who'd confided that fact almost conspiratorially to Tia as if she might find that of extra-special interest sometime soon.

Later that morning, Tia called into the local convenience store, stilling as she saw a copy of the same letter face up on the counter. The owner of the store followed her eyeline.

'When am I going to have time?'

'For what?'

He picked up the letter, waved it at her.

'What are all my punters supposed to do when I'm down some school somewhere and how do I explain that to the council when they come calling for their rates? Think they'll knock some off for me being so public-spirited?'

Then he snorted by way of a reply to his own question.

Tia maintained a diplomatic silence as she headed back to the door, her small purchase completed. But then she paused as he called out to her.

'So would it hurt?'

She looked at him.

'This test? It's needles, isn't it? Always hated needles.'

Tia held his stare, steady.

'Shouldn't hurt a bit.'

The next morning Tia woke to another letter from the police. For a time – about as long as her coffee took to percolate – she didn't open it. Then she unsealed the flap of the envelope, scanned the contents. I was fairly sure I knew what would be inside, yet another instalment in the now-ongoing campaign to pile on the pressure but I was wrong.

Tia laid the letter down on open view. It thanked the community for its co-operation in the investigation into the Eddie killing. And the police were pleased to announce that an arrest had been made.

Tia just stared in space, her expression betraying nothing.

43.

DETAILS OF THE arrest circulated pretty quickly and, once those details became common currency there was general agreement that the police had their man.

The man in question was a thirty-something male. He was reasonably well known in the local area for begging, mostly in a supplicatory manner, but occasionally more aggressively too. Most of the time he was pretty harmless but once he managed to score even a small amount of cash he'd head for one of the cut-price drink shops that had recently infested the neighbourhood. There were always deals to be cut with the different shopkeepers over and above the normal ones on offer which made the buying of booze cheaper – and considerably cheaper in some cases – than buying water.

His aggression would be in direct proportion to the success of his exploits out on the streets. If he'd had a spectacular day he'd be spectacularly aggressive to whoever he encountered. A poor day and he'd be his usual meek, mild and cowed self. Someone once tried explaining that if it was the other way round then people might be more inclined to unload the odd coin into his outstretched hand. There was precious little incentive in doing so when you knew it virtually guaranteed you a drunken rant.

It didn't sink in. Nothing seemed to. The begging became more and more desperate which in turn only alienated his prospective punters all the more. Small wonder then that he'd graduated to petty burglary.

He'd broken into Eddie's flat, that much he freely admitted. He'd passed the shop a couple of times, had heard a couple of his regular customers complain to each other about the place being closed. They took it almost as an affront. Eddie, in their view, provided something akin to a local service. He had no right to simply withdraw it like that with no warning.

He hadn't taken too much notice the first couple of times. But when one day turned into another, the conclusion had become inescapable. Eddie must have gone away. Whether that was for a holiday or a business trip wasn't really the point and he didn't care. The point was that if Eddie was away, then the shop was unmanned. That didn't really mean that much, Eddie – given the nature of his business – had the premises secured with all the latest alarms. But his flat, as Tia and myself had similarly deduced, might be a different proposition.

The vagrant cased it out that same night. The locals were used to seeing him encamped in various doorways so no-one really took much notice. From his new vantage point he watched the flat all evening, observed as lights came on in adjoining flats and curtains were drawn. But no light came on in the flat he was watching. No hand drew the curtains. Eddie's home was as silent and as apparently unoccupied as his business.

Which was, however you looked at it, an opportunity. The flat didn't seem to be secured by any sort of alarm once you negotiated the communal front doorway anyway. That was partly due to the fact you had to negotiate that front door and that wasn't always the easiest manoeuvre to complete. The old trick of ringing every bell until someone simply hit the access button had been consigned long ago to the pages of lazily-plotted novels. No-one was that stupid any more. But partly it was also due to the fact that Eddie had never exactly been house-proud. His flat was a place to lay his head as well as the occasional and clearly-desperate female customer. Creature comforts had never figured high on his list of priorities, meaning he really didn't have a lot to steal. But what wasn't a great deal to most people was riches beyond the dreams of avarice to the character huddled in the doorway across the street and, as for entry to the communal hallway, he had all night to wait for some visitor to emerge, uncaring whether they'd secured the door behind them, allowing it to swing free for a few moments during which time that same character huddled in the doorway across the street would be inside.

It took three hours but finally his opportunity presented itself. It took some ingoing partygoers to act as Fairy Godmothers, but with just one wave of their magic wands the door was swinging open behind them and as they disappeared, laughing, up the stairs, he was in. The flat door was the next obstacle but it didn't prove much of a barrier for long.

Some few months before he'd equipped himself with a long-handled screwdriver for purposes of personal protection. No matter how far you'd fallen, he'd discovered, no matter how little you might have, there were always those who would try and take it from you. The long-handled screwdriver wouldn't deter the more desperate or the genuinely insane, but the rest had been frightened off more or less successfully as he waved the blunted blade in their faces.

He dug the metal into the thin wood around the lock. He didn't really care what sort of damage he might do, he didn't plan to be in there too long anyway. It was possible one of the neighbours might head down that part of the hallway and see the splintered wood, but so long as they didn't do so in the next ten or so minutes that wasn't going to give him too much cause for concern either.

As it happened he didn't cause anything like the damage he expected. The lock gave after just two twists of the blade and from a distance, certainly the distance to the communal front door, there didn't seem to be too much amiss.

He slipped inside the flat, quickly, closed the door behind him and then, a moment later, really wished he hadn't.

His first thought, as he told the police in his initial statement, revolved around personal hygiene. He had the grace to acknowledge that might sound curious from a man whose last acquaintance with anything resembling soap and water was very much a distant memory, but some smells you get used to particularly when they're masked beneath several layers of clothing bolstered by a few layers of old newspaper.

But some smells you could never get used to. And the smell that hit him in that enclosed hallway was something he never wanted to experience again. The problem was that curiosity – or maybe the desire to profit in at least some way from his evening endeavour – drove him on where common sense, survival instinct, call it what you will, really should have sent him back down the hallway and out into a night which he'd never regarded as particularly fragrant before but which was now going to smell like something created by the finest parfumiers.

He moved on into the kitchen and was then almost sick on the floor. Eddie was lying there, or at least what was left of Eddie after the parasites had started to consume him. And then he'd turned, gagging all the while, as he stumbled down the hall and now he was actually sick on the floor as his fumbling fingers tried to find the handle before he slammed the door behind him and dashed back out onto the street.

Which was what had nailed him, of course. Forensics had a fair bit of work on their hands but they did eventually get round to those traces of vomit. No-one paid much attention to it at the time, it could even have belonged to Eddie; but when the men in the white coats finally put it under a microscope or whatever they used these days, it was found not to have originated in Eddie's gut but in the gut of a petty local criminal who'd been taken into the local nick on several occasions in the recent past, mostly in connection with his overly-aggressive style of begging and generally threatening behaviour.

The vagrant put his hands up pretty quickly to the crime of entering the flat and depositing what was left of the contents of some dustbins at the rear of a kebab shop on the High Street on its floor. He described in detail the smell that hit him as he'd walked in, which wasn't difficult as no matter what he'd done, no matter how hard he'd tried to disguise it in one way or another, he simply couldn't get that smell out of his nostrils.

The police had listened without comment, recorded everything he said.

And then they'd delivered their response.

Bullshit.

As far as they were concerned this tied everything up nicely. By his own admission this vagrant had broken into the flat. By his own admission he was a desperate man looking for something to steal. They couldn't know the exact sequence of events – whether Eddie had returned unexpectedly and surprised him – or whether he'd misread the situation and Eddie had been inside the flat all the time – but they could hazard a pretty shrewd guess as to what had happened next.

Eddie had come across his unwelcome visitor and had protested his presence. That unexpected and unwelcome visitor had become overly aggressive and generally threatening once more. And the ensuing confrontation had ended up with Eddie dead on the floor, his visitor back out on the street with plenty of time to prepare his story for the day – which would almost inevitably dawn given the presence of his DNA in the hallway – when he would be picked up and questioned.

The police acknowledged that as stories went his was fairly skilfully constructed. He must have realised it was impossible to deny his actual presence so adjusting the timescale was a neat way of admitting the break-in while attempting to evade the consequences of a larger crime. He had the grudging admiration of the police for it all even though, as they also pointed out, he didn't exactly have too much else to think about.

But their reaction was still the same.

Bullshit (again).

He was charged, remanded in custody and spent the next few hours protesting his innocence in various remand centres in and around London. During that time his clothes were peeled from his body and that body itself was subjected to various cleansing processes which removed assorted termites and parasites from his skin. Once that skin was returned back to a condition that might be regarded as almost human, he was given new and clean clothes. At the same time he started to adjust to decent food at regular intervals and began to enjoy simple comforts such as heat on a cold night.

Over the next day his protests gradually lessened in tone and volume. Then they dried up completely. That coincided with the arrival of a legal aid solicitor who'd been summoned to work with his new client on his defence only to find that client really didn't have too much to discuss with him.

The vagrant had already established, via discussions with various other remand inmates and prison staff, that a guilty plea on his part meant he'd be looking at perhaps six to eight more years of this sort of treatment. And he'd done some long, hard thinking which hadn't actually taken him too long or involved him in all that much effort either.

What the hell was he doing? For the last two years his life had been one long struggle to find food, warmth and shelter. In one fell swoop he'd achieved all three. Strictly speaking he hadn't achieved anything of course, but that was a minor quibble. It had been decided that he'd achieved all three and who was he to argue with wiser minds than his own?

He could maintain his innocence and, given a decent brief and the lack of anything other than circumstantial evidence, he might well secure an acquittal at some dim and distant point in the not-too-attractive future and his reward would be a return to the constant struggle of searching for food, warmth and shelter which were currently being handed to him, literally in one of those cases, on a plate.

He changed his plea at that very first meeting with his hard-pressed brief. He put his hands up to all the charges and signed a statement to that effect. A dispassionate observer might have been surprised at the similarity between his statement and the theory rehearsed by his interrogating officers immediately after his arrest. The police officers themselves simply congratulated themselves on their perspicacity. Their killer disappeared into the system. There'd be a court case at some time in the future which was just a formality now the defendant had decided he wasn't a defendant at all but any further investigation was, effectively, closed.

One thought now dominated the vagrant's mind. Why hadn't he done this before? He'd come across a couple of people in similar positions to himself who'd talked dreamily of life inside; of turkey dinners at Christmas, kippers on Father's Day, three square meals every other day, not to mention hot showers. At times he'd even let his mind drift towards the undeniably attractive vision that wafted before his eyes.

But he'd never acted on it and deep down he knew why. The sort of crimes he was capable of committing would never have sent him down for that sort of stretch. He was a man afflicted by that most troublesome of curses given his previous predicament and circumstances – a conscience. OK, he might run to the occasional petty theft but that was basically it as far as any criminal intent on his part was concerned. Even his well-documented sporadic aggression was all bluster and little substance. For all the complaints against him, there were precious few, if any, who ever witnessed that aggression spill over from the verbal.

The truth was that all this had never been an option because he simply didn't have it in him to commit a crime of this kind. He could never have lived with himself if he had. He couldn't imagine how the person or persons who had committed that crime could live with themselves either.

He didn't need to of course.

But Tia did.

4 4 .

T HE MEMORIAL SERVICE wasn't to be held in a church. Not an ordinary church anyway, nothing so conventional for Tia. She'd put as much thought into the venue as she'd put into the order of service and the guest list and I'd have expected nothing less from a woman who spent her days organising events that would live in the minds of oft-jaded attendees for months to come as well as unlocking the wallets of assorted sponsors. Tia, it had to be said, always had known how to throw one hell of a party.

The service was to be held in a hotel we'd come to regard as our second home, certainly in the early years of our relationship when trifles such as cost hardly figured. The hotel might have been a hundred or so miles from the capital but the prices had always rivalled anything to be found there. Other touches, revolutionary at the time, ordinary now – roll-top baths in the bedrooms and the like – all contributed to the impression, deliberate of course, of louche decadence. As well as a home from home.

It certainly felt like that to Tia and myself arriving in the middle of a rain-drenched night for our first visit. There was no reception desk, just a friendly face who appeared from a side room we later discovered to be a games room, complete with full-size snooker table lined in blue baize. She didn't bother checking our names. Passing trade was something of a rarity in this establishment, those who'd successfully decoded the somewhat tortuous directions to make it to the front door had usually booked in advance. She led us out of the hotel, past what looked like a particularly welcoming bar – it was, we were to later discover – past a dining room that smelled of smoke from a wood-burning fire in the centre of the room – not unpleasant, anything but – then out past a rack of Wellington boots and into a converted coach house where our room on the first floor led up to a mezzanine landing containing the biggest bed we'd ever seen. It felt immediately like a small piece of paradise and our tour of the hotel and grounds the following day did nothing to dim the favourable first impressions.

The spa was the first port of call for Tia, a converted range of outbuildings that at one time were cowsheds although the proportions looked almost too elegantly symmetrical for such a previous purpose. A range of treatment rooms led off the main reception which also looked out over two pools, one indoor, one outdoor, the outdoor infinitely preferable, heated to almost Jacuzzi-type temperatures making it the pool of choice for just about every guest whatever the weather. In fact, the worse the weather the more popular it became.

I spent an hour in there on the first morning while Tia refused to leave the outsize bed. I called the restaurant to ask when they finished serving breakfast only to be told that they didn't adhere to set times for different meals. If you wanted a bacon roll at three in the morning or afternoon, then call down and someone would rustle it up for you. I was briefly tempted to put this to the test one early morning on our first stay but decided against it. The staff seemed cheery and laid back but there was little point in pushing our luck.

On the afternoon of that same first day we came across the church. Had we not been so preoccupied with deciphering the almost incomprehensible travel directions – the hotel was tucked in the middle of a whole maze of minor roads that very definitely defeated Sat Nav Mapping – then we'd have seen it as we turned onto the main drive. But we were so relieved to see anything that even remotely resembled journey's end that we really didn't take in anything of the surroundings. But once we found the small building at the top of the drive, realised it wasn't just some relic of a former age, that it was open, that indeed it was always open, and walked inside, we were captivated.

The church dated from the middle of the eighteenth century and was used by the hotel as its principal venue for weddings and christenings. The hotel had hosted several such functions in the past. The whole experience so the wedding coordinator promised conjured up a bygone age of country weekends and shooting parties.

We'd watched one of the weddings on one of our stays on our third or fourth visit, a relatively small-scale affair that hadn't, unlike most of them, booked out the entire place. A dreamy Tia told me that if she was the marrying type – which she wasn't – and if we were ever to be married – which we weren't – and if she ever had a dream venue in mind – which she didn't – then this would be it. It made a sort of sense after a bottle each of the house red over dinner and I told her I knew what she meant.

But if the church was never destined to hold our wedding it was destined, it seemed, to host something else.

It was relatively easy for Dom to place the bugs. There wasn't exactly too much in the way of security around the place. The hotel was patrolled at night just in case any light-fingered locals decided to chance their luck with the belongings of distracted, probably drunken or wired guests, but those patrols didn't extend to the grounds and certainly not to the church. There was nothing in there of value anyway and so nothing to guard.

Besides, it was a point of pride that the place was always open day and night for those who might seek solace there. There was always the risk of some sort of mindless vandalism but in the eyes of the hotel and in the view of the minister who attended and presided over the occasional upmarket wedding or celebration, it was a risk worth taking. And it was a faith that had up to now been rewarded. No incident of any description had ever been logged by the local police in respect of the building or its environs. And Dom was too much of a professional to leave any trace of his activity behind, so there wasn't about to be any incident of any description logged now either.

Dom didn't quite see the point of it all and told me so. He understood the attraction of recording the actions and activities of persons engaged in private pursuits. That was all fairly obvious. Put a bug in the bedroom of your lover or the office of your business acquaintance and there could be all sorts of gold uncovered.

But what on earth could I learn from a bug placed in a public place like a church? There'd hardly be any confidences exchanged between the guests that I could observe. There'd hardly be any indiscretions that could be studied and analysed later. It promised to be one of the most anodyne occasions ever recorded in that sense so why on earth bother with any sort of recording at all?

For the first time since our curious liaison began in that anonymous hotel, I kept something back from Dom. Even as I was keeping it back I didn't quite know why. I'd hardly formed any sort of coherent plan at that stage after all. But something was forming, somewhere on the very edge of my mind, on the fringes of anything that could be called conscious thought. It took another day or so of watching Tia make plans, contact well-wishers, arrange speakers and rejig again and again some sort of running order for the service, but finally I knew what I was going to do.

Which was when I realised that given what I now had in mind the bugs placed by Dom were going to be somewhat superfluous to requirement. There was going to be no need for any sort of hidden surveillance at all in fact. From now on everything was going to be out in the open.

4 5 .

THE NEXT MORNING there was yet another development in the search for Eddie's killer. Much to the chagrin of the formerly-happy vagrant whose somewhat convenient confession was now coming under fresh scrutiny, new information had come to light.

According to a press release issued by the local police, DNA identical to that found at the recent train crash site – and identified as that of the deceased Jack Connolly – had been found inside Eddie's flat. An interview with Connolly's long-time partner had confirmed a massive row as having taken place between Eddie and her partner just a short time before his disappearance.

The police simply reported the development. Investigations into the development, they made clear, were continuing. But it provoked something of a feeding frenzy among the press in general and the tabloids in particular. And behind the latter, the hand of Toby Vine was all-too evident, indeed Toby himself featured prominently in a couple of the more lurid speculative pieces masquerading as reports.

As he'd made all-too clear to Tia in his visit to the loft, Toby did not believe for a moment he'd been mistaken that day outside Millbank. Toby had seen me and I'd seen him too.

Toby also hinted – hints that were forensically followed up by the same tabloids – at certain issues and questions connected with me in the past. And alongside the interview, those same tabloids duly reprinted a selection of headlines from the time of the Trooper Rohl incident. Words such as 'Fraud' and 'Cheat', picked out in bright red ink, once again screamed from the side of the page.

Nothing was actually said. It didn't need to be. You didn't need a weatherman, as the old song had it, to know which way this particular wind was blowing. It was those levers and pulleys again. That old pendulum effect. Build a star up to the sky and then watch it fall all the way back down to earth again. Destroy what once you'd created.

Tia's TV appearance had created a tragic and sympathetic victim.

Now an all-too-likely villain was taking her place.

In the veiled opinion of the press, what had actually happened here was obvious. Mr Connolly had killed a local businessman with whom he'd already clashed and had then taken advantage of a sudden and genuine disaster to do what he'd done once before.

Mr Connolly had fed the world, in short, a total lie.

46.

W E MET IN a pub which couldn't have been constructed more than twenty years before, but certainly wouldn't be standing in another ten. Then again the estate it served – a vast wasteland of grey concrete – hadn't even lasted that in places.

Already a process of selective demolition had started as contractors fought a losing battle against the onward tide of dry and wet rot, wood and metal fatigue and simple shoddy workmanship and bad design. Communal walkways had quickly become ambush alleys. The local police had equally quickly designated the estate a no-go zone, advising ambulance and fire services to adopt the same unofficial, but strictly observed, policy. Inside the four streets that bordered the estate it was a case of anything goes and much did. The few families housed there quickly moved out. A local school closed within two years of opening, mainly due to lack of demand from an ever-dwindling supply. A church still clung incongruously to its original site on the very edge of the estate and still opened its doors for three services each Sunday as well as the usual celebrations marking the religious festivals of Lent, Easter and Christmas. Local rumour had it that the parish priest ran a lucrative sideline dealing in the softer drugs but that was probably just an urban myth.

It should have made for a largely deserted and almost exclusively feral locale but the estate was still fairly heavily populated and most of the local shops still did a brisk trade. The local pub maintained an equally steady trade too. It was a weekday lunchtime when I walked in and it was packed to the rafters and business wasn't just confined to the bar. Itinerant traders moved from table to table with offerings as diverse as baby wear and mutton. It was the proud boast of many of the locals that you could buy anything and everything in there.

Including muscle.

Tia had sourced her own via her agency contacts. I'd sourced a similar species through a simple trawl of the internet and while this outfit weren't exactly offering their services on eBay, it was a close-run thing.

My new companion – who was very much cut from the same cloth as Gene – studied the picture of Tia I'd printed off from my computer. Then he looked at the various shots of the loft I'd also supplied. For a moment a flicker of unease crossed his face but that wasn't anything to do with the quarry he'd been asked to target or the location from which she was to be removed; it was the very specific instruction regarding the physical well-being of the cargo he was deputed to deliver.

Because Tia, as I made clear from the start, was not to be harmed. Which was tricky.

My new companion showed me a list of charges his outfit had printed up in turn. The whole thing came in a laminated cover and looked like a fairly downmarket takeaway menu, but the charges were exotic enough. A simple broken leg would set the customer back around a thousand pounds depending on the age and location of the victim. Curiously, the charge was lower for someone younger rather than older and the other anomaly was the charge for two broken legs – two legs broken on the same person at the same time that is, not a bulk purchase. The price for the double break rocketed to almost four times the price for a single break, the reason being that health issues became acute with a double break. There was, apparently, a much greater risk of blood clots and complications. The target could even die, particularly if the man or woman in question was elderly, hence the increased charge for persons of advancing years. Death came at a considerable premium and my new companion wasn't in the charity business. He didn't want to quote for a double leg break which then turned into something more terminal particularly when, as had happened in the past, he suspected that the client in question had such an outcome in mind all along. There were, as he pointed out, a lot of devious people about.

But I was causing him even more difficulties. A simple abduction was something his oufit had often handled, but it was usually a prelude to some serious injury visited on the person or persons abducted so there was never any reason to treat them with kid gloves. This required thought and planning and some considerable time and expertise in carrying out surveillance on the loft, not to mention a full risk assessment being carried out on the target.

This went on for some time until I brought matters to a head by proposing a fee roughly equivalent to two broken legs which was immediately accepted. I asked when he might be able to carry out the thought, planning, surveillance, risk assessment and deliver the abducted target to the specified apartment and delivery was promised for later that same day, suggesting there wasn't going to be anywhere near the thought, planning and surveillance that had so exercised him just a few moments before and which was beginning to look increasingly like a bargaining ploy. But as he'd said himself, there were some devious people about.

I checked on Tia via my laptop less than an hour later. She was putting the finishing touches to the running order for the memorial service which was scheduled for ten the next morning. Dom had been back in touch to confirm that all the bugs had been installed in the church and were functioning properly. He couldn't connect to a power supply but each bug had a forty-hour battery life, so some of the speakers at that service would have to wax seriously verbose if we weren't to capture the whole thing.

By now, I think Dom was beginning to suspect something else was going on. He'd developed a sixth sense when it came to all matters subterranean and his in-built antennae was well and truly twitching. But I didn't enlighten him. I just made sure the link to the loft computer was working OK. I'd need to take it over sometime during either the night ahead or in the early hours of the following morning and couldn't risk any problems. For all this to work there couldn't be any loose ends.

I waited till Tia was in the shower. Within moments I had remote control of her desktop and every keystroke I was making on my laptop was immediately transferred to her screen. I checked the camera monitoring the bedroom. The sound of water running from the shower was coming through loud and clear and steam was percolating around the slightly-open bathroom door.

I turned back to my laptop and typed a message which immediately transferred to the screen in the loft. The message was simple and to the point. It told Tia that I loved her. I stared at the simple message writ large on her computer for her and for the whole world to see. I kept it on screen for as long as I dared and then deleted it moments before she reappeared towelling her now-damp hair, comforting myself with the thought that in just a few short hours she'd know that for herself, totally and completely and without any fear of contradiction.

One hour later there was a ring on the loft doorbell. It wasn't the buzzer from outside which had announced the vast majority of visitors up to now, meaning whoever had rung that bell was inside the complex. Meaning, so far as Tia was concerned, that it must be some neighbour again come to talk over some detail of the memorial service perhaps and she didn't even stop checking another detail of the service on her mobile as she headed for the door. She was already pasting on a polite smile as she reached for the handle.

I wasn't smiling. I knew exactly who'd be waiting on the other side. As her hand reached out some small part of me wanted to call out, to protect her from what I knew would be that instant of total shock and fear, terror even – but I contented myself with the reassurance that the game was a long one and the moment of shock and terror was just that; a moment, an instant that would fade, that would even be forgotten in time.

As Tia opened the door there was a sudden white light. She was almost literally blinded for a moment as a flare exploded just before her eyes. Given her disorientation it was the work of an instant to secure her arms and legs with tape at the same time as a bag was placed over her head. More tape fastened over her mouth meant she couldn't shout out, couldn't alert anyone else in the block to the fact that on top of all her other recent misfortunes she now seemed to be the object of a burglary, or an assault – or possibly even something worse – at the hands of some more than usually heartless example of local lowlife.

Tia, secured and trussed, was then bundled into a laundry bag and packed inside a stiff-sided cart. I could now see her assailants as they briefly came into view of the bug in the radio alarm clock and I'd have been fooled by them too. Their overalls were exact replicas of those worn by operatives from the cleaning company who serviced the complex. The laundry bags and wheeled laundry carts were exact replicas of the genuine article too. Perhaps they were the genuine article. Perhaps somewhere in the depths of the building two operatives were currently tied up without their uniforms and missing their laundry cart.

It hardly mattered. By the time they were discovered – if that was the means whereby my internet contact had completed his deception – the object of that deception would be far away from the scene of the apparent crime and, I was already confident, without leaving any trace behind.

The door closed behind the men and Tia. For a moment, as they exited, the lead muscle glanced back towards the bedroom. For that moment he too seemed to stare right into the concealed lens of the radio alarm clock almost as if he knew it was there.

It was impossible of course. I hadn't told him any details of the larger plan at work here. He hadn't asked, wasn't interested in all probability. In his line of work he simply carried out instructions and left anything else to his paymasters. Yet in that moment he not only stared straight at the bug as if he was staring straight at me, but there was something in his expression too, something knowing, but of what I couldn't divine. Then the door closed behind them and they were gone.

I shook myself back to the land of the living and away again from the world of fanciful imaginings, a by-product I knew of too much time spent by myself. But that, as with everything else, would soon be over.

I took over Tia's desktop once again by remote control. As before all I had to now do was type on my keypad and everything I typed automatically transferred to her screen all ready for onward transmission.

I'd already drafted the message I wanted to send but I still took care reading and rereading the draft before I sent it out. Again, the tone had to be spot on. There were several people in Tia's online address book – friends and long-term colleagues – who'd be alert to any false note in any messages Tia might be sending right now. A couple of them had already called round concerned as to the strain she was under and I didn't want anything in this communication to provoke a similar response. I was aiming for a dignified, almost resigned tone. Something that invited sympathy rather than anything that might panic a recipient into any sort of call to arms.

The message was fairly simple and to the point. On reflection, Tia had decided that she could not attend the memorial service after all. She thought she was strong enough to bear it, but as the time had approached she'd realised she wasn't. She wanted the service to go ahead; in fact, she was insistent it do so. Cameras and audio devices had been installed to record the service and it was going to give her a great deal of comfort in the days and weeks to come to be able to watch all the individual tributes that were going to be paid to her partner that day.

That last touch was, hopefully, a neat one. It told any concerned friends or colleagues that Tia was looking beyond the trial of that service, was already looking forward to a process of repair and recuperation. The message ended with an expression of heartfelt thanks to those who'd sent messages of comfort and support and an assurance that she'd be in touch with each and everyone of them in the next few days to convey those thanks in person.

A few hours later, Tia was taken out of the stiff-sided laundry cart. She'd become impossible to restrain, even with the tape restricting her movements and my new contacts had been forced to resort to using a disabling drug more commonly used to subdue small to medium size animals in transit. So when Tia was carried into the rented apartment she was seemingly just a collection of recently-cleaned clothes.

There'd be a delay of another few hours while she came round but that actually suited me. I hadn't particularly relished the prospect of her first glimpse of a dead man taking place with my internet companions looking on. Now they'd be well out of the way and Tia and myself would be alone as we should be, as we perhaps always would be from that point on.

Those few hours later, Tia opened her eyes. She took a second or two to focus, to adjust to her new surroundings, even to, briefly, luxuriate in the new-found freedom from her recently-imposed bonds before she looked across the room and met my eyes.

47.

Dom was right. His latest surveillance technique was nothing if not extraordinary. He was also right that it was hardly likely to ever be offered for general sale even if it offered the promise of the most intimate form of surveillance imaginable. Because for the first time, if everything worked as it should, it was going to be possible to actually inhabit another person's thoughts, to take up residence in effect in another person's mind.

Tia stared at me as I started to explain all this. She hadn't spoken since coming round, hadn't asked a single question or made any sort of response. Only her eyes betrayed her struggle to understand the new world into which she'd been catapulted from a world she probably hardly recognised any more.

The operation was simple, hardly meriting the rather grand-sounding term in truth. It involved little more than a simple incision in both our upper arms. Once the incision was made a small silicon chip, enclosed in glass, would be inserted. I'd already practised the incision, if not the actual insertion, two or three times and the minor wound had healed within moments. I showed Tia the almost invisible scars that had been left behind but she still didn't make any sort of response. I had the impression that enduring a minor cut of the kind I was describing was the least of her concerns right now.

Once inserted the chip would read the electrical signals coming from nerves in our arms. It's long been accepted scientific belief that electricity coursing up and down the nervous system is actually a snapshot, not only of a person's physical state, but their mental state too. In other words, those signals could encode how that person – or in this case two people – were feeling at any given moment in time.

If the signals from one arm could be fed into a simple laptop, of the type I had on the small table between myself and the still-staring Tia, then this would then be sent on to the other person's chip and thereby to their nervous system. If that all performed as it should, then Tia's nervous system would be temporarily possessed by mine, enabling me to feel the emotions she'd be experiencing at the exact moment she herself was feeling them.

It wasn't all to be taken on trust. The software had come with a small DVD presentation showing a volunteer with a temporary chip inserted moving through a house in an attempt to prove that silicon and flesh can recognise each other. As the volunteer walked by, a television switched on to a pre-selected channel. As he walked into the kitchen, a kettle began to boil. The demonstration was intended to show that similar chips, if used by the disabled, could be used to power similar household appliances.

But, and as Dom had already pointed out, that was nothing compared to the more interesting, indeed dramatically more interesting, possibilities on offer.

OK, there were risks. Few, if any, had actually attempted to go the whole way with this, had effectively wired themselves to another human being with these sort of surveillance intentions in view, although plenty of scientists had linked computers with the human nervous system in the past. A college in Augusta, Maine, had used the technology to treat victims of multiple sclerosis, enabling them to achieve basic controls over key motor functions. In Atlanta, Georgia, after a transmitting device had been implanted into his brain, a stroke victim had been able to move a cursor on a computer simply by thinking about it. Many similar and well-publicised experiments had also been undertaken by well-respected practitioners in the UK, all with the same altruistic ends in mind.

But to attempt to access another person's emotions, feelings – and even memories – in this particular way, and without any of the more usual scientific and medical checks in place, was uncharted territory. So no-one could know for certain just what the outcome of all this might be and in the interests of fairness I did feel duty-bound to point that out to Tia. Nobody could really guarantee whether the human brain could actually cope with this kind of outside invasion. It was possible, though hardly likely, that the brain might simply shut down in the wake of the literally unprecedented event it was experiencing.

I explained this to Tia as I explained everything else. It was a full and frank summary of everything Dom had explained to me plus additional pieces of information I'd sourced from various outlets while I waited for her to be delivered.

Tia still hadn't spoken. Her eyes just maintained that almost unblinking stare. I didn't know what I'd expected but I did expect some sort of reaction at least. I was just about to check that the disabling drug with which she'd been injected hadn't caused some unfortunate side effect, whether she was still drifting in between levels of consciousness.

But then there was a reaction. Sudden, piercing and raw. Tia screamed. At the top of her voice and she didn't stop screaming either, so all in all I really didn't have any choice.

The memorial service started on time. Courtesy of Dom and his unofficial bugs and Tia and her official audio and video recorders I could see virtually every attendee, could monitor not only what was said by the guest speakers but the reaction on the faces of their audience. It was the kind of experience that really needed to be shared so it was good in one sense that Tia was with me, watching it all. It was just unfortunate that circumstances had dictated the reinstatement of the tape covering her mouth and securing her arms and legs. But as I said, recent events had left me with very little choice.

Tia had taken me by surprise with her sudden scream. I knew she was always going to find aspects of all this highly curious to say the least, but I did expect some sort of dialogue. Perhaps not any sort of extended debate – that was always going to be too much to hope for given the enormity of the discoveries she'd be making – but at least some exchange. I was disappointed, I had to confess, that no exchange, or even the ghost of such, had taken place. I wanted the chance to guide Tia through the twists and turns of the events that had enmeshed us, try and make her understand if not exactly empathise with all I'd felt impelled to put in place. None of that had been possible and that wasn't just because of that piercing, unbroken, scream.

I'd stood to restrain her and Tia had dashed past me. She'd taken me by surprise with the scream and even more by surprise with the wild fist she'd lashed out, catching me full in the face, scarring my cheek courtesy of the small collection of rings on her fingers, turning my whole world momentarily blood red. By the time I'd regained some semblance of vision, could reorientate myself to some limited extent at least, Tia was scrabbling at the front door which fortunately I'd had the foresight to deadlock.

I reached out my arms, tried to pacify her, what the hell was this, did she really think she was in some sort of nightmare, a real-life horror-flick, did she imagine that I really was dead and that she'd entered some sort of parallel universe in which the deceased walk again and live in rented apartments in dormitory towns? Surely by now she'd have started to piece things together, work out in part at least what this was all about?

Tia lunged past me again but this time I was ready for the flying fist. I grabbed her, prevented her moving towards what she probably hoped was a rear door or some window through which she might make an escape that was simply unnecessary. All this was motivated by love after all. Why should she seek an escape from that? But all I succeeded in doing was diverting Tia into the smaller bedroom just off the main hall and that was actually the last place I wanted her to be at that point in time.

Natsuo had been a more willing audience at least at the start. I always knew she would be. She was always more receptive than Tia to what might be called the wilder side of human experimentation. For those first few moments, as I'd taken her away from that café and as she pieced together all that had happened, all that I'd put in place, there was something almost child-like in the sense of wonder that illuminated her eyes.

If only it had lasted. If only she hadn't spoilt it. It made it doubly worse that having surpassed my expectations, having seemed to grasp just what it was I was attempting to do, Natsuo should so quickly fall back into the mindset I'd more traditionally associate with what I suppose you might call the man or woman in the street. All this had never been designed for that sort of creature. This required an altogether higher sensibility to grasp and understand.

Tia was certainly of the right mindset, although even I'd have to acknowledge there were personal issues that might prevent her grasping its full beauty at least at the start. But in time I was more hopeful that a more open attitude and acceptance might prevail.

But Natsuo was different. And when her face – always pale – whitened even more in shock as I explained the next stage in all this, as I showed her the components of the experiment I was about to initiate, as I wondered – late thought – whether she might like to trial it herself with me, she disappointed me cruelly it had to be said. It wasn't just the blank refusal to even contemplate it at all, it was the incautiously-stated avowal – incautious as I think she realised the moment she said it – that Tia could not be allowed anywhere near either myself or this grotesque undertaking.

How could I tolerate that having come so close to the climax of this mission? How could I watch it snatched away at the eleventh hour? It was unthinkable, untenable; and I'd like to think Natsuo realised that.

Tia had no idea which door led where. She'd just dashed into the bedroom hoping it would provide an exit of some kind, only to realise within moments that she'd very much taken a wrong turn. There was a small window looking out onto the private garden but that window was secured with locks, and even if they were breached it would have been far too small for anyone of average height or weight to get through with any sort of ease. And such a manoeuvre would be absolutely impossible with a pursuer, albeit one with blood still stinging their sight, following close behind.

Beneath the window Tia turned. For a moment she looked behind me, computing the possibility of another assault and a dash back to the front door maybe. She stood precious little chance of success, but I'd reckoned without her innate enterprise and ingenuity and one part of me admired her next initiative even as another part was as appalled as Tia to witness its result.

Tia turned to the only freestanding piece of furniture in the room, the wardrobe by the bed. Then, employing a strength I really didn't think she possessed, she snaked an arm behind it, sending it crashing to the floor between us. As a tactic it was likely to do little more than delay things, in actuality it achieved more than I'd managed in the last few minutes in robbing Tia of all movement and resolve. Because, as a horrified Tia watched, the door crashed open as the wardrobe smashed onto the floor and the trussed and bound body of my old partner – and, apparently, her new friend – spilled out onto the floor.

Natsuo's head twisted as it came into contact with the thin carpet. A cracking sound echoed across the small room. Natsuo stared, fixed and unblinking, at Tia who stared back at her, unable now to move or to speak. She'd even been robbed it seemed, of the power to scream.

I approached from across the room, slowly, carefully, but any precautions were unnecessary. I don't think she even registered my approach. She was looking down at Natsuo whose eyes were screaming in silent pain, some bone in her neck or shoulder now quite clearly broken.

I touched Tia on the arm, intending to steer her away from a sight I knew would be distressing. Later, once I'd explained everything, once we'd submitted ourselves to the experiment, I was sure I'd be able to make her understand along with everything else. She'd know, as I knew already, that this, while hugely regrettable, was a necessity in the circumstances. All I had to do was complete the task.

Then all of a sudden, I realised that perhaps I wouldn't even need to explain it. Perhaps – extraordinary thought – Tia would simply know because she'd be possessed by me as I'd be by her. Cumbersome contrivances such as explanations would be rendered unnecessary. If that was true, if that was part of the bright new future that lay just around the corner for us both, then everything else, surely, must pale into insignificance, even – forgive me – Natsuo.

It also meant I wouldn't even have to bother with the questions that had been tormenting me ever since I staged my disappearance. The identity of the mystery visitor would now be revealed, not via Tia, but directly into my brain. Thanks to the diversion provided by Natsuo in that nearby café, I'd missed that encounter, of course. Just why Tia would be walking that day down the Strand hand in hand with Natsuo herself would also be laid instantly clear. And so much else besides – the keys in the pannier of the Duke – that strange code – the scar I'd seen on her back all that time ago now.

Tia felt my hand on her. She just looked at me, didn't speak. I couldn't divine what I was seeing in her eyes as she simply stared up at me, still not speaking, still not making any sort of response but soon I would.

Soon I'd know everything.

4 8 .

T HE MEMORIAL SERVICE began with a small slideshow of photographs taken by myself in different locations around the world. There was a whole range of subjects and moods from the more conventional war shots to character stuff; a striking image of an elder from a tribe I'd come across in Namibia as well as a human freak show I'd happened upon in Panama.

Trooper Rohl was, tactfully, omitted as was the recent tabloid speculation as to whether I was actually dead.

With Tia once again restrained opposite me, a sad but necessary precaution in the circumstances, I paused as I reviewed my life along with the attendees in the packed church, feeling – an immodest response I know – a certain admiration for the man who'd captured those sometimes extraordinary images.

A couple of the shots had even been referred to in august journals as masterpieces. I looked across at Tia. If only I could have placed a live feed from the rented apartment into that church right now. If only they could all have seen what was happening, not a world removed as it still sometimes seemed to me, but just time and distance away. If they really believed a few snatched photographs contained within them elements of greatness, then what would they have made of this?

Because even now, even at this late stage, new elements were being introduced all the time. The latest refinement had occurred to me as I was inserting the chip. I couldn't help it, as the needle penetrated her skin and as Tia recoiled, instinctive, at the sudden sharp pressure, I stroked her forearm, a gesture of comfort, of reassurance. For a moment she looked at me, her eyes focusing and for the first time there was some connection made, some old link re-established, nothing compared to what was to come but still a small step along a road which already promised so much for us both.

And the next refinement was suddenly obvious. It had been so long since we'd been together, properly together in what we always joked was the biblical sense, although there was nothing in our shared experience of religious education in schools or the occasional church that even remotely conjured up images of the activity we had in mind when we used that phrase.

But we could be together now. All that, along with so much else, was now not only possible but somehow right. In practical terms it would mean I'd have to release her bonds to some degree, but by then Tia would be connected via the chip to the computer and would be wired via my chip into my own nervous system. All thoughts of flight would by then have been rendered redundant with the experiment under way.

I removed her clothes, peeling away layer after layer from her uncomplaining, if still unresponsive, body. She didn't even seem to feel the slight chill that had crept into the room. Then I removed my own clothes. We faced each other naked now, about to be naked in so many other ways too.

I fought, again, against the brief flash of irritation that surged inside me as I looked at her, as I tried to read some reflection of the almost overpowering excitement I was feeling in her own eyes. But that would come. I'd lived with this for some good while now. This was all still new to her.

I kissed Tia – still sadly with no response – then turned to the computer. I hesitated, not out of any late second thoughts but simply to savour the moment. It wasn't often in life that one stands on the brink of something that will change that life forever, and not just for oneself but for others too. This was truly one of those moments and I wanted to remember what it felt like to balance on the edge of one existence before plunging headlong into another. I reached out, caressed the naked back before me, felt skin react, instinctively, almost involuntarily, then clicked on the control icon on the laptop that would begin the programme.

On the monitor the memorial service was now well underway. I could see so many old colleagues and acquaintances. Even Toby had made the trip. Most would have travelled with one eye at least on the possibility of their own advancement – the day was going to provide an unparalleled networking opportunity if nothing else – but some would have descended on that small church to register their own more genuine tribute. There was, as one of the speakers was saying right at that very moment in time – a picture editor who'd given me one of my first breaks – always an element of the pioneer in the approach I'd taken to my work.

I looked at Tia, naked before me, the software humming, her impulses and thoughts about to become meshed with mine as my impulses and thoughts were about to become with hers. If I ever talked about this, wrote about it, demonstrated it to the wider world in any way then that simple word – pioneer – would seem peculiarly apt.

I began to have trouble breathing. At first I thought it might simply be the heightened emotion of the occasion, an understandable side effect; but then I began to realise it was something more. My second thought was that it was the first physical effect of the process that was now beginning, but then I realised the sudden difficulty was actually more of a symptom than a cause. It was as if the space inside me was being squeezed somehow, as if the cavities inside not just my brain but my whole body were becoming inhabited in some manner. I couldn't yet identify just what it was that seemed to possess me in this way and there was always the possibility that this was my own mind playing tricks, some sort of wish-fulfilment so I had to keep monitoring the new sensation. But it was definitely intensifying all the while.

I looked at Tia who seemed to be in some sort of stupor now, not connecting with anything that was happening. But perhaps that was because all that was happening now wasn't happening to her, it was happening to some new being that had been created out of the union of two formerly separate people. Her thoughts, emotions and responses were now becoming inextricably melded with the thoughts, emotions and responses of another, and the overload all that was creating seemed to be shutting her down in some way. Perhaps it was a reflex action, a defence mechanism while her mind adjusted to the strange new world in which two people thought, acted, even breathed as one. It was, as Dom had been at pains to stress, totally new territory.

On the monitor another guest speaker had taken up the baton, was talking about the early days of mine and Tia's relationship, the conviction shared by so many of our friends that this was one of those unions that was destined to last, all of which made it all the more devastating that I was now gone.

Once again I felt like shouting at the monitor – Look! For just one moment, look upon the totally extraordinary and feel a tiny fraction of all I'm feeling right now. And all I was sure Tia was feeling too. Glimpse a life, two lives, a world being changed for all time.

I was now inside Tia, joined physically as we had been so many times in the past but now joined in other ways too and I was seeing pictures, her pictures perhaps, I couldn't yet know, it was still too early in the process for me to be sure what was my imagination and what was her reality. But even now, even at this infant stage in the process, I knew that something from outside was now in my brain and I had to decode new signals, as if I was learning a new language, separate everything out from the massive rush of feeling that was sweeping through me and that was surely sweeping through Tia too, learn to read all that was happening, search amongst it for answers.

Suddenly and out of nowhere came a picture, clear as the most blinding shaft of sunlight, a small child playing on a beach, building a sandcastle, watching the tide lap against it – not my memory, so it had to be hers, her childhood, not mine, a memory that was banal in one sense, everyday, the kind you wouldn't normally share so how was I seeing it now if the process wasn't moving on, if I wasn't beginning to access the innermost reaches of her mind as Tia presumably was now beginning to access mine?

I looked round the nondescript rented apartment, at the monitor relaying my memorial service, at Tia, her body and mind conjoined with mine. For a moment I savoured the experiences that were to come as I explored the mind of another, possessing her as she would possess me. I looked deep into her eyes, saw my own eyes reflected inside and I knew – without a shadow of a doubt – that if this experiment was a step too far, was destined to spell the end for the two of us, then no-one – absolutely no-one in the history of Christendom – would ever have died as happy as this.

Then came the pounding on the door.

49.

T HE OFFICER IN charge of the raid had the face of a thirty-year-old but eyes that seemed to have lived forever.

There was a wounded quality to them, damaged; as if she'd looked for too long on a world that never ceased to ambush her with its capacity to astonish and in all the wrong ways and for all the wrong reasons. And the way she was looking at me right now was telling me more eloquently than any subsequent interrogation could ever have managed that maybe she'd just stumbled across one of the most extreme examples of that.

I hadn't actually needed to respond to the hammering on the door. The specially trained officers massed outside weren't politely requesting entrance. They were using a jackhammer to break down the cheap plastic barrier that separated Tia and myself from the rest of the world. Another unit had already been stationed at the rear to prevent flight in that direction. I only had time to turn, stare at that thin plastic door in bewilderment before it gave way and police officers flooded inside.

Inspector Munroe – the owner of that face of a thirty year old and eyes older than time – came in behind the advance party. The first officers had been armed. They had no real idea what to expect to find and clearly weren't taking any chances. The fact Tia was inside and unharmed was quickly established as was the fact that I wasn't in possession of any sort of weapon. Indeed, I didn't seem in possession of even my limited faculties right now if my slack-jawed incomprehension was anything to go by.

All the time Munroe just stood before me and stared, making little attempt to hide the feelings clearly etched in those tired eyes.

I didn't know what the hell was happening. I didn't know how they'd found us, how anyone could have traced the address although – those faculties now slowly returning – I was already beginning to have my suspicions. I also didn't remotely expect what was to come next.

One of the armed officers – perhaps signalled by Munroe, I was sure I caught a half-nod from her in my direction – suddenly smashed me across the back of the head with a chair leg, broken as it was thrown against a wall on their entrance just a few moments before. I pitched forward onto the table only for my head to be yanked back by Munroe herself.

For a moment she stared deep into my eyes as I stared wildly back at her. Then she spat, literally, spat, a great globule of phlegm exploding all over my face, trickling into my mouth, stinging my eyes and clogging my nostrils. I gagged and choked as Munroe twisted my hair tighter and tighter as across the room Tia screamed, another reflex action, before Munroe finally released me, smashing my forehead back down again on the table

So it was I achieved my first insight into the more general attitude of a world that felt it had been duped, that felt – with considerable justification – that its emotions had been toyed with; that it had believed something to be true only to discover it had been presented with pale fiction in place of cold fact. The Trooper Rohl lesson yet again, perhaps. Then I was bundled into the small kitchen and an armed officer was stationed at the rear door as I was handed my clothes and commanded to dress.

As I was hustled away I could already see another female officer with Tia, placing a blanket around her shoulders. Then the kitchen door was slammed shut and I was left alone with only an incommunicative armed escort for company.

Outside in the street I could hear now-constant activity as police tape was unrolled, securing the apartment. Inside I could hear footsteps everywhere – in the sitting room, the bedrooms, the hall, checking out a hitherto-undiscovered basement. Then a short time later the door from the kitchen to the sitting room was flung open. Tia remained in the far corner shielded by that same female escort, the blanket still draped around her shoulder. Munroe was standing in the doorway and behind her Natsuo was standing there too, supported by another officer, waiting for the arrival of a paramedic to examine what would turn out to be a hairline fracture of her collarbone. Her face was as alabaster white and inscrutable as ever. Her hair was a little less perfectly groomed than usual perhaps, but aside from the slightly stiff posture Natsuo was adopting courtesy of her injury, that was about the only evidence of her recent incarceration.

'So – and just by way of warming up – you waste a lowlife pawnbroker. Then you nearly cripple an old girlfriend for life.'

Munroe kept staring at me.

'You pay some losers to kidnap your current girlfriend.'

My hired muscle.

They'd got to them already.

'OK, in the sicko stakes it's tasty, although coming from a man who lets his partner think he's been wasted in a train crash, what would we expect, but this – .'

Munroe gestured at the laptop, the software still active, the program – interrupted on their entrance – still running.

Dom?

Had they got to Dom too?

I kept my eyes level, staring back at Munroe as she proceeded to deliver her verdict on a man who not only counted murder, kidnap and deception among his dubious list of achievements, but who apparently had a strange and as yet unexplained compulsion to conduct grotesque experiments – her words not mine – on a scale that rivalled some of the more twisted excesses of the SS – again, her words not mine.

For some reason and as with Natsuo, it was the computer

program that really seemed to get to Munroe. Perhaps in some distant universe she could see some bizarre explanation for everything else I'd done so far. In no universe, distant or otherwise, could she understand how anything might explain all this.

In my pocket an untraceable mobile I'd recently acquired briefly pulsed, a text message delivered as Munroe turned back to Tia and Natsuo. I stilled, hardly now seeing Munroe or indeed anyone else.

Only one person had that number. Meaning only one person could now be trying to contact me. As casually as I could, I turned, hunched over the kitchen chair as if cowed by the enormity of my sins and sneaked a look at the screen.

The text was indeed from Dom.

It comprised just a single question mark.

I looked at it, then stared across at Tia.

For that moment I wasn't in that rented apartment, for that moment I wasn't with any of my present and unwanted companions. For that moment I was back with Dom in his surveillance store feeling his eyes on me as I left after that first visit, almost hearing the unspoken message that followed me outside, silently predicting my return.

Then I was actually listening to him, recognising again the tone in his voice as he leant close to the phone.

'Is that Jack?'

A millisecond later I was with him in that anonymous hotel watching as he stared, seemingly bewildered, at a whole array of bugs that had apparently failed at exactly the same moment.

Then I was listening to him again as he told me every one had miraculously reactivated once more.

All the time too I kept staring at my partner who wasn't even aware of my stare, who didn't indeed seem aware of anything right now. And all the time too, as that single question mark in the recently-delivered text echoed inside my head, a chill feeling crept over me.

While I was being taken into custody, while I disappeared into the system – much like the ultimately-innocent vagrant who'd visited Eddie – Tia was going to be examined, was going to be checked over but was then going to be released back to her old life, returned back home where she'd be monitored for a while, called on by a network of friends and family no doubt, but then allowed to return to some semblance of a normal life at least at which point…

And then my brain closed down, refused to visit the sudden vision of the immediate future that simple text had just ushered into my brain.

I palmed the mobile, looked through the open door at Tia again who was now finally looking across at me and – the strangest thing – it was as if she could now read my mind. She was staring straight at me as Munroe barked instructions into a handset, arranging for transport for Tia, ordering an even more minute sweep of the apartment, checking for any further evidence of human habitation, enforced or otherwise.

All the while Tia kept staring at me and her eyes seemed to bore into mine as if she was seeing all I was seeing right now, maybe not in its exact detail but as if she could read my fear, a fear not for myself, but for her, some instinct seemingly at work inside her, survival mode kicking in perhaps, telling her that while she was apparently being gathered inside one protective embrace she was being opened out at the same time to the sort of threat her current protectors couldn't even begin to envisage.

It couldn't have been my imagination. I knew her too well. And as if by way of confirmation of all that, there was now a faint nod across the room, a silent signal unobserved by anyone else, telling me that I had one chance and one chance only and that chance would be upon me at any moment and that I had to seize it right there and then.

I had no idea what she'd do. I didn't really know how she'd play out whatever it was that was behind her eyes right now. But what I didn't expect was for her to fly at Natsuo.

Natsuo clearly didn't expect the sudden attack either. For a moment that alabaster face cracked in shock, those hooded eyes flashed wide as Munroe stared across at the sudden and shocking display of violence unfolding before her for reasons she couldn't even begin to understand. Perhaps it was the almost-inevitable backlash of a soul bent out of shape by its recent experience at the hands of a more than usually venal example of human pond life.

But any explanation was very much for later, for now the matter of the moment was separating one victim from another and Munroe stepped in quickly to do that followed by the rest of the officers.

In the mayhem the escort guarding the door had eyes only for the developing mêlée, granting me one millisecond of an opportunity to escape.

In that millisecond I'd lashed out and was past the now doubled-up guard and outside in the small garden. With the house secured inside I was hoping against hope that the unit deputed to prevent flight from the rear during the initial raid would have been stood down and I was right.

I vaulted the fence at the end of the empty garden, dropped down into the street and began to run away from the apartment, but I knew that was always going to be a doomed endeavour unless I could access the sort of safe haven I now had in mind and quickly too. I turned a corner but there was nothing, turned another corner but there was no opportunity there either.

Behind, I could hear sirens exploding into life. I turned another corner and nearly missed it for a moment but there it was. An opportunity, not much of one but an opportunity at least. My fingers were ripped and bleeding in seconds but I did manage to lever the iron manhole cover up from the road and then I slid inside, slamming it shut above me.

Then I stood for a moment on the metal steps in the near darkness, my pounding heart drowning out every other sound, effluent running below me, a small army of vermin scuttling away.

In my pocket my mobile, briefly, pulsed once more.

I STAYED IN the sewer for the rest of that day and most of the following night. Once the rats became used to the new presence among them and realised I had no interest in doing them harm, they scurried around me on their usual business. As night-time companions they were among the less appealing I'd experienced in my time, but compared to some of the companions I seemed to have endured recently they were very definitely a cut above.

All the time one name reverberated round inside my head.

Dom.

I'd also gambled that the police would have instigated a house-to-house search in the immediate area, spreading the net ever wider as the initial trawl failed to produce any result. If I was right then once the first tranche of houses had been visited and eliminated there would have been nothing but a token presence left behind and again I was right. By the time I emerged from the main sewer a street or so away from where I'd first entered my subterranean hiding place, there was no sign of anything that resembled a thin blue line.

I hot-wired a nearby car – I was clearly becoming adept at acquiring illicitly-acquired transport – and drove away still under cover of darkness. I drove through the night heading west. Either consciously or unconsciously – I had no way of knowing by that stage – I was heading for Wales, where everything had begun, in a sense, with Trooper Rohl.

I drove for four hours. The motorway ended and a dual carriageway took over. That ended in turn at a small town. Taking a random exit off one of the roundabouts that next presented itself, I journeyed along a succession of lanes before coming on a small settlement on the banks of an estuary. There didn't seem to be any way out save back along the road that had brought me there so I abandoned the car in some nearby woods. With luck it wouldn't be spotted for a few days. Then I set off across a neighbouring field and had the immediate good fortune to encounter a tributary which probably fed into the nearby estuary and which offered a welcome opportunity to cleanse that close encounter with the sewer from my body and clothes.

Ten minutes later, I came across what looked like an old farm with a random collection of attached outbuildings. I checked them out, selecting one that didn't seem to be used for housing either crops or machinery – or indeed very much at all – and settled down to do some much-needed thinking.

I took out my mobile, looked again at Dom's text containing just the single question mark. There was no way it was purely by chance that Dom had delivered his message at the very moment I was in the middle of a police raid. The point and timing were obvious.

Dom was gloating and he wanted me to know it. He was well aware of the situation I was in, of the impossibility of my doing anything other than walking out of that rented apartment in the company of armed protectors and he obviously wanted to make sure I did so in an imprisonment of mind a hundred times more acute than any physical confinement I might have faced.

I slept without intending to do so. I woke to find sunlight bleaching the opposite wall. There was no sound of any human activity outside. I'd clearly picked well, the farm had few, if any, animals to tend. I kept watch from the small windows of the outbuilding and eventually saw a youngish couple emerge from the farmhouse, the woman carrying a small baby in a papoose, a young boy scurrying along by the side of a man. In the daylight

I could see the farmhouse looked more of a country retreat than anything more traditionally agricultural.

The young couple, who looked more and more like city exiles, settled the baby in the back seat of a spotless Range Rover and the young boy in the front before heading off down a small lane towards the road.

At which point another possibility presented itself and while I'd no real wish to add breaking and entering to an already lengthy list of crimes, it was undeniably true that it wouldn't add a great deal to any subsequent sentence I might now face. An old saying floated through my mind, something I'd first heard from an old grandparent I think, oddly appropriate given the setting and circumstances I found myself in right now. You may as well – one of them had once said to me – be hung for a sheep as a lamb.

5 1 .

THE INTERIOR OF the farmhouse was anything but agricultural too. It looked like the young occupants ran some sort of business from there, but the product or products they sold or the services they offered didn't exactly detain me too long.

I was looking for one thing only. In a traditional farmhouse I wouldn't have stood a prayer – or at least I assumed I wouldn't have stood a prayer. In truth I could count the number of traditional farmhouses I'd visited in my life on one finger. Maybe they were all state-of-the-art these days.

I needed, desperately now, to be online. Everything was kicking in again, just as it had done in the immediate aftermath of the train crash. A few hours before it had all been about getting out, getting away. Now it was all about getting back in touch in some way at least with all I'd left behind.

I came across a couple of up-to-the-minute desktops squatting diagonally opposite each other in what was clearly a designer-led conversion at the rear of the building – a home office presumably – but they really weren't much good to me. I didn't want to leave any cyberspace fingerprints behind by using any of those machines and anyway I needed to stay online for the next day or so at least while I worked out what the hell was happening here. I was hardly going to be able to haul a twenty-four inch behemoth up and down the countryside behind me. I needed portable technology, a laptop instead.

In something approaching desperation, I went into a smaller bedroom. From the brief glimpse of the family as they drove away, I guessed it belonged to the boy who didn't look much more than five or six. All of which made it all the more surprising that on the bed was a brand-new MacBook Air, all gleaming aluminium. I powered it up and, a few moments after I opened the display, a social networking site was on full view with some fourteen messages on screen awaiting the user's return.

I marvelled briefly at a world where children, barely toilet-trained, surfed on these sorts of sites, but not for too long. I should really have just grabbed what I needed – adaptors – a couple of the memory sticks I could see lying next to the Mac – and headed away. But the computer was already online and I simply had to make an immediate check on the loft. How was I to know when or where I'd next be able to find an accessible network?

I waited a moment for the laptop to connect. All the bugs would have been taken down by now, by the police if not by Tia, although I suspected it would have been one of her first tasks too. I'd told her about every one of them, aside – and I wasn't sure myself about this omission – from the radio alarm clock. I'd no wish or need to keep on spying on her so why I should have kept that one active was difficult to explain. Maybe it was some sort of instinct at work, some second sight perhaps. Or something else. Something I already didn't want to think about too deeply.

I went to the window as I waited for the computer to log on, looked down at a playground and a swing, slide and a climbing frame all standing on bark spread over the ground, providing some sort of protection in the event of a fall. Briefly I thought of the darkroom back in the loft, the room we'd once earmarked, via allusion more than anything else, as a nursery for some time in the hopefully not-so-distant future.

Would things have been very different if those unspoken plans had borne fruit? Would I then have fallen prey to all the insecurities that had claimed me? Was there still time to put that right? Would Tia even remotely consider the possibility after all that had happened? Or was all that just wishful thinking, Band-aid on a wound that, now, could never heal?

I turned back to the laptop. The software was now active. I bent over the screen and the first thing I saw was Tia, which was a blessed relief in itself. At the back of my mind lurked the ever-present fear that, courtesy of Dom, something might already have happened to her.

And then, all of a sudden, I saw something else.

I'm still in the same room. I'm still looking at the same laptop monitor. I'm still seeing images of Tia. Or at least the person who previously resembled Tia. But now it really is like looking at a total stranger.

On screen extraordinary pictures are dancing before my eyes. Is this Dom again, is he manipulating these images in some way, aware I wouldn't be able to resist logging on? Or is something else happening here instead?

Tia is with the – long-dead – Eddie. And the story I'm now seeing is apparently the story of what happened when my partner and her former tormentor were alone. Sometimes the action is being captured as if via a third party, although the way the images remain rock-steady even in the middle of what is to become some quite seriously heavy-duty action leads me to suspect – professional photographer's eye clearly working even under these circumstances – that some sort of stand is being used to secure the camera. Either that or the recorder really is the ultimate dispassionate observer.

Sometimes the action seems to be recorded by Tia herself. I can see part of her arm here, some small expanse of her leg there as the camera swoops and circles over the scene.

And what a scene. I'd watched Tia while she was in the company of Eddie many times before. I'd seen her tense as he looked at her. I'd read only too clearly her contempt as his eyes washed over every part of her body, felt the revulsion coming off her in great crashing waves as he stood just that little bit too close to her in his fetid shop packed full of so many broken dreams and dashed and disappointed hopes.

But I'd never seen her straddle him as I saw her do now, naked flesh on naked flesh, had never seen her grab huge fistfuls of his wobbling fat as she rode him, as his excited cries made clear, to something approaching ecstasy in his world, although from the evidence of her own accompanying cries Tia wasn't that far behind, meaning this wasn't some reluctant deal with the devil, some necessary evil forced upon her by the pressure of circumstance. This was choice, her choice and this recording, if that's what it was, had presumably been made to tell me that.

Then there were another set of images, far from steady, the camera definitely hand-held this time and now all that was happening was taking place out on the street.

Now the sound was muted, now only small snatches could be heard, the odd word heard here and there. Tia was in a shop doorway, bent close to a figure I identified fairly speedily as the vagrant, another bit-player in the Eddie saga, the unfortunate soul who'd done his own deal with the Devil, who'd taken the fall for the murder charge in exchange for some nice clean bedding and three meals a day. As I watched, Tia was urging him on, clearly inveigling him into that flat across the street where she knew a dead body was already lying on the floor.

Meaning this was Tia apparently setting someone up for an inevitable later fall, securing herself a mark.

A patsy, in US movie parlance.

A beard.

I straightened slowly, deciding – belatedly – to spare myself further revelations, totally unable to take in what I was being shown anyway. I knew better than anyone that images could be manipulated, but there was something about the easy familiarity

Tia exhibited in both the extracts I'd unwillingly watched so far that didn't seem to have the leaden hand of manipulation laid upon it all. Far from being controlled in some way by the actions of some sort of celestial film editor, she looked to be in total charge, in complete control.

Then suddenly a new thought crashed into my brain, one of dozens now crowding in.

The poster shop.

The poster shop run by the American with the strangled vowels. The poster shop that had vanished only to be replaced by the surveillance store. A location previously introduced to me by a partner I then set out to track.

Had some unholy alliance been forged in some way? Tia and Dom? And then, hard on the heels of that unwelcome thought came another.

Natsuo.

Who'd suddenly materialised like that outside that same shop that day. Not to mention inside that café near to the rented apartment.

I looked back at the monitor but all I could see now was Tia again moving around the loft, no more pictures of Eddie, no other trace of the vagrant and for a moment I began to fear I really was losing my mind, that I was hallucinating images where none existed.

And then, crashing in again, came the next thought, the one that eclipsed all others.

The experiment.

The program.

I stared at the screen, not seeing anything at all now, hardly able indeed to breathe.

Was that it? Had I started something which wasn't, now, to be stopped? That maybe couldn't be stopped? Was that why more and more images were, apparently, being force-fed into my brain all the while? Was I now seeing the world through Tia's eyes, her memories truly becoming mine?

From down the road, distant, came the sound of an approaching engine, a car making its way along the tracks, perhaps approaching the house, perhaps about to head off on one of the other tracks surrounding the property. I'd have no way of knowing until the family, if indeed it was they, swung onto their lane, disembarked from the vehicle and headed for the house effectively trapping me inside.

It really was no time to take chances. It was definitely time to get out. Besides I'd achieved all I wanted to for now courtesy of a precocious five year old and a prized laptop which would definitely be missed in one of the more peculiar burglaries the family would ever experience, in which one item and only one was removed. But something about that well-furnished bedroom in that upmarket house told me it was destined to be replaced fairly speedily.

The engine was sounding louder now, the vehicle getting closer. I was about to close the display to put the Mac back in sleep mode before heading away with another illicitly-acquired prize when suddenly I stopped.

On screen, Tia had moved again from the balcony to the sitting room. She seemed unable to settle once more. The moment she went out onto the balcony she came back inside, the moment she came inside she moved into the kitchen and then the bathroom almost as if patrolling some preordained route, completing a curious kind of circuit.

It was just the one gesture that gave it away. One simple upward movement of the head, a single glance towards one of the skylights set into the roof of the loft as the sun briefly appeared through the intermittent cloud.

Outside the approaching engine hadn't deviated in tone, meaning the approaching vehicle hadn't turned off, meaning it was becoming increasingly likely that this was indeed the family returning home.

But I didn't move. I didn't do what even now, even as my brain was almost totally consumed by a new and overpowering suspicion, I knew I should do and get out of there.

I'd seen that exact same gesture just a few moments before. In one sense that was hardly surprising, Tia had walked out onto that balcony a few moments before too, before walking back, heading around the open-plan sitting room, picking up a paper, discarding it, picking up a work notebook and discarding that as well. In times of stress she always did take refuge in distraction and repetition, would even touch the same item again and again as if to reassure herself of its solidity, finding certainty in the presence of everyday objects perhaps.

It was the sun on her face that gave it away, the way the sunlight illuminated her features in exactly the way it had done just a few moments before, only that was impossible of course. A calamity of biblical proportions would have had to occurred in the last few moments to make the event I'd just seemingly witnessed assume any sort of reality.

But the world had not stopped turning. That shaft of sunlight should have struck her face at a slightly different angle, should have highlighted her hair in a different way to even those few moments before.

Outside, the engine suddenly dipped in volume as the driver eased off the throttle, preparing to slip the car into a lower gear to traverse the final few hundred metres from the road up the winding path that led to the front door.

What the images of Tia with Eddie – or Tia with the vagrant – were all about I still had no idea. But the images now playing out on the laptop screen before me were on a loop. For the most part it had been cleverly disguised with small variations built into the repetition, but the giveaway sunlight had been missed. It meant that I was watching a composite of images from previous observations. It meant I was witnessing an illusion, a sequence of events that bore no resemblance to, or relationship with, present-day reality.

A confidence trick in fact.

So what was the present-day reality? The laws of physics, if nothing else, rendered the apparent evidence of my eyes irredeemably flawed, meaning it wasn't Tia I was watching on that screen. Or at least not the Tia I wanted to see and needed to see, the Tia in the here and now.

So where was she?

Outside, the car was swinging up towards the yard. I exited the programme, clearing all history and associated cookies at the same time. With luck there would now be no reason to alert the police or raise the alarm.

Things had changed. I wouldn't now be depriving the precocious five year old of his prized laptop because there was no point. Whatever I'd expected to access with it was not only illusory but a dangerous illusion at that.

Someone was clearly well ahead of me in this game.

And not for the first time.

5 2 .

THE NEXT MORNING as dawn was breaking, and not daring to leave it before with the family now home, I exited the outhouse.

Through gaps in surrounding trees I could see the estuary again. Despite the early hour I could hear the sounds of engines making their way across exposed sands heading for cockle beds that sustained, so I'd later discover, the fragile economy of the area. The sound of animals stirring in nearby fields also punctuated the early morning mist. It wouldn't be long before that mist cleared, before children walked down nearby lanes heading for the local school and postmen drove past on their rounds.

Ten minutes later I was standing on the platform of a small railway station. In amongst the early morning noises wafting on the air up to the farm I'd also heard the whistle of trains as they approached, including the warning siren of the only high-speed train that passed through each morning apparently, but didn't stop.

For want of anything better to do – and desperate to fill my mind with anything other than all I'd witnessed – or at least all I'd seemingly witnessed – I read a notice pinned on a small shelter petitioning the train company for this halt to be included among the high-speed calling points. Next to it a letter from the train company boss flapped damply in its polythene sleeve, informing petitioners that the platform was simply too short to take more than one carriage. There was a reply from the organiser of the petition in turn, but by then my mind had drifted back to the sights and sounds I'd attempted to banish on the walk into the village and which clearly would not be kept at bay for much longer.

Half of me now just wanted to run. There was no grand master plan at work as to where I would be going, even what I would do once I reached a destination as yet unknown. But I knew that wherever I went and however far I travelled I'd never be able to outpace what was fast becoming a comprehensive pincer movement of enlightenment and pursuit. Something was already telling me that in some hotel room somewhere, in some other rented cottage or apartment, walking down some street or sitting in some coffee shop, I'd look up and suddenly a new twist in this tale would unfold before me.

The answer lay, as all answers had perhaps always lain, with Tia. Only when I saw her, talked to her would I even begin to understand. I didn't know if she was back in the loft or somewhere else entirely. She certainly had been, but whether she was there now I couldn't know for sure. So there was only one thing I could now do and that was get back and find out for myself

I didn't notice the woman coming onto the platform, shoulder bag in hand, heading off presumably to work. The Welsh capital was just over an hour or so away making this commuter territory. I was still consumed by all that had happened, still trying to decode and understand it all, hopeless task though that might have been. But she noticed me.

I turned, a distant noise sounding, a hum on the rails as a train made its approach in the distance. She glanced at me idly, clearly in no mood for early morning conversation with a stranger but then she froze. For the last few hours all that had happened or not happened with Tia had driven everything else from my mind but then I realised why she'd stopped, why she was staring at me in that way and why she was now taking her iPhone out of her bag and was – as I kept watching her – already checking on something.

Then she looked back at me and, then, looked quickly away again as she saw me staring in her direction.

She'd recognised me. She recognised me as the sicko who'd been plastered across the tabloids for the last day or so and who was now on the run. She kept her face averted for now, concentrating instead it seemed on the approaching train now visible some few hundred metres down the line, willing it towards her with its complement of fellow passengers and with its guard and driver; safety in other words.

The train was now just a hundred metres or so away. But I could see much further ahead than that. My mind was already at the next station along the line, the doors on electronic lockdown, except one.

Through which a squad of armed police had already stormed.

The woman stole a last, quick, glance at me. And as the train came to a halt I turned and walked away from that small station as fast as I could.

5 3 .

I DIDN'T KNOW what I expected. Press, TV cameras, hordes of uniformed police maintaining round-the-clock surveillance perhaps. I encountered just a *Big Issue* seller in the doorway of the local convenience store – not the usual *Big Issue* seller who normally stood there, a different one for which relief etc., etc.; certainly not a police officer or a neighbour. Not a single challenge rang out as I headed down the street and made my way towards the loft.

It was as if nothing had ever happened. Or more accurately, as if the world had moved on and was already putting even the genuinely affecting events of the past week or so behind it, let alone any spurious versions of the same.

I passed the old harbourmaster's house. Briefly I thought of the blonde journalist and the photographer who'd visited us just before Tia and myself had set off for that poster shop and the *Badlands* surprise, and what a lifetime ago that seemed now.

Walking on as if I had every right to be on that street, as if – like Wakefield – I hadn't disqualified myself from what might be called civilised society, I let myself into the apartment complex and walked up the stairs.

At the loft door I paused. Now I actually had to encounter whatever was on the other side all resolve suddenly left me. There was no way to prepare, nothing I could do to steel myself for the experience that lay ahead. Those latest surveillance tapes had been doctored, I knew that now, but for what purpose? What had the unseen hand wanted to hide? And what else, if anything, had been doctored; and why?

I put my key in the lock, felt rather than heard the click of the internal levers and pulleys as they recognised and sanctioned my entrance, took a deep breath and pushed open the door.

Nothing.

As in totally normal.

Nothing out of the ordinary, nothing out of place.

And no sign of any sort of struggle either, no evidence indeed that Tia had actually returned to the loft at all aside from the tape which clearly showed she had been there at some point even if her actions had been compromised by trickery.

I crossed into the kitchen and for want of any other sort of clue checked the dates on the milk cartons. There were two inside the fridge, their sell-by dates a couple of days hence, which didn't tell me a lot. They could have been purchased a day ago or four to five days ago and I couldn't think of anything else that might tell me how long it had been since Tia had been there.

I went out onto the balcony, looked down at the river, at the clippers plying their trade. I stood there for a moment or two, blocked as to what to do next, then went back into the loft and headed for the bedroom. Maybe, even if I had no way of knowing how long Tia had been gone – or where she'd gone – then a quick check on the clothes left in her wardrobe and drawers might tell me. Only I didn't get there.

I stopped as I saw the open door to the bathroom. For a long moment I just stared across at the facing mirror, the same mirror that had reflected back to me that small scratch on Tia's back following her Edinburgh trip.

My face was reflected in the mirror but something else was etched on the surface too, something that looked like dried blood.

5 4 .

I WAS OUTSIDE the Covent Garden shop in less than fifteen minutes.

I knew exactly what to expect and, in that sense, wasn't disappointed. The rest of the shoppers and shop owners wouldn't have given the closed shop front a second glance. One day a movie memorabilia store, the next a surveillance outfit, tomorrow who knows? Who cares?

I moved round to the back, tried to peer in through the boarded and shuttered windows. The interior looked empty, stripped of all that oh-so-enticing software, the shelves bare. Aside that is from one item in the very centre of the room, squatting on a small stool, a laptop, its display open, the screen blank at the moment, but just waiting for one stroke of the keypad to coax it back into life so it could then display... what?

I was inside the shop in under another minute. There was precious little finesse about my forced entrance and I knew I was running the risk of another of the local shopkeepers coming to investigate the sound of the smashing glass and splintering wood, but then again why would they? The capital was packed full of madmen and this part of the gilded city had its share, but why would even the most seriously deranged and delusional soul want to break into an empty shop?

I crossed to the laptop and hit the space bar. Nothing happened and for a moment I wondered briefly about Dom and his sense of humour, about a man who'd quite obviously gone to all this trouble just to present me with, effectively, a blank page.

I stood before the laptop in the place where this had all started, now more lost than I'd ever been at any stage in the process, as far away as ever from any sort of resolution to it all.

Then, suddenly, I heard Tia behind me.

'Can I ask you a question?'

I wheeled round to see her standing in the smashed doorway. Unlike the last time we'd met she was calm now and sounded in control. There wasn't any fear or anger in her voice either. There was something else instead, something I couldn't place at first.

'Why did you do it?'

I stared back at her, unable to respond.

'All those devices.'

Tia nodded at me.

'Why?'

I hesitated. Now I could identify what it was that was lending that particular timbre to her voice. It was sadness; and something else too, something for now anyway I again couldn't quite place.

I hesitated again as she kept staring at me, waiting for me to answer.

'I explained all that.'

Tia nodded again. I had, back in the rented apartment and she knew it. Perhaps she just wanted to double-check, but she didn't.

'You wanted to be sure I loved you.'

It was more of a statement than a question.

'Yes.'

'I don't think that was the reason.'

I just looked at her, once again didn't respond.

'I don't think it was anything to do with me loving or not loving you.'

I kept looking at her, evermore lost.

What was she talking about?

She held my stare, steady, her eyes meeting mine full-on.

'I think you wanted to find out if you loved me.'

That same stare continued to hold me, unwavering now.

'So have you got your answer?'

Behind Tia, someone else came out of the shadows.

Munroe.

Then, behind Munroe, a couple of uniformed police emerged as well. And in the yard at the back I could now see Dom, a defeated-looking Dom, his hands encased in what looked like handcuffs.

For a moment Tia just stood there looking at me, seeming almost to be unaware of their presence.

Then she moved forward and kissed me, light on the lips, the softest, saddest of farewells.

5 5 .

E VERY MORNING THE routine's the same.
I wake at dawn, a dawn that appears almost instantly,
seemingly by magic. First, a small streak of light appears in the
dark. The next moment shadows assume shape as the rising
sun bathes the landscape, defining it all the while. It's then
that I rise, pull on a pair of shorts and a T-shirt, put on some
comfortable shoes and walk out of the small hillside cottage
overlooking the sea and keep on walking.

I walk down lanes which still see precious little traffic.
Always, the sea is close at hand. This is a small island, just
sixteen miles long and, at certain points, less than a mile
or so across. On a map it looks totally lost in the vastness
of the Atlantic Ocean. Innumerable smaller islands are
dotted all round its coast, some linked to the mainland by
small bridges, some accessible only by boat. Most of these
surrounding islands are uninhabited but here and there
houses can be seen, individual dwellings all painted one of
the local, traditional, pastel shades of blue or yellow, the
ultimate private retreats.

I walk each morning and each morning I'm met with
unfailing courtesy from young and old alike. Children on their
way to school bid me good morning. Their accompanying
parents smile at me as their offspring do so, including
themselves in the salutation. Other walkers, also passing, pay
me the same respects. No-one sees me as a man apart.

As I walk I review the primer. Maybe I should have read

it a little more carefully all that time ago. Maybe all that had happened would never then have taken place.

Go quietly to thy bed, foolish man; and, on the morrow, if thou wilt be wise, get thee home… remove not thyself, even for a little week, from thy place.

Occasionally the routine varies. A dozen or more ferries ply these coasts, taking commuters, holidaymakers and shoppers from one end of the island to the other. Now and again if one's docking close by – and if it's not one of my volunteer days – I hop on board, heading across a large expanse of water called the Great Sound, stopping off sometimes in the small capital, sometimes heading further north visiting another town near to the only airport, linked to the mainland by a causeway little more than a single carriageway in width.

From the quayside in the capital I walk up winding streets. Even here I rarely travel more than a few steps before someone bids me a greeting. Coming from London it was more than slightly unsettling at first and the usual business dress for men on this island – knee-length shorts – only added to the generally incongruous feel. But it's miles away from everywhere I know and everyone I've previously known and for now that's all that matters.

In one sense it's only time away of course; a simple plane ride. But consult the primer again.

An almost impassable gulf divides his hired apartment from his former home. 'It is but in the next street!' he sometimes says. Fool! It is in another world.

I've been here two years. I came in on a visitor's passport but managed to find work in a local museum. It was strictly on an unpaid basis which suited me fine. I still had some savings from my former life and even though this isn't exactly a low-cost island in terms of living expenses, I found some fairly cheap lodgings well off the beaten tourist track. With what I'd managed to bring from my old life I can survive for another couple of years without having to look for paid employment. And the stultifying routine of life in the museum – opening up in the mornings, greeting the occasional tourist and school party, selling a guide book here and there – has been perfect. The equivalent, I guess, of studying the arrival and departure times of river clippers in a world far away from this.

When my visa expired and it came time for me to leave one of the museum trustees learnt that I'd like to stay. I didn't enlighten him as to the reason, being much less to do with a burning interest in all matters connected with the island and its history but having much more to do with the simple fact I had nowhere else to go.

The trustee in question made representations to a couple of highly-placed government officials – friends or relatives from the little I could glean – and my residency period was extended.

The deal, while unspoken, was clear. While I remained working in my volunteer capacity I could stay. If I tired of those duties then my benefactors would presumably tire of me too.

I've not seen Tia for years now. I've had no contact with anyone else from my former life either but I think Tia may still be in contact with Natsuo. Despite that isolated attack in the rented apartment – occasioned, I discovered later, by her disorientated belief that Natsuo was somehow complicit in all that was happening – they'd remained close. It would be appropriate if that were still so. Once she'd dismissed her previous and unfounded unease regarding Tia and Joseph, Natsuo had become the leading light in the network of support Joseph himself had set up for Tia after the train crash. Some relationships endure and I like to think that one might.

Perhaps it was Natsuo having a previous and special connection with myself that made her support and presence all the more welcome to Tia at that time. It helped also that Natsuo would meet her whenever and wherever Tia requested. They even met once at a spot referred to by Tia as the usual place, although she more commonly met her old school friend Trudie there it seemed, to catch up on gossip, chew over old times.

Because of the connection we'd previously shared, Natsuo had also done what Tia had never done, indeed could never do, in visiting the crash site, although she was unaware that the simple memorial she'd left there – some small mementoes from our time together – would later alert the authorities that my all-important DNA had finally been found.

All those people seem to be from some other life completely now, a life populated by creatures from another world. No doubt they feel the same about me.

The clues were there all the time, of course. When I first read the original story it was the audacity of the trick that dazzled me. Reading it again – and then again – and again – I saw what I'd missed the first time round. This time the constant warnings embedded in the text almost from the very start of the story screamed out at me where previously my eyes had glided over them, only too anxious – I now realised – to reach the next incident in the unfolding plot. Perhaps it was the same for Hawthorne.

We know, each for himself, that none of us would perpetrate such a folly, yet feel as if some other might. To my contemplations, at least, it had often recurred, always exciting wonder.

More than anything I'd have liked a conversation with the great man. Knowing all I now know, my suspicion is that Hawthorne went back himself after finishing his original tale, placed in the text all those admonishments for the unwary. And knowing all I know now, I understand only too clearly why he was reluctant, why indeed he refused, to follow his fictional creation across the threshold at the conclusion of his cautionary tale.

Would that I had a folio to write, instead of an article of a dozen pages! Then might I exemplify how an influence, beyond our control, lays its strong hand on every deed which we do, and weaves its consequences into an iron tissue of necessity.

My suspicion also is that such a folio existed. I've no basis for that suspicion other than the fact that for that period of time I became his creation, walking almost literally in his shadow. So could Hawthorne have resisted journeying with the object of his own obsession for longer than the dozen or so pages he finally presented to the world?

What happened when he did journey in that way? What did he find out, not only about Wakefield, but about himself? What hinterland did he travel and what demons did he attempt to exorcise thereby?

And at what point did it descend into madness for him? At what stage in that journey did his imaginings turn into something else entirely? If the clues, once again, are anything to go by, then it seems to have been fairly early on.

There were footsteps, that seemed to tread behind his own, distinct from the multitudinous tramp around him; and, anon, he heard a voice shouting afar, and fancied that it called his name. Doubtless, a dozen busybodies had been watching him, and told his wife the whole affair.

Within hours of uncorking the genie from its bottle, that same genie it seemed had turned on the man who'd released it. In that sense perhaps I fared better than Wakefield although there were some who'd say madness had already claimed me the moment that half-notion first crossed my mind. But there was still time, both then and later. Time to turn back.

Later still, when there was no possibility of turning back, when my imaginings turned into something else again, when the line became blurred to the point where all actions, all characters previously known or otherwise twisted into something incomprehensible, then I suppose madness really did descend; but at what precise point that happened in the events in which I became enmeshed I'll leave to others to decide.

By the time I was in that farmhouse, looking at pictures that seemed to be dancing on a monitor in front of me, but which I know now were dancing before my eyes only, I'd certainly crossed that line. I'd even cast an inadequate loser who ran a surveillance store as chief architect of what was very much my own self-inflicted misfortune. Madness again, as became all-too obvious later. But by then it was too late. By then I'd already travelled too far down a road I'd been journeying too long, a journey in which simple aides to memory such as a code for an office alarm left in the pannier of a motorbike somehow attained the status of a portent.

A lot of loose ends were cleared up in the aftermath of my arrest. Tia made what in the pages of police procedurals would be described as a full and frank confession to the authorities for one thing. She seemed to want to get everything out of her system too and the whole Eddie story came out as a result. Aside from everything else, and as she made clear to them, she had no wish for the police to look again at the innocent vagrant in the wake of my return. To escape detection was one thing. To visit upon the shoulders of another responsibility for her own crime was something else.

Tia was prosecuted but in the light of her confession and in the light of the clear evidence of Eddie's unprovoked attack – evidence provided, ironically, by my very surveillance – her sentence was suspended. I'd played no part in the Eddie killing but I still had plenty of other misdemeanours to account for and so I served my sentence in full. So all in all I had a lot of time back then, sitting in that prison cell and subsequently, to try and decide just when everything turned from a simple exercise to anything but; a puzzle that time hasn't quite succeeded in unlocking.

Sometimes I pause on my walks, not for rest – these exertions never seem to tire me – but for something else; a moment where my brain might pause along with my body perhaps. At those moments I do start to sense some thought, some idea, some realisation perhaps, once again at the very edge of conscious thought which seems to want to usher itself centre stage. But for now it remains just out of reach. I sit instead on a small beach I've come to frequent having walked across a clifftop to get there and watch the waves come in and fill a variety of small caves before lapping at my feet and retreating again.

If truth be told, I still can't be sure that my present isn't in mortgage to a past that cannot be trusted. I spent a whole week once trying to work out what it was I'd sensed in Tia's voice that last time we spoke, unable to rid myself of the conviction that, in some way, it was triumph. Evidence, if any more were needed, of that same corrosive – and perhaps still present – self-delusion on my part.

But maybe, in the end, what I'm really doing is simple. Maybe I'm revisiting all that, trying to reinterpret, reinvent it all because – and even at this late stage – I'm looking for a way back, a path home; a course of action doomed, of course, according again to the primer.

Amid the seeming confusion of our mysterious world, individuals are so nicely adjusted to a system, and systems to one another, and to a whole, that, by stepping aside for a moment, a man exposes himself to a fearful risk of losing his place forever.

But Wakefield did not lose his place forever. Wakefield did return. He did cross that threshold again albeit after all those years had passed. And even though Hawthorne didn't follow him, he did record that from that point on Wakefield became a loving spouse until his death; even more ballast to my suspicion that somewhere in his papers there existed the folio he claimed he didn't write.

After Hawthorne's death, his wife and son – for reasons that were never explained – burned a whole collection of stories and novels on which he'd laboured, sometimes for decades. Maybe it was among them. Maybe they read all that happened after Wakefield re-entered his home and decided the world was better off not knowing.

Or maybe that's those same imaginings again. Maybe even now it's all not quite so consigned to another place and time as I'd like to believe. In darker moments – and there's still plenty of those – I wonder whether I'm simply paying lip-service to the warnings and admonishments I now read in every sentence of the tale. Whether in truth it's still the actions that entrance me, regardless of their consequences.

And perhaps I'm not alone. There's certainly those who listen to the Wakefield story as you'd listen to the rantings of a madman. But there's also those – and lately I seem to have come across more and more of them – who toy, sometimes briefly, sometimes for a more extended period with a similar scenario, wonder – sometimes briefly, sometimes for a more extended period too – whether one day, perhaps, they might do something of the same.

Only as an experiment of course. Little more than a relatively harmless prank. At that point I could call out like Hawthorne those centuries before, utter the same admonishments and issue the same warnings. But it would make no difference.

They're the ones who don't abandon the story in the first few paragraphs, whose eyes don't glaze over after just the first few words. The ones who read, then read on and then reread again, initially perhaps out of puzzlement, but then out of something else.

The ones who keep on reading for reasons they don't as yet understand.

The ones who won't stop until they've reached the end of the tale.

Also by the author:

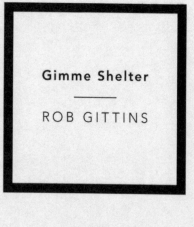

'Visceral, strongly visual and beautifully structured... powerful, quirky characters.'
Andrew Taylor, Winner, Crime Writers' Association Cartier Diamond Dagger

Gimme Shelter

———

ROB GITTINS

£8.95
£17.95 (hb)

Dylan Thomas's last days – and someone's watching...

THE POET &
THE PRIVATE EYE

ROB GITTINS

£8.95
£14.95 (hb)

Investigating Mr Wakefield is just one of a
whole range of publications from Y Lolfa.
For a full list of books currently in print, send
now for your free copy of our new full-colour
catalogue. Or simply surf into our website

www.ylolfa.com

for secure on-line ordering.

TALYBONT CEREDIGION CYMRU SY24 5HE
e-mail ylolfa@ylolfa.com
website www.ylolfa.com
phone (01970) 832 304
fax 832 782